IVIVIN

J. Nick Fisk

◊

Illustrated by: Orlando Guerra

Dedicated to Elise, for whom I started this story
-and-
to myself, for whom I finished it.

Preface

Hello and welcome to my book. I am not sure why you decided to pick this one up when there are literal libraries full of more worthwhile books, but I am honoured and humbled nonetheless. Thank you for taking the time to read this, my first book. I wanted to preface the meat and bones of the story with some supplemental information about how it is structured and why I structured it in that way.

This book started, originally, as a story I told my girlfriend at the time. We were enduring the struggles of a long-distance relationship. We were both dorks and enjoyed fantasy stories and settings represented across a variety of mediums. Due to our varied and oft conflicting schedules, as well the monotony of trying to keep each other updated in each other's mundane day-to-day happenings, regular exchanges began to lose their luster. As a result, I decided to spin a tale—an adventure—of a young fellow named Ivivin. Rather than write it all at once, I would instead send daily or near daily updates of the story to her. I was inspired by the positive feelings induced by being in love to be creative, even if it was in a silly, rough, and dorky way.

The original story was never finished, but I had most of the main beats of the story laid out (in my head). I ended our relationship for regrettable reasons. However, being with her taught me a lot about myself and being without her helped me to decide to change myself for the better. At first, I shied away from writing anything creative at all because I associated it so closely with her— she had helped me find and develop my love of writing, after all. With time and reflection, though, I realized that I shouldn't dismiss parts of me simply because she had helped me find them. If I wanted to treat the past with the respect and fondness I felt it deserved, I figured I should do the opposite and embrace those parts of me. To that end, I decided to finish the story of Ivivin. However, because the story was told over SMS and email, I have lost pieces of the original story to electronic oblivion. I scoured all the sources I could and compiled them, incomplete as they may be, and attempted to recapture, reconnect, and retell the story. As a sort of tribute to the reasons I decided to begin this tale in the first place, I have tried my best to not significantly alter the original tidbits I did recover.

The story of how this book came to be has a few interesting implications. I have lived life since I last touched the story of Ivivin. As such, it may be possible, if not easy, to distinguish when different pieces were written and who wrote them—the me of the past or the me of the present. Some may criticize this and it is fair criticism. A story should have a sense of continuity, both in its plot and its style. However, I feel this melding of my past and present is symbolic and I hope you can look past any flaws in this self-expression. Another interesting implication of the history of this book is that it is not structured into traditional chapters. The way the story was originally distributed was episodic. I sent out the story as texts or emails and intended it to almost be read out loud, day by day, reading the story as if one was reading a book to a child over the course of weeks or months. To recapture the original episodic nature of the story, I, again, wrote entries episodically. I bound myself to these, with each entry becoming immediately and immutably canonical—there is no changing the past, after all. Some entries were tremendously short and pointless. Some were overly serious. Some were comedic (or, at least, tried to be). At the end of the day, though, this story represents an attempt to communicate and express myself—at first, for a woman I loved dearly and now for myself and anyone kind enough to take the time to read this.

Thank you.

The Beginning

1

Ivivin sighed as he wiped his brow and looked longingly to his favourite spot on the farm—an elder tree nearly as tall as a barn. It served as a sort of reminder of his ancestors. His great grandparents had settled this land, clearing it of trees to be tilled and used for crop. They had succeeded in clearing all the trees in what is now their family fields. All but one, that is. Still standing was this behemoth of a tree. There were axe marks lining the westward facing end of the tree—a memento preserved from Ivivin's ancestors' attempts to bring the beast down. In the end, they failed to conquer the giant and left it be, as did his grandparents and even his own parents. While Ivivin found this familial tale amusing and would oft think of it fondly, the victor from that ancient scuffle had another purpose that Ivivin found much more appealing. It was a perfect place to lay under for a nice rest. Birds of all varieties came and went, their songs bringing life and peace to an otherwise mundane landscape. The roots of the tree were mossy and unexpectedly soft, making them a perfect place to lay one's head. Naturally, such a large arboreal wonder would not be complete without a thick canopy of leaves providing respite from the scorching sun of summer.

"It is time for a break," Ivivin thought.

Make no mistake, Ivivin was not a child of sloth or laze. Nor were his breaks under that oak tree usually born from the physical toils of farm work. Rather, his time under the tree allowed him to think. It gave him time to dream. And what fantastical thoughts and dreams they were! Over the years, he had been a seafarer, a king, a merchant in a busy market, and even a court jester! However, about two years prior to this very day, Ivivin had first imagined himself a most honourable knight. He built life after life where he was a hand of the king. He imagined himself as the strongest and most chivalrous knight the world had ever known. He imagined great services and adventures he would undertake all around the world. He basked in the gratitude of imaginary townsfolk and in the fear of ne'er do wells. Since that day he first saw himself as a knight, he had held fast to that fantasy and it had become a central part of who he was.

"*I wish I could be a knight*," Ivivin thought as he laid his head below the comfort of his tree. "*But I must live my life, the one I have. I love my family very much...Father...Mother. I am the sole heir to this land. Their livelihood will become mine and I shall care for them as they age. A knight's destiny is not my own, this I know. But, oh, how I want it!*"

Indeed, Ivivin often recollected and retold himself these thoughts, trying to ground himself so that his fantasies did not sweep him away. Only then, once he had reminded himself of his life and its requisites, did he allow himself to dream. On this day, Ivivin imagined himself atop a battle forged steed adorned in the king's own colours. He imagined himself riding across open fields. He could practically hear the galloping hooves of his imagined horse.

Da-thwump
Da-thwump.
DA-THWUMP
DA-THWUMP!

The sound of the hooves grew louder and louder until Ivivin jerked up from his resting ground. A horse neighed not but inches from his face. As Ivivin's eyes adjusted to the harsh sunlight once more, he could see the horse and his rider were adorned in the royal colours.

"*A knight!?*" Ivivin thought excitedly. "*No,*" he realized with his excitement deflating more by the second "*he is a royal messenger. He has probably come to make an announcement of a royal wedding to be had in Castletown. It is not unusual for such announcements to be spread even this far nowhere, after all.*"

"Boy!" called the royal messenger, unusually gruff in his voice for a man of his petite stature. "Hear my message and relay it to all you encounter. The king shall be travelling through your small village in twenty short moons. On this day, after twenty-moons have passed, the village of Gemi should have modest gifts of water and meal for his highness and his accompaniment to aid in their return to the castle. Again, tell all you know, boy! Leave not a detail out!"

The messenger looked into Ivivin's eyes for just a moment and departed, surely to continue to deliver the message to any villagers who would listen. Ivivin's slight disappointment turned to great excitement. He would have a chance few others with his destiny had. He would get to meet the king, his highness. Ivivin was not alone in admiration for the man. The king was widely considered truly benevolent and an unreasonably fair ruler. Indeed, taxes were no higher than they needed to be and the royalty was more than understanding when calamity prevented payment of these taxes, often offering aid and charity. That is not to say the king was a pushover. Ivivin had heard tales of the swift and mighty justice the king often spearheaded or how his knights were the fiercest warriors in all the lands. Any foreign attack against the castle not only failed, but failed swiftly.

"I cannot wait to tell mother and father!" Ivivin thought, skipping and bounding towards his house.

3

Ivivin burst into his home, startling his father, who was preparing supper. His mother followed Ivivin in moments after his dramatic entrance. She and his father both were finely coated in soil and weary from the day's labours. Ivivin's mother, still standing in the doorway with a hoe laid across her shoulder, noticed Ivivin's unusual energy.

"Ivivin, my child" she said "I haven't seen you this excited since your father last made sweetbread. What has you so joyous?"

She set the hoe down after wiping it clean. Ivivin took a deep breath, ready to spill the wonderful news of the king's approach.

"Today I—" Ivivin was cut off by his father.

"Ivivin, did you tend to the eastern fields as I asked of you? You know that we must finish before the ground freezes."

Ivivin, though frustrated that he was interrupted, responded promptly and proudly. "Yes, father, I even finished early!"

Ivivin's father smiled warmly and gestured at Ivivin to continue. "Today, mother and father, I encountered a messenger of the king!"

Ivivin's mother and father looked at each other uneasily and warily. Although Ivivin's youthful optimism had initially suspected marriage or other pleasant news, Ivivin's parents had been alive long enough to know warnings and news of danger came just as frequently to these parts.

"And, what did the messenger say?" Ivivin's father said cautiously. And so, Ivivin recounted his run-in with the messenger to his family as they sat down for supper together. His parents were relieved and they themselves were excited by the news. Ivivin's father noted matter-of-factly that he would have to go into the village proper to discuss what they could contribute to the king's provisions. It was apparent, however, that they were all eager for the passing of the moons.

Ivivin approached his daily work with a renewed passion and vigour. He aspired to finish his chores early each day so he could indulge in his fantasies. No later than the second moon passed, however, did Ivivin abandon his imaginings under the oak tree. He instead wanted to fashion a gift for the king. After a bit of thought and much pacing under his oak tree, Ivivin stubbed his toe on one of the many roots and was struck with much pain, but also much inspiration. He would whittle a piece of this root into a talisman of sorts. This tree represented his family and his destiny. Ivivin knew that he could not become a knight. He was not born of the right blood or into the right family. He hadn't the education nor the skill.

"Still," Ivivin thought *"if the king were to accept my token and return to the castle with it, then it will be as if my family themselves have a small place in that castle."*

And so Ivivin imagined an ornate token as he cleaved a large root to fashion. Each evening, Ivivin would whittle and whittle until the moon before the king's arrival. He eagerly ran a string through the token and held up the newly completed necklace to be admired. Ivivin's ear-to-ear grin invoked by the completion of his creation soon faded to a stoic consideration of his work.

"No doubt about it..." Ivivin whispered to himself. "This necklace is ugly."

Ivivin took a moment to reflect on his work. He had these grand and intricate visions of how he wanted his once-in-a-lifetime gift to look. Ivivin did temper his expectations a bit—he was a farmer and not a craftsman, after all. But the work of 'art' he had created was lumpy, uneven, and clearly the work of an untalented commoner.

Ivivin smiled.

"Still, I am proud of my ugly creation. I can only hope the king can bear to carry such an unpleasant thing."

Ivivin hurried himself to bed, clutching his creation tightly and waited for the new day to come.

4

Both Ivivin and his father awoke even earlier than usual, this, the morning of the King's passage through their humble settlement. Few words were spoken between them, but Ivivin's father could so easily see the excitement on his son's face. Truly, Ivivin was beaming with excitement. His mother volunteered to stay behind and complete the necessary work for the day. She cared far less for the affairs of royalty than either her husband or son. After a quick breakfast, Ivivin and his father made the short trek to their village's vendor area. It was the heart and soul of their community, as small as it was. Today, though, it was fuller than Ivivin had ever seen. Although there weren't any large settlements very close, there were a fair number of farms and other small homesteads. Folk who caught word of the king's passage made the trek to come see the royal entourage as they passed through. It was not until about midday that the king and his companions could be seen in the near distance. The buzz of the market had long settled, but it erupted anew with the royal party on the horizon. People ran about, organizing their offerings and clearing the path. Though the king was in sight, it took what felt like an eternity for the king to arrive in the market. When he finally did, his companions began to take account of the materials and offerings brought forth for the king in the center of the market. They began to load the material meticulously and unprompted. Ivivin, though, still clutched his token in his hand. He wanted to give the king this gesture himself.

"Now that he is here," Ivivin panicked *"I have no idea how to approach him to ask him to take this gift."*

The king, the capable orator he was, gathered everyone in the center of the market and announced that he would speak. Ivivin, as well as the other denizens, hung on every word.

5

The king was infamous for, well, a lot of things. But amoung those many talents was his ability to give moving speeches. Rumor had it, too, that he wrote all of them himself or improvised them on the spot. Ivivin liked to imagine it was the latter. He liked to imagine that the king was so inspired by his subjects and the events in the world around him that the words flowed naturally. Truthfully, it did not matter. The king had a mastery of speech in either case. He had all his subjects in a circle, with him at the center. Necessarily, this meant that some of the attendees were to the king's back, but the king worked his imagined stage so well that no one ever felt neglected or ignored for long. The king's speech truly was inspirational, but lasted a little too long. Ivivin, for as excited as he was, lost focus, like a few other boys his age.

"I would like to thank you all personally for your offering of aid in my return home." The king started. "The amount far exceeds our need and capacity, however. I urge you all to share this rich bounty amoung each other tonight in a celebratory feast! It is not often man gets the chance to celebrate goodwill and..."

Ivivin again lost focus on the king as he turned to face a different fraction of the audience. Instead, he turned his attention to the crowd and noticed that some odd shuffling not far from where he was standing. Then, in the corner of his eye, Ivivin noticed a brief shimmer of steel and heavy, almost panicked, breathing.

6

After the fact, Ivivin could not recall what went through his mind or motivated him to act, only that he was glad he did. A hooded figure broke from the crowd and charged at the king from behind. Almost simultaneously, Ivivin, too, sprinted into the circle. The king turned to face the apparent assassin no further than a yard away, assuming a stance to counter this wild man. The assaulter reeled back his arm, readying a thrust. At this moment, though, Ivivin intercepted the assailant before he could loose his blade—a simple tackle sufficed. The blade nicked Ivivin's cheek and scarlet splattered outwardly. The attacker, stunned but not incapacitated, attempted to flee. The knights, who had already been moving onto center stage, easily disarmed and apprehended the would-be killer. The king then approached Ivivin, who was still bleeding, and pressed an ornate cloth to his face to ease the flow of blood. The crowd went wild but was silenced when the king rose his hand.

"Brave child, you have my gratitude. What is your name?" The king spoke clearly and directly at Ivivin.

"I-Ivivin, your highness. My name is Ivivin and I hail from a farm a short trek northward." With each word, Ivivin gained confidence and momentum. "The land there will be mine one day, but now it is my father's. And before him, his father's and his father's father." Ivivin held out his lump of wood. "I made this token for you out of a tree that has felled my family since they first settled here under the rule of your family. It would do me great honour if you would take it with you back to the castle." Ivivin finished.

The king stared for a moment and then laughed heartily. "Child...no... Ivivin. You are certainly a strange boy. You intervened in attempted regicide at great personal risk and yet your first words are that of a gift for your king!"

The king succumbed to another fit of laughter. Composed, he continued "I would be honoured to carry such a token with me on my journey." The king gently took the token from Ivivin's hand and, for the first time, had a chance to look directly into Ivivin's eyes— eyes which lusted after adventure and some greater purpose.

"Child, speak openly and honestly." The king addressed Ivivin once more. "Is there something your heart desires? Declare it and, be it in my power to grant it, I shall make it so." Almost as instinctually as Ivivin had acted to stop the assailant, Ivivin knew what he would ask of the king. He looked first to his father, who nodded approvingly, and then opened his mouth to address his highness.

7

"I want to become a knight." Ivivin stated resolutely to the king. The king was noticeably taken aback. He surely had seen wanderlust and an adventurous spirit behind the boy's eyes, but he did not anticipate this request. Though, in truth, it was not a unique occurrence. The lad was just so...young.

"Ivivin... are you sure that this is what you request of me? The life of a knight is romantic—this much is true—but it is also fraught with duty and with danger. Do you understand this?"

Ivivin nodded.

"It seems like you have thought about this for some time, child. If that is the case, surely you know the traditions and laws concerning knighthood and who may become a knight?"

Ivivin's heart sank but he piped up nonetheless, though half-heartedly. "Yes, your majesty, only those with ties to nobility may become knights."

The king nodded. "That is indeed the tradition and law handed down to me by my father, and his father, and his father's father..." The king held Ivivin's gift out for all to see. "Not unlike the tree and farm that this token represents. You understand, then, that I cannot simply knight you."

Ivivin stared blankly at the king. *"I should have known better than to ask for such a thing. It is beyond me and beyond my family."* Ivivin thought to himself, cursing his lot in life.

Before Ivivin could apologize for his arrogant folly, the king continued. "However, there is another way I may come to grant you knighthood, my young Ivivin. This is my contribution to the tradition that has stood for generations. It is no simple task, nor a short one. Will you hear it?"

Ivivin nodded.

"For one of common blood to become a royal knight," the king said, almost reciting the words. "the prospective knight must prove to the king that their honour, bravery, chivalry, and dutifulness far exceed that of an ordinary citizen." The king stopped there.

"Your highness...is that all? It seems incredibly..." Ivivin started.

"Vague?" The king said with a chuckle. "Yes, Ivivin, it is a tad vague, isn't it? Tradition has it that the knight-to-be and the king come to an agreement on what this means. So, here, now, I shall tell you what you need do to become one of my esteemed knights. First, you must travel to the southeastern edge of the kingdom to the city of Rumi. The citizens there have been plagued by a great and evil creature. It is your job to fell this being. Secondly, you must find an esteemed squire to follow you, as all knights have. And lastly, you must collect a great and valuable treasure on your travels. Once you have accomplished these three tasks, journey to Castletown and present to me the fruits of your travels. If I am satisfied, you shall be knighted by my hand. Do you understand, most loyal Ivivin?"

The king awaited a response.

"I do understand, your highness, but…" Ivivin trailed off.

"I see…" said the king "such a decision is immense and will alter your life's path greatly. You needn't tell me your decision. This trial of knighthood will always be available to you. I trust that destiny will run its course, one way or another."

The First Step

1

Leaving home was a decision that weighed on Ivivin's mind heavily. He was the only son and sole heir to his family's farm. To set forth on such an adventure with no guarantee of success nor survival meant, in essence, abandoning his family and their way of life. Indeed, Ivivin might not have decided to set forth on his journey had it not been for the insistence of his parents.

"Ivivin, my sweet, tender boy. I can see the struggle in your heart and the doubt in your mind. I am your mother, after all. Your pain is my pain. I, too, can feel your itch to challenge destiny and follow your dream. Go, voyage and make tangible your dream." Ivivin's mother said, tears in her eyes.

"But mother...what about you? And father? And the farm? And what if I... what if I..." Ivivin trailed off.

"Fail?" Ivivin's mother finished.

Ivivin nodded.

"Son, you needn't worry about your father and me. We love you dearly and we know you love us too. We will love you even if you fail. We will love you whether your journey ends in wild success or if you quit with your tail tucked between your legs. We will love you no matter where you go. We will love you no matter who you share your heart with. And we will love you even when you don't feel deserving of love." Ivivin's mother finished her speech tearfully.

"Go, my son. The king clearly sees something special in you, as do I and your mother." His dad tacked on.

Now, one might imagine that Ivivin's father spoke his brief and encouraging line with complete composure. However, the truth of the matter was that, if Ivivin's mother was a little teary, then his father was a complete and blubbering mess. Ivivin recalled this scene in his mind over and over, smiling, as he took the first steps towards the rising sun.

2

Travelling alone by foot, it turns out, is a bit laborious and boring, as Ivivin soon found. Still, in the isolation of travel, Ivivin found new things. He discovered a new appreciation for the fauna and flora of the land. Ivivin and his family did not own much beyond farming equipment, but they scraped together what they could for his adventure. Ivivin took account of his belongings as he was resting by a nearby stream.

"Let's see here" Ivivin muttered to himself, removing everything from his rucksack. "Some clothes, rope, flint...what else..."

Ivivin stopped, drooling as a result of his findings. His mother had prepared him some salted fish—one of Ivivin's favourite dishes. It was even more appealing in that it would keep a long time without care. It also helped that Ivivin had been subsisting mostly on berries and other scavenged material. He was starving, but he had resolved to save his mother's fish for a special occasion—perhaps when he strongly missed his family.

"Still..." Ivivin said to himself sheepishly. "I need to eat something soon. I can't rely on my meager food stores for long. Which means...I need to hunt something."

This idea did not particularly please Ivivin. He was a gentle and tender heart. Ivivin knew of the circle of life but had grown up on a farm, raising plants, and trading for meat at the market. On occasion, his family would tend an odd chicken or rabbit for slaughter, but Ivivin could not bear to be near when his mother ended their lives.

"It seems like I really don't have a choice." Ivivin sighed. He then noticed a faint glimmer from the stream.

"Aha!" Ivivin exclaimed. "I will catch some fish this afternoon." Ivivin said, plotting his afternoon's hunt.

3

And so, it was on this fine afternoon that Ivivin fought his first formidable foe. A small pike meandering in the stream. Ivivin had tried and failed to fashion a proper lure from his surroundings. Frustrated, he took to the stream to catch his dinner by hand. He saw his first opponent —this small pike—and prepared himself to do battle. Ivivin actually succeeded in catching the pike with his bare hands after about a dozen attempts. He was so shocked, however, at his own success that he had no clue what to do with the fish! He struggled to keep hold of the fish as it floundered about until...

WHAM!

The pike landed a solid upper-cut square to Ivivin's jaw, knocking him over and forcing him to release the fish, which wasted no time in putting as much distance between Ivivin and itself as possible. And so Ivivin sat dazed in the stream, contemplating the loss of his first battle.

4

Despite the absurdity of his duel with the honourable pike, as Ivivin continued his journey, hunger became a more apparent reality and poised a more apparent, and very real, threat. Out of necessity, Ivivin had eaten a few salted fish his mother had packed him. But by his estimation, there was still quite some distance between where he was and the next town over. Ivivin couldn't read a map, nor did he own one. But Ivivin had settled on going to the next closest major town to the east, Smithton, for several reasons, the primary of which was that he could find it relatively easily. All he had to do was follow the stream until he arrived. At this rate, though, Ivivin wasn't sure he could make it to town without starving to death. Both the thought of dying from starvation alone, as well as the hunger pains themselves kept Ivivin up through the nights—nights which afforded Ivivin time to think. To think about his place in this world and how big it really is. To think about the relationship between all things. Man and nature, animals and plants, and even worms and the earth. He came to accept life for what it was. A struggle. Survival was a struggle that humans had gotten good at minimizing through specialization and trade. But for life here in the wild—for him—it was still a struggle. An intricate dance to prolong one's life and survive to fight another day. Many nights, these thoughts haunted Ivivin. It made him realize how fragile and exposed he truly was. But, on occasion, it brought Ivivin comfort. He was not alone in his hardship. It was possible to live away from the safety and relative comfort of his home on the farm—the animals around him knew not of farms nor of houses, yet they got along in life just fine. Yes, Ivivin would occasionally feel comradery with nature and those apart of it. Most of the time, though, he was scared and alone in the dark, his belly aching of hunger and his mind screaming for rest that never was fully fulfilled. But, nonetheless, Ivivin had accepted life.

5

Ivivin knew he must hunt or fish or scavenge to survive. He did have basic knowledge of local plant life. But as he got further and further from home, the familiar species of plants grew rarer and rarer still. He was also wise enough to know not to just eat any old plant. That would be a one-way trip to an early grave. Ivivin's hunger was vast and pained him, but he pressed on towards town. One evening, just as the sun was setting, Ivivin caught sight of a rabbit retreating into its home in some shrubbery. He told himself he would catch it the following morning. But, when morning came, Ivivin could not bring himself to go forth and collect his meal. He just imagined the look on the rabbit's face and he remembered the rabbits he himself had tended at home. Unfortunately for Ivivin, though, hunger had made him weak. He found himself unable to continue his journey eastward. That night, still just a stone's throw from the rabbit's den, Ivivin did not sleep. He stared at the stars, his mind blank and tired. Out of the corner of his vision, he saw a huge, feathery mass descend from a nearby tree and snatch up a vole that had been foraging in the nearby grass. Naturally, he was startled. Both by the sudden appearance of the owl, but also by how quickly the vole's life escaped it. He became aware that death was not this abstract thing looming on some far-off horizon. It was here. He realized death was ever present for all living things. It would come and it could be unpredictable. More importantly, he realized that death made way and provided for life. Death was unpleasant and ugly. Dying frightened Ivivin on a primal level. But, nonetheless, Ivivin had accepted death.

6

The next morning, as soon as the sun had risen, Ivivin walked over to the shrubbery. He found the hole the rabbit had been residing in quite easily. His hands and knees were trembling, but still, Ivivin simply reached into the hole and pulled from it the rabbit. Much like Ivivin, the rabbit was young, male, inexperienced, and scared. Ivivin could see the fear and confusion in the rabbit's eyes. Realizing the torture he was inflicting on his prey and knowing he could not show mercy on this day, Ivivin snuffed out the life of the rabbit.

7

Ivivin had recovered his strength and recovered his resolve. He took his journey slowly at first, hastening as he began to gather and trap food more effectively. One evening, Ivivin was watching the moon rise as he was preparing to sleep for the night. The vastness of the world still terrified Ivivin, but tonight, under the light of the moon, was somehow tranquil. He looked at the moon and the stars for quite some time before deciding to call it a night. Just as he was preparing to lay down, however, he saw a silhouette appear in front of the moon. Ivivin squinted and looked to the sky once more, trying to resolve the figure.

"It's getting bigger." Ivivin said to himself aloud, perplexed. *"Wait, it's not getting bigger...it's falling!"* Ivivin realized too late as the mysterious object crashed into his face, knocking him over onto the ground, though more by surprise than by force. In fact, the impact was surprisingly light and soft. Ivivin sat up and realized that some sort of animal had fallen from the sky and now sat dazed in his lap. His first judgement was that it was a dirty mouse of some sort, but this mouse had feathers. Upon closer inspection, Ivivin found it was…

"An owl?" Ivivin said, almost not believing it himself. Not because the creatures were terribly rare. In fact, they frequented Ivivin's family's farm, hunting rodents that infested the fields. No, the question was not posed in surprise at seeing such an owl. Instead, Ivivin found it hard to believe that such a dirty, thin, and sickly-looking creature could be of the same sort of the majestic hunters he came to know on the farm and had thus encountered on his journey.

The owl recovered from his daze and looked up and around. It quickly, if clumsily, flew to the small pile of fish scraps that Ivivin had from his dinner, grabbed a small morsel of meat, gave Ivivin a look of terror, and then, as suddenly and frantically as it arrived, it departed.

Ivivin stared again to the sky, dumbstruck at what had just transpired. It took only moments for him to chuckle uncontrollably at the absurdity of this, the second 'battle' of his adventure. He laid down to sleep and, for the first time since leaving home, fell asleep with a smile.

8

The rest of his journey to Smithton was, well, frankly a bit boring. Sure, Ivivin had come to accept some profound truths of the world, but he was still just a lad.

"Better uneventful than dangerous, I suppose." Ivivin would often tell himself. It wasn't that he didn't appreciate the beauty around him. Indeed, if an area was particularly scenic, Ivivin often would end his day prematurely and stay there for the night. But isolation was setting in. Ivivin hadn't spoken to another person since he left the Gemi market, shortly after leaving home. Ivivin missed home. Luckily, though, on this day, Ivivin scaled a hill and could see the western face of Smithton on the horizon.

"If I walk all day, I can make it by nightfall!" Ivivin encouraged himself. His first checkpoint in sight, Ivivin continued towards the city. It was, perhaps, for the best that Ivivin did not suddenly stumble into town.

"I don't really have a plan for once I arrive, do I?" Ivivin allowed himself to realize. He spent the day's trek particularly

engrossed in thought. Despite all the time to think, though, Ivivin did not have much to go on by the time he arrived.

"I know not where I can find a great treasure…" Ivivin checked his coin purse *"…and I certainly cannot afford to purchase one. And I imagine I must have some renown in order to convince someone to become my loyal scribe."* The thought of having a follower of sorts was so absurd that it made Ivivin giggle.

"So, what remains is to dispatch the…the monster plaguing Rumi. But, I already knew that. That's why I am headed to Smithton in the first place." Ivivin was growing increasingly frustrated as he thought himself in circles.

"Well, I will stay on the outskirts tonight and go into the city tomorrow to gather as much information as I can." Ivivin said, trying to convince himself that he actually did have a plan.

And so, Ivivin approached the city and, no more than a few kilometers from the west entrance to the city, he stumbled upon a stable, seemingly abandoned. There was evidence of a house that had burnt to the ground not far from it. It had been so long since Ivivin slept in a manmade structure that he instantly and boldly decided to claim it as his own, if only for the evening. Ivivin was beaming as he took the first steps into the barn.

"I did it! I made it to Smithtown!" he yelled, both to alarm any animal residents and to express his elation.

"Here's to the journey of a thousand miles!"

Smithton

1

"It seems I can't resist poking around the town after all." thought Ivivin as he entered the city of Smithton. He had left his gear back in the stable, extremely 'well hidden' under a few pounds of hay. He did, however, keep his dagger on his person.

"One can never be too careful." He thought. As he walked about, he saw a vendor's area not unlike the one he saw with his father in Gemi. It spanned from one side of town all the way to the other. It was huge! Ivivin scoped out all the places excitedly, trying to guess what each vendor sold. As he carefully gathered his clues, he decided on the stores he would visit first in the morning. He also reminded himself that he needed to find someone who could tell him how to get to the mountain. He decided he would ask as many vendors as he could the next day. Anxious for the morrow, Ivivin decided to head back out to the stable. After quickly washing off in the stream that led him here, Ivivin fell fast asleep on the soft, albeit dry and scratchy, hay.

2

Ivivin woke the next morning to a feeling of extreme homesickness. He had been saving his mother's salted fish for a time like this—for when he missed home. So far, Ivivin had been eating mostly greenery and whatever he could catch in a poorly dug pit.

"It is due time for a proper meal." Ivivin thought ravenously. Hungry and homesick, Ivivin retrieved his bag from its hiding place and quickly opened it. To his utter horror, it seemed as if something had crawled into his bag and died! Upon further inspection, though, he noticed it was breathing. Suddenly, the mass erupted from the bag and Ivivin found himself face to face with...the peckish, sickly owl from a few nights ago.

"He must have snuck into my bag while I was in the forest that morning." Ivivin thought. Despite its dramatic and bombastic entrance, the little owl now seemed exhausted. It hastily stumbled back into the bag, recently dropped by a startled Ivivin, and resumed its stay. Ivivin opened the bag and saw bits of leaves and grass the

owl-invader had imported to cushion its new homestead. More strikingly, Ivivin noticed he had only two of the fish his mother had packed for him left.

"That wretched owl!" Ivivin thought. He snatched the fish from the bag and wrapped them in his spare clothes, effectively owl proofing his precious keepsakes before returning them to his bag.

3

When Ivivin arrived at the market, he was not disappointed. There were so many people, stands, booths, exotic foods, weapons, and knickknacks. Although saddened he was not actually there to shop, Ivivin had a great time looking from store to store to store. He imagined faraway lands and unknown people acquiring untold treasures that these merchants surely held. Ivivin then came to a sudden, striking realization.

"I AM headed to a faraway land!" he thought.

"Speaking of," Ivivin reminded himself *"I need to start asking people for directions."*

And so Ivivin started his task of pestering the locals for directions. Oddly enough, very few people seemed interested in Ivivin when they realized he wasn't a customer. Having obtained very little useful information, Ivivin headed towards what seemed to be the loudest area in the market. He figured that, the more people that were around, the more likely he'd encounter someone who was willing to help him.

4

As it turns out, following loud sounds is not always the smart thing to do. The source of the noise, Ivivin found, was an argument between a blacksmith and...

"Are those knights?" Ivivin wondered. And knights they were, though not from the kingdom from which Ivivin hailed. These knights had apparently travelled far and wide just to ask this smith to forge them weapons and armor. The smith, it seemed, denied their request. But the knights were not taking 'no' for an answer; they attacked the smith. Ivivin, acting on impulse, rushed to the aid of the smith. He was, however, brushed aside easily by one of the two knights. Persistent, Ivivin charged into the fray yet again, this time

making one of the knights stumble and allowing the smith to land a solid left hook. Annoyed at this slight, the knight turned to Ivivin and pointed his blade at him and prepared to thrust. As he did, the smith tackled him, getting a sizable cut on the arm as a result. The smith then leered at the knights with such ferocity and intensity that they both scurried away.

5

After the skirmish had ended, the smith returned to his forge, literally dragging Ivivin in tow. He sat by the fire and stuck a flat piece of steel in the flames. With neigh a wince, he calmly pressed the steel to his wound and seared it shut.

After methodically wrapping his burn in a somewhat tattered cloth, he turned to Ivivin.

"Who told you to interfere, boy!?" He bellowed.

"I'm sorry." Ivivin peeped. "I'll take responsibility."

Ivivin, burdened by incredible guilt, took the same hot steel and pressed it to the very same spot on his arm where the smith had on his own. Caught off guard by this gesture, the smith ripped the tongs from Ivivin's hands. The smith looked at Ivivin's arm, evaluating the damage. The steel had burnt and it would certainly leave a scar. But it was not nearly as severe a burn as the smiths' own and he appraised that Ivivin would suffer no lasting injury from it.

"Oh, you'll take responsibility all right!" the smith declared. "How much money do you have? I'll be taking all of it."

Ivivin firmly told the smith that he didn't have any and the smith didn't have a hard time believing it, looking at the boy.

"I do not have any money. None at all. You see, I am on a journey to the village of Rumi, far to the southeast. If I call fell the beast that plagues the town, I will be one step closer to becoming a knight."

When the smith heard Ivivin's last statement, he grimaced, but then addressed Ivivin. "Boy, the merchants of this town head to that city regularly. It is a port settlement of much commerce. But it is difficult to reach because it is nearly surrounded on three sides by mountains and by water on the fourth. If you do not have a guide, you will have to go around the mountains—a trek that could take years for an inexperienced traveler."

Ivivin's heart sank at these words.

"I cannot waste time here. I must help those people! Isn't there a…" started Ivivin, before the smith interrupted him.

"If you have a guide, then the trek takes no more than 3 or 4 weeks." Ivivin looked relieved. "I'll just follow the guide and the merchants, then." The smith sighed "As much as I would like to have you outta my sight, boy, the merchants left about a week ago. It'll be a few months, maybe even a half year, before they're back and ready to make the trek again."

Ivivin was heartbroken. "Must I really wait idly for the merchants to return?' he said, dejected.

"Wait idly!?" the smith exclaimed. "You will do no such thing! Have you forgotten that you are to take responsibility for my arm? It'll be at least a month before I can use it again somethin' proper. So, no, you will not be waiting idly, boy. You will act as my left arm for a while. That *is* what an honorable knight would do, after all."

Ivivin, although heartbroken, had no claim to refusal. He simply stood there, dumbfounded.

"I will see you here before dawn tomorrow, boy. There is much work to be done."

Ivivin returned to his stable on the outskirts of town. After again failing to shoo away the owl, Ivivin became so frustrated by his situation that he started kicking old hay around wildly. He was hopeless on his own! He couldn't even stand up for himself, let alone protect another person! He eventually wore himself out and collapsed onto his hay pile. Ivivin found the owl's continued presence frustrating. He had tried his best to get that message across to the little bugger, but the owl just didn't seem to get it. It saw an upset lad and raised him a scruffy animal cuddle. After numerous failed attempts at keeping him at bay, Ivivin eventually compromised by setting his bag near him and shoving the frayed creature inside. Despite all his frustrations, he was somehow able to fall asleep in no time at all.

6

At daybreak, Ivivin arrived at the smith's forge.

"You're late." grumbled the smith. "I said be back here before dawn."

Ivivin hastily, if half-heartedly, apologized.

"I don't know where you've been staying, boy, but from tonight onward you'll be staying here in the forge since you can't seem to be on time. But for now, it is time to get to work!"

And get to work they did. Ivivin was to make two-hundred nails by the day's end. He fumbled around amateurishly with the materials constantly. The first ten nails he made were scrapped immediately for being of an inferior, unusable quality. After that, Ivivin worked all day, stopping only for the occasional drink of water. After the first twenty nails, Ivivin's arms ached. He had worked a hoe all his life, true, yet this kind of pain was different. The heat, the weight of the tools, and the pressure on him to do well wore him down at every moment. Throughout it all, though, the smith simply stood there, watching him. So Ivivin forged on.

And on.

And on.

At the end of the day, Ivivin hadn't even made one-hundred 'acceptable' nails. The smith sneered and remarked that he would have to finish them himself. He sent Ivivin to gather his things.

During his walk to the stables, Ivivin was washed in disappointment in himself. He was also extremely worried for the future.

"Would every day be this hard? Was that request even possible?" Ivivin considered taking his things and running, but remembered the intense gaze of the smith and couldn't fathom escape. Before he knew it, his thoughts had brought him back to the stable. The owl, it seemed, had caught a vole (or, more likely, the vole died a peaceful, non-avian death and the owl had the luck to stumble upon it). The owl had seemingly placed half of the vole deliberately on the haystack Ivivin had been using as a bed. Oddly touched, but unwilling to eat the vole, he scanned the room for the owl but didn't find it.

"Maybe it was a goodbye gesture." Ivivin thought. That notion, he would soon find, was ill conceived. When he opened his bag to verify that he had all his possessions, there was the imp,

tucked away and now glaring at him for the disturbance. The owl flew from the bag and looked to the vole, then to Ivivin, and back to the vole expectantly. Ivivin handed the owl the remainder of the vole, saying that the little guy had earned it.

"So, I take it you are here to stay, huh?" said Ivivin, looking at the owl with mixed feelings. 'Well if you are going to be bugging me from here on out, I should give you a name."

While a thousand grotesque and cruel names soared through Ivivin's head at that moment, he knew he could not actually name the owl in that fashion.

"I dub thee Icarus, Imp of the Owls." The owl seemed genuinely confused, but Ivivin had come to expect that of the little monster by now. He was confident if he called it by that name enough, it would eventually get the picture.

"Speaking of names," Ivivin realized "I should really ask the smith for his name when I return to the forge. Icarus! Are you coming?"

The owl stood there blankly but suddenly realized the meaning of Ivivin's words when Ivivin shrugged at the lack of response and started to leave. It tumbled through the air and crashed onto Ivivin's shoulder and, subsequently, crawled into Ivivin's mobile owl home...er... bag. The new duo headed back to town, both ready to start a new page in their lives.

Smith the Smith

1

"You can't be serious" Ivivin said incredulously to the blacksmith.

"Did I stutter, boy? That is my name. It always has been and it always will be."

Ivivin couldn't cope with what he had just heard. Ivivin had simply asked the smith for his name.

"Alright then, Mr. Smith the Smith. Where should I put my belongings?" Ivivin said to an increasingly impatient Smith.

"Is that all you have?" Smith asked, genuinely surprised at the extent of the scarceness of Ivivin's resources.

Ivivin nodded.

"You'll be staying here, in the back room past the forge. There is an old, battered bed back there. I'm sure it is older than you are, but I am also positive that it's better than your previous arrangements." Smith said, picking stray hay off Ivivin's back. Sensing a disturbance, Icarus the owl crawled out of Ivivin's pack and revealed himself to Smith.

"My god, boy! What are you doing with that rat in your pack!?" Smith exclaimed, startled.

"What are you talking abo—OH! You mean the little imp! That's no rat, it's a bird. At least, I think it is..." Ivivin responded.

Smith's first instinct was to toss the owl outside to fend for itself, but the longer he stared at the disheveled beast, the sorrier he felt for it.

Smith relented. "He can stay too, I suppose. Just keep him out of the rest of the forge. Especially the kitchen. Understand?"

Ivivin and Icarus nodded in unison.

"Good. Get settled, boy. We have a full day ahead of us."

2

The first two weeks at Smith the smith's forge was hell for Ivivin. The work was grueling and there was no shortage of it. Ivivin, under constant scrutiny and criticism from Smith, learned to make amateurish nails and chain links. More time than that, though, was spent on learning to care for the forge and how to handle the tools. Ivivin quickly resigned himself to the fact that he would spend the rest of his days caked in ash and soot. It was grueling and monotonous work. Every night, Ivivin would collapse into his bed with whatever food Smith sent his way. He would ravenously inhale his meal, saving a little bit for his new pet soot-ball, Icarus, and then fall asleep almost instantly. When he woke in the morning that always came too soon, he was greeted by sore muscles and a dry mouth.

"I am not going to survive until the merchants' return" Ivivin thought each morning. Nonetheless, he continued working day in and day out until his second full week came to a close. Ivivin was surprised, then, when on the dawn of his fifteenth day at Smith's forge, he was instructed not to set up the forge right away. Instead, Smith instructed Ivivin to run to a bakery at the market and pick something up.

3

Ivivin knew better than to question Smith first thing in the morning, so he grabbed his bag and started to the market.

"I wonder if we are going to repair some kettles or pots?" Ivivin thought to himself, suddenly excited by the idea of learning to do something more complex than he had been doing for the last few weeks.

He had a bit of a skip in his step as he headed to the market. Smith had made Ivivin go introduce himself to as many market tradesman as he could, so his trip to the baker's shop was riddled with smiles and waves. Ivivin was startled by sudden movement in his bag before remembering that Icarus had been using it to roost. The winged vagabond poked his head out of Ivivin's bag, obviously nettled at the disturbance.

Ivivin recognized the smell of the bakery well before he saw it. He entered the baker's shop and was greeted by the owner. The husky, muscular woman was caked in, well, cake mix. She saw Ivivin and immediately gave him a box. It was much smaller and lighter than Ivivin expected. He opened it, his curiosity getting the better of him. The contents were simple. Three sweetrolls—no pans, pots, kettles, or trays.

He must have been visibly confused, as the baker chuckled and then commented "This is a bakery, hon, what did you expect?"

"Oh, nothing in particular, I suppose. Thank you very much, ma'am." Ivivin managed to spit out as he headed for the exit.

"It is no trouble, hon, and congratulations!"

"Congratulations?" Ivivin thought to himself as he made his way back to the forge. *"And what is with these sweet rolls? Does Smith have a sweet tooth?"*

4

When Ivivin returned to the forge, sweets and sooty owl in tow, he was shocked to see that Smith hadn't gotten the place ready for the day's work. Instead, Ivivin walked into the unusually cool forge perplexed. Smith heard his return and joined Ivivin.

"Took you long enough, boy!" Smith growled.

"Sorry, sir. I brought you your order from the bakery." Ivivin said, obviously a bit unsettled.

"Well, they won't do us any good here. Come with me to the dining room. And bring your blasted bird with you."

The three of them went to Smith's dining room, which was unusually clean and pristine. Ivivin set the sweetrolls and his bag on the table. Icarus rolled out of the backpack and stumbled a bit about the table, finally succumbing to dizziness and collapsing next to a document of some kind and a small box.

After a brief pause, Smith spoke up.

"Ahem. Ivivin, I can see you are a little confused. You see, it is tradition around these parts to celebrate when a craftsman accepts a new apprentice—it's a ceremony of sorts. I am not a fan of frivolities, so this is all you are getting. Deal with it."

Ivivin was awestruck. He was under the assumption that he was only here to repay his debt. He never expected for Smith to declare him an apprentice. Moreover, he had his own quest to pursue. Smith, almost as if reading Ivivin's mind, addressed this issue.

"Do not fret about your little quest, boy. You will be free to go with the merchants once they return. I just can't have you running around here representing my forge and you not be my apprentice. It just wouldn't be proper. Open the box." Smith gestured to the small box on the table.

Ivivin opened the box and found a plain, steel ring. Ivivin picked up the ring and inspected it. There was a small engraving on the outside surface, but otherwise it was a plain band. Ivivin recognized the engraving as the crest of Smith's forge. He slipped it on. It was a bit loose, but Ivivin liked the weight on his finger.

"Alright then, boy. All that's left is to enjoy these sweetrolls and have you read over and sign the contract."

Ivivin handed Smith a sweetroll and took one for himself. "Who is the third roll for, Smith?"

"I figured your dirty friend there would appreciate a share." Smith said, almost abashedly.

Icarus seemed to understand and started on his own sweet roll. It was only a minute or two before they all had finished.

"Alright, Ivivin, give that document a read over and sign. It essentially just authorizes you to act on my behalf in this city. Hence the ring." Smith explained lazily.

"Sounds good," Ivivin said. "But there is just one problem."
Ivivin seemed embarrassed.
"What is that, boy?"
"I can't read."

5

Life at the forge only picked up after Ivivin formally became Smith's apprentice. Every day, without exception, Ivivin worked the forge. And every night, without exception, Smith would help Ivivin learn to read. At first, Ivivin was dreadfully embarrassed by being illiterate, but Smith never seemed to treat it as anything special. Rather, it was just like when he showed Ivivin new techniques at the forge. Smith's arm was healing, but he still lacked the strength to work the forge all day. Instead, he supervised Ivivin almost constantly, critiquing and criticizing every motion of the hammer and tong—which is why it came as such a surprise to Ivivin when one evening, after his writing lesson, Smith approached Ivivin about working the forge alone the next day.

"Ivivin, I have some errands I need to run tomorrow. I will get the forge ready before I leave. I trust you can make the repairs to the carriage and finish up the sickle?"

Ivivin was startled by Smith's nonchalance, but nodded. "Yes sir, I can handle it."

Smith and Ivivin both retired to their rooms. Icarus greeted Ivivin happily with a scratchy hoot, obviously expecting scraps of his dinner. Over the course of the last few months, Icarus' coat...well it was still mangled and dirty, but it certainly was fuller. The little bugger really was starting to grow on him, but something was starting to bug Ivivin a bit.

"Icarus...maybe you should go out and start hunting your own food again?" Ivivin said to the scraggly bundle of feathers. Icarus looked at Ivivin, clearly hurt, and flew out the window. Ivivin felt a little bad, but it didn't stop him from being excited and anxious for his first day manning the forge tomorrow. Weariness eventually beat out excitement as Ivivin fell into a deep sleep.

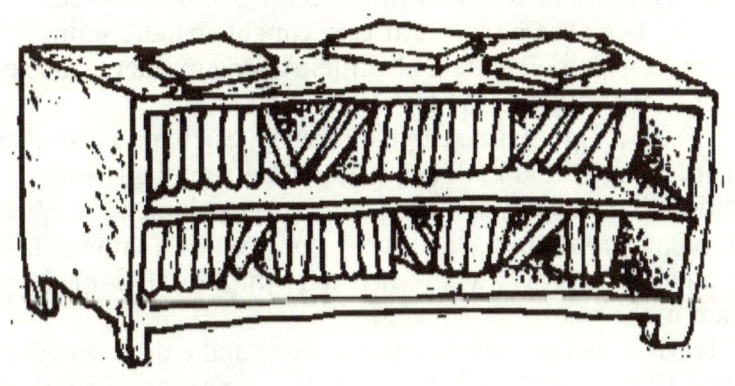

Just as Smith said, Ivivin awoke to an empty forge that, nonetheless, was prepped for the day's work. Ivivin took special care in his craftsmanship this day, knowing that Smith trusted and relied on him. Unusually, Icarus decided to come sleep in the forge on this day, perhaps sensing that Ivivin would start to feel lonely. More likely, though, was that it was a particularly cold morning and the forge was warm. It didn't matter to Ivivin which. He was glad for the company. It was a simple, yet complex art that Ivivin felt he was starting to get the hang of and, for the first time, Ivivin felt some individuality go into his work. He grinned with a sense of pride.

That afternoon, an older farmer woman came to pick up the repaired sickle. Her hands were calloused and her skin wrinkled, but she was vibrant and full of energy.

"How much do I owe you, sonny?"

"Let me see what Smith left me…" Ivivin said, looking through a stack of papers. Smith had started writing down the work and billing information—something that he never used to do—so that Ivivin would have to practice reading.

"Ah, here we go. It says that you owe him a booshell…"

Ivivin stopped and stared at the word a moment.

"Sorry, a half bushel of wheat come next harvests"

The woman smiled. "Oh, that Smith, always so sweet on me. Where is he? I'd like to thank him."

"He is gone running errands today. He left me in charge of the forge" Ivivin said, a hint of pride leaking into his voice.

"Oh, I can see he left it in very capable hands, sonny." She teased Ivivin with a chuckle and smile. After a moment, she seemed to realize something and she frowned.

"I see, it is that time of year already. Such a travesty." She looked at Ivivin, with a look expecting understanding—an expectation that was not met. She gave another look of somber realization and continued. "I suppose you wouldn't know. He is not very open about it. Anyways sonny, tell Smith I will come by next time I am in the market to say hello."

Ivivin was left with many questions and a drive to have them answered. But, more than that, he was left concerned for the wellbeing of his master.

7

Ivivin finished his work on the carriage a little bit ahead of schedule and decided to inform the patron that the work on it was complete. It involved a bit of a trek, sure, but Ivivin needed to clear his head a little bit from his encounter with the farmer woman. He tidied the forge a little bit, grabbed his ring (now hanging from a chain of Ivivin's own fabrication to prevent it from getting damaged while forging) and bag, and departed for the market.

"If I hurry, I can catch them at the market before they head home for the day!" Ivivin thought as he hustled, despite his whole body being sore from the day's work.

The walk was uneventful and he delivered the news without incident. The fellow told Ivivin he would be by before the market opened tomorrow to pick up the carriage. He paid Ivivin the agreed amount and Ivivin decided to wander the market for the last half hour before it closed. Ivivin was starting to become quite recognizable as Smith's apprentice. However, Ivivin thought it was strange.

"Do all apprentices get this sort of attention?" Ivivin thought aloud as he waved to a passing carpenter. Ivivin's absentminded wandering lead him to the same bakery Smith had ordered sweetrolls from. Ivivin was inspired by the sight. Smith did not pay him for his work—then again, apprentices were seldom paid to begin with. But Ivivin did occasionally get tips from generous patrons. It wasn't much, but Ivivin decided that he would use what he had to get some sweets for them to share. He entered the bakers, eager to surprise Smith with a small gift.

8

The baker, Isabella, smiled as she welcomed Ivivin. Ivivin explained that he was there to get a gift for Smith and to celebrate his own first day manning the forge alone. The baker smiled with a surprising amount of gentleness for her stature.

"You do remind me of him, you know." she said softly.

Ivivin was a little confused. He didn't think Smith and himself had all that much in common.

"Who, Smith?" Ivivin asked.

"No, hon. Smith's last apprentice, and the last we thought he'd ever take." She answered.

Somewhere in the back of his head, Ivivin knew that Smith must have had apprentices before him, but Smith was pretty reserved. He seldom spoke about his past. Ivivin figured that Smith would tell him eventually.

"Oh. Who were they? The apprentice before me?" Ivivin asked, his curiosity getting the best of him.
The woman paused thoughtfully before replying. "His son, Wayland. He was his apprentice about a dozen years ago."

"Oh." Ivivin said. "Where is he now?" Ivivin was unsettled by the mere utterance of his own question.

The woman snickered a sad snicker. "The Northern side of Smithton. Maybe three or four miles north of here, and about six feet straight down."

9

Despite the setting sun and his own judgement, Ivivin found himself walking north, a box of sweet rolls in hand, to the cemetery. Even after the sun set, the moon was exceptionally bright this evening, with barely a cloud in the sky. Ivivin felt shuffling in his bag when his scraggly bird friend appeared on his shoulder, yawning and looking a bit irate. It seems Icarus had failed to catch any prey during his hunt the previous night and had some hunger pains.

"Before you head out, Icarus, will you stay with me for just a little while?" Ivivin said, still being spirited away by his own legs to the cemetery. Icarus let out a small, affirming growl and settled down on Ivivin's shoulder.

Ivivin had never been to the cemetery here. Or any cemetery at all, really. He had always imagined them as unwelcoming and borderline creepy monuments to the dead. He was surprised, then, when he arrived at the gates to the cemetery. The whole place was tranquil and seemed to be at peace with nature. It was surrounded by hills on three sides, with lush trees forming the border. Ivivin never thought he'd find such a place welcoming, let alone beautiful.

"Still, I can't just walk in there. I didn't really have a plan, did I?" Ivivin thought.

Half driven by morbid curiosity and half by the entrancing beauty of the area, Ivivin decided to climb up on the hills and look at the cemetery from above. There Ivivin saw graves of all sorts, scattered across the ground. Something mesmerized him about the disorder and inconsistency of it all. There were maybe ten or so torches shuffling about the cemetery. Ivivin just sat on the hillside with Icarus and watched. Lights began to leave the cemetery, one by one, as time passed. When there was only one light left, Ivivin moved as close as he could while still being on the hill. Sure enough, it was Smith, hunched over in front of a simple grave.

Ivivin stood there, watching Smith, for what seemed like an eternity, ignoring Icarus nibbling at his ears, awaiting permission to go try his luck at hunting once more. When Smith finally started to move once more, the moon had already passed overhead. Before he started off, Smith touched two graves and patted them. Ivivin gestured to Icarus that he was free to go.

"Thanks for your company, Icarus. Good luck." Ivivin whispered to the owl as it stretched before taking off. Ivivin hurried, almost running, to ensure he made it back to the forge before Smith. With his last glance at the cemetery, he saw Smith looking up at the owl flying noisily past him overhead.

10

Ivivin had indeed returned to the forge before Smith. He sat waiting for Smith's return, unsure of what he should say, if anything at all.

"Is it really any of my business?" Ivivin questioned himself. *"Am I concerned for Smith or am I just curious for my own fulfillment?"*

As he recalled all the reading lessons and all the bread broken with Smith, the answer came to Ivivin naturally.

"I want to know more about this man. He is my mentor and friend. I want to be able to help, if I can."

Smith took his time walking back, arriving a full hour after Ivivin, with the sun starting to come over the horizon. He entered the forge, presumably to get the fires tempered for the day's' work. Smith was surprised to see Ivivin awake and waiting for him, but the look of surprise soon settled to one of resignation.

"I assume you have something to say, boy?"

"Just one thing." Ivivin replied.

"Out with it then." Smith pressed.

Ivivin reached out and offered Smith a sweet roll. "Tell me about your son."

Wayland

1

Smith sighed. "I suppose I shouldn't be surprised that you found out. A bunch of gossips these lot are." Smith looked at Ivivin squarely. "I suppose I trust you well enough, boy. But fair warning, if I am going to tell the story—my son's story—I am going to do it something proper. It'll be a long tale. You going to be able to keep those lazy eyes of yours open?"

Feeling invigorated, Ivivin nodded confidently.

"Alright then. I suppose I should start with his mother. My wife. Grandia. She was a wonderful woman. Her life's story could fill one-thousand tomes." Smith said with a hint of nostalgia in his voice.

"Is that a lot?" Ivivin asked.

Smith chuckled.

"Yes, boy. It is a lot. Grandia and I met here, in Smithton. She was born in Castletown. A writer, storyteller, and poet, she travelled all over this country of ours and even made her way to the far east for a time. She got by on her charm and her wit, I imagine. As for me, I was born here, in Smithton. An orphan, I was. Never did learn what happened to my own folks, but there was a smith here—a fellow by the name of Vulca. He took me in as his own. Was an elderly sort, so when he passed I was not much older than you. But he raised me right and taught me the fundamentals of smithing."

"This was his forge, then?" Ivivin interrupted.

"No, actually. He was a fair smith, sure, but he was not so gifted nor sought after to as need a forge of this caliber. This place was of my own creation. Though I suppose I do not need one quite so expansive now, either." Smith responded thoughtfully.

Ivivin had always thought that they didn't use much of the equipment or area of the forge, but he had always figured it was to keep things tidy.

Smith continued. "When I met Grandia, she was travelling with a group of merchants. They were headed north and wanted to wait a few weeks for warmer weather before continuing. When I saw her first, she was singing at Old Man Grey's tavern."

Ivivin was already imagining the scene. A beautiful woman singing melodically and sweetly, winning over the heart of his master.

"Was it her voice that won you over, Master Smith?" Ivivin asked excitedly.

Smith seemed to misunderstand Ivivin's question for a joke, as he started to bellow in laughter.

"No, no, Ivivin. In fact, her voice was something awful. Like a dying toad or a breathy hag." Ivivin couldn't help but notice Smith beaming as he recounted the tale.

2

"So... if not for her voice, what caught your eye about Grandia?" Ivivin asked excitedly.

This was really the first time Ivivin had talked about this with anyone besides his parents. He was surprisingly enthralled by the story of Smith's youth and romance.

Smith sat and thought for a moment before responding. "Well, she certainly was a beautiful woman. But beauty is more common than you might think, boy. If I had to say one thing that caught my eye at first...it was her confidence."

"Her confidence?" Ivivin asked, puzzled. He wasn't expecting such an answer. In the tales told around his hometown, the knight was always wowed by the beauty or kindness or gentleness of the woman.

"That's right boy. You have got to be pretty confident to get in front of a packed tavern and sing like that when your voice is so horrid. She seemed so secure in who she was and who she wanted to be. The moment I recognized that is probably the same that I came under her spell." Smith continued.

"So, what happened? Did she notice you too?" Ivivin prodded eagerly.

"I am getting there, boy. I am not so eager to recount all the times she rejected any offer of mine to spend time together. She just wasn't having it. I musta approached her dozens of times during her stay here. She was always so kind and gentle and... well, she did flirt quite a bit. But she never accepted my company. Until, one day— the time I said would be my last attempt—she did."

"What changed?" Ivivin asked, genuinely curious.

"I wondered that same thing for quite some time, Ivivin. It wasn't until I asked for her hand in marriage that she gave me an answer. Apparently, she had, by chance, walked by my forge the morning prior. I was so absorbed and focused in my work, I didn't notice her passing by. But she noticed me. She...Grandia told me that I was so focused and so artful in my discipline that she was awestruck. If her singing her scratchy song in that stale tavern was the moment when I fell under her spell, well, I suppose that morning is when she fell under mine." Smith said with a warmth that Ivivin had never heard from him.

3

"Grandia and I... courted each other for quite some time before we wed." Smith continued. He stared at Ivivin a moment and chuckled. "In fact, she refused my proposal outright my first attempt. Made the ring myself and everything. But she refused to spend her life with a man who could not read and write."

Ivivin couldn't believe it. Smith's home was filled to the brim with books and, as far as Ivivin could tell, he was an excellent teacher.

"You mean, you couldn't read either?"

"That's right, boy. I was older than you by the time I learned the written word. Writing is an art itself—an art so dear to Grandia that the idea of committing to one who couldn't appreciate it repulsed her. Her wanderlust, she could set aside. But not her words."

"So, did you teach yourself how to read? Is that even possible?" Ivivin asked.

"No, no. Luckily I had a master of the art wrapped up in my arms. Grandia, she was my teacher. Harsher and stricter than I, but infinitely more eloquent. It took me quite some time to learn, in no small part because learning from your lover entails a certain level of distraction. But I learned nonetheless."

"And you proposed again?" Ivivin prompted, attempting to get Smith to progress his story.

"Yes, Ivivin. I proposed again. This time, with the written word. I finally spoke her language. There was no longer any doubt in our minds that we wanted to become family."

"What did you write to her?"

Smith was taken at the frankness of the question, but shook it off.

"A poem."

Ivivin opened his mouth again, undoubtedly to ask him to recite the poem. Smith stopped him in his tracks.

"That poem is not for you and it certainly is not for today."

There was silence for a while as Smith reflected on his own words. He continued "Well, we aren't here to talk about my wife, are we? I had started to garner a name for myself as a smith. Not long before the time that we wed and were with child, people began arriving from all over the country to ask specifically for my services. You can imagine, with a child on the way, that I was glad for the increase in business. But I was only one man. Luckily, just as people journeyed for my wares, others came to me to learn."

4

"Before my son, I had three apprentices. That makes you my fifth, I suppose." Smith told Ivivin. "Helmschmied was my first and the first to ask me. I won't pretend as if I appraised him carefully. I took him in because he seemed trustworthy and I needed the help. His previous master had passed before Helmschmied believed himself ready. In truth, he was only a few years younger than me and had much more formal instruction in the art than I ever did. Nonetheless, he was rough around the edges. His personality was cold and pragmatic. But, in the forge, he found his passion. He loved making exquisite armours and folk loved to buy them. He learned the fundamentals from me to that end. Over the course of just a few months, we had developed a style and method for armour making that only increased our renown. I would have thought it a miracle, our success. That is, until I saw a real one."

"A miracle? What was it?" Ivivin hung on Smith's every word.

"The birth of my son."

5

"I fell in love with Wayland the moment I laid eyes on him. And I was so grateful to my wife, his mother, for bringing him into our lives. Helmschmied took more of a lead role in the forge for a time. Within about two years of his apprenticeship with me, not terribly after we celebrated the first anniversary of Wayland's birth, I formally graduated him to a master and we became partners. It was a happy time." Smith recalled fondly. "I had a healthy son, a loving wife, and a dear, if distant, friend. I was recognized as a master of my art, which brought about change. One day, a royal messenger came to our forge." Smith laughed. "I don't care much for knights, but even I have to concede that our king is unusual and kind. You see, he wanted me to be his smith. He could have ordered it, but, instead, sent a messenger and directed him to ask me if I would."

"You were the king's smith!?" Ivivin interjected.

Smith shook his head. "No, boy. This place was my home. I had my family. I had this forge I built from nothing with my own two hands. I was happy here and nobody, not even royalty, would take that from me. Instead, I sent the messenger back with two things. The first was a beautiful shield that was as durable as it was majestic. It was the finest piece Helmschmied and I ever made together. It was also our last."

"Why was it your last? Did something happen to him?" Ivivin blurted.

"No, no. The second thing I sent back with the messenger was Helmschmied himself. My first pupil, my partner, and friend.

He had long outgrown this forge and we agreed that he would go in my stead. And so, he did."

6

Smith continued with his story, despite the sun having risen and the forge being unprepared for the day's work.

"So, there I was, down a partner and up to my neck in work. My wife, bless her, helped the best she could when she could. She also convinced me to take fewer contracts and, eventually, we had settled into a happy little routine..." Smith trailed off.

"Routine... I suppose routine is what did it. You see, my wife had spent her whole life travelling and writing. Though it was not an agreement we reached quickly, I could see that being bound to this town wore on her. So, we agreed that she would travel, alone, once more. She had always wanted to visit the Giganta Valley in the city-state of Olympia, not terribly far south from here. Relations with that country are a bit more strained now, but, at the time, the trip was a relatively safe one."

"How long was she gone?" Ivivin asked

"Three-hundred and sixty-four days. She promised to be back within a year and left on the day after Wayland's fourth birthday and returned just before the fifth. That woman sometimes, I swear. She returned and it was like she was never even gone. She said she had enough material for a few years and we returned to our happy lifestyle, for a time."

Smith's face had been extremely emotive during his story. Taking a moment to compose himself before continuing, Smith adopted a sullen look, as if he had tried to numb a great pain.

7

"Grandia was a hearty woman. Well-travelled and smart enough to keep herself safe and healthy. I don't think I had seen her sick a day in her life. But, while in Olympia, she contracted an illness that did not set in right away. You may have heard of it. It is one of the reason's travel to the south is more difficult. It is called Diakopí-tharros in their ancient tongue. We call it Crumbleheart disease in these parts."

Ivivin shook his head. He hadn't heard of many illnesses, let alone ones from a foreign land.

"Apparently, it is caused by some curse or parasite found in food and water there, though no one is exactly sure the precise cause. The people there, they have grown to tolerate it. Very few people get sick from it, though those that do ail just as intensely as the rest of us."

"What happens?" Ivivin asked with morbid curiosity.

"It is called Crumbleheart for a reason, lad. It erodes at the heart, both one's body and one's spirit. The cause of death is simple. The heart weakens and weakens until it eventually falls apart all at once under the force of its own beat. But..." Smith hesitated. "Those who get it often die well before their death."

"I don't understand." Ivivin said, genuinely confused. Even Icarus seemed perplexed.

Smith, the hulking mass of a grizzly man he was, started to cry and sob. Ivivin knew not how to comfort the man, so he just moved closer to him and waited.

"Boy, those cursed with that horrid sickness...they slowly lose the ability to feel all things good. No hope. No happiness. No joy. No love. They die long before they draw their last breath."

8

Ivivin could hear roosters rousing as he waited for Smith to continue.

"The doctors here, they were able to identify the illness with relative ease. They had not the means of curing her here. But there was hope. The illness was much more common in the south. The doctors there might have had a solution. Unfortunately, Grandia would quickly lose her ability to travel. It was unlikely she would survive the venture once more. Our remaining option was to get a physician or medicine and bring it back for her. I had neither the money nor the desire to leave my wife's side. She had spent much of our savings on her journey and I had not been accepting nearly the volume of contracts to have been able to save much. This led me to bring on my next two apprentices. Brothers, twins in fact, by the names Tubal and Cain. I was pressed for time and for money. I put out word that I was accepting any and all contracts. Tubal, Cain, and I, we did quality work. Rushed, unlike with my first apprentice, but still fine work. But, as we were no longer being choosey with our work, we crafted many more weapons than Helmschmied and I had ever done, and for people whose causes we neither knew of nor cared to know." Smith sighed, got up, and put a kettle on over a fire.

Ivivin watched him in silence. Smith's hands were quivering. Smith resumed his seat and continued.

"My goal was to earn enough to convince someone to go in my stead. Tubal and Cain sensed my desperation. They had not the talent of Helmschmied or I, but they thrived under the pressure and devoted themselves to the cause. I went beyond dedication, though. I became obsessed. I was consumed by the idea of saving my wife. Obsessed to the point where I neglected her at the start of her decline. I did so many things wrong. So much that I regret. Once I noticed her health starting to decline, I put out word that I sought a speedy traveler to journey to Olympia and seek a physician or cure and bring them back. I thought my bounty would be more than sufficient to motivate any journeyman. But word of the illness and its effect had started to spread and there was tension at the border of our two kingdoms at the time. No one heeded my call. So, I did something horrid. I asked Tubal to go… No, I ordered it. A command from his master. I threatened to denounce him as my student should he not go. Tubal, the kind man, could tell how I hurt and departed on the journey without a word of hesitance or objection."

9

Smith paused his story once more and prepared tea for Ivivin and himself. They sipped on it a while before Smith continued.

"I had largely ignored my wife in favor of work, trying to secure funds to secure her life. It was not until after Tubal left that my wife, she pleaded with me to work less and spend my days with her. I am so glad she had the courage to put me in my place. I supervised Cain and aided him when he needed it, but my days became filled with time with my wife. When she could walk, we walked around the town and talked and sung and even skipped. When she lost strength in her legs, I carried her. Eventually, she had not the stamina to leave the house, but her heart...it was still whole. She smiled and laughed as I played with our son. She read and wept for the characters in books. She wrote and wrote and wrote. I watched her write for hours and days and weeks. She was fighting as hard as she could to live and live full of love."

"Eventually, I began to worry, as did Cain. Tubal still had not returned. It hadn't been so long that we were seriously concerned for his well-being, but it was ample time to make the voyage and return. And... Grandia...was dying. She could no longer sit up. I could see deadness behind her eyes when she thought she was alone. One night, the night of our child's...of Wayland's 6th birthday, she asked to speak with me in private."

"Smith, my dear husband, dry your tears. I haven't even had a word yet." She told me gently. "Is Wayland in bed?"

"Yes, Grandia. He sleeps."

"Good, good. Smith, my sooty lover, I have some favours to ask of you."

"Of course, my dear Grandia. What are they?"

"I do not have the strength tonight to write, but I am so very close to finishing my book. Will you write as I say?"

I picked up the tome, already bound, and turned it to where her writing ended and I listened to her words, putting them to paper. My coarse and ugly script contrasted her elegant words. It was not much, perhaps only a single page.

"Is that all, my Grandia?"

"I am afraid not. I have a much crueler favour I need of you. I know not when Tubal will return. When he does, please give him my gratitude, but I fear I will not last to his return. And I do not think I could recover even—"

"Shut your mouth!" I exclaimed in anger, which subsided and devolved quickly to sadness. "You are going to make it. Look how hard you've fought. You still feel wholly. You have time yet left!"

She shook her head. "No, my dear lover. I am just barely hanging on. I can feel this evil thing seeping into my core. I know not the words to describe it, but I can feel the cold. My body may live a while yet, but my soul is battered and torn. I am whole, but only just."

"So, what would you have me do? Call Tubal back and just watch as you become hollow?"

She smiled at me faintly. "No, I do not wish for that fate. I do not wish to know a world where I do not feel love for you and our son. Please, Smith. I lived a life of wonder and amazement before we met, but nothing can compare to this feeling. I won't let it leave me. So, please, while I love you both still so fiercely…" She trailed off.

I knew what she wanted. As if in a trance, I brought Wayland, still sleeping, from his room to her side. I followed her instructions and brewed a noxious drink. I wanted so badly to drink with her, to slip away. A world without her seemed devoid of happiness. Wayland, though, he anchored me here. Grandia, she insisted that she drink it herself, with no help from me. I am unsure if it was to go out on her own terms or to spare me from delivering the toxin, but she did not hesitate when the draught touched her lips. The night was long as I held her in my arms with Wayland in resting in her lap, but by morning she had passed. Her last words to me…she sang that same song she sang on the day first we met. With her same, scratchy voice, she let me know she was whole until the very end.

10

"And that is how the life that could fill a thousand tomes came to an end" Smith muttered, his cup trembling in his hand. Ivivin knew not what to say, or even if he should. They sat in silence until Ivivin could stand it no longer.

"What of Tubal?"

Smith sighed deeply. "Tubal returned. He had gotten caught in a skirmish on the border and had lost an eye and was wounded badly. A kind family took care of him there and nursed him to health. He brought back news that there was no cure. Only rumors and superstitions. The family that nursed him back to health, they were Olympian." Smith stared at Ivivin. It slowly dawned on Ivivin the implications of that statement.

"You mean…?" Ivivin managed

"Yes, Tubal, too, had been cursed with the very same disease he went to find a cure for. Moreover, we now knew there was no cure. Cain, he was livid—furious at me for sending his brother on that fruitless trip. He had seen the devastation it had brought on my wife and I had doomed his brother, his own twin, to the same fate. One night, I noticed that one of the swords we had made together had gone missing. I assumed Cain intended to take my life, so I took Wayland and asked Isabella, the woman at the bakery, to watch him for the night. I returned just in time to see Cain thrust the blade into

42

the heart of his brother. I could not move. He stared at me from across the room as he plunged the same blade into his own chest. My selfishness...it was the hand that guided his blade."

11

"The following years were...complex. I am going to skip ahead to thirteenth anniversary of the day of Wayland's birth. I had refused every apprentice that came my way and had resolved to never take another apprentice. But, at thirteen, Wayland convinced me that he wanted to learn my trade and I relented. He became my fourth apprentice. I had changed since my wife's passing. I cared very deeply for my son, sure, but I had become isolated from anyone else. I had become obsessed with money. I felt that, if I had more, I might have been able to help my wife. So, I still fulfilled any contract, as long as it paid well enough, given Wayland and I could handle it ourselves. Wayland learned the trade well and everything went smoothly until a few weeks after he turned seventeen."

Ivivin knew already how this story would end, but Smith's words held him at attention nonetheless.

"We were approached by a group of men to make weapons and armour. They were knights from a distant land and they made a very generous offer. This was the first and only time Wayland spoke back to me. He did not trust the men or their money. He refused to work on those weapons and begged me not to. But I carried on without him, assigning him other work since he would have nothing to do with it. What a fool I was."

Smith took a moment to compose himself.

"Those men...they were indeed knights, but sworn to a king not so noble as ours. When I had completed their order, they did not pay their balance. Instead, they beat me near death and took it all from my forge. Then they took the armaments and pointed them at the townsfolk. They robbed every vendor, killing any and all who resisted. My son tried to convince them to just leave—told them that they could have the armour and weapons if they just left. They struck him down with blades that I myself forged. Yet again, my selfishness was the hand that guided the blade that ended the life of my only son, Wayland."

Growth

1

Ivivin and Smith had undeniably had grown closer after sharing in Wayland's story but, other than that, not much changed. Ivivin continued working for Smith day in and day out. Ivivin carried on with his lessons in the written word. Icarus was learning through rigourous trial and error how to better hunt. Some nights, he didn't need to eat any of Ivivin's food at all, though sloth still plagued the owl on occasion and he was more than happy to just feast on the scraps of Ivivin's dinner. As the days came and passed, Ivivin grew more satisfied in his work. But a thought lingered in the back of his head—a fear of growing so comfortable here that he might abandon his quest here, at its first juncture. Nonetheless, Ivivin took great pleasure in his work and all the people he was able to meet because of it. Indeed, Ivivin often handled orders and deliveries, giving him ample opportunity to speak with a great deal of people. He often had to turn people looking for weapons or armour away and had become quite adept at it. So, when yet another fellow walked in this day looking for weapons and armour, Ivivin was ready to give him the same spiel.

Ivivin now knew why Smith refused to make weapons and armors. And, though he knew and understood the reason, that did not stop Ivivin from wanting to learn how. He had restrained himself for the sake of Smith and had never even tried to make one, but the itch persisted.

"It would be incredibly useful to know how to make and repair such things on my journey" Ivivin thought to himself. *"But I couldn't ask that of Smith."*

And so, Ivivin turned to his visitor to refuse their services.

"I am sorry, sir, we don't produce weapons or armour here. It'd be best if you took your business elsewhere."

"Drat." said the visitor, who was very apparently well-travelled. "I was hoping to get a new set and break it in before leaving with the merchant escort to Rumi."

"Rumi...that is the town which the king has tasked me to save! The merchants, they have returned and it seems they are preparing to leave once more!" Ivivin thought excitedly.

The rejected traveler was already halfway down the street when Ivivin realized that he was his best chance and finding out about joining the expedition. Ivivin chased the fellow down and pressed him for information. Ivivin was directed to the head of the merchant group, who was more than happy to have Ivivin along, free of charge, given he didn't have cargo for the escorts to defend and helped the caravan as needed.

That evening, Ivivin sat down to dinner with Smith.

"How do I bring this up…" Ivivin deliberated. It certainly seemed like a delicate issue to Ivivin. After all, he and Smith had grown quite close. The struggle must have been very apparent of Ivivin's face, because Smith growled at him suddenly.

"Spit out boy!"

Ivivin, shocked, nervously spilled the details of the merchants' departure and his plans to join them.

"The next full moon, eh?" Smith said deep in thought. "That doesn't give us much time to prepare. Perhaps three weeks with change."

"Us?" Ivivin thought.

"Well, no use dwelling on time we do not have." Smith continued. "Ivivin! Tomorrow, and each day thereafter, you shan't be working in the forge. You must prepare for your journey."

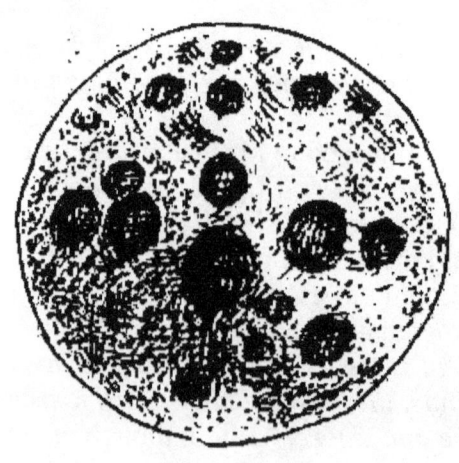

3

The next morning, Smith beckoned Ivivin towards the part of the forge that had not been used even once since Ivivin's return.

"I don't know much about it myself, but I am going to help you learn the basics of the sword." Smith told Ivivin. "Take this armour, a light training mail, put it on and meet me out back."

Smith left Ivivin in the forge alone. Ivivin stood before the mail and a dusty mirror. He removed his clothing to put on the armour. A quick glance in the mirror caused him to take pause, however.

"Is that really me?" Ivivin thought, dubious of the mirror's quality. A combination of age and the toils of smithing had made Ivivin more hearty and muscular. He certainly was nowhere near as large and developed as Smith, but, at the same time, it was hard to believe that he had changed that much.

"I don't know that my own parents would believe it" Ivivin whispered to himself as he strapped on the mail and walked to meet Smith.

4

Ivivin savoured every day that passed. Smith, perhaps because of his experience with Grandia, was extremely helpful in helping Ivivin pack and prepare for his journey. His writing lessons reached a natural conclusion, he was taught the very basics of swordplay (though he had no sword), and he finished up all the smithing projects he had started. Ivivin, though not a master of any of these trades, felt empowered by his new skills. He couldn't imagine trying to have continued his adventure as he was when he first arrived. He was scared still, sure, but he, for the first time since his journey began, felt like he had tools to help him survive.

Though Ivivin's departure was imminent and Smith helped with many facets of preparation, the two didn't speak much about the departure itself. Instead, they spoke mostly about the same things they always did—the tasks at hand, what is for dinner, and the like. It wasn't like they were avoiding the topic, but there was just never a place where it seemed appropriate to bring it up. Smith and Ivivin had been spending less time together during the day—Smith would often give Ivivin tasks to do on his own or go attend to some errand. The time they did spend together didn't need to be sullied.

Just a few nights before the merchants planned on departing, Ivivin finished gathering the essential travelling supplies he would need for the trip. He was sitting in bed, eating supper, and watching Icarus as he returned from his hunt empty-handed.

"Icarus," Ivivin said to the noisy would-be-hunter "I have a question for you."

Icarus looked at Ivivin intently.

"Does this owl understand me or not?" Ivivin wondered when, suddenly, Icarus swooped to his side and began prodding around his plate.

"Maybe not…" Ivivin sighed.

"Icarus, are you coming with me or are you staying here with Smith?"

Despite his rugged exterior, Ivivin knew that Smith had a soft spot for the feathered mongrel and thought that, maybe, it might be best if Icarus stayed.

Icarus looked at Ivivin, confused, but slowly seemed to realize the meaning of the words. Icarus responded by tucking himself in Ivivin's bag and refusing to leave it for the remainder of the night.

As Ivivin laid to bed that night, he smiled.

"I know Smith would really like to have Icarus around, but I think I might get kind of lonely without the little devil."

5

The passage of time is inevitable, of course, but the day of Ivivin's departure still seemed to arrive rather suddenly. Ivivin was all set, having loaded up his provisions in the days leading to today. All that remained was one final breakfast with Smith. Well, that and to make sure Icarus didn't break anything. Ivivin was anything but surprised, then, when he walked out to the dining area. Smith was reading, waiting for Ivivin and his scrappy sky-rat, with three sweet rolls and tea set out on the table. Smith set aside his tome and the three of them indulged in this, their little tradition, one last time before Ivivin once more set forth on his adventure.

6

After the last of the tea had been sipped and the last of the sweet licked from their fingers, Smith and Ivivin both stood.

"Now, now boy. Don't be in such a hurry. Stay here a moment. I'll be right back"

Smith gestured to Ivivin to resume his seat. Ivivin obliged, scritching Icarus's chin as the bird began to doze. In the distance, Ivivin could hear the clanging of metal but thought nothing of it. That is, until Smith returned with what looked to be new armor and...

"A sword!?" Ivivin said in disbelief.

"Aye, that it is. Glad you learned something in the months you've been here." Smith retorted and he handed Ivivin the sword.

"I had always heard that Smith was renowned for his weapons, but this is more than just a sword. It is almost like a sculpture—more art than blade." Ivivin thought, inspecting the piece. It was not a needlessly ornate blade. Sure, there was some flair to it, but the beauty came from the impeccable metal work. Every angle and juncture seemed intentional and deliberate, as if predetermined by destiny. Indeed, Ivivin would not be surprised if the blade came from nature itself, before man had tainted the name with its crude mimicry.

"I figured a shorter sword would be best for you. Despite all your growth, you're still not a large fellow and a short sword should be easier for you to adapt to as you continue to age. How is it?" queried Smith.

"It's incredible. When did you have time to make this?" Ivivin asked, stupefied.

"I started the day you told me of the merchant's imminent departure. I couldn't send you out there with only a dull dagger to protect yourself."

"Only three weeks!" Ivivin exclaimed in his head. *"This sword seems like it would have taken a lifetime to craft. Smith truly is a genius!"*

"The armour next, boy. It is a bit simple, but it should fare you well." Smith said, handing Ivivin the mound of metal. Ivivin slipped on the armour. It was incredibly simple, especially compared to his sword. Mail that covered his torso and back, stopping just shy of halfway down his arms. The left shoulder was fortified with a spaulder. Ivivin bounced around the room, surprised at how light it all felt, especially in comparison with the training armour he had used in the days prior.

"Make sure you maintain—"

Smith was cut off by sudden embrace from a teary Ivivin.

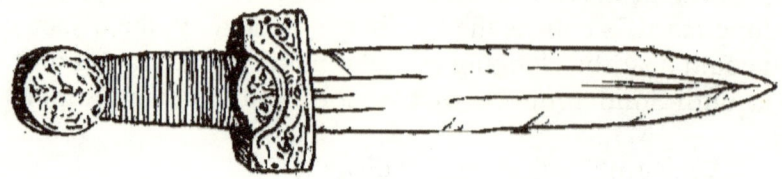

7

Ivivin and Icarus made their way to the east most side of town, past the market, where he was to meet up with the merchants. In addition to his new sword and armour, Smith had given Ivivin a small amount of ink and parchment to practice his letters. Ivivin was so giddy and excited that his anxiety seemed small and far away. He basically skipped all the way across town, much to the annoyance of Icarus who was trying fruitlessly to sleep in Ivivin's pack.

His enthusiasm would soon fade as he arrived to a bit of a disorganized mess. This trip was announced on far shorter notice than others and no one seemed quite ready. Eventually, the caravan set out, a full three hours later than they had planned. Ivivin was in no rush to chat with the merchants, as they seemed to all be doing with each other—there would be plenty of time on this trip to get to know them. Instead, every so often, Ivivin would look back to Smithton and, each time he did, it became smaller and smaller. When the city was nearly out of view, no larger than his little finger on the horizon, Ivivin snickered to himself.

"It's funny how a place I once thought so grand and expansive seems so tiny from here. Or maybe I've just grown big." thought Ivivin, giving his second home a final look before scrambling to rejoin the caravan.

The Journey to Rumi

1

Ivivin found travelling with the merchants to be infinitely more enjoyable than travelling alone. While all were careful to ration their provisions and still lived a life of scarcity, just having company made all the difference. It certainly was less boring and helped Ivivin feel a little more secure. As they travelled to the southeast, Ivivin learned more about the situation in Rumi. It was a port town surrounded on every side either by mountain or ocean. As such, it did fairly well economically, as it attracted exotic wares and sellers, though they could barely produce enough essentials for their own populace. For years they flourished as a shining example of trade and commerce. That is, until the monster arrived and took up residence in the mountain and began demanding tribute, straining the population's ability to sustain itself. That is why the merchants were so eager to return—they were fetching outrageously good prices on commodities and some were even returning with exotic wares that would be worth far more inland.

Ivivin did his best not to imagine the monster he would eventually have to face. It was, after all, a way off. Instead, he inquired about the details of their journey and why the path the merchants were going to take. He learned that there was a series of caves that they could use and cut straight through and under the mountains. It was, apparently, very dangerous to go without folk who had already been, as it was very easy to get lost. Likewise, the journey was always made in large groups as it is well known that dire wolves lurked in and about the caves.

"But don't worry," one merchant told Ivivin "they are too timid and scared to attack large groups. Especially when we have our secret weapon!" he finished confidently, gesturing to the campfire.

It seemed as if the merchants had a very good idea of what they were doing, so Ivivin and Icarus passed their days with very few worries. Travel could be wearisome, but nowhere near as exhausting as working the forge. And it could be unexciting and monotonous, but Ivivin had learned to enjoy his companions and the scenery around him.

The rest of the journey to the caves, which Ivivin now knew were called the Wolfelaw Caves, was uneventful. They arrived at the mouth of the caves about midday, but, rather than enter, the merchants started setting up camp for the night.

"How strange." Ivivin thought *"We've always travelled all day—until sunset and sometimes even beyond. Why are we stopping now? It will be dark in the caves anyways."*

Sensing his confusion, a merchant approached him. "I bet you are wracking your mind trying to figure out why we've stopped for the night already, huh? I'll let you in on the not-so-secret secret, my lad. On the surface, it is to ensure we are well rested for the journey, which will take two full days. But we also want to make our presence known to the wolves. Wouldn't want to startle them. A wild beast is dangerous, but one that feels backed into a corner is deadly." The merchant warned.

Ivivin nodded, feeling a sense of foreboding that only worsened when, around the campfire that night, the merchants pointed out shifting silhouettes of the wolves in the distance. Ivivin struggled to sleep, anxious about their journey the next day. He clung to his sword closely this night.

3

Ivivin was surprised at the light spirits of the merchants as they awoke before dawn the following day. They were chatty and seemed excited—far more than Ivivin had expected, given his own unease. As they approached the entrance of the caves, Ivivin quickly realized why. The walls and ceilings of the cave were riddled with blue gems that sparkled and illuminated the cave. A nearby merchant noticed the look of amazement and perplexedness on Ivivin's face and grinned.

"It's amazing, isn't it? I heard that, once upon a time, this entire cave was filled with these gems. But they were excavated for a monarch in a kingdom across the sea. They had the sense, though, to leave the crystals at each entrance intact, so that travel through the caves was still possible."

Ivivin and Icarus took in the sight of the crystals while the lasted, which was only about a half mile into the caves. At the edge of the illuminated area, the merchants dipped their torches into a barrel of oil they carried and lit them. As they left the majesty of the twinkling stone-stars behind them, Ivivin thought he heard faint growling in the distance.

4

Once away from the comforting glow of the entrance, Ivivin came to realize how grand and terrifying the caves were. A visceral fear pervaded the atmosphere, despite the nervous chatter amoung the merchants.

"I could have sworn I heard a growl!" Ivivin thought over and over again as they continued to walk.

"I must just be so scared that I am hearing things." Ivivin tried to rationalize.

"I wish these fellows would be silent!" Ivivin muttered to himself, desperately wishing to disprove his fears by listening. But they chatted on and they walked on, deaf to Ivivin's internal cries of frustration.

The plan, Ivivin recalled, was that they would stop for a short rest about halfway through the cave. It would take about two days to make it through. In the interest of preserving their rations and especially their oil, they wouldn't stop for more than a couple of hours. Every step they took was followed by a sincere wish by Ivivin to reach that halfway point. And, every step he took without that respite was an exhausting disappointment. After what seemed like an eternity, the fellows leading the caravan called them to stop.

5

Ivivin sighed in relief, initially, at the prospect of getting to rest. That briefest of feelings did not linger, though. Although he was surrounded by people, he felt incredibly alone. His chest tightened and his breathing became strained. Ivivin wanted desperately to call for help, but couldn't muster even a whisper. His muscles tensed tighter and tighter. Tighter than they ever had been before, until they started to ache. His stomach felt as if he had swallowed some of Smith's ore and he felt faint and dizzy. The lanterns laid about started to wobble back and forth and blur. The walls of the cave seemed to contract, surrounding him and suffocating him. With a primal sense of urgency, Ivivin gasped for air as he was strangled by some incorporeal force. Just as his vision started to fade to black and he began to lose consciousness, Ivivin felt a hand on his shoulder.

"Calm down, young one, you are going to be alright."

Suddenly snapped back to reality, Ivivin recognized the man as one of the guides. All at once, Ivivin breathed and relaxed. He panted, sweating ice, on all fours as he laboured to regain his breath. Icarus made his way from his space in Ivivin's pack and pecked gingerly at his fingers. Ivivin slowly recovered from the assault born from his own fears, panic, and anxiety.

6

Needless to say, Ivivin had a hard time relaxing after his breakdown. Icarus and the guide stayed with him, trying to comfort him with their presence. Ivivin hadn't really gotten a chance to speak with the folks leading the caravan—they were too busy fielding questions and, well, leading them. Ivivin looked at the man. His expression was outwardly warm and gentle. He was older, considerably older than either Smith or his father. It was hard to tell in this poor lighting, but his cheeks seemed rosy and flush, despite the grimness of the caverns. Seeing this man eased Ivivin, if only a little. After some time, the guide spoke up.

"Ivivin, was it?" He asked gently.

Ivivin nodded meagerly.

"Was this the first time you've experienced that sensation?"

Again, Ivivin nodded.

"I see. Well, Ivivin, may I share a secret with you? I have lived nearly five of your lifetimes and I still feel the way you feel at times. There is no shame or weakness in it."

Ivivin felt immediately disheartened. "I do not ever want to feel like that again." Ivivin told the kindly guide.

"Unfortunately," started the guide "you are human and a moral one at that, the best I can tell. These things are unavoidable, especially for those living bold lives, such as yourself. To feel is to be healthy, to feel deeply is to be human. Do not shun these feelings. Do not attempt to control them. Instead, control how you react to them and what you learn from them."

"You make it sound easy." Ivivin retorted, with a youthful bitterness in his voice.

"I suppose I do. It is not my intent to give that impression. Like all things in life, some people are better than it at others. I was pretty bad at it myself, when I was your age."

After a brief pause, Ivivin realized that this was one such opportunity to learn and that he shouldn't let it escape him.

"How do you control yourself?" Ivivin blurted.

The guide smiled, expecting the question.

"I take a moment to think. To think of love. To think of trust. And to recognize my role in this world. That I am just the smallest piece of this grand puzzle that is existence. Even the greatest man will eventually die and fade away, his story to be distorted and fitted to the needs of those who follow. For me, this realization is what calms me. I am not important, but that which is dear to me is."

Ivivin thought back to his voyage to Smithton, where he killed that rabbit. He remembered the feelings from that time, being part of this great cycle of life and time. He felt so arrogant in this moment. He had left Smithton confident and assured, as if the skills and knowledge he acquired there changed his role in or, rather, decoupled him from the world, giving him power over it. He realized now it was an arrogant sentiment. Ivivin couldn't come to completely accept this man's words. He didn't fully understand what he meant. But the sentiment, at least, allowed Ivivin to reframe his world. He was scared yet, but ready again to take another step into the darkness and face himself.

7

The guide left Ivivin alone with his thoughts to go ready the caravan for departure. Ivivin pet Icarus and set him back in his pack. He gathered his things and prepared to continue. Before he knew it, they had begun moving once more. Ivivin felt oddly at peace, despite still being afraid of what was to come. He was less aware of his own thoughts and more focused on that which was around him. The cave walls were just that—walls. But each stretch of wall was unique in a way, too, with different concave and convex curves. If Ivivin looked closely, he could even see slight variations in the colors. He realized suddenly that he could hear once more, despite the merchants' continued chatter. The uproar that prevented him from hearing—from listening—came not from the perceived cacophony of his surroundings but, rather, from a storm in his own mind and heart. Ivivin sighed. He felt a little silly, but also kept in mind that what he felt was real and was dangerous. He started enjoying the sounds of the cave. The sounds of rodents scurrying out of the way of the caravan, the dripping of water from the ceiling, and even the occasional swear of a merchant who had lost his footing. Ivivin even closed his eyes while he walked, using the sound of footsteps to ensure he didn't bump into his neighbors. Smiling slightly, he listened and listened.

And then, a growl.

8

Ivivin sprinted to the front of the caravan to warn the guides, but was too late. The kind old man who he had just spoken with was gripping his arm, barely standing at the four-way junction, as the sound of blood dripping drummed against the cave floor. The mercenaries were in a panic, waving the torches around to fend off any other wolves from approaching. Between flickers of torchlight, Ivivin could see the shimmering of eyes and teeth down two of the paths ahead of them. Just as he saw this, yelling could be heard from the back of the caravan. The other guides and mercenaries fended off the wolves while the rest of the caravan went down the only presumably wolf-free passage available to them. Those who went first were soon panicked when they realized that they were forced down a short path that ended prematurely with a subterranean lake. A literal dead end. Water fell from the ceiling and many of the merchants had a hard time keeping their torches aflame, not to mention the first few who stumbled and fell into the lake, instantly extinguishing their light. These beasts, whom the merchants had assumed timid and dumb, had trapped them. Ivivin could see only a sea of fangs over the shoulders of the mercenaries.

9

More frightened than he had ever been in his life, Ivivin found himself moving more on instinct than intent. He pulled one of two barrels of oil from the cart and quickly stuffed the cloth from his own unlit, makeshift torch into the bunghole, grabbed a nearby merchant's lantern, and lit the cloth ablaze. He rolled the barrel as fast as he could towards the wolves, yelling at anyone who would listen to move. The mercenaries managed to dive out of the way at the last moment as the barrel careened into the pack of wolves. Those at the front scattered.

Then, a deafening explosion.

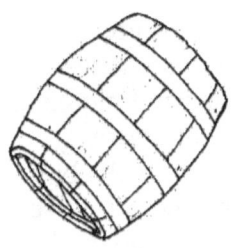

10

Ivivin couldn't say whether had slain or simply scared off the majority of the wolves. But, other than the injured guide, all of the others were generally fine. Ivivin, it seemed, had saved the caravan if not from annihilation, then from colossal losses. There was danger still, though. Ivivin had fended off the wolves, sure, but at the cost of a whole barrel of oil. They had brought two, of which they realistically expected to use about one and one-third. They were left, then, with just under a third of a barrel left with a little less than half of the voyage remaining. They waited for the fire to subside and tended to the wounded. It was not long before panic started to seep into the caravan. Icarus didn't seem to mind terribly, but he could see very well in the dark. Ivivin himself started to succumb to the fear of the soon-to-be mob when the injured guide erupted.

"QUIET!" yelled the man, much louder than Ivivin had imagined the guide was capable of yelling, based on his demeanour from their earlier conversation. Despite a slinged arm and a pale, worn face, the guide spoke with confidence.

"We need not give way to panic and fear! The path forward is the same as it always has been. Oil or not, we will get out of here. The other guides and I will lead the way. As for oil, only those at the front and back will use fire."

"But that leaves the rest of us blind!" yelled an audibly frightened merchant. "You'll have us unaware of the path? Of the wolves?"

"Yes." replied the guide simply. "Trust and have faith and have a chance at life. Or, if you'd prefer, you can have a fully illuminated view of your death."

The fire from the explosion was fading fast. The guide spoke once more.

"We don't have time for you to fruitlessly push fear from your heart. Just carry it with you as we move forward, step by step."

He divided the guides and mercenaries in half and sent half to the back and half to the front. Slowly, the lights faded into the distance. Ivivin who was towards the back, could make out faint light of those at the back, but not of those up front.

When the last nearby flame died, blackness enveloped them. When the last flame died, they took their first steps into the shadowy unknown.

11

Ivivin was a little shaken, but eventually found himself listening yet again to the things around him. He closed his eyes as they walked and walked for hours. Over time, the merchants started getting lively again. There was still a distinct air of worry hanging about, but it seemed as if everything was going to be alright— just as the guide had said. Faster than Ivivin could believe, he could see a familiar and enchanting twinkle a way ahead of him. The luminescent gems that adorned the exit were in sight! Ivivin stopped a moment, just before stepping under the first of the thousands of gems riddling the ceiling and walls, to stare and appreciate these beacons. Ivivin had never seen a lighthouse, nor even the sea, but he imagined that this must be how sailors feel when they lay eyes on the guiding light. Merchants hurriedly passed by Ivivin as he sat there and stared. It was only when he found himself at the back of the group that he realized the pressing need to walk on. He scritched Icarus, who was perched on his shoulder, also mesmerized by the shining stones. Ivivin could see the light break at the cave's exit less than a quarter mile off. He picked up his pace excitedly.

Suddenly, Ivivin was thrust to the ground, face first, by some great force. He turned around and realized that he was knocked over by one of the mercenaries who had blocked the lunge of a lone dire wolf. Ivivin could see singed fur on the wolf. The mercenary swiped at the beast forcefully, but just barely scratched the agile creature. It growled, turned, and ran off. Ivivin sighed in relief... that is, until he noticed both the lack of weight on his shoulder and the sound of frantic wings deeper in the cave's reaches.

12

Ivivin gave chase to the wolf, leaving behind a confused mercenary. Ivivin did his best to follow the sounds of clumsy wings and pounding paws. He had exited the safety and comfort of the gems and had re-entered the labyrinth, haphazardly turning wherever the sound guided him. He fumbled to light his own borrowed lantern, which had only minutes of oil remaining at best. Ivivin heard a nearby crash followed by silence. He turned the corner to see that the wolf had trapped Icarus in a small crevice at a dead end. Any attempts by the exhausted owl to escape would lead it straight into the jaws of the beast.

Ivivin could feel every beat of his tumultuous heart. Primal aggression raged within him as he was faced with an equally primal foe. He almost acted on this instinct and charged the beast, but he was grounded by the memory of the wolves' planned assault. These were not mindless, base beasts. These were intelligent creatures. The look in the wolf's eyes cemented this notion.

Ivivin assumed a defensive stance and kept the wolf at bay. Both combatants knew that one wrong move—just one rushed motion—would mean the end. Ivivin slowed his breathing and desperately tried to find something in his environment that could help him. Time was working in the wolf's favour and Ivivin knew this. Once the light of his lantern went out, Ivivin was as good as dead. He tried to calm himself and again found himself listening to this, the whole world, around him. In the distance, he again heard the distinct sound of paws on stone. This time, though, they were much lighter and much less coordinated. Ivivin slowly backed away from the wolf towards the junction. The wolf watched intently, expecting Ivivin to head back from where they came and abandon the bird. Instead, Ivivin started sprinting towards the sound. The wolf, suddenly realizing the gambit, gave him chase.

When the wolf turned the corner, it froze. Ivivin held in his arms a young pup, hastily muzzled with rope. Ivivin held the tip of his blade to the pup's throat. Just as Ivivin thought, the wolf understood his intent. He allowed Ivivin to pass and return to the crevice where Icarus was shuddering in fear. He reclaimed the shaking heap of feathers and shoved it in his pack. He returned to the junction, set the pup down, and released its muzzle. The wolf and Ivivin locked eyes before both the wolf and the pup vanished into the void. Ivivin stood at attention until the now-too-familiar sound became one with silence.

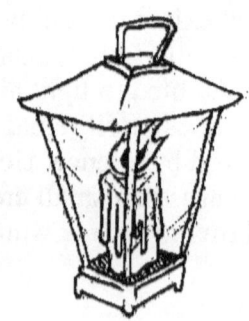

13

Icarus was saved for now, but the duo faced another hurdle. Ivivin's lantern was beginning to flicker out and, in his rush, he did not commit to memory the paths down which he had chased the wolf.

"Little good staving off that wolf does if we starve to death!" Ivivin exclaimed in frustration.

Icarus, still trembling, crawled from the pack and resumed his place on Ivivin's shoulder. Ivivin stood there, desperately trying to recall his path.

"It's no good. I can't remember anything after the first turn."

Icarus, frustrated that his transportation was inert, began nipping at Ivivin's ear. Ivivin swatted at the bird.

"Icarus, stop that! What is wrong with you?! I don't know where to go!" Ivivin shouted, half at the bird and half at himself. The owl hopped onto Ivivin's hand and stared at him a while. Eventually, the owl gave Ivivin a fed up and irritated look and took flight.

"What?" Ivivin said, dumbfounded. The owl doubled back and saw Ivivin standing there as his lantern began to flicker. Icarus screeched in the same manner he did when Ivivin teased him with food, keeping it just out of his reach. Ivivin's lantern finally died out. Icarus resumed flight and Ivivin followed the sound of the ungraceful hunter's wings. Ivivin's heart soared when he turned a corner and saw that comforting twinkle once more. The exhausted owl allowed itself to crash into Ivivin's arms and the duo exited the cave together.

14

Ivivin returned to the surface only to be met by thunderous cheering and applause. The merchants, now safely out of the cave, showered Ivivin with their gratitude. It did not feel like it while they were still in the grasp of the labyrinth, but Ivivin had indeed saved the lives of many that day. Ivivin felt himself blush as he received embarrassing compliment after embarrassing compliment.

Though they were all worn, there was a village with a very accommodating inn only a few miles away. The inn would not be able to bed all the merchants, but they would have a warm meal and spirits, both of which were desperately needed. The hike was filled with people coming to speak to Ivivin and learn of his story. Ivivin began to give the same rehearsed spiel about becoming a knight, but the merchants never seemed to bore of asking. Before long, they arrived in the village. They were welcomed warmly by the inn. What was a dreary average day in the village suddenly became busy and frantic as the villagers jumped at the opportunity to make some coin from or, better yet, trades with the merchants.

The people of this village, known appropriately as Wolvesbane, prepared a small feast of sorts and the caravan celebrated. Everyone's aches and worries gave way to drunken amiability and full bellies. The tale of how Ivivin warded off the wolves was told no fewer than a dozen times, with each recollection becoming more grand and picturesque than the last. Ivivin himself got drunk for the first time in his life, as the merchants wouldn't leave his hand be without a cold one. Ivivin and the merchants partied into the wee hours of the night before letting the sweet embrace of sleep take them.

Ojasa

1

Ivivin and the merchants woke up the next morning or, rather, afternoon, feeling rejuvenated, if not a bit hungover. They departed for their goal; the port city of Rumi!

"At this rate," Ivivin thought *"we'll be there in less than a week!"*

The merchant group walked and walked and walked until they finally arrived at the city. It was huge! Ivivin stared. The market alone was larger than the entirety of Smithton.

Once they arrived in the town center, Ivivin said his farewells to the merchants, who told him when they planned to return to Smithton and parted cheerfully. Ivivin rushed to the market, excited to see the wonders it held, only to find it all but empty. Minimal supplies, food, or much of anything, really, was for sale. All the salesmen seemed to be down in the dumps.

"Ah," Ivivin realized *"the lack of materials and goods here must be why the merchants have come. There is no competition."*

Ivivin decided to do some information gathering about this supposed 'monster' he'd been hearing about. Ivivin had never seen a monster, so he was skeptical. Though he couldn't keep his mind from wandering to the thought of the cave wolves he faced with the merchants. They weren't monsters, but they were scary nonetheless!

2

Ivivin asked many people of the city about the monster. Most of the people he asked seemed too afraid to answer—they simply didn't believe that Ivivin could stop the monster or didn't want to send him to an early grave. After asking what had to be the 200th person he asked, an older woman overheard his question and invited him to her house to hear the truth. She described for Ivivin the monster: It was gargantuan, standing at least twelve feet tall and had scales of steel. It stood on two legs with fangs larger and sharper than daggers. By her account, this was a terrifying creature that, on occasion, comes down from the mountain peak that he calls home to demand a large offering from the city. Moreover, he usually picks a person or two to kill to set an example, even taking their carcasses

63

with him back up the mountain, likely to be eaten. Icarus trembled in fear and began to sweat.

"How do I face something like that!?"

3

Ivivin saw Icarus shuddering and nuzzled him affectionately. Poor owl. He asked the old woman how long until the monster was due to strike again

She simply and grimly responded. "It should be any day now."

The woman offered Ivivin and Icarus a place to stay for the night, albeit just a spot on her floor. However, it was much nicer than his sleeping arrangements had been while travelling. He was woken midway through the night to the sounds of panic and despair. The old lady had barricaded her door.

"He has returned! Ojasa the Beast!"

Ivivin grabbed his things and convinced the panicked old woman to let him out of the house. Icarus remained sleeping in the bag, blissfully unaware of the danger to which Ivivin was taking him. Sure enough, Ojasa had returned. He was setting houses ablaze on the outskirts of town, declaring that his tribute was late. As town officials scrambled to gather goods for tribute, Ivivin rushed toward him. But, once Ivivin got close to the monster, he became petrified by fear before scrambling pathetically around a corner. This sudden jolt woke Icarus, who crawled out of the bag and perched on Ivivin's shoulder. When they peeked back around the corner at the beast, Icarus remained surprisingly calm. Noticing their presence, the beast glared at them and, in the moment, Ivivin fled. He ran and ran and ran until he was far from where he started. There, he fell to the floor with weak, trembling legs.

"What a coward I am!" Ivivin exclaimed as he began to sob.

Much to Ivivin's surprise, Icarus had remained exceptionally calm, considering the sequence of events. Ivivin felt even worse knowing his cowardly friend was braver in this situation than he was. After this, Ivivin wallowed around the city for days, struggling with the fear still lingering in him. Fear of the monster Ojasa and the idea of having to abandon his dream or face his fears immobilized him. Icarus seemed almost perplexed at Ivivin's struggle, but was supportive nonetheless, staying by his side during the nightly nightmares and cold sweats.

4

About two weeks after Ivivin's encounter with Ojasa, Ivivin caught wind of a knight who rode into town. Well, more like an ex-knight. He was missing an arm. He questioned the townsfolk about the monster, just as Ivivin did. When told that it would be some time before Ojasas' next visit, he asked where the beast resided. He was told of the monster's lair atop the Mirage Mountains, so named because of the shimmering reflection of the sun on the range. The one-armed knight left as quickly as he came to go and face the beast, headfirst and headstrong.

Ivivin began asking the residents of the city where the one-armed man went. The answer was the same. He had gone to the mountains to the north, where many a knight have attempted to ascend and slay the monster, but from where none returned.

Ivivin grabbed his gear (and Icarus) and left town after the knight.

"I cannot afford to be frozen by fear. I must act."

Ivivin realized on the outskirts of town that this was easier said than done. The initial kick of bravery had worn off and each step felt like a death sentence. He could see the one-armed knight getting farther and farther ahead as his own feet started to drag. Again, Icarus seemed unusually calm about the whole situation and climbed back into the bag for a timely nap. Eventually, well after the other knight arrived at the base of the mountain, Ivivin, too, arrived. At the base of the mountain was the knight—tired, quivering, and pale. He was speaking mostly gibberish, but Ivivin could tell he had just barely survived a nightmarish encounter.

Icarus, upon seeing the man, flew off towards the top of the mountain. Ivivin's heart sank as Icarus ignored his pleas to return. It was not only dangerous for the scraggly owl—now Ivivin would have to brave the mountain to save his friend, save the town, and slay the monster without the company of his owl friend. And so, Ivivin reluctantly set up the mountain, though much faster now that his friend was in danger. He ascended, terrified of the perils to come.

After a solid hour of quick paced hiking, Ivivin noticed that he had barely moved from the base. In fact, he was illogically close to the base, almost as if he hadn't moved since Icarus flew off. Confused and tired, Ivivin sat down for a moment

"What is going on!?" He thought, frustrated. Almost as soon as he sat, he stood again. *"This is no time for rest—I must retrieve Icarus!"*

And so, he set off up the mountain once more. After another hour of hiking, he noticed that, again, he hadn't made any progress. It was beginning to get dark, further complicating things. Ivivin trudged on, however, convincing himself that his mind was simply playing tricks on him.

When night fell, things got very creepy very quickly. There were bats everywhere and the floor had an eerie, faint red glow about it. He could hear a whistling sound and echoes of what he swore were the voices of children. As he continued up the mountain, he began to see strange creatures. Large, acid-spewing lizards skittered about the landscape. Bears with razor sharp claws and teeth, much larger than any bear he'd ever heard of, patrolled the area. It was now that fear truly and fully returned to Ivivin.

"Icarus must have flown past these creatures." He reasoned as he sneaked past the unnatural monsters. In his gut, Ivivin found it hard to believe the owl would have survived this journey, but he continued nonetheless. As his surroundings became increasingly terrifying, so too did the intensity of his trembling.

Things only continued to worsen as Ivivin climbed. He began to see volcanic pots with odd, flaming creatures emerging from them. There were winged, black creatures dripping lava from their mouths. Large boars with obsidian tusks and killing lust in their eyes populated the landscape. Ivivin started into an outright sprint! That is, until he looked behind him and saw he still hadn't made any distance up the mountain.

Ivivin decided, remembering the words of the guide from the merchant caravan, that running from his fear was what kept him from ascending the mountain. He slowed to a walk. And he walked and walked and walked. Though he still made no visible progress, Ivivin continued his hike. After what seemed like hours of trudging through what seemed to be a living nightmare, suddenly it was all gone—vanished—and he was at the peak of the mountain, miles away from where he was just moments ago. More strikingly, it was no longer night, but midday! Confused and tired, but somewhat relieved, Ivivin fell to his knees and regained his composure. Much further and he might have gone insane. In fact, he still wasn't sure that he wasn't now, already. He looked up and saw a short flight of stairs which led to what appeared to be a castle tower, ornate in structure and design. No doubt it was made possible by the riches the monster has accumulated over years of terrorizing Rumi. Recomposed and with a renewed sense of resolve, Ivivin took his first steps up the stairwell.

6

When Ivivin got to the top step, there was a short path leading to the tower. Atop the sign right by the door was Icarus, the disheveled owl, perched and looking at Ivivin tauntingly, almost as if to say, 'what took you so long?'

Half relieved and half annoyed at the owl's calm safety, Ivivin went to reclaim his friend. As he got close, Icarus flew defiantly to the top of the tower and perched. Suddenly, the cocky bird was snatched up by a large, scaly hand and pulled out of sight. Ivivin burst into the tower and began sprinting to the top. He vaguely noted his surroundings. In particular, he noticed that the tower seemed relatively normally furnished, but had no time to take mind. He burst open the door leading to the flat roof of the tower. Directly in front of him was Icarus in a cage, guarded by the monster, Ojasa. He even larger, scarier, and more fearsome than Ivivin remembered him back in the city. After belching fire, the beast addressed Ivivin.

"Child, I know not why you have ascended my mountain and my tower. If you have come to play hero, I assure you that you will be sorely disappointed. You, and this mongrel bird, are trespassing on my land—a mistake I shan't let you repeat. BOY! Have you forgotten all the terrible things I am capable of? I can melt the flesh off your bones effortlessly. I can crush you with no more than a sneeze. I am the worst nightmare of man!"

The beast gazed at Ivivin menacingly a moment before continuing. "However, I will make a most generous deal with you. If you leave me all your possessions, here and now, then I shall allow you to attempt to make the trek down my nightmare mountain.

Though I cannot guarantee you will survive, boy, that is the smart choice. Make the smart choice. And make it quickly, else I shall end you in the most gruesome of ways."

Ivivin stood dumbfounded and petrified for a moment before he made his choice...

7

Ivivin dropped his gear.

Ojasa smirked "Smart choice boy—be you gone!'

Ivivin walked towards Ojasa and, more specifically, Icarus.

"What are you doing, boy!?" Ojasa bellowed.

"I am getting my friend owl and going on my way." Ivivin said firmly, if with just a hint of terror in his voice.

Ojasa laughed heartily. "Fool! That owl is one of your possessions. Leave it here and be gone!" Ivivin turned and walked back towards the entrance. Icarus looked hurt and betrayed. Ivivin stopped in front of his gear and suited back up. Ojasa looked at him perplexed—or, at least, as perplexed as a beast as himself could look.

"Boy! What are you doing!?"

Ivivin drew his sword and looked the horror straight in the face. "I will face you, nightmare of man, and then I shall reclaim my friend."

8

"FOOL!" screeched Ojasa "You cannot hope to defeat me!"

"Maybe so, but...if I leave here without Icarus, I am already defeated!" Ivivin retorted.

Ivivin rushed the nightmare, sword drawn. His heart was weighed down by fear, but driven forward by his feelings for his feathery friend. As Ivivin got closer, Ojasa grew even more huge and even more fearsome.

"Will you still fight me, boy?" The horror questioned.

Although Ivivin had paused for a moment out of both surprise and fear, he resumed his charge and struck the beast in the highest place he could reach—just below the knee. Ojasa screeched a strangely human scream. Ivivin swung again, this time much lower and the beast let out yet another oddly human yelp.

Then, before his eyes, Ojasa disappeared. In his place was a short, old, fat man. He had a cut across his face and another on his arm. They were shallow—not nearly as severe as the wounds Smith the smith had gotten when he and Ivivin first met in Smithton. Despite this, the man fell to the floor, crying, and swore he was a weak old man and that he was sorry. He pleaded with Ivivin, begging him to spare his life. Ivivin ran past the man to release Icarus. Once free, Icarus again showed the same indifference to what should be a stressful and confusing situation. In fact, he looked rather unimpressed by the whole situation.

Then it clicked

"This man is a magician. The beast Ojasa is his illusion. The whole mountain was an illusion—a nightmare. The weapon of Ojasa was never his fangs, claws, or size. No, his weapon was fear." Ivivin realized.

Ivivin was correct, the man was a sorcerer—an illusionist—using his magic to deceive and cheat people out of their goods by making them live a nightmare. Ivivin tied the man up, using scraps of clothing from around Ojasa's lair to stop the bleeding. He harassed the man to ascertain the source of the power and his illusions. He reluctantly told Ivivin about the bracelet he wore, about its magic, and how it was the source of his power. Ivivin stripped him of it, put the man in a cart, and started to wheel him down the mountain. Icarus perched happily on Ivivin's shoulder the whole trip back.

9

When Ivivin arrived back in the city, he was shaken and exhausted. His weariness was compounded by the fact that he decided to bring the one-armed knight with him as well. But, with a bit of resolve, he made his way to the city council. Although it was in the early evening, the leadership of the town was still hard at work, trying to cope with the economic situation brought on by their nightmare. Ivivin pounded on the door to the hall as hard as he could until finally someone relented and answered. At first, the responder looked annoyed, but, after seeing the condition of the three travelers (minus Icarus who was now sound asleep in Ivivin's bag) rushed to fetch a physician. Other members of the city's leadership and concerned townspeople came forward, startled by the noise. After the physician had given Ivivin some water and food, the council questioned Ivivin about the ruckus he was making. It was there Ivivin recounted his living nightmare to the city folk, as well as the quest he undertook to end it. He showed them all the magic item and presented them 'Ojasa', reduced from his nightmare form to the battered, lazy old man he truly was.

The city rejoiced. They declared that a feast for Ivivin would occur the following day and swore that every man, woman, child, and even horse who travels here shall learn of his name. They called him such names as 'Ivivin, Slayer of Nightmares' and 'Ivivin, the Man Who Knows Not Fear.' Much like with the praise he received from the merchants after their escape from the Wolfelaw Caves, Ivivin was terribly embarrassed to hear such words. Before Ivivin could further hear the lauding of the townsfolk, however, he collapsed from his exhaustion. The last thought that swept across his mind was that he was now one step closer to being a knight.

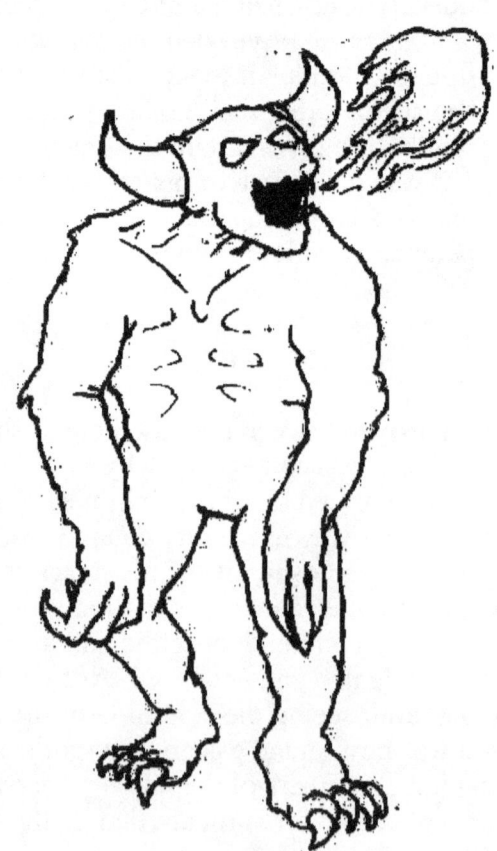

Crosstown

1

Within the week, Ivivin had gathered enough supplies to carry on with his adventure. There was a lingering problem, though—Ivivin really didn't know where to go next. He sat at a table at the inn with his map splayed out.

"Well, now that I've finished the first of the king's requests..." Ivivin thought before glancing at the armlet he got from Ojasa *"Well, two of the king's requests, perhaps. Where should I go next?"*

"How about you? Where would you like to go, Icarus?" He asked Icarus sarcastically.

Icarus hopped onto the map, pointing north, about halfway between Rumi and the Castletown. He was currently on the east most bounds of the kingdom. The castle was nearly the west most locale of the kingdom.

"I'll have to go back that way eventually anyways." Ivivin considered.

"Alright Icarus, you win. We'll head north. We leave, hopefully, within the week." He told the mongrel. He still needed to convince a guide to take him back through Wolfelaw.

"But," Ivivin reasoned to himself *"it shouldn't be too hard given my new reputation in this city."*

Indeed, it was as easy to find a guide as Ivivin had anticipated. Although the travelling merchants were a little sore about Ivivin ruining their monopoly, the city's residents were more than willing to help. After generous donations of supplies were packed up, Ivivin scooped up Icarus and tossed him in his bag. Then, just as simply as he had arrived, he left. Ivivin made it through the mountain much easier this time, locking Icarus firmly in his bag to avoid another incident. Ivivin was certainly fearful—that hadn't changed—but this time he never allowed his anxiety to boil over as he had during the previous expedition.

Once through the caves, Ivivin sought out the next major northward town. From there he'd have to pass by a legendary lake, stop in Crosstown for supplies, and make a short trek through desert to get to the northern half of the kingdom.

"It's good to be back on the road again!" Ivivin thought. *"Especially by ourselves; I had nearly forgotten how liberating it is to travel alone!"*

At this rate, it seemed Ivivin and Icarus would arrive to the desert in no time. Given, they'd have to stop and gather supplies before headed to Crosstown but, even so, Ivivin was confident they would arrive in no time at all. The pair took their time and minimized their reliance on supplies, instead electing to live off the land the best they could.

One day, as they were approaching a village, Ivivin saw a huge body of water on the horizon. He panicked, checking the position of sun to make sure he hadn't accidentally ended up on a coast somewhere. He realized that the water was not a sea at all, but a lake. Specifically, Saeber Lake. The water was so different than the sea around Rumi. Its water held no salt and was clear nearly to the bottom. Ivivin and Icarus lingered on the lakeside for a few days. Food and, well, water were both plentiful. He could see why the residents of the nearby village had settled there. After a few days, they blew in and out of the lakeside homestead, only restocking their expended essentials. They had caught their stride and Ivivin didn't want to do anything to disturb that. So, the dynamic duo hurried along towards Crosstown.

They soon entered an area known as the Hollow Hills. It was a unique geological marvel. If any sound, even the faint sound of a single needle falling to the floor, was made at the height of a hill, it tended to echo and reverberate for miles. Conversely, you could barely hear yourself talk at its troughs. Ivivin suspected that he could very well detonate another barrel of oil here and someone just feet away would be none the wiser. He often played with both these features as they journeyed. As they got closer to Crosstown, Ivivin had already all but forgotten the horror he struggled through at the mountain, having come to peace with himself and his fear. He had honestly expected more strife on his travels, but was pleasantly surprised by the lack thereof...that is, until he saw some smoke pouring from the other side of the hill he was climbing.

3

When Ivivin peeked over the hill, he set his eyes upon a bandit camp. It was at the bottom of a basin of sorts. Or, more accurately, it was completely encased by hills, rendering it virtually silent. It was not far from the desert and the near-desert settlement of Crosstown. Ivivin decided he had better sneak around and alert the townsfolk to their presence. He moved swiftly and with purpose to make it to the town before the bandits. He was sure he could outpace them—he was one person and it is much easier for one person to travel, right? Not wanting to risk finding out, Ivivin hustled until he arrived at the town. However, it was so late he was struggling to find the town's leadership, having fruitlessly wandered the streets in search of it. Frustrated, Ivivin returned to the outskirts of town and stared at the stars while he considered his options.

"Maybe I will just rest my eyes a minute..."

Ivivin woke to Icarus poking and prodding. He had overslept! Hoping it wasn't too late, Ivivin sprung up and sprinted into town. Crosstown was just that—a town placed on the thinnest span of the desert, making it the fastest way cross the desert and reach the north. Else, Ivivin would have to go all the way around the dessert and then head north. It would likely add months to his trip. Besides, this place had all the supplies he would need to cross the desert here.

But they wouldn't if bandits got to the town first!

Ivivin asked the first townsperson he stumbled upon where town hall was located. He sprinted straight to the building and sought an immediate audience with the mayor. He addressed the leader of the town, who was appointed by the old king—the king that ruled before the current one. He was an old man himself, with slicked back hair, peppered with grey, accompanied by a patchy mustache and beard.

"Sir, I have grave news! There is a large bandit camp stationed not a day or two's march away from here!" Ivivin exclaimed.

"What!" exclaimed the old man, clearly shocked. He composed himself. "Oh! I think you mean the nomad group about fifteen miles from here, do you not?"

"Yes, though I'm not sure they're noma—" Ivivin started.

"You worry for naught boy. We have already spoken to their leader. They are nothing to worry about."

"But..." Ivivin tried to object.

"Get you from here, boy. I will hear your slander no longer!"

Ivivin thought something was fishy, but he didn't have time to question it. He had to figure out a way to resolve and diffuse the situation.

4

If the townsfolk wouldn't believe an outsider, maybe the knights and military at the nearby fort would. Ivivin knew he had to hurry if he had any chance of returning in time with soldiers to stave off the bandits. He left everything he didn't absolutely need, save Icarus, at the local inn. He ran and ran and ran. Even when he felt as if his calves would split and his lungs would burst, he kept sprinting.

When he arrived at the fort, he was shocked to see it was is in a total state of disarray. He learned from the first able bodied soldier he encountered that bandits had poisoned their well. About half of the troops had drank from it before they realized what had transpired. Ivivin tried his best to rally what troops he could, but morale was low and no one listened to him. He just didn't have the pull or influence to convince them to act, especially given the present situation. Ivivin began to get flustered when he noticed, on the horizon, a familiar person riding in on a horse. It was the one-armed knight he saved from Ojasa!

5

The one-armed knight was, apparently, a former commander of this fort. Upon hearing Ivivin's account of the situation, he gave a moving and motivating account of Ivivin's bravery in Rumi (as well as his own failure). The soldiers were in absolute awe at this young, unthreatening man conquering a quest that had felled so many experienced warriors. They were inspired and rallied who they could. Besides, as the one-armed knight pointed out, they would need supplies from that town to save their poisoned comrades and to get clean water for the rest of them. After they readied themselves and met at the entrance, Ivivin asked the one-armed knight, who was suited up for combat, for his name.

"I am Miroslav, the Free knight." Said the one-armed man.

"Miroslav..." Ivivin thought. *"Wait..."*

"That's a northerner's name!" he blurted out.

Miroslav chuckled at this forwardness.

"Yes, Ivivin, I was born a slave in the far north. When the father of the current king led a crusade into the northern wastes, he happened upon me. He saved me when I was just a lad and brought me around the world with him. When I returned, he made me a knight. He gave me my title: 'The Free Knight'. When he was on his deathbed, I made a sacred vow to protect his son. However, when I lost my arm training him, the current king was so overcome with guilt that he sent me on a voyage, likely to ease his guilt, but also to let me see the world before I am no longer able. When I decide to return, I'm sure he will welcome me back with open arms."

"Miroslav," Ivivin said, touched by the story. "I am Ivivin. My goal is to become a knight of the king. When I do, will you be there when I am knighted?"

"If we live that long, then I will arrange it so." Miroslav stated with a grim smile.

6

The freshly motivated troops marched to Crosstown. Ivivin could only hope they'd arrive in time! He went ahead, borrowing a horse from the fort. He hadn't ridden a horse before, but it seemed to come to him naturally.

"This IS a skill a knight should have." He thought, a little proud of his natural knack for it. Icarus was terrified of the horse, though, and flew what he decided was a probably safe distance from the strange creature. Ivivin found it funny, how Icarus found this horse entirely terrifying, but had managed to be unaffected by the nightmare wizard.

He arrived at Crosstown and was surprised to see....

...absolutely nothing out of place.

Everything seemed to be fine. In fact, no one was particularly worried about anything, save a small child crying over their torn doll.

"Good," Ivivin thought *"We still have time."*

Ivivin knew that no one would believe his cries and the town's leadership had already renounced any possibility of the attack (which Ivivin still found incredibly fishy). Acting on this gut feeling, Ivivin left his borrowed horse on the outskirts of town and ran to the town center. The sun was starting to set. Ivivin knew he needed to get to the bottom of this before nightfall, as that is when the bandits would be most likely to strike. He hustled to the strangely quiet town hall.

Closed for the day

The sign plastered on the door was not a good sign. Ivivin felt a mischievous and curious compulsion to sneak in, so, he did. He heard voices within and listened into what seemed to be a business meeting of sorts. Except, as Ivivin was shocked to find out, the mayor of the town was striking a deal with the leader of the bandits!

Everything made sense now. The old man from town hall was trying to shake Ivivin off his tracks. It seems that he had been slowly sneaking bandits into the town hall for the last two or three nights. Just under half the bandit force was already inside the city and the other half was going to strike tonight! An attack on multiple fronts...

"There is no way the townsfolk can mount a resistance to that." Ivivin somberly realized.

7

Ivivin rushed out the building. He had to think of a way to isolate this building and fast. From there, he just had to hope that the troops arrived soon. Ivivin had several ideas cross his mind. He thought to set the building on fire, thinking back to how he handled the wolves. Somehow, that did not sit well with Ivivin. He doubted that anyone would believe his intentions afterwards, let alone allow him to do it in the first place. After all, the area still had people here and there, out and about.

No, he couldn't solve *everything* with fire.

Moreover, there seemed to be a distinct lack of an honorable, speedy, and effective solution to this particular threat. He could only think of one plausible course of action—and by no means was it a smart one. It was a gutsy plan, full of holes and terrible 'what if' scenarios. But, if there was something Ivivin had learned so far on his journey, it was to be less afraid of the evils in this world. Your fear would become their weapon. Instead, Ivivin had come to believe in facing evil with both fear and fearlessness. He recognized there are indeed things in this world worthy of being feared, but he also had come to learn that strength is fighting anyways, despite your fears.

So, Ivivin stood in front of the hall, clad in his armor and with his sword in hand. His brave and trusty owl companion, Icarus, stood firmly next to him...

On the rooftop...

Several buildings away.

8

While Icarus shivered in his metaphorical boots on a safe roof far, far away, Ivivin was doing the same, just directly in front of a building bustling with a bushel of bloodthirsty bandits. He could hear soldiers and the bandits beginning to skirmish each other at the edge of town. It remained, then, that Ivivin had to stop, or at least stall, the bandits in town hall. As they exited, it was quite clear to Ivivin who the leader of the bandits was. He was a colossal man, but somehow didn't give off the air of one. He had the air of a craftier man—one who never had to rely on force or raw power. Yet, at the same time, he did not seem entirely dishonorable. Ivivin approached the man boldly and openly.

"I challenge you to a fight. If you can kill me, I possess great treasures from my travels and they will become yours. If I can best you, however, then you will call off your men. Half of your men are currently engaged with the remnants of the soldiers you so cowardly poisoned, so I will stand in to fight you lot on their behalf! Send your strongest warrior to face me, scoundrels" Ivivin proclaimed, sounding more confident than his trembling legs would lead one to believe.

All the bandits paused their advance, shocked at Ivivin standing his ground and making such an absurd suggestion. Well, all but one, that is. The hulking head bandit seemed enraged, but not by Ivivin's declaration itself. Rather, it was as if Ivivin accused him of something he did not do.

"Boy, I am Xaivier the Fierce. I am an honorable warrior, albeit not a lawful one. I would never poison my adversaries!" The bandit leader spoke calmly, but with great presence.

"Which means..."

Xavier turned to the mayor of the Crosstown and thrust his sword straight through the man's chest.

"Wha—Why?" gasped the mayor as fell to the ground. "I just wanted to give you the upper-hand..."

Xaivier spat at him in disgust. "I did not need your help, trash. This was to be your fate at any rate—my hand was just forced a bit earlier than I had planned. Any man who sells out the people to whom he is duty bound to serve for mere chump change is not obviously not in possession of enough honor to deserve to so much as walk this earth. There is a difference between giving yourself an advantage and disadvantaging your adversary. Now lay there, pitiful man. Breathe your last breaths and know that not even hell will look kindly upon those who lived and died without honor."

Xaivier turned to Ivivin. "Normally, I would not even consider such a request. After all, it could render my cunning plan worthless and the effort of my loyal men would go to waste. However, since that...swine...has interfered, I suppose shall grant you your duel. And why should I not? If you were more cunning than I, you would have solved this problem instead of facing me head on. You knew not of my character or if I would even entertain, let alone grant, your request. You took an uninformed and reckless gamble. Apart from that, well, you are much, much smaller than me, young warrior."

Ivivin assumed a defensive stance, prompting Xaivier to chuckle.

"Very well, let us begin. But know this. When I duel, I duel until death."

The unreasonably large man pulled his sword from the mayor's chest. Xaivier ripped the small amount of untainted cloth from the mayor's body and used it to wipe the blood from the blade.

"You seem an extraordinarily honorable young man, if lacking in smarts. It would be dishonorable to taint your blood with that from a parasite like that loathsome insect. Here is your final warning, young man: I am no ordinary bandit. I am a renegade knight. I am charged with slaying seven of the other nine top knights from the country from which I hail. I dispatched them all, without mercy, for simply being dishonorable. Not one of them landed a single blow. So, kill me if you can."

They both readied their weapons, prepared for a battle.

10

It quickly became apparent to Ivivin that this was not his very best idea. Every blow he tried to deliver seemed to be easily parried and, indeed, felt as if he was on the receiving end of the swing. What seemed to be Ivivin's only advantage was his speed. It was not enough to land a blow, but it was at least enough to not get hit himself. Rather than block, he could dodge—or, rather, he had to. He didn't want to find out what'd happen if he tried to deflect the bandit's blow. It was clear that Ivivin had to think of a plan—he couldn't keep this up forever. He looked over to Icarus, who looked as if he were shrugging at Ivivin.

Close.

The blade of Xaivier's sword passed right by his face. He couldn't afford to divert his attention. It seemed Xaivier wasn't quite giving it his all yet either. Ivivin needed to act before Xaivier's arrogance and pride gave in to boredom.

"All or nothing!" Ivivin thought.

Ivivin stepped forward, fast, and swung upwards. Xaivier just barely dodged the blow. Ivivin didn't ready himself for another strike. Instead, he let his sword fly from his hands into the air. He slid Xaivier's counterblow off the armor on his arm and slid along the floor under and between Xaivier's legs. Ivivin's sword then came down hilt first on Xaivier's head, stunning him for just a moment. Ivivin readied the chain which bore his apprentice's ring, jumped deftly onto Xaivier's back, and used the chain to strangle him. Xaivier thrashed around violently, knocking Ivivin into walls, pillars, and even a lit torch.

But Ivivin endured. He attempted to stretch out his legs against Xaivier's back to put even more pressure on the bandit-knight. Eventually, Ivivin could feel Xaivier's strength start to fade. Even though Ivivin's hands were bleeding—cut deeply from the chain—and his muscles screamed out in agony, he pulled even tighter in an attempt to end the fight. Xaivier fell to his knees, then to his stomach. Just as Ivivin felt the life slipping from Xaivier, he released his hold. Xaivier rolled about coughing, hyperventilating, and swearing. Ivivin had won.

But could the bandit king Xaivier be held to his word?

As it turns out, Xaivier could be held to his word. His men did not even attack Ivivin after their battle concluded, though Ivivin wasn't convinced they weren't simply shocked into immobility. Once Xaivier rose from his floor, the arrogance in his eyes had vanished. He rushed to call off his men at the outskirts of town. This time, it was the soldiers who were so shocked they could do nothing—all the bandits (minus those already felled to the knights) were all able to escape. Xaivier had left behind, however, a scarlet cloth—a handkerchief of sorts, with his crest on it. He told Ivivin to wear it proudly, as it is a sign of his defeat. Ivivin tied the cloth around his waist and collapsed. Never had his body ached so much or for so long. His hands dripped blood. His muscles burned. The soldiers took him to the local inn and called a doctor. The last moment of consciousness Ivivin remembered was Icarus nuzzling his forehead apologetically.

Ivivin was down and out for a while. His hands would be scarred from the chain cutting into his hands, but it seemed like he would retain all the function of both his hands once they healed. Additionally, his muscles were strained, maybe even slightly torn, from the stress of exerting that much force. But it was done. And the town was saved.

After a few days, maybe a week or two, of rest and some supplies to get through the desert, he resolved to cross the desert. He didn't need to be at one-hundred percent to cross, as there would be as little exertion as possible in his trip anyway.

As the details of the assault came to light, Ivivin was brought fruits and things from the Crosstown citizens. The soldiers recovered, obtained supplies and medical help from the town, and then returned to their fort. The knight Miroslav had left Ivivin a note. He was glad Smith had forced Ivivin to hone his reading skills, as Miroslav had left quite the note. From what Ivivin could gather from the messy script, Miroslav had decided to return to the fort to gather his thoughts and things. He would make sure that the fort was attended to and prepared, then he would return to the side of the King. It seemed that Miroslav took great pride in his ability to write, much like Smith. Ivivin decided that he would find a book to read and carry it with him on the rest of his journey—he wouldn't want to disappoint Smith by losing the skill they had forged together, after all! Of course, that would have to wait until when he could actually get up and leave. Luckily, his recovery went without complication and the people of Crosstown decided to give Ivivin a gift.

The gift was a shield bearing, you guessed it, a cross across the front. It was the town treasure, unanimously given to Ivivin by the inhabitants. It was a simple, yet intricate shield. More functional than beautiful, there was still a stunning property in its simplicity—not unlike Smith's work. Ivivin gratefully accepted it, adding it to his steadily growing pile of gifts, most of which were supplies he would need to cross the desert. Included were clothes to keep the sun's harsh rays off him and an unusually large supply of water. Ivivin sighed in relief that he would not need to go shopping himself. Bartering was, in Ivivin's humble opinion, the absolute worst.

Out of the Desert and into the Cave

1

Within the week, Ivivin said his farewells to the people of Crosstown and began his journey to cross the desert. Icarus was being fussy. He found the sun far too harsh outside the bag, but found it too hot and stuffy on the inside. He was constantly shuffling in, around, and about Ivivin and his person. It wasn't even the hottest part of the day. Ivivin had left later in the day, but while there was still sunlight. From here on out he would only travel under the moon's light, but this first day he needed to cover some distance. Plus, setting up camp in the desert for daytime use would be a little different, so he wanted to give himself a bit more time to prepare.

2

"IT'S SO HOT!" Ivivin couldn't stop thinking as he waited the day out. Not nocturnal like Icarus, Ivivin found it difficult to sleep during the day, even in the shade he set up. Icarus was either dead or sleeping incredibly peacefully. Either way, Ivivin wasn't terribly concerned—the heat kept him from thinking about much anything for long. He needed to find a way to relax. He started to read his book, one he had picked up in Crosstown. It was an interesting story, sure, but Ivivin found it too difficult to read.

"I should have started with an easier book." he thought, a bit disappointed in himself. This book recounted the story of the first king. Specifically, Ivivin was struggling with the first part of the story, where he had slayed a bunch of wolf-man monsters. It was lore of old, thus accounting for its incredible difficulty. The only parts Ivivin could understand, at least at first, were fight scenes. But he tried his best to reread the parts he didn't understand, getting a little bit more out of the text with each pass.

It took Ivivin days or, rather, nights to cross the desert. He was fatigued, but incredibly happy, when he saw the last dune of sand on the horizon. He had made it to the north.

3

The temperature seemed to drop steadily with each and every step Ivivin took further north. He followed a river up north, reasoning that he was more likely to find a town built along it. It was fall, sure, but there were already bits of ice drifting down the river, if only now and again. Finally, he spotted a town on the horizon and was instantly excited—he was long out of food that was not dried. He would kill for a bowl of any soup to help fend off the cold. As he got closer to the town, however, he was shocked to see that it was in a chaotic state. There were some fires and a lot of screaming. A group of men, clearly of the rough sort, fled the city on horseback. Much to Ivivin's surprise, a lone young woman set after them on horse shortly thereafter. Even at a distance, the fire in her eyes was clear.

Ivivin entered town to investigate and, if he could, help.

4

Ivivin helped the townsfolk douse the fires and there didn't seem to be much wrong with or missing from the town, all things considered. Except that a single girl was kidnapped. They reasoned that the kidnappers had set fires as a distraction. The girl they kidnapped seemed ordinary, if generally talented, according to the townsfolk. They could think of no reason for anyone to target her. The young woman who followed her, though, seemed far less ordinary. She was the self-proclaimed 'knight' of the town. The town was fairly small and far from the nearest fort, so this young woman had made a habit of helping the town out and the title sort of just fit. Ivivin also learned that the young girl who was kidnapped was the younger sister of this knight-girl.

"That explains the girl on the horse, but why would they kidnap that girl and just that girl?" Ivivin thought. He knew slave trade was a thing, but if they were slavers, there was no reason they couldn't have taken more captives. There was more to this story, he suspected.

Ivivin asked Icarus what he thought.

Icarus looked at Ivivin as if to say *Dude, I'm an owl, what did you expect me to say?* Icarus shook his head and flew off. Or, at least, he tried to but instead crashed into an older woman passing by. Ivivin went to scoop up his owl-wreck and apologize to the older woman. She looked at Ivivin, suddenly grabbing his hand, and stared at him intently. Ivivin, understandably confused and creeped out, tried to talk to the woman. She seemed not to hear him. She just stared at his palm intently. She jerked herself back into this world and commanded Ivivin to her house. He felt compelled to follow, although he was not sure why. In her house, the woman revealed she was a seer of sorts and that she was the one who brought these two girls from the east in the past. She told Ivivin that they were orphans and grew up with the seer woman. She also told Ivivin (and a still very dizzy Icarus) that it was in the stars of his eyes and the lines of his palm that Ivivin was destined to go after the young woman. If he ignored this call to fate, she insisted that his dream of becoming a knight would be shallow and unfulfilled. Ivivin had told no one here of his goal and the fact that she knew it startled him. He decided that, at the very least, he would investigate the crisis further.

5

Just as Ivivin had made his decision, the old seer lady suddenly pointed.

"Venture due north. There you will find a cave. That is where they have taken her."

Ivivin, a bit shaken with all the recent lunacy in his life, knew it was probably best to just leave the crazy lady alone and leave this town. But there was this nagging feeling at the back of his head that he should investigate further. As it turns out, this feeling was actually just Icarus pecking at the back of Ivivin's head, but he decided to explore further in any case. He found that the girls had indeed come here years ago under mysterious circumstances, but were eventually accepted as members of the town. From there, they lived fairly normal lives. Ivivin recalled the young orphan-knight giving chase to the horsemen. He was, admittedly, a bit entranced by the young woman and decided it was worth listening to the seer to see how fate would unfold.

"After all, knights help ladies, right?" Ivivin thought, trying to rationalize the irrational. He decided to set out after the determined young woman, much to Icarus' frustration.

So, Ivivin trekked due north, just as the seer-woman had instructed. Every step he felt an increasingly bitter cold sweep over him. As he headed towards the mountains, the difference between the town's climate and the mountains was obvious. He arrived at the cave at sundown. The horse that the young woman had used in her pursuit laid slain by the entrance. From there, Ivivin saw a clear trail of blood headed towards the mountain. He had a bad feeling it belonged to the sister and decided to follow the trail, rather than enter the cave. Night was accompanied by an even more severe and penetrating cold. Ivivin was sure to remove his armor to avoid frostbite. The cross wind caused by the mountain made it difficult to ascend, reminding Ivivin of his time on the Mirage Mountains. Snow began to fall fresh. Ivivin had to hurry or the blood trail would vanish beneath the cruel powder. He arrived at a crevice in the mountain side, out of sight from the undiscerning eye. The trail of scarlet seemed to end here. His investigation revealed a cavern, which harboured the woman, who herself harboured a fresh slash across her arm.

6

As Ivivin approached the woman, she lunged at him ferociously with a dagger. Ivivin stopped it. Barely. The blade was just short of his throat. She looked at him faintly, with delusive eyes, and collapsed. Ivivin could tell she was running a fever. He felt a draft, chilling him to the bone. The wind was picking up and the snow was coming down harder. Ivivin decided he needed to help the young woman.

First thing was first. He needed to drag her further into the cave away from the wind. It would prove incredibly awkward for

Ivivin as, although she was currently covered, she was not clothed properly. She had bundled her cut with some of her clothes, stripped herself of her armor as the cold weather worsened and frostbite loomed. The remainder of her clothes she tattered and spread about her whole body, rather than in the manner they were intended. He dragged her as delicately as he could across the cave, to the furthest point from the entrance. He then went out back into the storm and grabbed some wood, miraculously still dry from being hidden underneath a peculiar stone formation. He started a fire for her as quickly as possible, but her fever was getting worse still. Ivivin began to panic and decided he would have to go back into the town to get her medicine and clothes.

Well, ideally, Ivivin thought he should carry her back to get professional help in town. But the state that she was in and the weather was making that an extremely dangerous move. He took Icarus and stuck him on top of her by the fire. He pointed to the pile of wood he had gathered and instructed Icarus to put what he could in the fire, praying the little bugger would understand. Icarus gave Ivivin another *Dude, I'm an owl* look, but seemed to generally understand what he meant. After all, the fire would keep the sentient ball of muddled feathers warm, too. Ivivin left his armor, shield, and sword behind in the cave so he wouldn't be weighed down. He even left his spare clothing with the young woman to help keep her warm. He took off as fast as he could. The snow slowed him, but he was still able to make good time. Despite the cold wind, Ivivin figured he could make it to the town and back in about half the time—by midmorning or so.

7

"So cold!" Ivivin thought over and over, reminding himself how unbearably hot he was in the desert not too long ago. But he persevered. Less than an hour from the town, however, Ivivin was struck by disaster. The snow picked up even further, sure, but that wasn't the worst of his problems. He had stumbled upon and crossed paths with a mother-bear, looking for her cub. She saw Ivivin and attacked him in a frenzied rage.

Ivivin was swordless, shieldless, and armorless.

"Damn bear!" Ivivin thought.

He was just barely dodging bear swipes, each coming much faster than he imagined such a large creature to be capable of. He grabbed a loose, thick branch to try and defend himself, but the bear cleaved it in two with ease. However, that was what Ivivin had planned! Now his big stick had been masterfully transformed into...a slightly smaller, but now sharp stick! He went to strike the bear and the bear swiped at him in turn. Ivivin managed to cut one of the bear's eyes and the bear landed a moderate blow across Ivivin's shoulder.

Blood.

All of a sudden, they stopped fighting, as if they both decided the fight wasn't worth the cost. In fact, Ivivin suddenly focused on the horizon. There lay the baby cub, trapped under a tree fallen to wind. He scrambled that way. The bear followed confusedly at first, but realized shortly after what was going on. They jointly lifted the tree to free the cub, who was a bit torn up and battered.

The mother bear looked at her wounded cub with a profound sadness. It laid next to it to keep it warm. Ivivin rushed back to town. He scrambled to find someone to give him supplies on credit. Once he did, Ivivin first rushed back to the bear cub. He cleaned cub's wounds the best he could. He then began his terrible sprint back, though with renewed enthusiasm after seeing the grateful look on both bears' faces. He ran through the rapidly intensifying storm until his lungs felt like they were going to burst. And then he ran some more. He arrived not a moment too soon, as he fell to the floor of the cave exhausted. Once he had collected himself for naught but a moment, he made his way to the back of the cave. Icarus' kindling had run out. The mass of freshly singed feathers was cuddled next to the girl, obviously exhausted from moving wood onto the fire.

8

Ivivin treated the woman's wounds and fever with the medicine he got from the town. He knew there was no dry wood left outside, but he went out to get the least wet wood he could. He gradually dried out kindling and then firewood by the embers of the original fire. He tended to the young woman until night came once more. He, himself, then fell prey to sleep. He awoke in the morning to find that the storm had tapered and died. The sun was back in the sky, blessing the landscape with its lovely kiss of radiance once more.

The young woman was faded in and out of this world as her fever passed. She eventually sprung up with a look of great concern. Ivivin, startled, forced her back down, which proved incredibly difficult, despite her injury. She questioned Ivivin about what happened and about how long she was laying here in the cave. When Ivivin answered truthfully, her face became coated in dread. She spoke:

"It is tonight. I must go."

The Shaa'Ilii

1

Without so much as introducing herself, the woman gathered up her things and rushed from the cave, despite Ivivin's protest. Ivivin, too, gathered his things (making sure to scoop up a chilled Icarus) and burst from the cave after her.

"She's fast!" Ivivin thought. She had already had escaped from Ivivin's sight. It didn't matter, though. Ivivin knew well where she was headed: The bloody entrance to the first cave, where she was wounded. If Ivivin hurried there, he could stop her from injuring herself further. He ran as fast as he could to the cave. The entrance had two new bodies laid next to the horse. Two fully grown and fully armed men had met their end there.

"Did she take those men down by herself!?" Ivivin wondered to himself, starting to feel like leaving Icarus alone with the strange woman was not a very responsible decision. Not far into the cave, however, Ivivin discovered the young woman leaning on the wall and breathing heavily. She didn't seem to have any new wounds, but the original ones were obviously bothering her. Ivivin tried to help her sit down and ask her what she was doing, but she pushed him away. The hellbent woman continued to walk down the cave, leaning instead on the wall for support. Ivivin, a bit frustrated, swept her feet out from underneath her with a swift, if clumsy, trip, forcing her to sit down. She was startled, but took the not-so-subtle hint.

2

Ivivin, still quite irate, began to interrogate the unstoppable woman, who had finally begun to calm down. She implored Ivivin to keep quiet, as their presence was hidden yet. She explained to Ivivin why she was so desperate to save her sister and why it had to be tonight. She revealed that her sister was the subject of a grand prophecy—a prophecy that promised great power to whomever brought her to this cave. This power was so great, in fact, that it was said to be able to bring any king to his knees and make any knight tremble and tear.

Not only was keeping this forlorn power from the wrong hands of the utmost importance, but the older sister feared what

89

would become of her sister in the process of summoning the power (or after, when the cult realized they did not need her anymore).

Ivivin was startled that such a power could exist. Thinking back to his fight with Ojasa, though, he decided that stranger things could be true. Icarus, frightened by the story, quivered in Ivivin's shirt as he helped the still-unintroduced and informal knight to her feet.

He looked her sternly in the face.

"I will help you...."

"Elara. Sister of Idalia."

3

Cliché as it may be, Ivivin and Elara devised a plan to infiltrate the cave. Ivivin would disguise himself as one of the cult-bandits by covering his face with one of the odd, demonic looking masks they sported. He would then lead Elara, feigning capture, as a prisoner to the center of the cave. From there, well, they would ad lib an escape strategy. It wasn't a great plan, but it was a fast plan. And time was of the essence. And so, he tied up Elara's arms with a clever slipknot and they began their trek into the deep reaches of the cave.

With every step they took, Ivivin felt more and more that his plan was fairly stupid. He even had to stuff Icarus into his pants as not to draw attention to himself. Icarus, understandably, was less than pleased and swore a secret owl oath that he would have his revenge. This feeling, however, faded when they started to sneak past the other members with ease. It was almost as if the demonic masks existed only to make their infiltration easier! In passing, Ivivin ascertained that these cult-bandits called themselves the Shaa'Ilii, which apparently meant 'The followers of Shaa'. He also picked up that they worshipped a mythical demon they referred to as 'Shaa'Ra'.

And, like every good adventurer, Ivivin knew that demons were bad business.

4

    Elara and Ivivin needed to get to the Inner Chamber fast. That is where they had heard that the leader of the cult, going by the mantle Shaa'Id, was waiting for the stroke of midnight with Idalia. They hastened their pace. Save for a few suspicious glances, nothing seemed off about the whole place.

    That is, until they entered the inner chamber.

    "IT'S A TRAP!" Ivivin thought to himself. *"But how did they know we were coming!?"* He pondered fruitlessly as the members of the cult moved aggressively in on their position.

    Elara slid loose her knot and readied herself to fight. It seemed unlikely to Ivivin that it would do very much good, however. They rushed still further inside the very large inner chamber, but quickly found themselves surrounded by what seemed to be the entire cult—about 40 people or so. They were quickly captured, restrained, and forced to their knees to wait the arrival of the Shaa'Id.

    Ivivin took the chance to look around to try and devise an escape strategy. Despite the obvious alterations made to the chamber by the Shaa'Illi, the cave was verily majestic. The walls were embedded with pale charcoal colored gems and the walls themselves emitted a semblance of serenity, reminding Ivivin of the gems from the Wolfelaw caverns. Unfortunately, there seemed to only be one way in and one way out.

As the Shaa'Id entered the room, Ivivin realized this fight would not be an easy one. The cult leader was, for lack of a better phrase, absolutely shredded. Ivivin had been expecting a crusty old man or something of that nature. Icarus poked his head out, saw the Shaa'Id, and immediately went back into hiding. The Shaa'Id smiled as he approached them. He gestured to one of his followers to bring him something.

"Or someone." Ivivin realized as the man drug Idalia into view.

5

"We are doomed." Ivivin thought.

That was, bluntly, the situation. To make matters worse, the Shaa'Id would not stop laughing maniacally. It was terribly worrisome. Ivivin could see no notable means of escape. He figured, once again, that he'd have to wing it.

"Wing it..." Ivivin thought. *"That's it! Icarus! He has some sharp stuff on his face, even if it's oddly shaped and mostly dysfunctional. He can tear at the rope!"*

Ivivin looked down, as if he was praying, and whispered to Icarus "Hey buddy, anytime you're ready."

Icarus looked back at him exasperated, throwing him a look that clearly said, *'This is not my job'*.

The Shaa'Id saw Ivivin's 'prayer' and stopped laughing. He exclaimed. "Boy! It is far too late to pray to Shaa'Ra! I am his speaker and your fate, as well as these girls', is sealed! Mauhahahaha! It is part of an all-too-brilliant plan whispered to me by Shaa'Ra himself. I will describe to you the true misfortune that has befallen you and the true repercussions of your foolish actions so you may all know true anguish before your death!"

Shaa'Id began to elaborate on how his plan was pretty much the best plan ever, except for the part where he expressly told them his plan.

"You see, foolish Elara," Shaa'Id said "Idalia is not of the same bloodline as you."

This shocked Elara visibly—much, much more than Ivivin would have expected. After all, they were both orphans in the first place.

"So that means...." Elara trembled.

"Yes!" The menace exclaimed "*You* are the youngest and sole heir to the clan of Nomo, as well as the subject of the prophecy contained therein!"

Ivivin was confused, but both Elara and Idalia were visibly upset. Noticing the confusion on Ivivin's face, the Shaa'Id realized that the girls had not told Ivivin everything about this prophecy.

"He, he doesn't know, does he!?" Shaa'Id chuckled. "Well, we can't have that. Can't have that at all! He cannot fully understand his folly and despair until he knows. You!" He snarled, pointing at Elara. "Tell the boy, now, or I kill your sister."

Ivivin was bewildered.

"Why would they kidnap the Idalia just to kill her now? That's an empty threat, isn't it?"

But Elara obeyed quickly, much to Ivivin's curiosity.

As Icarus began to hack at the rope with what could arguably be categorized as a beak, Elara began her story.

6

"You see..." She started. "Idalia and I were orphaned at a very young age. She nor I can remember how we came to live with our current mother. But, from what she told us, she found us in the rubble of a village not too far from this very cave. It that was nearly burnt to the ground. She said we were both found in the remnants of the same house, in the same room. That, coupled with the fact that she and I look very alike, led our mother to believe we were sisters."

Ivivin took a moment to compare the two women. They were both very similar looking indeed, but there were some notable differences. For example, Idalia had fairer skin—Elara was tanner, despite living up north. Idalia also had a dark brown hair that was bordering on black. Elara's hair was very dark brown as well, but had a distinct clay hue when looking at the hairs individually. Their faces were a bit different as well, as Elara had a face that was a bit sharper in its features than Idalia's. Their body frame, height, eye color, and even voices were all very similar, though. It was no wonder they concluded that they were sisters.

Elara continued. "We grew up living a relatively normal life, despite the tragedy of our youth. But everything changed when our mother went into a sort of trance when I was about 13. She recited to us, Idalia and I, a prophecy of sorts—"

"A prophecy indeed!" interrupted the Shaa'Id. "This was the same wonderful prophecy whispered to me by the great Shaa'Ra! It spoke of an insurmountable power that the Nomo clan held. It seems as it was a last resort of sorts, capable of generating great power in a desperate time. And all it takes to unlock this infinitely great power is this chamber. That and..." He glanced at the girls, indicating for Elara to finish his statement.

"...The youngest pureblood daughter of the Nomo clan." She reluctantly muttered.

7

Ivivin started to assemble the situation, piece by piece. Elara was desperate to go after Idalia immediately because they both knew of the prophecy and the danger it posed to her sister's life, their home, and the world at large. Since Elara thought she was from the same lineage as Idalia, she thought that Idalia was the youngest daughter, as required by the prophecy, when, in reality, it was Elara herself.

The revelation must have shown on Ivivin's face, as the Shaa'Id smirked and resumed his rant.

"I think the simpleton's got it! You see, the Shaa'Ra came up with this ingenious plan. This girl, Elara, has quite the reputation. Some even call her the knight of her village! Undoubtedly her actions were linked to her desire to protect her sister and she would gladly die for her. The problem for us? This heiress of Nomo would likely resist our capture and could possibly die in the process. As fierce as she is, she was liable bring a few of us down with her, too. She would be useless to us dead. No, we needed fresh blood of Nomo pumping warm through her still. The mighty Shaa'Ra, in his boundless wisdom, instructed me to instead abduct her sister, very publicly, and allow the heiress to follow us here instead. My followers would then ambush, but not kill, her. She would live just long enough to fulfill her purpose here, all in the name of Shaa'Ra!" The madman panted, pausing to catch his breath a moment.

"...Of course," he continued "You, boy, threw off our plans, albeit an admittedly insignificant amount. And now, for that, you will die here. But only after you bear witness to the rise of Shaa'Ra!"

8

Ivivin didn't know exactly what the Shaa'Id was ranting about, but he was sure that he'd prefer to never find out. Unfortunately, Icarus was not making great headway on the rope.

"How did this bird survive in the wild?!" He pondered.

And so, the Shaa'Id approached the girls. He kicked Idalia with an impressive and cruel force directly to the stomach. He then dragged Elara by her hair to the centermost area of the cave. She had a look of frustration and powerlessness on her face, tied up as she was. Once the Shaa'Id had placed her in the center of the circle, Ivivin noticed the gradual luminescence of the cave.

Then, everywhere, light.

The dark crystals embedded in in the cavern walls shone brightly, containing a slight blue tint. It was not unlike the light of a full moon radiating on a clear night. Then, just as suddenly, the light began to focus just above Elara, forming a large, presumably magic, circle above her. It grew steadily larger and larger until it was about twenty feet in diameter. It looked just like...

"The moon." The Shaa'Id spoke. "The moon is the tunnel that connects, nay, intertwines the light and the dark. This power, this passageway is what will guide Shaa'Ra to this world. Unfortunately, though, his otherworldly form cannot exist in this world. That is, not without a vessel."

The mysterious light began to bear down in a column upon Elara. She struggled to move, clearly panicked, but it was entirely a vain attempt. The Shaa'Id approached the circle.

"Do not worry girl. You are not to be his vessel. Once he is revived, your suffering shall end by his hand. No, it is I, the Shaa'Id, destined to become his vessel."

9

The Shaa'Id entered the center of the moon-circle. As he did, black sparks began erupting from the floor, focusing on the Shaa'Id from all angles. As Elara basked more and more in light, the Shaa'Id cloaked himself yet further in darkness.

"Such power!" The Shaa'Id exclaimed. "Ra! I gladly give myself to you. Take this form I have sculpted for you over the course of a lifetime! With the coming of dawn, your presence in this world will be sealed and your wrath and power absolute!"

Ivivin, coming to his senses, began trying to fidget and break free. Icarus pulled through, shearing the rope. The rope fell away and Ivivin sprinted to where they had placed their arms. Time was of essence and, as Icarus scuttled away, Ivivin turned to face the man-demon.

The light stopped bearing down on Elara and the dark sparks had likewise vanished. However, the large bright circle persisted still above Elara and a new, dark circle was embedded in the ground directly below it. The Shaa'Id, or, rather, the Shaa'Ra turned to face Elara.

Ivivin charged, sword first, towards them.

10

Ivivin was repelled by the Shaa'Ra almost effortlessly. A simple wave of the hand created a huge impact that sent Ivivin flying. The Shaa'Ra smiled.

"Listen here, boy, to the hopelessness of your struggle. There are two ways to prevent me from reaching full power and wreaking havoc upon this realm." Ivivin shuddered. Something about the voice of this entity chilled him to the bone.

"This isn't even his full power!?" Ivivin thought in disbelief.

"If you wish to stop my arrival into this realm, then you must either destroy my vessel, the Shaa'Id, before sunrise. Or..." He smiled a sinister smile and gestured to Elara. "You can destroy the bridge that carries me here. You, with such a gentle heart could never do the latter. And you, with such a weak and unrefined corporeal form could never do the former. So, your only real options are to flee and die later or fight and die now."

96

Ivivin was scared to his core. The already intimidating Shaa'Id, now possessed by the Shaa'Ra, had an overwhelming demonic presence about him. But Ivivin believed firmly that no one was unbeatable. Well, perhaps the Shaa'Ra would be, if allowed to reach his final form.

Ivivin picked up his shield and his sword once more. He charged the Shaa'Ra again, only to be struck by the incredible force once more. This time, though, he bore the brunt of it and did not fall. Instead, he landed on his feet and charged again. This time, when he felt the force beginning to shoot him back, he cast it aside with his shield. He was stopped, but not repelled. His legs and arms burned from the strain, but, nonetheless, he charged again.

Ivivin charged and charged and charged, each time getting minutely closer and closer to the Shaa'Ra. Unfortunately, the Shaa'Ra seemed relatively unfazed. In fact, he seemed to be taking great enjoyment in watching Ivivin's desperate attempts to reach him. He began bellowing in laughter, which each one of his blows becoming stronger. Ivivin could feel his bones beginning to crackle under the force. The pain began to become unbearable.

Then, suddenly, nothing.

11

Ivivin isn't stupid.

You see, when Ivivin first charged, he caught, out of the corner of his eye (whilst being flung through the air), his little owl companion desperately tugging at Idalia's ropes. Idalia and Ivivin made eye contact for only a moment but, in that moment, a thousand words were spoken. As the Shaa'Ra became increasingly powerful and playful, he also became decreasingly attentive to his surroundings. Icarus had, eventually, broken Idalia's bondage. She wielded Elara's sword and thrust it through the heart of the not-quite-complete Shaa'Ra.

The Shaa'Ra left the body of Shaa'Id and was forcefully funneled back into the black circle on the cave's floor. The Shaa'Id, miraculously, seemed to be alive, though with a sword thrust through his chest. Ivivin felt relief, but the feeling did not last long. Although the followers of Shaa'Ra had let the Shaa'Ra and Ivivin do battle undisturbed (both out of fear and respect for their god), Ivivin now felt many a murderous glare fixed upon him and the young women. Their numbers were halved, however, as many had fled when the Shaa'Ra first came to be. Still, they were outnumbered. Ivivin doubted he could pull off the same stunt he did in Crosstown. Things were looking bleak.

12

The portals, both light and dark, remained open. New sparks of both moonglow and of darkness began to fly haphazardly. Behind him, Ivivin heard a scream. It was the Shaa'Id himself being drug by the sparks into the black portal. From what seemed to be the center of the world itself, Ivivin heard a demonic voice.

"You shall not go unpunished for your failure, my Shaa'Ilii. All those who bear the mark of Ra shall join me. Your blunder has ensured my entrapment between worlds. So, to entertain me in this dark eternity, I will torment you all for your failure. Come, my devoted followers!"

The bulk of the remaining followers were then gruesomely drug under into the abyss, with Ivivin unable to help even a single one. There were still five men left, though, who seemed to not have yet been branded with the mark of Shaa'Ra. And it looked like there was still fight in them yet.

Then, in an instant, Elara flew by, disarming and incapacitating all of them in one fell swoop. All of them, save one, seemed to be pretty gravely injured.

"I left one for us to bring back to our foster mother. She'll know what to make of this whole ordeal, if we bring him."

So, Ivivin bound the vagabond cult member and helped drag him into town, though firmly Elara insisted on dragging him most of the way herself. When they finally arrived in town, Elara, Ivivin, and Idalia all went straight to the old seer—their foster mother. In her home, Elara and Idalia's foster mother had a nice warm meal laid out for them, like she knew already of their victory and precisely when they would return. She had even laid out a plate (albeit less full and delicious looking) for the lone cult member they had brought along.

The Tear of Jupiter

1

After an odd and quiet (but undoubtedly tasty) dinner, Elara cleared her throat loudly to express her desire to talk about the day's fiasco. The seer-mother understood her daughter's impatient tendencies well and indicated that they should recount the day's events to her.

So, they did. Every detail seemed to be painstakingly conveyed. Ivivin, exhausted from charging the Shaa'Ra over and over, laid down and only really chipped in for his part of the battle. But he listened. And listened. And listened. It was almost as if the whole thing was a children's fable—he couldn't believe it actually had happened. So, naturally, he was surprised that when the trio was done so verbosely recounting their tale, the seer-mother simply asked:

"Are you forgetting anything?"

Ivivin and Icarus both simply shook their heads while sprawled on the blankets laid out for them, eyes closed and on the verge of sleep. When the seer-mother asked again, more sternly this time, Ivivin sat up and looked to the dinner table. She had an unnaturally serious face about her and was staring Elara directly in the eyes. Elara seemed taken aback before eventually regaining her composure and meeting her mother's glare. The seer-mother sighed and calmness returned to her face.

"Stubborn child, you do not need to protect the world from me. Or from anyone else in the room for that matter. Well, except, maybe, that odd rodent in the corner." She joked, nodding towards Icarus. After chuckling at her own joke, she continued. "I know you have the crystal, child. Show it to me, my dear daughter."

2

Reluctantly, Elara reached into her clothes and retrieved a crystal. Elara seemed terrified that it was exposed and out in the open. Slowly, and with nervous glances to and fro, she handed her foster mother the stone.

"What is that?" Ivivin thought sleepily.

As if reading his mind, the seer-woman spoke.

"Ah, yes, you did well to hide this crystal Elara. It is the legendary Tear of Jupiter indeed. Anyone even mildly versed in the arcane could easily conquer countries with the power this stone alone holds. Shaa'Ra tried to use it to break the seal binding him to his domain and enter this world. Fortunately, you three..."

Icarus looked a little hurt.

"You four. Sorry. You four stopped him and trapped him in the worlds in-between."

Ivivin was shocked to hear that stone had that much power. He looked at the crystal again. There seemed to be a sort of crusty mineral coating the already kind of dull-looking crystal. His dubious look must had been apparent, as the seer-woman continued.

"This is the Tear of Jupiter from lore, children. As the story goes, Jupiter had three children, all of divine, unnatural beauty. These, in celestial terms, are its moons Europa, Ganymede, and Callisto. Jupiter herself was known as harsh and cold, but also beautiful and strong. Bearing children softened her, though, and she came to grow warm alongside them.

Europa was very much the spitting image of Jupiter before motherhood. Ganymede was a handsome man who was moral and earnest, almost to a fault. He was also easily the weakest of the three. And, finally, Callisto was a gentle, soft-spoken woman who valued her family more than anything. When disaster struck in a faraway land, it is said that the celestial king called the children of Jupiter, now young adults, to arms and sent them here, to our Earth. Saddened by the departure of her children and the struggle that laid before them, Jupiter cried and cried and cried. Her tears reached even Earth. The tears, full of emotion, bestowed great power to her children. When they learned of this, Ganymede and Callisto cried soft tears of extreme happiness that their mother loved them so. But Europa, the cold and stoic young woman that she was, cried not and kept a still face. She could not fool her siblings, however. They could sense, if only for a moment, how lonely she truly felt. So, Ganymede and Callisto gave their share of their mother's tears to Europa. She was filled to the brim with emotion. Her cold heart could stay frigid no longer. Europa, too, began to cry. Her tears were as salty and large as her mother's.

But, with their gift, Ganymede and Callisto had given up their power to Europa. In the war that followed, Ganymede and Callisto both fell in battle. Europa, who had until that moment herself been fighting fiercely, stopped the battle. She began to cry and cry and cry, just as her mother had, until she herself became an ocean of tears that washed away the evils they were sent here to battle. Thus, disaster was averted and Europa was deemed a hero who gave her life for good. In reality, however, she could not bear to live in a world without her family. In death, the three became one with their mother once more."

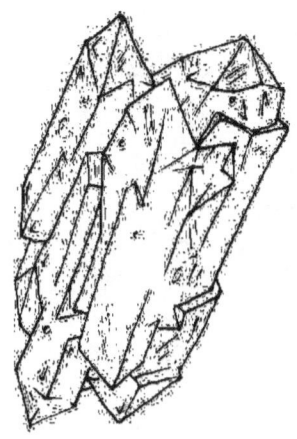

3

Ivivin thought the tale was both a heartwarming and bitter legend. But he couldn't quite understand what it all had to do with the stone. Again, almost as if reading Ivivin's mind, the seer quipped once more.

"This stone.... this crystal… is the manifestation of Jupiter's tears. The Tear of Jupiter holds the power of the demi-celes Europa and her soul-siblings. And you three.... you are the reincarnations of Jupiter's Children. Ivivin is Ganymede, Idalia is Callisto, and Elara..." She paused and smiled for a moment "You are Europa, my fierce and cold daughter."

Naturally, the three were shocked at the boldness of this claim. Ivivin made his way back to the table and sat down, staring intently at the seer-mother. She smiled and asked him:

"What do you think of all this, boy?"

Ivivin looked at both Idalia and Elara. They both seemed shaken to the core, as if they somehow knew all along. Ivivin looked back to the seer-woman.

"I don't buy it."

4

Idalia and Elara looked at him shocked, but the seer-lady kept smiling and asked him why.

"I won't deny that something felt unusually familiar about Elara and Idalia." Ivivin started. "But it is nothing so profound as being related, let alone being celestial-spirits of common ancestry. I just don't believe it. Well, not that I am Ganymede, at least. The rest of your story rings true to me."

The seer-woman did not seem particularly shocked, but she did seem curious. Elara was intently staring at her hands

"I somehow knew I was different. But...but not like this."

There was silence for minutes, which was finally broken by Icarus vomiting out a pellet of bones rather loudly, as owls are apt do.

"Elara, Idalia, Ivivin..." the seer-lady started. "You no longer bear the burden of who you once were. The responsibilities, the relationships, and the things that make you 'you' are separate from that. Live your life as if you were never anything but human because that is what you surely are now."

She paused.

"That is what I would say, if not for that, the artifact anchoring you to your past lives. It is a dangerous thing and we cannot leave it be."

She sighed.

"I had hoped you all could live normal lives but, as Elara just demonstrated, the stone emits a heavy pressure onto all of you."

Ivivin was listening and watching, trying to make sense of the woman's words. Elara and Idalia both seemed to be staring at the stone, unable to look away. Idalia was trembling and Elara was sweating. Ivivin didn't understand why. Even Icarus seemed to be watching it and keeping his distance from it. It was as if the crystal were exerting some tremendous pressure that bore down on their spirits themselves. But Ivivin felt nothing of the sort. Sure, he was aware of the power it held—he had seen and felt it first-hand. But, as far as he could tell, it just looked and felt like a stone. Even the rocks in the Wolfelaw caves seemed more impressive.

The seer-woman noted, just as Ivivin did, the behavior of the individuals in the room. She seemed to have discovered something and burst out in a fit of laughter. She laughed so hard and so genuinely that it tore the tension in the room into tiny shreds. Ivivin almost started laughing just from seeing her. It was as if the universe itself had been revealed as nothing more than a gag and this exact moment was its punchline.

5

Once the seer had finally calmed down, only releasing a snicker or two now and again, she decided an explanation was in order.

"It will be easier to show you all, rather than explain with words." She grabbed Elara's hand and pricked it with a needle. She let the blood drop onto the stone, which then shone brightly for a few seconds before fading. She repeated the process, but this time with Idalia. Again, the stone shone brightly.

"The stone will shine to indicate the true heirs of the tears of Jupiter. As such, it will not react to my blood." She said as she demonstrated by pricking her own finger and letting her own blood make its way to the stone. Just as she had said, the stone was unreactive and the blood simply evaporated.

Finally, she grabbed Ivivin's hand, pricked his finger, and his blood, too, fell onto the stone.

Nothing.

6

The old woman began laughing again, though not quite as fiercely this time around. Elara and Idalia were shocked—the man that they thought was their soul-brother was a stranger after all!

"Where is Ganymede then!" Elara outburst.

"Do you really want to know?" the mother-seer teased.

Ivivin knew it was not him. It was a feeling he couldn't shake. It just didn't ring true to him. He had no clue, though, of who else it could possibly be.

"It wasn't the Shaa'Id was it!?" Elara exclaimed.

"No dear, the truth is more twisted yet." said the seer-woman.

"The Shaa'Ra?" Idalia peeped.

The old woman just gravely shook her head, stood up, and walked to the corner of the room to retrieve something. It was then Ivivin knew what the old woman intended.

"But there is no way." Ivivin reasoned to himself. *"That would be absolutely ludicrous. A joke of the heavens played on mortals indeed!"*

Sure enough, the seer returned to the table holding what appeared to be a struggling tuft of dust and feathers. She pricked its bottom and again let the blood fall onto the stone.

The three young ones were mortified.

The stone shone brightly, as it had for Elara and Idalia, for none other than Icarus, the apparent reincarnation of a celestial spirit. Idalia and Elara were struck with awe and silent. Ivivin was shocked, too, at first. But shock quickly evolved into an uncontrollable laughter.

"The world is really a strange and wondrous place!" Ivivin thought as he laughed heartily. Not long after, Idalia and then Elara joined in the laughing as Icarus tried to straighten himself up and retain some pride in this absurd situation.

Ivivin picked up his 'all-powerful' bird and held him to Elara's face.

"Hey Elara! Say hello to your brother!"

Elara was a bit abashed but kept giggling nonetheless.

While the three young ones were busy joking around and laughing, the seer woman sat in her chair, smiling.

"This is the best possible thing that could have happened to these children" she thought *"There is no way they can take their reincarnations too seriously now. This will help them live their life unshackled. Thank you, winged-rodent. I suppose you are noble, too, in your own way."*

7

However, the seer-woman knew that not all was yet settled.

"The matter still at hand, children," She began. "is what we are to do with the stone so we can put this whole ordeal behind us. It cannot simply be hidden—there are arcane means of locating such objects and, even though it would not be at full strength if it were not wielded by the blood of the Moons of Jupiter, it would still possess a deadly and immense power in the wrong hands."

Elara, with a determined look, spoke up.

"I will be the bearer of the stone, mother. All who try to take it from me shall be sent swiftly to the grave."

The seer-woman sighed. "No dear. Firstly, if you were to get captured again with the stone, the full fury of Jupiter would be unleashed. Would be better to keep you both separate from the stone, I think."

Elara, although passionate to her duty, could see the logic in that argument and resigned that she could not be the one to carry the stone.

"Then you, mother? Can you keep it safe?" Idalia asked.
The woman paused for just a moment before responding.

"I cannot. The best I can do is look for ways to seal the powers of the stone away forever. And, if it is possible, it would take me quite some time to work out. So, no, it would be best if the stone were not left with me."

Ivivin could see where this was heading.

"I guess it defaults to me, then." Ivivin sighed. "Though won't it be dangerous for me to keep the stone AND Icarus? I mean…" Ivivin just barely stifled a snicker "He, too, has the blood of Jupiter. Wouldn't that be the same as Elara?"

"Well, yes and no. You see, if an unruly force comes seeking the stone and the incarnate of Ganymede, they will likely mistake you for him. After all, it is ridiculous to think that an owl, let alone Icarus, would be heir to the name Ganymede. As long as you stay close to each other, you would effectively act as a decoy. Of course, this involves a large personal risk on your behalf Ivivin." The seer woman responded.

Ivivin contemplated the situation and replied "Yeah it does. But I cannot think of a safer place for it than within the castle vaults. Once I become a knight sworn to defend the castle and the kingdom,

I will hide the stone there until such time we discover a way to seal its power away."

The seer-woman looked a bit suspicious. "You trust the king and kingdom to persevere that much, do you boy? Wars and strife and coupes are common in this world."

"I have made it my goal to become a knight of the king. The day the kingdom falls will also be the day I fall. The result is the same." Ivivin stated matter-of-factly.

"I see." The seer woman said. "I will trust your judgement then. Well, now that this matter is settled, you all should rest. Ivivin is weary from battle and I can tell he wants to be leaving in the morning."

Ivivin laid down and sleep crept up on him almost immediately. Icarus, in all his glorious divinity, could be seen cuddled up by the top of Ivivin's head.

8

Ivivin woke in the middle of the night to some clamor—it sounded as if there were people on the roof. He sprung up and quietly crept outdoors, worried it was yet another assailant. However, he found instead Idalia and Elara, sitting together on the roof. Idalia appeared just as fair as she always had, but Elara was unusually radiant this night. She had a rare smile on display as she giggled, joked with, and teased her sister. Ivivin could plainly tell that it was much more than just the risk of a dangerous power being unleashed that drove Elara to such lengths to save her sister. It was their bond that motivated Elara more than any other factor. He smiled silently and began to ease himself back into their home. Just as he was about to enter the house, however, Idalia caught a glimpse of Ivivin and invited him to join them. The smile quickly faded from Elara's face. She didn't seem upset about the gesture, but she also didn't look particularly enthused, either. Ivivin figured he would politely indulge Idalia for a few minutes and return her to Elara by resuming his rest.

So, the three sat on the roof and gazed upwards at the stars. Idalia was planted in the middle of Elara and Ivivin. For a while, she tried to make small talk by pointing out the constellations in the sky, talking about the seasons, and how warm it must be where Ivivin was from compared to out here in the north. The ordeal must have been too much for her, though, as she fell deeply asleep after just a short while.

9

Ivivin knew full well that he could leave Idalia in the capable hands of Elara and all would be fine. But something about sitting there and looking at the stars above was entrancing. Elara must have thought the same thing, because she, too, just continued to look at the stars (after, of course, covering her dozing sister with a blanket). Idalia remained a sleepy barrier between them for hours and the two did not utter a single word to each other.

Then, unprompted, Elara pointed to the sky.

"Lupus..." she said, briefly pausing.

"...is my favorite constellation."

Ivivin was startled by the sudden noise and motion and jerked, almost bumping into Idalia. Moreover, Ivivin had never learned anything about constellations, save the very basics of navigation, so he was left a bit confused.

"Lupus huh? What is it?"

"The wolf." She said

Ivivin didn't see a wolf. He made shapes in his head from the stars, but they didn't resemble anything. He just liked to look at them.

"I never learned about constellations. So, I can't see what you're talking about. I'm sorry." Ivivin said, not knowing quite why he apologized.

"That is a shame. It is very common here in the north. Our mother taught us." Elara said, putting her hand down at last.

Then, their silence resumed, unbroken, for another twenty or thirty minutes until Elara got up, put Idalia on her back, and worked her way back inside. Ivivin watched the girls vanish back into the house. He would stay a while longer, with Icarus eventually coming out so see where his friend went. They sat there together and gazed at the stars, shivering from the cold of the north. About 15 minutes after Elara and Idalia had gone inside, Ivivin and Icarus followed suit and embraced sleep.

The entire household would wake rather late the following day.

10

Ivivin packed his belongings. His shield from Crosstown, his armor, his sword—all his gear and equipment—he packed up snugly and prepared to take his leave. His plan was to head back west, slowly working his way back to the kingdom. He was also still lacking all the King's requirements for knighthood, but he hadn't seen the whole country yet. He felt more and more as if that was the true purpose of his journey. Of course, he still very much wanted to be a knight, but he also enjoyed his wandering about. The seer woman had suspended the Tear from a rope and tied it to Ivivin's bag. It was an awkward size—too large to wear as a necklace, but too small for Ivivin to feel comfortable enough that he wouldn't lose it if he couldn't easy check on it.

The seer woman left Ivivin once he exited the house, wishing him well on his travels and informing him she would send for him when she had discovered a manner by which to seal the Tear. Elara and Idalia, however, decided to escort Ivivin to the edge of town. Although they had known each other for only a short while, it felt like months, even years. Idalia gifted Ivivin with a pouch that could be easily strapped to his leg. It was full of medical supplies, ointment, and an owl embroidered into it, with the symbol of Jupiter (♃) on its chest. He donned it and hugged her goodbye. He expected a rather cold goodbye from Elara—that was just how she seemed. He knew they had bonded a bit, though, and was sad to part with her. Ivivin turned to face her to say farewell only to find her pressing a book into his face.

"Here." Elara said, not quite making eye contact with Ivivin "It is a book of the constellations. This is the one from which our mother used to teach us when we were young."

"Th-thanks" Ivivin said, pleasantly startled by the gesture.

"Now you don't have an excuse to be so ignorant of the stars. Next time I see you, you better know all of them!" Elara said, finally making eye contact. Oddly enough, Ivivin thought she looked a bit intimidating, but also a bit flustered.

"Oh!" Ivivin thought, struck suddenly with an idea. He rummaged through his gear, effectively undoing his attempts to stay organized and compact. He pulled from the bag the book he had acquired in Crosstown.

"It is beyond me, but I bet you, Elara, could power through it. You'll probably love it, too! It seems like quite the tale, from what I can tell." He handed the book to Elara. They shared in a smile for a moment before Ivivin turned to leave.

"Thank you both!" Ivivin said. "I'll make sure to bring back a gift from the castle when I come back to visit!"

As Ivivin left, he was unusually excited. He had never received a gift from a girl his age before. Today, he received two. Youth seemed to flourish and take form in his mind as he made his way east.

11

Elara and Idalia returned to their home. Idalia went inside straight away to cook for their worn mother. But Elara lingered outdoors, watching the horizon until Ivivin was no longer visible. Then, she went to join her sister and mother inside. Much to her surprise, she was met by her seer-mother at the doorway.

"Elara, I can tell you, too, wish to leave this place and set forth on your own adventure. Do not hold back for our sake. I have years yet left to live and Idalia is safe, as Ivivin bears the Tear. I will make arrangements for you to journey across the desert to the south with the next group of merchants to head that direction. Tomorrow, start your preparations. But, for now, would you keep your old mother company?"

Elara could not believe she was that transparent. She could do nothing but nod.

"Also, dear," the old woman said with a sly smirk on her face. "You are related to the owl, not the boy. Isn't that a relief?"

Elara could not believe she was that transparent.

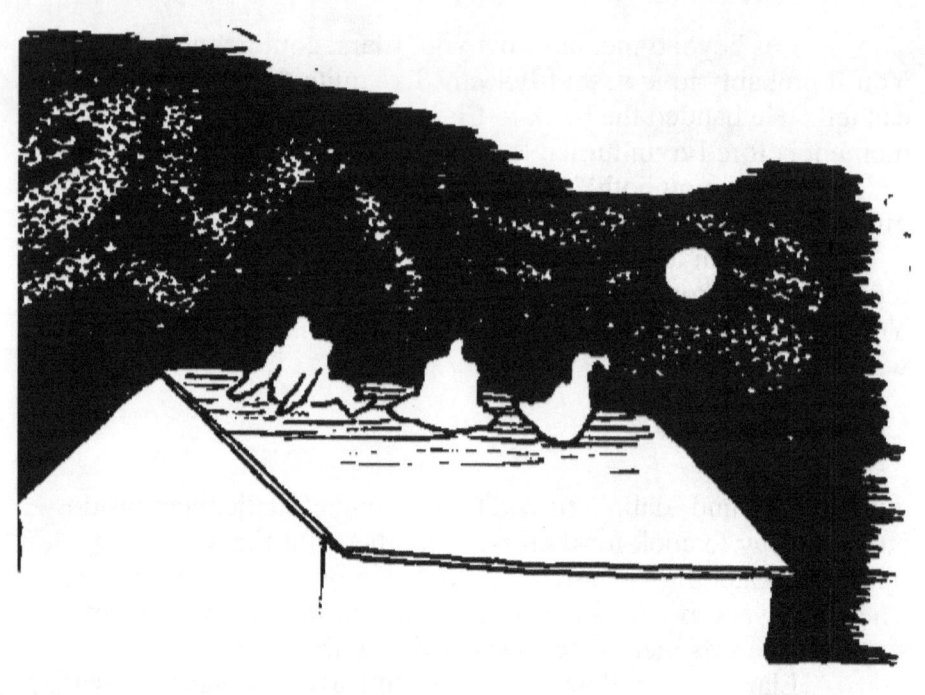

Northward Bound

1

And so, Ivivin and Icarus were off on their own once again. Ivivin decided that, before returning west, he wanted to see the mountainous peaks to the north. He had no intent of crossing the border, but he wanted to climb up a small peak so he could see the range clearly. He had heard from Smith that the mountains in the north are the largest in the world and easily were amoung the most beautiful. He decided he would head northwest, as a sort of compromise. His plan was to camp out at the first town he came across until an unusually nice day came around. He would then hike up the mountain and gaze upon the majestic range.

Icarus didn't like this plan much—the look on his face made it pretty apparent. Ivivin reassured Icarus that he could stay in or near the warmth town while he climbed. With that settled democratically, the pair refocused their trek northwest. It was similar to how they traveled before and, thus, very familiar. But Ivivin now had a lot to think about and reflect on. He thought about his trials thus far and wondered about how he even managed to do the things he did. He had little confidence in his ability to do so if the situations were to arise again. He thought fondly of his family back home. He wanted to go back on his way to the castle, he decided. When he thought of Smith, it helped him keep walking when his legs were sore and achy. And then there were his most recent of friends, Idalia and Elara. When he thought of them, he would get giddy for no real reason and spend the afternoons smiling. He was having a hard time reading the gift Elara had given him. It did him little good to look at it in the day, but the flickering light of a campfire made it very difficult to read at night. He decided that he would purchase a lantern the next time he found a town. Until then, though, he could not stop himself from anxiously and eagerly glancing at the book from time to time. He hoped more and more that he'd reach town soon.

2

Ivivin arrived at a small village on his way to the mountains. From the folk there, he learned that there was another town not terribly far from here and that it was by the base of one of the smaller mountains—a perfect fit for Ivivin's goal. Upon investigation, Ivivin quickly learned that this village had only 2 shops, a general store and a grocer, as well as a single inn. Ivivin decided he should stock up on supplies, including a lantern to read Elara's book of constellations once it got dark. He walked to the store, but was disappointed to find that they didn't have any lanterns available. Dejected, Ivivin fiddled around with some of the goods about the shop, looking for things that may be of use. When he grabbed a small stone with odd foreign lettering on it, he was shocked to see it start to glow. Ivivin wasn't the only one. The shopkeeper rushed over, fearing Ivivin had broken a ware. He snatched the stone from Ivivin's hand and the light faded.

The shopkeeper explained to Ivivin. "A few years ago, I bought this stone from a foreign traveler who said it possessed some sort of magic. I didn't buy any of it of course, but he was asking a very reasonable amount and looked desperately in need of money to eat. I figured the shape was unique enough that, one day, someone would buy it as a trinket. Apparently, it does possess some sort of magic. I'll tell you what, lad, if you can make it glow just once more for me, I'll let you have it at the price I bought it."

Ivivin grabbed the stone again. It glowed, but this time less brightly. Ivivin himself felt somehow worn from holding it.

"A deal is a deal." The shopkeeper said "It really shines a wonderful color. I am happy I got to see it."

Ivivin handed over a few copper pieces and wrapped the stone in a small piece of cloth, sticking it in his pocket.

"You are headed northwest, am I right?"

Ivivin nodded.

"I'll tell you something good, then. The town northwest of here is called Winter's Fort. It's not really a fort, but there are often soldiers there patrolling the border. Anyways, there is a man there, a childhood acquaintance, who became obsessed with magics and the such. He runs an inn there. I'm sure he could tell you something about that stone."

Ivivin decided he would do just that. He decided to stay in the village for the night and head off to the northeast the next day. That night, in the inn, he pulled out the stone once more. It glowed bright enough for him to read and the light was constant and consistent for at least a few minutes. Whatever the true purpose of the stone, Ivivin had found himself a new reading lantern. He set the stone down. Icarus, who was both disturbed and intrigued by the light, began to fiddle with it. It glowed again—this time brighter than any time Ivivin had grabbed it and it continued to glow even after Icarus had freaked out and flown away.

Ivivin, now fearing a connection to the lore of Jupiter, resolved to ask the innkeeper about the nature of the stone's magic when he arrived at Winter's Fort.

3

Ivivin had originally planned on leaving rather late in the morning, but ended up leaving the village as soon as the sun broke the horizon. From there, it took him about three days to arrive at Winter's Fort. It was substantially colder here, but the mountains nearby seemed to break all wind. It felt warmer than other places he had been in the north so far, as least. With a sense of purpose, Ivivin went to the inn. He wanted answers as soon as he could get them. The innkeeper was surprised that Ivivin knew of his arcane interests, but still eagerly agreed to investigate the stone and its magic. He offered Ivivin a small room at the back of the inn that was once occupied by workers. It would take a while for him to make sense of the stone, he explained. Ivivin decided that this would be a good chance to go out to the mountains. He planned to leave next morning and return at dusk, making a day of it. Icarus vehemently opposed the idea of going up the mountain and made it clear he would be staying in the warm room while Ivivin hiked the following morning. Ivivin spent the night eagerly preparing his supplies for the hike.

4

Ivivin departed the following morning for his hike, letting the inn's keeper and Icarus know where he was going and that he would be back before dark.

Elsewhere, Elara set out with a group of merchants to cross the desert into Crosstown. It was, apparently, a harsh journey but not an unmanageable one. People seldom died and, if they did, it was because they went it alone and unprepared. Elara had nothing to worry about. She would cross the desert with the merchants and set off alone from Crosstown. She planned to see the country quickly, but thoroughly, and return to her sister's and mother's side. She held a hope that she might run into Ivivin, but knew the chance was forlorn. After all, they were headed in nearly opposite directions. She thought back to the almost-too-cheery goodbye her sister and mother had sent her off with. She knew that they were just pretending to not be sad so Elara would actually set forth. She knew she would get lonely this trip, but she also knew that this is what she wanted, too, in her heart. Within a few days, Elara and the small group of merchants would arrive at the northern end of the narrowest stretch of the desert.

Ivivin climbed the mountain diligently, seldom stopping and only resting for a minute or two at a time. He was getting strong. His legs could bring him almost anywhere he wanted and, as he climbed and hiked, Ivivin felt for the first time as if he could do anything. In a bit less than half a day, Ivivin had made it to the top of the mountain. It felt, simply put, good.

5

Ivivin took a minute to look at the surrounding mountains. Or was it hours? Ivivin couldn't tell. The sublime feeling he had standing at the peak of the mountain distorted his sense of time. He was by no means on the tallest mountain. But he could see the other peaks in the range and, if he tilted his head just so, he could also see past them—out into the neighboring country. The original homeland of the one-armed knight Miroslav, Ivivin recollected. Ivivin realized then and there that, though he had been on the road for so long and seen so many places, he had barely made a dent. There were places still in this very country he had not seen. Moreover, this continent contained many countries. What's more is that Ivivin was sure that there were extravagant places to see in lands across the water! It was here on top of the peak of the mountain, at the peak of a difficult climb, at the peak of his life, and at the peak of his adventure, that Ivivin realized how truly small he was. He wondered if this feeling was how Elara felt when she looked up at her stars.

Ivivin would not be in this existential trance for long, though. A storm was headed in from the northeast, one that Ivivin did not see until it was rather close and he was already atop of the mountain. Upon seeing the storm, Ivivin decided he should hustle back down the mountain before it got dark and before the storm hit. Ivivin was absolutely right about being small in this world, though, as the storm headed his way was large and fearsome. And, unfortunately for Ivivin, it moved far faster than Ivivin's current experience could have ever allowed him to predict. The storm hit, Ivivin slowed, and night fell as wind kicked snow up in unpredictable and horrid patterns. Once again, it seemed, Ivivin would be fighting for his life.

6

Elsewhere, Elara was spending the night a very shallow way into the desert. They had planned to travel at night after this, so Elara was preparing herself by staying awake all night so that she might sleep during the day. She stared at the stars, as was her hobby. She immediately remembered the night on the roof with Ivivin and Idalia. She knew Ivivin must fancy her sister. After all, Idalia was the pinnacle of all things feminine and fair. It was not surprising in the least. So, she did her best to thrust these fledging but shallow feelings aside. She would sacrifice anything for her, big or small. She smiled and looked again to the sky. The stars soothed her. There was a legend, or, rather, a fable that said this planet and everything and everyone on it, was the result of a star bursting into bits and scattering itself across the night sky. Over time, the stardust clumped together to make the earth and its inhabitants.

Elara took comfort that she, too, was made up of dust of the stars.

7

"Well this is just the worst." Ivivin thought as the storm, now safely capable of being categorized a blizzard, pounded on him about halfway down the mountain. Unfortunately, he could not descend any further—if he lost his footing, he would likely tumble very easily to his death. The snow and wind in and of themselves were not the problems hindering Ivivin's decent. Rather, the issue was that he could not see. He crawled around where he was, looking for any sort of shelter.

No such luck.

The best he could do was a rotting, hollow tree log. He would have to will himself to survive until the storm let up. But when minutes turned into hours, Ivivin realized that if he did not make the climb down, he would freeze here and die. With no light source and nothing special to help him make the climb, Ivivin began to consider trying to slide down the mountain and just hoping for the best. He exited the log and again felt around for anything he could use to cushion his fall(s) and bump(s) and break(s).

He stuck soggy bark wherever he could without soaking himself. He grabbed the rotting log he was 'chilling' in and held it like a sled. He stared at the edge of his safe haven, breathing heavily and shivering. Fear gripped him thoroughly. It was as if he was merely choosing how he would die and staring was the only thing he could do to delay that choice. Staring. And staring, and staring. And then more starting still.

Eventually, Ivivin prepared himself for the ride. He looked up for one last glance into the distance, hoping for a miracle to relieve him of the leap he was about to make. The storm, if anything, was picking up. But Ivivin noticed out of the corner of his eye, an odd and sustained glow slowly, but steadily, ascending the mountain. Ivivin screamed and shouted to the light, relieved to even have an option other than becoming a human toboggan. To his surprise, it headed straight towards him, without regard to terrain. Was this a spirit come to claim his life?

No.

9

It was Icarus, the brave owl, holding the stone Ivivin had left at the inn. Icarus tumbled from the air into Ivivin's arms and the stone dropped to the floor right in front of them. Icarus had flown up the mountain with his...odd...wings in the middle of a blizzard just to bring Ivivin the stone, so that he might live.

But there was no guarantee that Ivivin could produce light enough to descend the mountain safely. Or that he could do it before he and his friend froze. Ivivin was still terrified, fear making him shake just as much as the bitter cold. But his friend had bet everything on him, so it was time to bet everything on himself. He tucked Icarus into the most inner layer of his clothing. He picked up the stone, still holding a faint glow from its tenure with Icarus. It did not light anew. Ivivin tried to focus. He gripped the stone harder and harder, hoping and praying it would light once more.

Nothing.

He thought to touch it to the Tear of Jupiter.

Nothing.

He thought once more of Icarus and of Elara and Idalia and Smith and how he wanted to see them again. He gripped the stone, barehanded in the storm, so hard he began to bleed.

Nothing....and then, something. The stone began to glow.

Ivivin began what was easily the worst experience of his life. The pain of the cold and the desperateness of his breathing not only fatigued him physically, but mentally as well. He thought about giving up and laying down and just dying. If here were alone, he surely would have faltered and his life would have flickered out. But Icarus had trusted him and so Ivivin fought through it. Looking back at it, Ivivin would not be able to understand how he kept going. The entire climb down he thought constantly about giving up, but it was as if his body moved on its own. Towards the base of the mountain, the light from the stone died. Ivivin stumbled through the remainder of the journey. He fell and fell and fell. But each time he fell, he rose. None of the falls were enough to stop him and, so, he got up and kept stumbling. When the inn finally came into sight, Ivivin suddenly returned to himself. He was desperate and he filled with the desire to live. He began to run in the snow which was already feet deep. His legs burnt and screamed and shivered. But he ran. He ran all the way to the inn. The innkeeper, being a smart and prepared man, had warm water ready for them. But instead of getting in himself, Ivivin slowly dipped Icarus into the water. After a few seconds, Icarus returned to this world. Ivivin grinned faintly before he collapsed and blacked out.

11

For days, Ivivin slept and rested. His body was weak and, even in the few moments of consciousness he had, he was frail and could barely move. Icarus was in a similar state, at least at first. The spry owl recovered a bit faster than anyone could have anticipated. Unfortunately, the storm had caused him to lose even more feathers. He couldn't sustain flight for very long and looked even more scruffy and unkempt than usual. The innkeeper alternated between feeding Ivivin and studying the stone. It was fascinating enough to him to put up with his resident cripple. He, of course, expected Ivivin to compensate him for the food, but fed him and housed him out of the kindness of his heart. This continued for quite some time, 6 days, before Ivivin even began to recover. He regained consciousness for longer and longer periods of time and could bathe and relieve himself unassisted. He had reached the turning point. It seemed that Ivivin would recover, given a bit more time.

12

During Ivivin's and Icarus' recovery at the inn, Elara had continued on her own adventure. She and the merchants had arrived safely in Crosstown.

"Finally," Elara thought. *"I can be free of these bickering merchants!"*

Elara knew travelling alone from this point on would be lonely, but she was sick of that particular crowd of people. She wouldn't have minded travelling with Idalia or...

"Ivivin" she muttered, wondering if he was safe in his travels. She knew that she would not see either of them for quite some time and tried to force herself to accept that.

"This is the hardest part of leaving home." she thought. *"Maybe I should find myself an animal companion, as Ivivin did."*

She decided to stock up supplies in Crosstown before headed southeast. Her plan was to loop around the country, southeast to south to southwest and back to the north.

"With this route," she thought. *"I may get to see Ivivin as a knight on my way home. Maybe we could even spar a bit!"*

As she was wandering around the town, she was surprised to hear that Ivivin was known here. He had apparently made quite the name for himself here in Crosstown. It was still the talk of the town how Ivivin single-handedly crushed a giant and brutal bandit king. And how he let the bandit live out of mercy and earned the bandit's respect and admiration. It did not sound like the Ivivin she knew. He hadn't mentioned such a conquest and her most vivid mental image of him was probably him being flung through the air repeatedly like a child's plaything by the Shaa'Ra.

"Then again..." she thought. *"It does sound foolish enough to be him."* She made her rounds to the shops and headed back out the very same day, doing just as she had planned, and headed southeast.

13

Ivivin, on the other hand, was still dealing with his delayed travel plans. He could still scarcely walk for minutes at a time, let alone travel and survive. He did, however, begin to help around the inn, even if it was only for ten or so minutes at a time. Soon, the innkeeper took notice of these little tasks and felt he should rededicate himself to studying the stone so that, when he was well again, Ivivin could be on his way right away.

Days turned into weeks as Ivivin got better and better. It got to the point where he was helping not only around the inn, but the town, all day. He did whatever he could to earn his keep. In fact, Ivivin felt strong enough to venture out again, but felt at peace here, doing day to day activities. It reminded of him of his days with

Smith. And, in truth, he wanted to stay for just a while longer. The innkeeper, being a bit of a romantic himself, saw this in Ivivin. He had already unraveled the secrets of the stone, but knew Ivivin would force himself onward the moment he knew. He decided to withhold the information from Ivivin for just a little while longer, so that he might get his fill of this daily life.

And so, Ivivin continued his role as the town's helper. The townsfolk slowly came to trust and rely on him more and more. The kids would come and ask Ivivin to tell them stories. Ivivin obliged. He would tell them stories of his journey, but, instead of himself in the lead role, he framed Icarus as the hero. They laughed at first, but soon they began treating Icarus like a king of sorts. Icarus, although grumpy from all the activity, obliged the children in their fantasy and played along with them, on occasion. Ivivin thought to himself that he would miss peaceful days like these when he became a knight.

The Flor Festival

1

The innkeeper struggled to find the right time to tell Ivivin about the magic of the stone: A Moon's Tear, as he had uncovered. It was not as if he had discovered anything earth shattering about it; in fact, it was quite the contrary. He had only a vague understanding about its powers and limits. But he knew that, once he told Ivivin, the young lad would place pressure on himself to leave this place. Although the innkeeper was confident that the boy had recovered physically, he somehow felt that Ivivin was still mentally and emotionally fragile.

"It is amazing," the innkeeper thought *"that this boy—this young man—has done so very much and has yet to break internally."*

The innkeeper sighed.

"Look at me!" he said to himself "I am trying to read this boy as if he were a tome. To study him like an artifact. How very foolish of me. But my dilemma is real. Ivivin, he feels like a man but looks like a boy. I will tell him, I will. But I will wait until the Flor festival. I at least want him to see it. After all, he travels to see the world. Why not show it to him?"

The innkeeper looked to the center of town. Ivivin, as was usual for this part of the day, telling tales to the children. And, as always, he told stories of his journey, but never with him as the hero. The innkeeper knew this and snickered.

"Maybe he is a bit like a boy after all."

2

Preparations for the Flor festival had long been underway, but it wasn't until about a week out from the 3-day long festival that Ivivin really noticed something amiss. People were cleaning their houses and getting ready for guests—for a fee—all over the village. Others were busy tinkering with trinkets to be sold at the festival. Several caravans had scattered to towns all over in an attempt to bring supplies (and guests) back with them. In just a few days, the scene had transformed from quaint, mountainside village to the hustle and bustle Ivivin had grown accustomed to during his time in Smithton.

Ivivin was rather confused, though. He truly had no idea what the festival was about. And the innkeeper intended to keep it that way. The innkeeper had told the residents of the village to keep Ivivin in the dark. Even the children took joy in teasing Ivivin with the knowledge.

"Of course," the innkeeper thought *"he will probably have the surprise ruined for him by the guests arriving with the caravans. But if we are lucky, maybe they won't spoil it for him."*

Ivivin thought it was both mean and endearing that the whole town was in on this sinister secret. He sighed to himself, resolving that he would do his best to stay in the dark until the festival.

3

It was the day before the start of the Flor festival. Ivivin had, more or less, managed to stay in the dark about the whole ordeal. However, he did learn the reason why the festival was to be 3 days long. There was to be a day of celebration on either end of the main event.

"That is," Ivivin thought *"the 2nd day of the festival will be what is truly revealing."*

Ivivin felt like a child again for the first time in a very long time. He had attended a few modest celebrations near his home, usually harvest festivals, but this Flor festival was already shaping up to be much larger than that. That Ivivin knew not what was to come only enhanced the tones of childhood anticipation he felt.

Unfortunately, Ivivin had stumbled upon another hint as to the nature of the festival when strolling by the vendors. He overheard some children, who had been brought to the village in caravan, consistently mention flowers and blossoming.

"Puzzling." Ivivin thought *"I don't think this can be a festival celebrating flowers or spring—there is snow everywhere around here. I don't think many types of flowers could survive here."*

Almost as if on cue, Icarus came frantically flying towards Ivivin away from a group of children who, upon Icarus' flight, hooted and hollered for the owl to return. Icarus crashed into Ivivin's chest and fell directly into his arms. Icarus had been adorned heavily with flowers. Ivivin's interest piqued as to where the flowers might have come from. He decided he would ask the children.

"Excuse me, before I hand over my friend here to play with you some more..." Ivivin started as Icarus looked at him, betrayed, "I'd like to know where you got these flowers from?"

One child, who always seemed very eager to play with Icarus peeped up immediately. "The vendors are selling them! We got some of the ones that were ruined in the journey here for free!"

"Ah, I see." Ivivin said, trying not to let his disappointment show in his voice. *"Of course, there are no flowers here, it'd be absurd."*

"Ok, here you go!" Ivivin said, handing Icarus to the little girl who answered him. She immediately began to smother Icarus in her chest and face. The children, having saved their king, ran off to play some more. Ivivin would just have to wait to see how the festival would play out.

4

The first day of the festival was quite odd, in Ivivin's opinion. There were all manners of food, game, and festivities. However, it seemed like the prizes given in various events were unusual. They were all some manner of food or flower. It seemed like the whole festival was dedicated to flowers!

"But there is still fresh snow on the ground, there won't be flowers here for months, if at all!" Ivivin thought, perplexed. These thoughts puzzled him all day, as he refused to admit that the whole festival was simply in reverence of flowers.

"Be at ease, my mind." Ivivin told himself "The festival's purpose will be revealed to me tomorrow. Just wait."

Still, Ivivin found it hard to focus on enjoying all the events with these questions weighing on his mind. Indeed, he was even further perplexed when the time where the village typically settled down for the evening came and went, yet the festivities showed no sign of slowing. In fact, the village was up dancing and celebrating very late into the night. Ivivin gradually slipped into the mood. While the puzzle never left his brain entirely, he was able to enjoy, at least, the night of the first day. He even partook in some spirits, offered to him by the innkeeper. Icarus, too, enjoyed a festive beverage and could be seen wobbling about the village late into the night. Ivivin, on his way to bed, took note of signs that had been hung in all the common areas of town. They informed him that there were quiet hours being observed in the village until midday the following day.

"Midday!?" Ivivin exclaimed to himself drunkenly. "That is so late for the villagers here, who so oft rise at dawn!" His focus on the matter was short lived. The spirit of the spirits left him and he grew more and more weary. He fell hard to his bed and remembered nothing else.

5

Ivivin awoke to a very sharp and foreign pain, as if he was suffering the blight of some poison. Icarus, too, was rather pained in the morning.

"It seems as if the spirits left something behind for me to enjoy this morning…" Ivivin muttered to himself as he rolled back into bed, glad that the rule that baffled his drunken self was indeed in place. As he returned to his slumber, he could hear the faint sound of an owl getting sick in the distance.

6

Ivivin slept for a very long time. He was sure he had missed much of the festivities and was alarmed that he might have missed the secret to the entire festival.

"It must be nearly dusk!" Ivivin thought concernedly.

Sure enough, it was relatively late in the afternoon. When Ivivin poked his head out, however, he was surprised to see that he was not the only one just waking. In fact, it seemed as if the whole community had decided to wake up at around this time. The inns and food stands had been noisy since perhaps an hour ago and Ivivin was one of many who made their way to the street in search of soup. A lazy crowd gathered for rather fatty foods and soups, as well as herbal teas. Ivivin still could not divine the nature of the festival; however, based on the atmosphere, he was confident he was celebrating it properly. Slowly, though, things began to get livelier and livelier. Booths were again open for games and wares. Darkness came and, again, nothing extraordinary came to pass.

"Is the day really to end so simply?" Ivivin thought as Icarus clumsily landed on his shoulder. As if to answer this question, folk began to quiet down rather suddenly. They scrambled about for

blankets and things to sit on. Families and travelers formed groups all over the village, facing a small stage that had hurriedly been erected a short time ago. The innkeeper invited Ivivin to join him on the roof of the inn. Confused, but undoubtedly excited by the development, Ivivin eagerly followed him.

The cold was a bit bracing and brisk, but the innkeeper brought an assortment of cloths to keep them warm. As Ivivin looked out towards the stage and the stars, he couldn't help but remember the time he spent on the roof with the sisters.

7

A man appeared on the stage. Ivivin was unable to hear the entirety of the rather brief speech the man hurriedly delivered due to the slight humming of the wind in his ear. He heard, again, some words about flowers. He was sure that he heard something about a 'bloom incited by the sky' and 'a marvel of nature' but was puzzled still. However, he could not ignore how serene the night was. There were so many people gathered, yet the air was silent. The snow was largely undisturbed and unsullied in parts of the area, despite the huge crowds. The wind, while sharp, clearly carried the somehow calm anticipation of the crowd. As Ivivin was on the verge of losing himself to his thoughts in this moment, it happened.

Light.

The most beautiful colours of light Ivivin had ever seen stretched across the sky. The light of the stars faded to obscurity as these absurd lights danced through the night sky. Blues became purples became reds. Intense flashes of vivid contrast erupted from time to time. Ivivin had come to realize the miracle happening in the sky before him. He broke his eyes from the entrancing sky after what seemed like hours, curious to see the reactions of the village. It was then the festival truly made sense to Ivivin.

Flowers.

Flowers of the most amazing shades spread across the snowy ground. A field of flowers bloomed all at once in this winter, mountainous village. Or, at least, that is what Ivivin thought at first glance. The petals of these flowers, though, twinkled and changed color and shape. Suddenly it dawned on Ivivin. This beautiful field of flowers was an illusion—a reflection of the lights that populated the sky. The entire village radiated colour. The audience of this musing of nature was captivated in its entirety. Not a sound was made for the entire hour the lights shimmered and danced and celebrated. Ivivin could hear only the breathing of a ragged Icarus perched on his shoulder. The lights began to fade, transitioning from a fierce boil to a gentle simmer and then...

Darkness.

8

Ivivin was floored by the marvel he had just observed. For a while, his mind was blank as he stared into the night sky. Eventually, the light of the stars returned, as did Ivivin's thoughts. He thought of home, of his goal, and of Elara and Idalia. He snickered as he remembered that Icarus is the incarnation of a celestial being—of Ganymede. It also reminded him of why they had come to this village in the first place. He was both eager to continue his journey and saddened by the idea of leaving. He knew that once the innkeeper unraveled the secrets of the stone, he would set off. He would likely not see this village again any time soon. The children he befriended would be grown by the time he returned, if he returned at all.

"Nothing is static." Ivivin thought. *"Not people, nor even the skies above."*

Icarus sat there with Ivivin for a few more hours into the night. Ivivin finally came down, but only when the innkeeper called for him, checking to make sure they did not fall asleep in such a dangerous place.

"Remember, Ivivin, there is still another day for the festival. You should get some rest and enjoy the festivities again tomorrow!" The innkeeper told him.

Ivivin perked up a bit at the reminder and hurried himself to bed. He was excited for what would come tomorrow. He knew that the main event was over, but it had touched him deeply and he could not wait to celebrate and discuss it tomorrow with these townsfolk. After some time, Ivivin fell into a deep slumber while deep in thought about the beautiful, almost otherworldly lights he had witnessed that night. He could not help but speculate and imagine wild stories about what they meant or how they worked. He fell asleep with a small smile.

9

Ivivin spent the better part of the next day anticipating another big event, like the night before, even though he knew it would not come. It seemed as if all the stands were hustling and bustling, but nothing special was happening. A bit let down, Ivivin halfheartedly played a few games at the stands and managed to win some flowers before headed back to the inn.

"How childish of me!" Ivivin scolded himself. *"But I can't help but feel a little disappointed."*

Of course, the third day of the festival did have a purpose, as Ivivin discovered a few hours before sundown. The stands all closed and people were flocking out to the outskirts of town with flowers in tow. Ivivin struggled to think of any reason people would head that way.

"In fact," Ivivin thought *"I can't even think of anything on that side of town, except the...."*

It dawned on him.

People were walking to the cemetery. The snow there remained largely undisturbed and even covered some of the smaller tombstones in their entirety. People had begun laying their flowers all over the untarnished snow. Ivivin sat and watched as all the flowers that people had won over the course of the festival came to rest here, with the deceased. What struck Ivivin was that atmosphere of the ceremony. Rather than being a somber occasion, the flowers were spread festively and coated the ground in a thin layer. By the time night had begun encompassing the village, most of the ground was covered with flowers and smiling people. While this event was not fantastic in the same way as the sky-waves, Ivivin recognized the scene as a magic all its own. The innkeeper tapped Ivivin on the shoulder and indicated that he should follow. Ivivin grabbed his flowers and followed the innkeeper to one of the few bare patches left in the cemetery. Together, they laid their flowers on the ground, stared at the floor until the dark completed its migration, and then walked back to the inn together. Ivivin no longer had his sinking feeling of disappointment. He was so sure he would never forget this place or these people. This feeling led him to think of Elara and Idalia, which inspired him to resume his seat on the top of the inn and watch as darkness finally spread over the village.

10

The innkeeper went inside for just a moment before joining Ivivin and Icarus on the roof.

"Ivivin..." the innkeeper said, "I have discerned the identity of your stone and its magic. Here." The innkeeper returned the stone to Ivivin, feeling it was wrong to keep it from the lad even a moment longer.

"Lets you and I talk about it in the morning. I am beat from the festivities. Deal?" the innkeeper yawned. Ivivin nodded and thanked the man before returning his eyes to the sky. Ivivin sat on the roof looking at the stars. He tried his best to remember what Idalia had said about which constellation was which and what they meant, but it was no good. He passed the stone around in hand, fiddling around mindlessly with the magical artifact. Ivivin stared at the stars, which he found beautiful regardless of if he knew their stories, and remembered his own. The stone in his hand started to shine once more. Ivivin jumped, having forgotten the stone was special at all. This reminder was welcome, though, as Ivivin quietly crept down the roof and to his room to grab Elara's book of constellations. A faint light from the roof of the innkeeper could be seen until the wee hours of the morning.

Rumi 2: Electric Boogaloo

1

Elara was told of a great lake, one that would take several days to be clear of, due south of Crosstown. Though she ultimately wanted to journey southeast, she decided she could not pass up the opportunity to see such a landmark.

"After all, the whole point of my journey is to see the country for myself, with my own eyes. I would be doing my worried mother a disservice if I didn't see such a marvel."

Elara travelled south, then, and would head to the southeastern corner of the country from there. Her travels were much faster and easier than Ivivin's. She knew the stars well and was able to reorient herself without stopping for long. She often took breaks in the day to read the book Ivivin had exchanged for her own. Indeed, there were entire afternoons where she would come across a particularly large tree, just begging to be climbed. She would climb the tree and read the day away. Well, when she didn't fall asleep, at least.

Elara could see why Ivivin had struggled to make headway on the book. It was, by all accounts and in all regards, a classic. The language was archaic and the story was told with as many abstract metaphors as it had concrete happenings. It didn't matter, though, Elara savoured the challenge and was, frankly, addicted to the story. It revolved around the life of the world's very first king. He did not inherit the throne, though. Rather, he was put there by people he had helped at great personal risk over the course of his life. Much of the story revolved his travels and the people he met.

"It truly is a charming tale" Elara thought, putting her book away as the sun's light faltered.

"I guess I will stay here tonight." Elara thought to herself as she set to work lighting a small fire.

After a quick bite and some star gazing, Elara laid to sleep. She struggled to fight off giddiness as she imagined herself as the first king. Eventually, her fantasies turned to dream as she drifted off.

2

"Saeber Lake, huh?" Elara said to herself as she shielded her eyes from the reflection of the sun on the lake's surface. Truth be told, Elara was a little underwhelmed by the sight of the admittedly vast lake. It wasn't that she didn't recognize its beauty, but perhaps she had expected too much. It was, after all, just a lake. Elara walked along the lake nonetheless, reasoning that there must be at least a village somewhere along the lake. As comfortable as she was with nature, she still craved the feeling of a soft bed. It was, perhaps, the only thing she missed more than her mother and sister.

So, Elara walked about the perimeter of the lake, generally disinterested in it, until she saw bank of sand jutting outwards from the lake's edge.

"A beach?" Elara asked herself, having never seen one.

"I thought beaches belonged only to the sea?" She thought as she approached the sand. Recalling how long it took her to rid her shoes of sand after her desert voyage, she stopped just short of stepping in. Elara deftly bared her feet—something she loved to do on the rare occasion that it was warm enough in the north—and took her first step. It was warm, but not hot. It had a certain amount of give, sure, but far less than the sand of the desert's dunes. It was certainly easier on the eyes, as well. If Elara moved her head about, she could see faint twinkling of all different colors from the sand. She sat down and stared outwards towards the water for a while.

"Maybe this lake is pretty amazing after all."

3

As initially underwhelmed as Elara was with the lake, she now struggled to tear herself away from it. She stayed at that same beach for two full days after she arrived, just reading and fishing and lazing in the sand. It wasn't that she didn't ever want to leave this place, but she knew that she was unlikely to find another place like it for a very long time once she left it behind. Elara sighed.

"Alright, I will leave tomorrow morning." She thought as she looked around her, trying to memorize everything about the scene so she might describe it to her mother and sister when she returned to them.

As the sun was approaching the horizon, Elara noticed a strange shifting in the sand a few feet away. Then, sand all over the beach started to shift, gently rocking to and fro. From the sand burst forth hundreds of tiny creatures. Elara could not recognize the creatures at all. They had fins not unlike a fish, but skin that more closely resembled a snake. They also seemed to carry around some sort of plate armour on their backs.

"Whatever they are," Elara thought, *"they are extremely cute."*

She tried her best not to step on any of the creatures as they shimmied towards the water. The strange creatures assembled on the water's edge, forming a pattern that almost looked rank and file. All the creatures then opened their mouths synchronously.

"What are they—" Elara began before being cut off by an incredibly loud and high-pitched wail. Elara dropped to her knees and covered her ears. It was so loud that it pained her. It was made worse by the days of silence that preceded this moment. The wailing stopped as the army of screamers closed their mouths.

Suddenly, something began to rise from the lake. Two somethings, in fact. Elara looked closely. Her jaw dropped as she realized the sheer size of the figures emerging from the water. Then all the water and waves finally settled, Elara saw two more of these strange sand-fish-snakes. But, rather than small and adorable, these ones were colossal and, well, still adorable. The two house-sized creatures opened their mouths. Elara covered her ears, expecting pain to come once more. Instead, the creatures let loose a very low, almost melodic note. It was extremely loud, shaking the sand under Elara's feet. Still, it was pleasant to hear.

Just as suddenly as they appeared from the sand, the hundreds of strange creatures vanished into the water, as did their enormous counterparts. Elara stared at the water a while before gathering all her gear and moving it, and herself, a safe distance from the beach.

○

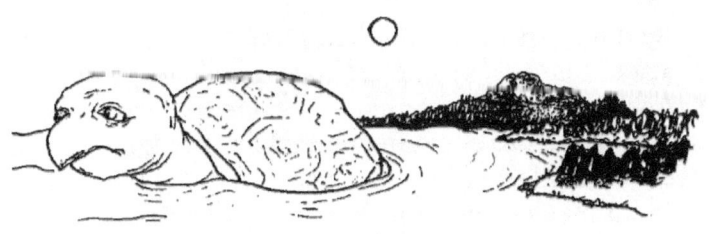

4

Elara eventually stumbled upon the village she was looking for. She must have seemed a little off, as the first thing she asked the very first person she saw was about the giant snake-fish that are born in the sand small, but go get big in the water, and make a tremendous amount of noise.

"Snake-fish?" The woman said. "Oh! Do you mean the Lake Riddlers? They bear a striking resemblance to a creature called a turtle, so I have heard."

The woman looked at Elara, who seemed troubled, before continuing. "Wait, did you see them? No wonder you are so terrified. Worry not, they are gentle creatures, though banshees when they first are born. Did you think them some sort of monster to warn us about?" The woman left Elara, poorly attempting to conceal her laughter as she walked away.

Elara scurried to the inn, her face a burning scarlet.

5

Elara did not stay in the village for as long as she had originally intended. In fact, she set off the very next day, still embarrassed and startled. She had only done two things—slept and asked the innkeeper about travelling to the southeast. She wanted to put as much distance between her and that village as she could. She followed the lake still, more out of habit than anything, but wanted that, too, out of her sight as soon as possible. After a couple days, she reached southernmost tip of the lake. She approached it to give it a final glance when she saw another beach. Her feet were bared once more.

6

After a non-specific, non-zero number of days on the southern beach, Elara kicked herself into gear.

"How could I have let myself become so easy going?" she tried to shame herself as she remembered her life up north. Elara and Idalia never wanted for anything, per se, but they lived a frugal life. Elara had spent much of her time helping the denizens of the village

with whatever she could. And, often, that meant struggle. She was a little ashamed that she felt softened and weakened by her journey. She would be sure to train a little bit each day here on out.

The innkeeper in the village had told Elara that the path she sought was not one she could cross alone. Wolfelaw Caverns was a labyrinth fraught with dire wolves. Even disregarding the wolves, one wrong turn could mean starving to death alone in the dark. Elara would need a guide to take her through the caves. Fortunately, the innkeeper also let Elara Rumi was once more a bustling center of trade and commerce, both foreign and domestic, after some brave soul saved it from a horrible monster that had been terrorizing the town for a few years. So, the innkeeper told Elara that, if she camped out by the entrance to the caves, she would likely encounter merchants making the trip within a week or two, tops.

This solution pleased Elara, who did not particularly enjoy her time with the merchants she crossed the desert with. She resumed her travels, hoping that she might even get to meet the hero who vanquished the monster of Rumi while she was there. It sounded like it could have been a story straight out of the book Ivivin had given her.

7

Elara, ever the efficient traveler, made it to the entrance of Wolfelaw Caverns in record time. It wasn't that she was in a rush to get there, per se, and she enjoyed the countryside as she travelled. She couldn't help but marvel in how different the rest of the country was from the north. She hurried, then, so that she could lounge. During her travels so far, Elara had grown to love living life on her own schedule. It was not always a lazy life—she still had to provide for herself and plan her travels, but she had really become fond of days where she might read or nap the day away.

"I love mother and sister, both, I really do." She would often think. *"But they can be such busybodies."*

Now that she had arrived at the caverns, she wanted to investigate the entrance to confirm that this was indeed the correct passageway. Elara was told that the entrance of the cavern, as well as the exit, would be lined with a sort of glowing stone. Elara was already a bit on edge creeping up to the mouth of the cave—she knew to be on the alert for wolves, which could easily outnumber and surround her if she wasn't careful. Her nerves were worsened as she recalled the shining stones involved in the summoning of the Shaa'Ra. She loosened up, though, the moment she saw how majestic the stones actually were. Indeed, she would likely have stayed and marveled at the phenomenon for hours if she had not been snapped back to reality by the far-off sound of howling deep in the caverns. Elara decided she would camp a safe distance away from the caves and come survey the area for travelers each day.

8

Four days had passed with no sign of travelers entering or exiting the caves. Elara had been lazing around at the peak of a hill each day that gave her a decent vantage point of both the caverns and her surrounding area. Elara had been enjoying resting and lazing about, but boredom was starting to set in. On this, the fifth day, Elara started to more often and more anxiously scan the landscape for travelers. Late afternoon, Elara saw some figures emerge from the cave's entrance. Disappointed that the traffic was not headed the other way but still bored and craving human interaction, Elara approached the small group of travelers.

Elara had no idea what she would say to the travelers when she arrived and got a bit bashful once she got close. Luckily, the travelers were actually a performing troupe. There were practitioners of music, acrobatics, story-weaving, and even animal taming! They invited Elara to join them for the night, as they were eager to have an audience to their practice. Unsure at first, Elara was won over by their warmth and sincerity. She decided she would spend the evening with them. And she was glad she did. She got to see a woman perform feats of balance and athleticism with her friend, a bear named Oso. The woman had many tricks, but Elara's favourite was when the bear balanced on a single foot and pointed its face upwards, towards the sky. Then, the woman climbed the bear and she too balanced on one foot in a most graceful pose. The very point of her toes rested on the small pad of the bear's nose. Elara had not realized how beautiful such acts could be. At first, she again felt the urge to find herself an animal companion, like Oso or Icarus. That feeling was supplanted, however, by an urge to feel that confident and graceful herself.

Despite her strength and her skill, Elara often questioned herself. She questioned her own appearance and intelligence, despite having helped so many people. This feeling brought Elara back to a time when she finally had gotten the strength to talk to her mother about it. The ever-wise seer-mother had given her advice that she had never forgotten.

"You needn't compare yourself to others, my child. And you needn't fret that some possess skill or circumstance that eclipses your own. If you want to, you can learn and change to be more like someone or do something they can do. But, before you do that, ask yourself: 'Do I want this simply because I don't have it? Or is this something I would truly like to do or be?' And if someone appears who incites such feelings in you, don't resent them. Instead, ask them to share with you their life's story and, if you are lucky, their talent."

Elara looked inside herself and then smiled confidently as she approached Petil, the beast-tamer.

9

Petil was a little shocked when Elara asked about her trade and how she learned it, but soon engaged in Elara's enthusiasm. By the night's end, Elara had learned all about her life. She had come from overseas as a young girl. Her father had died and her mother wanted to escape the memories of their old home. She was a fisherman and soon they settled in Rumi. While her mother was on the boats, Petil would often go into the wilderness and play. There, she met Oso, who was just a cub at the time. The two would play often. They'd roughhouse and nap. They grew up together. At first, Oso's mother was very defensive, but because Petil showed no fear nor aggression, they grew to like each other as well. Petil recounted with great laughter and fondness when own her mother learned of this friendship. Over the years, Petil had been speaking of her friend, who she named Oso, and how they played together. Petil's mother dismissed it as a friend of her child's fantasy. One day, Petil had asked if Oso could come to dinner. Her mother giggled, told her sure, and even set out an extra plate for her daughter's imaginary friend.

"Mother nearly died of shock when I brought a bear cub into the house!" Petil finished.

Elara was so glad to have met Petil and they chatted about all matters of things. Elara eventually complemented Petil on her performance, noting her grace and poise, and asked Petil how she could learn to perform such acts. Petil stared at Elara, clearly wondering what such a well-rounded adventurer would want with knowledge of such things. She saw honesty in Elara's eyes, however, and decided to indulge the young woman, whatever her motivations might be.

"You want to know how I started, Elara?" Elara nodded eagerly. "First, I learned to dance. The pose I struck atop of Oso comes from a dance I learned overseas, when I was a child."

"Dancing?" Elara asked. Petil nodded.

"Come to think of it...I don't think I have ever danced. Not since Idalia and I would together as small children."

She looked at Petil, expecting her to elaborate. Petil smiled gently at Elara, gestured at her to wait a moment, and walked away. When she returned, she was accompanied by music and some lively troupe-members. Petil took Elara's hand and they, as well as some other troupe members, began to dance. It was unsophisticated. It was clumsy. It was even a bit embarrassing. But as Elara danced with the members of this troupe, she learned something about dancing:

It was fun.

10

When Elara could dance no more, she took a seat next to one of the older women in the troupe by the fire. Together, they stared at their peers as the dancing and singing continued. The older woman, a storyteller, turned to Elara and smiled.

"Did you have fun?" The woman asked a still-sweaty Elara. Elara nodded and was a little embarrassed to know that this old and wise-looking woman was watching her dance, too.

"My name is Koza. You are Elara, no?" Elara nodded, stunned at the woman's voice. It was firm, yet subtly melodic.

"Well, Elara, I do not share in the talents of those dancing the night away. But I like to believe my craft is beautiful in its own way. If you will indulge me, may I tell you the story of the caverns you await guidance through?" Elara looked back out to the dancing, which was growing more wild and energetic. She had enough for one night, she figured, and asked Koza to tell her the story. And so,

Elara settled in for the long haul as Koza spun her the history of the Wolfelaw caves.

11

"You may have heard that the cave was mined clean of the shining stones that now serve as beacons for the cavern's entrance and exit. You may have even heard that they once illuminated the full path through the cavern. But that, my dear, is only part of the story. If you travelled about a day's hike to the west, you would happen upon some ruins. An old kingdom that now lays razed and forgotten. It once flourished in a time well before the reign of our king and the unification of the kingdoms into the one we know today. It was known as Attar. Rumi, too, was once the capital of an old kingdom known then as Sanai. For many years, the two kingdoms were at peace with one another. There was even a ritual— a rite of passage where, on the sixteenth year of their birth, the citizens would cross over the mountains and spend a year in the other kingdom before returning home. The journey was grueling. The path you seek and await, now known as Wolfelaw Caverns, did not exist at the time. It could take months to get through or go around the range. But, nonetheless, the countries did it as a way to promote goodwill and the exchange of culture, skill, and news. And, for a time, all was well.

One day, though, the queen of Sanai gave birth to a daughter and, on the very same day, the queen of Attar gave birth to a son. They were to live privileged, if uneventful, lives until the day of their sixteenth birthday. They each set off on their journeys and, as fate would have it, they would meet on the mountain range. The fell deeply in love and spent a whole month together in the mountains before their bittersweet parting. Upon arriving in Attar, the young princess needed to pick something to study for her year in Attar. She had told her father she intended to study horseback riding, as the people of Sanai had no horses. However, when she arrived, her mind was so occupied with the prince of this country that she dismissed all trades and arts and skills, no matter who the teacher. One day, she stumbled upon a fellow in the wilderness. A druid and geomancer— a master of the magic of nature. She saw him move and crumble rock with his power and thought only of clearing a path between the two kingdoms. She begged and begged the man to teach her. The

137

man agreed, but warned her that magic, especially that of nature, was difficult to control. It would be easy to become overwhelmed, if one had not the mental and emotional fortitude required. She would need to temper her emotion to be master the art. So, over the course of the year, she studied and studied, demonstrating an aptitude the druid never before had seen. On her seventeenth birthday, she set off to return to her homeland. The young prince, too, set off on his journey to return that day. He had studied the ways of the sea—navigation and warfare alike. The young royals once again met on the mountains and confirmed their continued love for one another. The princess and prince parted ways after only one day, as the princess assured the prince they would be able to see each other soon. Once at the base of the mountain, the princess called forth the power of nature to create a path to her lover. But, because of the strong and complex feelings behind her magic, she created the vast labyrinth we know today, rather than the straightforward path she had intended. But it mattered not to her—the cave was lit brightly by magic stones and she knew the way. And, so, she continued meeting the prince in their secret tunnel.

A time came though, where the two kingdoms became at odds with one another. The kingdom of Attar desperately wanted access to the port at Rumi and sought to conquer Sanai to achieve it. Likewise, Sanai struggled with crop and needed more fertile land to sustain its growing population. The two skirmished, but full on war was prevented by the mountains that separated the kingdoms. The prince, though conflicted, eventually betrayed the location of the tunnel to his father. He was ordered to guide the troops through the labyrinth to launch a surprise attack on Rumi. His fealty to his family surpassed the love he felt for the princess and so he obliged. He marched an army into the tunnels only to be met by his lover. She saw this betrayal of their love and rage overwhelmed her. She meant to use her magic to seal the tunnel, but her hurt and anger corrupted her magic. Instead, the magic willed the soldiers of Attan into wolves and, after much struggle and resistance, she too became transfigured. She became their Wolfess. Only the prince had remained human, as the princess, though devastated, couldn't find it in her heart's heart to do harm to the her once-lover. Unfortunately, she had lost her heart upon surrender to her bestial nature. And, so, she herself ended the life of the prince between the vice of her fangs. The wolves then attacked the people of Attar, who were now defenseless and overwhelmed. The remnant wolves then came to settle in what eventually became known as Wolfelaw Caves."

12

Elara stayed awake late that night, long after the troupe had exhausted themselves into their tents. She tried to make sense of the story Koza had told her.

"Usually, stories like this have some lesson to be learned-- some moral. But I cannot figure this one out." thought Elara as she again looked to the stars.

"Lupus...the wolf. How funny." Elara joked with herself as she traced her favourite constellation in her mind's eye. She could hear the howling of the wolves in the distance.

"Maybe the story has no moral." Elara entertained. *"Maybe the only moral is that bad things happen sometimes. That sometimes people make decisions and they must live with their consequences. Maybe it is about never really knowing where you stand in the hearts of others."*

Elara was hoping for a happy ending and resolution, but it never came. Maybe that was the lesson, that, sometimes, there is no happy ending, but life moves on regardless.

The howling of the wolves sounded especially lonely.

13

The next morning, Elara groggily parted ways with the troupe. Although they had only spent a single day together, Elara felt like she had known Petil for weeks and was disappointed to see her leave. Petil could see how Elara looked up to her. She wanted to leave her with something to remember her by and to remind her that she could do whatever she put her mind to. After a short period of consideration, Petil brought Elara an old hip scarf. It was nothing fancy, but it had seen a few performances. Elara, though initially hesitant to accept the gift, eventually let Petil tie the scarf around her hip. It was incredibly vibrant and stood out. Elara didn't think it suited her, but Petil reassured her that it was perfect before they said their goodbyes. Elara kept examining the scarf, somehow proud to be wearing it.

"Come to think of it… didn't Ivivin sport an embroidered red cloth in a similar fashion? Is he a dancer too? I'll have to ask him sometime." Elara mused as she slipped back into sleep.

She did not get to sleep long, however, as the sound of a crowd soon woke her. It could not have been more than an hour or two after the troupe left when Elara was greeted by a group of merchants preparing to enter the cave. Elara, still grumpy from a lack of sleep, struggled to convince the merchants to let her tag along. After a few glares and grumbles, though, the merchants relented and allowed Elara to join them. Unlike Ivivin, who felt panic and fear in the darkness of the cave, Elara was struck with lethargy and lassitude that was only enhanced by the same dark of the cave. She closed her eyes not for peace, but under the weight of their containers. Elara and the merchants made it through the cave unscathed. The merchants marched onwards to town, but Elara refused to travel any further than she had to. Despite her weariness, though, she was proud of having come this far and, before succumbing to her exhaustion, made sure to practice some of the motions Petil had taught her.

A whirl of twirling orange persisted for some time before eventually settling on the floor.

Return to Smithton

1

Ivivin woke early, both eager and anxious to learn the exact nature of the magic stone from the innkeeper. He already sported one extremely dangerous artifact on his person—Ivivin wasn't sure his heart could bear another such surprise. Ivivin was disappointed, then, to find the innkeeper still asleep.

"I suppose it was a very long couple of days." Ivivin considered as he exited the inn to pass the time with a little stroll. Out and about in the village were travelers packing to leave and locals tidying up from the mess. Feeling particularly altruistic, Ivivin decided to help the people he came across along his walk. He cleaned windows, loaded wagons, scrubbed troughs, and much more. Before Ivivin knew it, the sun had already passed overhead. It was afternoon before Ivivin realized how long he had been out. Ivivin rushed back to the inn to speak with the innkeeper.

When Ivivin returned, the innkeeper was sitting at his private table, reading a large and old looking book. The table was set for two. The innkeeper gestured to Ivivin to join him as he removed his spectacles. Ivivin did as he was prompted and they sat in silence for a time, neither wishing to cast the stone to shatter the illusion Ivivin had been living here. Eventually, though, Ivivin piped up.

"So…" Ivivin removed the arcane object from his pocket, "About this stone."

2

With the silence finally broken, the conversation seemed to flow naturally. The innkeeper could see resolve had returned to Ivivin's eyes and his conflict about telling the boy evaporated.

"Ah yes, the stone. It truly was a joy to investigate, Ivivin. Thank you very much for indulging an old man in his far-out hobby. That stone you possess?"

Ivivin looked at the stone nervously.

"It is of no danger to anyone in and of itself, as far as I can tell. It is very minor magic. You have seen the extent of its power. It simply illuminates the area around it. This kind of artifact is well known, if still very rare. They call these artifacts 'Tears'."

Ivivin had never gone from worried to relieved to worried again so quickly.

"T-tears" Ivivin managed, recollecting the fierce power contained in the Tear of Jupiter.

"Yes, Ivivin. Tears. There is indeed very fierce magic that exists in this world but, generally speaking, tears are not amoung them. It is said that tears are remnants of old spirits who grew too close or attached to humanity and their struggles. And in doing so they came to understand our pains and felt how we felt. Whether tears of happiness or tears of sorrow, there were spirits that wept openly with early humanity. Their tears, they hardened and became empowered. Not with the power to vanquish foes, but, rather, the power to comfort those who feel the aches of being mortal—of being human. I know not which spirit wept the tear you possess, Ivivin. If you wish to know, the people of Olympia are far more in tune with the history and happening of the spirits, though perhaps the library of the castle might also contain such knowledge. Regardless, though, that stone is perfectly safe. It does exactly what you've used it for. It lights the way."

Ivivin returned again to his state of relief.

3

With the knowledge from the learned innkeeper, Ivivin had no further business meandering in this town. The people and the experiences he had would be etched into his mind forever. It reminded him of Smithton. Ivivin decided he would stay no longer than a few more days, tops, and would leave as soon as he had his affairs in order. He went to inspect and inventory his belongings. He had long since unpacked his pack into his modest room and moaned at the idea of packing once more. It looked like all he really needed before venturing back out was for the cobbler to have a go at his boots and to stock up on some provisions. Ivivin didn't know where he was going, other than west, so it was best he be prepared. Ivivin looked to his armour, which laid about on a chair.

"I should probably look this over, too, and make sure it isn't damaged." Ivivin said to himself. He held up the armour and inspected it, looking for any fatal kinks that his brief tenure as a smith's apprentice would allow him to recognize. It was certainly worn—Ivivin had been roughed up a few times since he first donned the armour, but it seemed to be in great shape, considering.

"Nothing I can see." Ivivin thought. *"Smith certainly is the best."*

Ivivin went to put his armour on and... couldn't.

"What the—do I have it on backwards?" Ivivin exclaimed to himself, waking a napping Icarus. He removed the armour and reoriented it. Still, something was wrong with the armour.

"Ah!" Ivivin realized "It must be the leather straps. They got wet with me fiddling about in the snow and dried and shrunk."

Ivivin rushed to the market to get whatever animal oil he could and beeswax to recondition the leather the best he could. After several hours, the leather seemed fine and Ivivin tried the armour on once more.

Still, nothing.

And that is when Ivivin finally realized that there was nothing wrong with his armour. He had simply outgrown it.

4

Ivivin looked at the fine chain work and binding of his armour and quickly came to terms with the fact that he could not meddle with its construction without ruining the armour. Ivivin was heartbroken, at first, that the gift his teacher fashioned him was no longer of use to him. He played with the idea of making his own armour, but he had never really gotten the chance to at the forge. However, this problem led Ivivin to his next decision—he would return to Smithton and ask Smith not only to make him new armour, but to show him the basics needed to repair or alter that armour should he ever need to again.

"Yes," Ivivin mused to a half-asleep Icarus "I can return to Smithton and ask Smith for new armour. I have missed him so and I want to share with him all that I have seen on my journey. Oh! And I still need a 'esteemed squire' for the king's trial. I don't know quite where to find a squire, but they aren't unlike apprentices right? Maybe Smith can point me in the right direction for this task while he is at it." And so, just like that, Ivivin's heartbreak was replaced with a giddiness at the idea of seeing Smith again.

5

After a few days of preparation and packing, Ivivin was prepared to leave the town, but he wasn't exactly ready. The inhabitants here had all gotten to know Ivivin rather well and Ivivin carried around a sense of guilt at the prospect of leaving. These people had welcomed and trusted Ivivin and allowed him to build his own place here. Not all of them knew of Ivivin's goals and Ivivin was sure a few of them even expected Ivivin to stay indefinitely. It certainly was tempting for Ivivin. It wasn't that he had lost his passion towards his goal. It wasn't that he had lost his ambition. It was, rather, that the gentle liveliness of the town and its people had given Ivivin new goals and new passions, too. They didn't detract from his original goal and passion. They enhanced it. Ivivin felt he was living life far more vividly with every day that passed. If Ivivin's life was a picture, then he considered his path to knighthood an outline, but all his experiences, here and elsewhere, as the colors that make the art brilliant. Ivivin struggled with this guilt, unsure how to relieve himself of the burden. He wanted to sneak off in the shadow of the night, telling no one. He also wanted to tell each person he had come to know goodbye individually. Ivivin felt truly conflicted and, to his own surprise, it was not some grandiose decision that caused this conflict. It was a simple matter of trying to leave.

In a logistic sense, too, Ivivin was not quite ready to leave. There was still the matter of Smith's armour and what to do with it. Ivivin considered carrying the armour back to Smith to see if he could salvage it. But Ivivin also did not think hauling around several extra pounds in pack space that he did not really have to be a wise decision. At the same time, Ivivin didn't want to sell the armour. That seemed disrespectful to Smith and his intentions. Just as Ivivin was thinking to himself how unexpectedly difficult departing this place was becoming, he was approached by the gang of children who oft begged Ivivin to continue the tale of Icarus. They, of course, wanted Ivivin to continue the story. Ivivin's worries fell to the back of his mind as he agreed. Ivivin went to fetch Icarus. He met the children in their usual place. There, Ivivin sat on a tree-stump with the children circled around expectantly.

"Let's see here, where did we leave off...?" Ivivin asked the horde. It had been since before the festival that Ivivin had told his story to these kids. He had lost exactly where they had left off. In no time flat, though, a particularly mucusy child reminded Ivivin in a tone most matter of fact and sniffly.

"You had just gotten to the part where Icarus got trapped on the mountain during a blizzard! We've been waiting ages to find out how he survives!" The stuffed-up child wheezed.

Ivivin was taken aback. He was, in essence, at the end of his story. Once he spoke of how they braved the blizzard and returned to the town to recover, that will have brought the pack up to speed. Ivivin was distressed at this, having reached the present in the story. In his story. It was unsettling, to not know what to tell these children next. Ivivin considered his options.

"I could fabricate more for them...or I could tell them that this is the end of the story...or..."

Ivivin smiled as he settled on the course he would take.

So, Ivivin told the ensemble of children the tale of how Icarus braved the mountain with the help of his close friend. It was a short tale, though Ivivin did not skimp on the theatrics. When that part of the story ended, however, Ivivin sat in silence for a moment, waiting. It wasn't long before another child, a young girl with a perchance mischief, prompted Ivivin to continue.

"What happened next?"

Ivivin expected the prompt and continued. "Icarus recovered in a wonderful town where he got to see and know wonderful people. Icarus grew quite fond of the people of this town and worried about their wellbeing. He knew he must continue his journey, but his love for both the town and its inhabitants weighed heavily on his mind. That is, until he met twelve brave souls." Ivivin gestured to the twelve children who sat before him. "Icarus saw these brave souls and, even though they were young, knew that they would protect the village. That they would make sure no one wanted for anything. That the chores got done and that no one would feel alone in the village if they were around. Icarus, though on a journey to become a knight himself, proclaimed these twelve to be the knights of the village." Ivivin held Icarus like a sword, much to the critter's displeasure, and proceeded to 'knight' each of the twelve children.

"And then, knowing the village and its people were in good hands, Icarus and his companion set forth on their journey once more."

Naturally, the rather pungent one of the group spoke up.

"What happens next?" they inquired.

"Whatever it is that you want to happen." Ivivin responded. Ivivin stood up, handed Icarus to the mob, and went back to the inn. From the doorway, Ivivin could see the children whose story time had evolved into fantasies of protecting the town from a great dragon, of which Icarus was unusually eager to fill the role. Ivivin smirked and went to tell the innkeeper that he and Icarus would be on their way around midday tomorrow.

7

Ivivin decided that he would only say goodbye to the innkeeper, which he did that morning, and anyone he ran into on his way out of town. It would be simpler this way. Around midday, Ivivin gathered Icarus and his things, left the inn, and headed to the same stump where he been telling stories to the children. He laid out Smith's outgrown armour on the stump. He started at it for a moment and thanked it for serving him so well for so long. Ivivin and Icarus headed to the west most edge of town to leave. They didn't run into anyone on his way to the edge of town, which disappointed, but did not surprise, Ivivin. That is, until he rounded the corner only to be met with a crowd on each side of the path. As he walked, he passed through a small sea of familiar faces. The townsfolk waved and cheered with each of Ivivin's steps. Ivivin was in a sort of emotional stasis as he faltered to process the scene. He could make out the innkeeper at the end of the tunnel, smiling at Ivivin.

Ivivin was used to praise and gratitude. Sure, he was still embarrassed to be on the receiving end of them, but scenes like this had played out in Rumi and Crosstown. But in those places, Ivivin had saved the people, as fluky as the circumstances may had been. Their actions were those of gratitude and appreciation. But the people here, in this little town so far from home, Ivivin had done nothing of the sort for these people. He didn't defend the village from a monster. He didn't fend off bandits or prevent some calamity. He just lived life alongside them, through both the mundane and the exciting, day by day being himself. Through that and through that alone, they had slowly nestled into one another's hearts.

The stasis of Ivivin's emotion gave way to a river of tears as Ivivin passed through the sea of fond faces and warm sentiments.

8

The sound of his own footsteps bore into Ivivin's mind. It had been quite some time since he was alone and, while he generally enjoyed travelling, he forgot how boring it could become, especially now that the grand mountains of the north were behind him. Ivivin had to focus, though, as he was travelling with purpose. He needed to pass between the Unyk River and the Onabi desert. He was too far west to cross the desert. It was significantly wider than near Crosstown and the voyage would put his life at risk. At the same time, Ivivin did not want to double back and cross the desert the way he came.

"What is the point of my journey if I don't see new things?" Ivivin rationalized.

This left only one real option. Head west and go around the desert. Ivivin knew if he hit the large river Unyk, he had gone too far. Ivivin considered stopping by his home—it would add a significant amount of time to his trip, but he would also be closer than he had ever been since he had departed. In the end, though, Ivivin decided he wasn't ready to return home. He felt that, if he stopped again so soon and in a place of great comfort, he might never leave again. So, Ivivin pressed on, a little homesick, but determined to see as much of the world—even the boring bits like he was experiencing today—as he possibly could.

9

Ivivin and Icarus made their way southwest uneventfully (well, save for the fiasco in a small village in which Ivivin almost died from excess consumption of pastries at a local festival). The topology and surroundings were dull. That is, until Ivivin reached the area between the desert and the river—roughly where he would shift his direction to the southeast. The landscape was incredible.

There were shrubbery and cactus of the desert that had grown to sizes larger than most trees Ivivin had seen. There was a bounty of wildlife that Ivivin had never imagined he would see together in his lifetime. Perhaps the most startling happening in this unique geographical wonder was when Ivivin barely avoided being trampled by a stampede. Not one of hooved creatures, as one might expect. No, instead, Ivivin was almost squished by a swarm of lizards. And not just any lizards. These lizards were the size of horses! Ivivin saw them several times during his brief time in the area between these two environments. They would run several times a day from the desert to the river and back. On the way to the river, the reptiles were lean but on the way back they were huge and swollen. Most notably, their cheeks and bellies puffed out as if they had been inflated. It was a small marvel in Ivivin's mind. These lizards would bring river water back to the desert several times a day, presumably for a colony or family to share. Ivivin was impressed and might have watched the incredible feat with awe and admiration had the lizards not also looked incredibly silly scuttling about so pudgily.

10

Ivivin had seen Saeber lake on his way to Crosstown, but that was the east most edge of the lake. Ivivin had heard that the lake was incredibly large and, sure enough, when he first saw the lake, he could not see across to the west-most shores. Ivivin wanted to see the huge body once more, this time, from a new perspective. So, he travelled a bit more east than south, knowing it would add a few days, maybe weeks, to his travel time. Icarus didn't complain, as there was always easier prey around such bodies of water. The feathery heathen hadn't had much luck since they passed the river-desert junction. He was getting tired of eating Ivivin's scraps.

They spent their days hiking and their evenings learning more of the stars from Elara's book under the light of the tear, which always cast a gentle and comforting glow. Sure enough, Ivivin and Icarus eventually stumbled back to Saeber Lake, though they had overshot east just a bit. Ivivin was proud of how well he had done though—he half expected to miss the lake altogether. They traced the perimeter of the lake westward and after a few days, they arrived at the west most point of the lake. Ivivin couldn't make out the other end. Ivivin took a little pride at having been to both ends of this natural wonder. He wondered how many other people could say the same. As he pondered this, Ivivin saw an odd shadowy figure to the southeast, still near the shore of the side of the lake closer to Smithton.

"Is that... an island?" Ivivin wondered.

His curiosity drove him to approach it. He even considered swimming out there when he was closer to see if anything was hidden on the island. As he got closer, though, it appeared to be more of a rock than an island. It had an odd pattern and was strangely glossy, as if covered in slime. Ivivin squinted at the figure in an attempt to resolve its identity when it suddenly turned to look at Ivivin. It was as if one of the lizards from the desert had donned armour and taken up residence in the lake! A morbid curiosity built in Ivivin, trying to get him to get even closer to the beast. Ivivin looked at Icarus, perched nervously on Ivivin's shoulder. They both shook their heads, performed a volte-face, and moved away from the lake as quickly as they could.

11

As Ivivin headed further and further south, he began to recognize the landscape more and more. No features or landmark in particular stood out to him, but he became incredibly nostalgic for the beginning of his journey. He remembered meeting Icarus. He remembered almost starving. He remembered the lessons he learned—harsh ones—before he had even really set forth on his journey. He remembered how weak and, frankly, ignorant he was when he left home. He was again filled with gratitude for Smith and all that he had shown him. Ivivin still felt ignorant and still felt small, but that was because he had gotten a taste of how large the world really was. Ivivin was happy that he could sustain himself. That he could trap and fish and scavenge and survive. That he was, in his own way, free—not from the cycle the world followed, but free to move around within the constraints of that cycle.

Ivivin anticipated smooth travels from here until to Smithton, but Icarus seemed to be getting nervous in this area. Ivivin had long since come to trust the owl when it came to sensing danger, so he too raised his guard. But no amount of attention could have prepared Ivivin for what happened next.

12

One evening, just as the sun began to sink below the horizon, Ivivin was attacked! He didn't see the perpetrator, he only felt himself get hit five times in rapid succession, almost simultaneously. Ivivin was knocked to the floor. Ivivin guarded his head in anticipation of further blows. Je imagined that he must have been attacked by a skilled fighter who could throw punches faster than the eye could see. He worried that it was someone after the Tear of Jupiter, perhaps some remnant of the Shaa'Illi. He winced as he anticipated the next round of blows, but they never came. Instead, he felt a light weight or, rather, a bunch of light weights shifting around on his chest and belly.

"What the?" Ivivin said as he stared at his chest. There, five owls were scurrying about, tugging at Ivivin's clothing, as if they were looking for something.

Upon closer inspection, Ivivin reasoned that these might be the same kind of owl Icarus was. Ivivin was never really able to identify the species to which Icarus belonged. The scruffy ball of haphazard feathers was hardly a model specimen. Still, if Ivivin squinted and turned his head a bit, he could see the resemblance. Unlike Icarus, these owls were well-kempt and majestic. They were all larger than Icarus too, with sharper beaks and talons. And, whereas Ivivin could hear Icarus flying nearly a mile away, all five of these owls had silently approached and assaulted Ivivin.

At that moment, one of the owls emerged from the sleeve of Ivivin's shirt dragging a distressed Icarus by his tailfeathers. The owls all surrounded Icarus, now on the ground next to Ivivin. Now that Ivivin could compare them, there was no longer any doubt in Ivivin's head that they were of the same species. They even looked like they could be related. And, as it turned out, they were. These owls were Icarus' siblings. He had four sisters and one brother. They sat there silently staring at and judging their sibling. Ivivin sat up to assess the situation and try to understand what exactly was going on. Ivivin's heart warmed a little at the sight.

"Maybe these were Icarus' friends before we met. Maybe he got separated from them and now they're going to catch up. That must be it, they probably thought I captured their friend and wanted to save him!" Ivivin mused to himself.

The other owls suddenly started to shriek at Icarus. Icarus took flight, but the others quickly took him back to the ground, just a few yards from where they started. Ivivin was shocked by the sudden movement of the birds and was paralyzed until Icarus' cry pierced Ivivin's ears.

Ivivin had never felt much anger in his life but, for the first time, his rage boiled over as he saw these owls pecking at Icarus, tearing out his feathers and cutting him. Ivivin bolted over as fast as he could and scooped Icarus into his arms and hid him tightly against his chest. The owls persisted, however, and started to pelt and peck Ivivin with the hopes of getting him to release Icarus. Again, anger built inside Ivivin. He raised his head and faced the assailants. Ivivin's glower stuck a primal chord in the birds. In a scramble and flurry of feathers, they fled.

Ivivin inspected his friend. He didn't know much about owls or how much they could weather, but he knew Icarus had handled worse. Icarus looked up at Ivivin, even more in shambles than he was previously. Filled with shame, Icarus took flight to be alone awhile. He didn't make it far before he lost control and began to tumble from the air. Ivivin sprinted and caught the bird before he hit the floor. Icarus looked at Ivivin apologetically and defeated. Ivivin understood well in that moment the life Icarus had led before they met. Ivivin dropped to his knees and held Icarus close. Ivivin cried there, his friend in his arms.

"I'm sorry." Ivivin said to the Icarus over and over, rocking the bird back and forth.

Ivivin woke to the sound of Icarus' frustration. The owl tried time and time again to ascend and fly, but could stay in the air no longer than a few seconds before tumbling back to the ground. In the light of the morning sun, Ivivin could clearly see that many of Icarus' flight feathers had been wrenched from his body. Icarus tried for what felt like an eternity to fly. Each failure broke Ivivin's heart a little more. Eventually, Icarus plummeted once again and stayed down. After a few minutes, Icarus let loose a heart-wrenching sound. A raspy and elongated keen—a lamentation over the loss of self. The pair sat there, silent, until the sun had long passed overhead. Ivivin scooped up his friend and placed him on his shoulder. Under an unusually harsh sun, the two made their way to Smithton.

Elara in Rumi

1

Elara walked the streets of the market aimlessly. The magic of the enormity of the city of Rumi had not even come close to wearing off. Elara had never seen a large city and had not considered how overwhelming one might actually be. Elara had arrived three days prior and, every day since, has walked through the huge expansive market, a spectacle in and of itself, to see the sea. The majesty of the immensity of the water and the unique way the light shimmered hypnotized Elara. She was fascinated with how the waves would come from seemingly nothing, how the water looked so different at different locations or times of day, and how the water would retreat into the distance, revealing pools containing little critters and other assorted treasures. Indeed, most of her time had been spent at the water. And, while most of the beaches were rocky, she had found herself a sandy haven. When she arrived, she kicked off her shoes and welcomed the warm grains of sand between her toes. She checked to see if anyone was watching before partaking in a healthy amount of frolic in the sand, incorporating some of Petil's movements into her otherwise aimless running about. After spending her wind, she planted herself onto the sand and stared out to the waters.

Elara spent some time trying to decide what to do here. Despite the size of the city, she had essentially only seen the path from the inn, to the market, to the water. She knew very little of the people, of their traditions, or of their problems. She had not avoided all gossip, though, as the merchants of the market often chatted nervously with one another. The first thing she gathered was that Ivivin had been here and that he had apparently vanquished a mighty beast by the name of Ojasa. Initially, Elara was impressed. But she found out later that the beast was an illusion of an old, portly fellow that ruled by fear, not substance.

"Ivivin was just the first person to figure it out then." Elara reasoned, becoming far less impressed with the feat. *"He didn't really face any real danger."* Still, Elara thought it was neat that she knew a local celebrity.

Not everyone lauded Ivivin's accomplishment absolutely, though. Apparently, Ojasa had quite the accumulation of wealth and treasures. Ivivin nor the townspeople had thought to reclaim these goods immediately. Indeed, the residents of the city still generally feared the mountain. Eventually, though, the city council put together a task force to investigate Ojasa's castle and its contents. To their surprise, however, the castle was occupied anew by well-known figure from Rumi named Ajaxx.

2

Ajaxx was, by all accounts, a racketeer and ruffian. For years, he had essentially run or facilitated most all the shady, underground dealings taking place in Rumi. On the surface, he ran a major shipping and warehousing operation in Rumi. But his all-but-confirmed illicit activities ranged from intimidation of competitors to human trafficking. When Ojasa first arrived some years ago, he was amoung the first to leave Rumi, though his influence, albeit diminished, could still be felt. Now he had laid claim to Ojasa's castle and all the treasures and wealth therein. Obviously, the city of Rumi would have liked to reclaim their goods and either occupy or demolish the castle, but Ajaxx had obtained an abundance of resources at a time when Rumi was struggling. He used these resources to assemble what amounted to a small army and to exert his will over Rumi and its people. While he was no king nor mayor, Ajaxx had, essentially, become the ruler of Rumi.

Some people had actually benefitted under this rule thus far, from what Elara could tell. Although they were subject to the whims of Ajaxx, many merchants enjoyed a recuperating economy—even with the new Ajaxx operations 'tax'. Unfortunately, those not in the business of making money or looking the other way did not always fare so well. Those who publicly criticized Ajaxx or his company were often found battered or, occasionally, dead. What's more is that those who worked for Ajaxx, from the accountant to the hired muscle, were, in essence, immune to the law. Intimidation was the norm. It was not a violent location, nor a peaceful one. Ajaxx was slowly trying to irreversibly ingrain himself in the people, infrastructure, and laws of Rumi. While he had never dirtied his own hands, this informal rule was a natural place to start.

Elara continued to stare out into the waters. Thoughts of this man had sullied her mood. No matter the economic benefits, she could not abide such a man nor respect his rule. She stood, brushed herself off, and made her way back to the market.

3

Elara was filled with a particular sort of frustration. This sort of frustration comes with the desire to oppose—to resist—but against not an individual or monster. Rather, she felt a strong urge to revolt against an abstraction—not just Ajaxx, but everything that allowed him to continue exerting his influence. Many people thought it best to keep their heads down—that the king would eventually send help in the interest of preserving his rule. But in Elara's heart and mind, she felt the people affected would be irreversibly hurt and the damage would be done. As her days in this town turned to weeks, she could feel more people coming to consider the situation normal, despite it amounting to an absurd travesty of the rule of law. So, Elara spent her days looking for likeminded people.

"Surely, there must be some gathering of people who oppose this man and his dealings" Elara would think as she wandered the town. But if there was a faction of resistance, Elara couldn't find traces of it.

"I suppose that makes sense." Elara reasoned, trying to stay optimistic. *"If opposition is met rather brutally, then secrecy would need to be paramount beyond all else."*

It was not until her funds began to dwindle and she took up employ at a tavern that she found her first lead.

4

Elara's work at the tavern was exhausting—not because the work itself was particularly laborious. She cleaned, which, in contrast to her travels and her previous knightly work, was quite easy on her. Rather, she found dealing with drunken patrons at the wee hours of the night began to annoy her. She longed for the freedom of travel again and the thought of leaving this place oft crossed her mind. She often wanted to get back on the road and leave this city to its problems. But that Ajaxx and his fellows were also said to be involved in the trafficking of humans—treating people as property. Elara couldn't live with herself if she ignored it. As luck would have it, though, Elara's search efforts for a faction would pay off. But not because of her active effort. Looking through the town in the day was misguided. Instead, it was the loose-lips of a young woman in a drunken stupor at the darkest of hours of the night that cued her in. The lady was quickly stifled by her two companions, but Elara had heard enough to know her next move.

5

The Drifter's Roost was a popular inn: 'was' being the operative word. It had since grown and developed into much more than that. It still housed an inn, sure, but a wide variety of other crafts and artisans had also found their home under the roof of The Drifter's Roost. From what Elara had gathered from her initial tour of the surprisingly large building (or, rather, bunch of buildings patchily connected) was that the owner had facilitated and protected the business of many small-time, local merchants who could not keep up with the eruption of the larger businesses burgeoned by advancements in marine trade and commerce. From haberdashers to butchers, Elara was stunned at the variety represented in the people operating in The Drifter's Roost. They did share one thing in common, though, and that was that they were small operations indeed. Still, it seemed most of the members got by, at least, and the building was filled with lively people, both vendors and shoppers. Elara lost sight of her goal as she wandered the aisles. It was not until she happened upon the inn proper that she remembered why she was investigating this location in the first place. She suspected, based on the words of the drunken fellow from her work, that whatever resistance to Ajaxx existed was centered here.

Elara may have found a lead, but she really had little idea to how she would approach identifying the faction or its members. Elara supposed she could just ask whoever was in charge what they thought about Ajaxx and use their reactions as a metric of alignment. She walked to the young woman currently helming the inn.

"Excuse me?" Elara asked the woman, who was busy looking over paperwork.

"Yes?" relented the young woman, not even bothering to look up at Elara.

"May I speak to whoever is in charge of...this? All of this?" Elara mumbled, realizing how silly her request must sound.

The young woman took pause before continuing her task. "Madame Cantabelle? I suppose she would be running about the brewery this time of day." The woman, still looking downwards nudged her head towards a hallway Elara had yet to explore.

"But," she continued "I wouldn't expect her to have patience nor the time to entertain you."

Elara wandered away from the counter to collect herself a moment, still peeved at not even earning a glance from the inn's worker.

"Madame Cantabelle, huh?" Elara mused. *"That name sounds...regal. And, from the sound of it, she has no patience for common folk like myself."* Elara sighed, realizing how fruitless interacting with such a woman would be.

"Still, it may be worth a shot to speak with this 'Madame Cantabelle'. After all, you never know." Elara thought as she made her way to the brewery.

6

The Drifter's Roost's brewery was expansive. Elara knew not the inner workings of the craft, but even she could tell this was a large and modern enterprise. It was not uncommon, of course, for inns and even families to make their own drink, but the scale of this operation was exceptional. It was filled with barrels and tools and people. It took Elara a moment, but one of the things that stood out to her most was that many of the workers were women. The vast majority, in fact. Elara didn't know if this was typical, but it struck her all the same. She kept her eyes peeled, looking for a someone fitting her image of Madame Cantabelle. In her survey of the brewery and its people, however, she bumped into a worker. A large, middle age woman. And when Elara bumped into her, she could feel how solid that woman was. Elara had just barely kept herself from falling to the floor, but the woman seemed undisturbed as she carried a barrel across her shoulder. Indeed, it was not until Elara apologized that the woman even seemed to recognize Elara's presence. She turned slightly to face Elara, handling the barrel with ease. The woman's face was covered in soot, presumably from the malting flames. She towered over Elara and was truly imposing.

"She would have given the Shaa'Id a run for his money." Elara thought as she admired the woman's intumescent arms. Her

thoughts were cut short, however, as the woman opened her mouth to speak.

"Oh, didn't notice you there, you wee thing. Wait a minute… you are assuredly not one of mine, are you dear? Did you come here looking for work?" The woman said to Elara.

Elara was stunned. Not at the question, nor her accent, nor even the titanic woman's gentle demeanour. No, instead, Elara was stunned at the sheer pleasantness of the woman's voice. The timbre alone captivated Elara and she was silenced by her own entrancement.

"Dear? My young lady? Can you talk?"

Elara snapped to and meekly replied "I am looking for Madame Cantabelle. I was hoping to ask her some questions…"

The woman smiled. "Of course, my little hummingbird. I am Madame Cantabelle. Welcome to my Bohemia!"

7

"Follow me, my peckish hen." Madame Cantabelle said as she set the barrel down. They made their way to an office, near what seemed to be the entrance to a cellar. "Come, sit. You're safe here. No need to worry." The Madame said in her most melodic of voices. Elara, again mesmerized by the woman's voice, sat across from The Madame at a small table in the corner of the room.

Elara took a moment to look around. She had a hard time nailing down the style of the office's adornments. It was, for lack of a better term, a hodgepodge of different trinkets, styles, and decorations. As disparate as the items were from one another, though, there was no denying their uniqueness and quality. Eventually, Elara's eyes met with those of Madame Cantabelle, who had been waiting for Elara to finish her inspection.

"You'll excuse me, dear, but, while I always have time for people in your position, my schedule is filled to the brim. So, I'll be frank, how did you manage to get away?"

Elara was following until the last sentence.

"Pardon, get away? Get away from what, exactly?" Elara asked, thinking back to the Shaa'Ra and the large creature at Saeber lake.

"There is no need to be shy with me, my darling dove. I know it must be hard to talk about, but I handle this all the time. You can trust me. I mean, that is why you sought me out in the first place, no? My sterling reputation? Even if you don't want to stay here, I can give you work until you get back on your horse, little one."

Elara was brought no closer to understanding this woman's inquiry.

"I am sorry, ma'am. I don't understand. I am a traveler from the north. I blew into town a few weeks ago now. I just had some questions I was hoping you could answer." Elara said, trying to be as clear as possible.

The Madame seemed to understand and her demeanor changed quickly.

"I am sorry for the misunderstanding then, but, if you aren't here for my services, I must get on with my day. I would appreciate it if you would take your leave." The woman stated as flatly as her voice would allow.

As Madame Cantabelle stood to see Elara out of the office, Elara was again reminded of the sheer density of presence this woman possessed. Despite being intimidated by the woman, Elara had come too far to shy away now. In the doorway, Elara blurted her question.

"What do you think of Ajaxx?"

8

Madame Cantabelle stopped in the doorway and locked eyes again with Elara. "What do I think of Ajaxx?"

Elara nodded.

"Ajaxx… I suppose I have never really thought about it too much, my dearest finch." The Madame stated, resuming her more sweet tone. "But...if I had to say…I suppose he's rather good for business in these parts. I have met him a handful of times, terribly polite. He is a shrewd businessman, as sure as geese have feathers."

Elara was sickened to hear praise for this man and turned to leave the woman. Her disgusted reaction must have shown clearly on her face, as the Madame put a hand on Elara's shoulder to stop her. Elara turned to face her, this time, and saw the hulking woman sporting a sly grin.

"Oh, my feisty little sparrow." The Madame whispered fiercely. "You are far too easy to read, but we'll make use of you yet."

Elara's own strategy had been turned against her. She stared at the woman in a daze of disbelief. Madame Cantabelle opened the heavy cellar door with ease and smiled sharply at Elara.

"Welcome to my Bohemia."

9

Elara followed The Madame, who just barely fit through the cellar's entrance, down below the brewery. It was a narrow passage lined with barrels on each end. At the end of the passage was a plain grey stone wall with a vibrant blue silhouette sparrow adorning it. They made their way to the end of the passage, where Madame Cantabelle made a point to stop and point out the two candlesticks on each side of the passage. She turned the one on the left side of the passage slightly and pushed open the wall...er...door.

"The one on the left opens the door in. The one on the right alarms those inside that something is wrong without entering. I must be on my way, my spring dove, but I must know your name before I away."

"My name..." Elara considered lying to the woman, but was reassured once more by her voice. "...is Elara."

"Elara! Oh, your name is simply *divine*! No time for doting, though, I must be off. Bennu will help you settle right on in!" Her sweet voice turned serious as she started back the cellar's entrance.

"I look forward to working with you."

Elara had an extremely difficult time reconciling what had just happened with this strange and gargantuan woman. She stood at the entrance of the hidden doorway, still agape, when she was suddenly grabbed and pulled inside. The hidden door closed behind her.

"What about a secret entrance makes you think you can just stand there like you have no sense, girl!" screeched an unknown woman. The shrill voice of this woman contrasted acutely with that of the Madame. Elara felt herself being examined—judged—by this woman and decided to reciprocate. She was quite small and slim and had skin the closest to bronze Elara had ever seen. Her features were nearly as sharp as her voice. What stood out most, though, was this woman's hair. It was red as flame and it shimmered as such as the woman restlessly bobbed back and forth. The silence was broken with an outreached hand.

"The name's Bennu. Welcome to the Sparrows."

Elara hesitated only for a moment before she let their hands meet.

10

Elara learned about The Sparrows and its members quickly and was, frankly, in awe. Madame Cantabelle was a sailor in her youth and her office was adorned with items from her travels. Bennu said there was a rumor about The Madame floating around that she was the offspring of a siren. Whatever the case, the Madame had settled here from overseas because this port city of Rumi reminded her of time as a sailor. She established the inn and eventually the consortium by means of her good relations with merchants and transporters alike. The Sparrows, then, arose when The Madame first caught wind of the human trafficking happening right under her nose. She found and freed the six girls being held and invited them to work for her. Those women became the founding members of the Sparrows. Since then, they have been involved with uncovering human trafficking rings, freeing those involved, and offering work to those who decide to stay in Rumi. Those who stay and become impassioned to help the cause are vetted and invited to join The Sparrows.

"Well, that explains why The Madame was offering me work, but why do you all operate in secrecy?" Elara asked Bennu.

"Well, our methods can be a little...unsavoury and the leadership here isn't always understanding of our occasional vigilantism."

Bennu's expression turned sour.

"Like how they are letting that filth Ajaxx walk all over them nowadays. Blast! I thought we were done with him. I'd take Ojasa over that ball of sleaze any day."

Elara was conflicted. She had taken lives in the protection of her sister and her village. Yet things were also so black and white for her in those times. This organization...The Sparrows...they seemed to operate in a more moral grey area. Elara agreed wholeheartedly with their mission, but breaking the law to do it felt wrong. This conflict, like many of Elara's emotions, were all too easy to read. Bennu tried to assure her.

"Don't worry Elara! I have been working with Madame Cantabelle for years and she has never once been wrong. Her singsong voice and her sheer size mask how cunning she truly is. If we follow her word, then we are sure to make a difference! Which reminds me..." Bennu pulled out a brooch and handed it to Elara. She recognized it as the same as all the workers at the brewery wore—a roosting bird made of bronze.

Bennu explained. "These are our badges for work at the brewery, at the inn, wherever the Madame puts us to work. Each badge has a coloured embellishment on the sides, you see. But, for some of us, the Sparrows, well, they're all blue."

Elara recalled the badge she had seen on the innkeeper—green. And the brewery workers, they had all sorts of colours.

"Hold onto that, it is the best way to prove you are one of us. If the secret base didn't tip you off, we don't trust a lot of folk. Hell, if you weren't so easy to read, I wouldn't trust you either."

11

Elara quit her job at the tavern and took a similar job at the tavern at the Drifter's Roost, where she could be close to the Sparrows. Elara could hardly grasp what had happened in this short time. She couldn't help but feel like she didn't have a lot of say in joining the Sparrows. She suspected the Madame used her conscience against her to ensure her silence and participation. By just thrusting her into the group without asking, the Madame essentially used guilt against Elara to ensure her support. Elara realized the cunning of this woman, now, and was initially livid about feeling used and manipulated. After a few nights on her beach, though, she realized that it didn't matter. She wanted this, the Madame just realized it before she herself did.

Soon, Elara would be participating in her first ever mission with the Sparrows. They had been gathering information and planning it for quite some time. When Elara first met the group, she was not as surprised as she would have once been. This resistance faction—this group of honourable outlaws—consisted mostly of women from all over the world. Elara had to stop herself from constantly inquiring about and indulging in the heritage of the members. She learned quickly that many there wanted to discard their past. There were those, though, like Bennu who were very open about their past. Elara came to learn of many distant lands, just as she wanted, but she also came to learn of many heart-shattering histories. About being kidnapped as children. About being sold to old men for favours. About being beaten over and over to 'train' them. Elara had villainized the act of human trafficking long before she knew what that even truly entailed. Now that she was faced with those who had lived it, it was much more real for her.

A silver lining of it all in Elara's eyes, though, was that she found those who had suffered in their lives—people like the members of the Sparrows—to be particularly real. That is, they all had such whole personalities. They were easier to want to connect with, even if they were immeasurably harder to understand. Elara's life hadn't exactly been a walk in the park but, compared to some of these fighters, she couldn't help but feel she had lived a blessed life. She had felt pity, at first, for these people. But that pity was gradually and genuinely replaced with comradery and concern.

Elara was ready for her first operation with the Sparrows.

12

Elara did not help much with the subterfuge or aggregation of information leading to this point. Though she was tight-lipped, Elara wore her emotions on her sleeves and did not play the role of an informant well. So, she trusted in the Sparrows and the Madame.

Finally, it was her turn to contribute. There was to be a boat docking in the dead of night that the Madame was confident would have a number of young women aboard. Their mission was simple. Free them before Ajaxx's men smuggled them out and away. This was their best and only chance. This being Elara's first mission, she would not be entering the boat, nor would she be helping spark the distraction. Instead, she would be keeping watch, both on the happenings of the boat and on the movement in town. The Sparrows had taught Elara some bird calls, at which she was...proficient. These would serve as her means of communication with the women from her perch. She had an excellent view of both locales from her position. On one side, the smaller-than-expected boat was anchored under the over-hang of another cliff. On the other, Elara could keep an eye on the beach where the distraction plan would come to fruition.

Elara kneeled at her nearby cliff, watching everything from a spyglass lent to her by The Madame herself. The distraction plan was a bit ingenious, at least, Elara thought so. Frequently, the members of the Sparrows, as well as other employees of the Madame, were known to, well, party. Party hard and into the wee hours of the night. They set up a fair distance from, but still uncomfortably close to, the boat. The fellows on the boat would have to go and convince them to leave and the partygoers would simply entice them with drink and dance. The crew would send more people, who would be ensnared themselves. The infiltration crew would make their move once they were sure there were few enough people aboard that they could handle it. And the plan worked and worked very well. The crew trickled out until Elara thought she saw even the captain drinking and dancing jovially on the beachfront. She (poorly) loosed a nightjar's cry and several silhouettes boarded the ship.

13

"It wasn't supposed to be this way!" Elara thought as the light of a cruel fire reflected off her eyes. The fire sparked to life not moments after the last of The Sparrows' infiltration team made it onboard. Likewise, a fight had broken out on the beach between the crew and the party-goers. The fire spread unnaturally fast along the boat.

"What do I do!?" Elara asked herself. She was frozen by her own powerlessness. She was not particularly close to either location and wasn't sure how much she could do to help at either. A single thought thawed her, though.

"Lives are at stake." Elara thought, coming to terms with the reality of the situation. She would trust in members on the beach to manage. Those on the boat, they were who Elara would help.

"But how...?" Elara thought, trying to think of ways to put out the fire. *"There is no way I can douse the flames myself, neither by water or sand."* She noticed townsfolk gathering at the burning boat, no one to each the boat's deck with their meager buckets of water. Elara was struck by inspiration.

14

Elara hurried as quickly as she could to the dock and the group of worried townspeople. Elara knew that pouring water on the surface would be impossible. There was simply no way to deliver the water that high and in that quantity. However, there was another way. Elara had been to the docks and the beaches almost every day since her arrival. She had seen everything from stray cats to bickering lovers to garbage dumped haphazardly. She recalled, nearby, old rusty chains amoung other, abandoned materials from the lazier shipwrights of the area. She deftly found what she was looking for. She dragged the heavy chain over to the crowd and directed people to hold fast to it. On one end, Elara fastened a hook. She faced the crowd and spoke.

"I will attach the boat to the chain and then we will tip it over! There are people aboard, so please, make haste!"

There was a murmur of agreement as Elara drug the chain to the boat. There was no easy place to attach the chain. Elara would have to use the gunwale. She stepped back, wrapped the chain around her waist, and, with all her strength, ran and leapt towards the boat. Elara managed to grab hold of the edge of the gunwale.

Pain.

Elara's hands bellowed in torrent of torment and she was sure she could hear her own flesh sizzling by the heat of the flame. She almost let go and fell to the water. It would have been all too easy.

But she persisted. She struggled to hook the gunwale for what felt like an eternity. In reality, it took no more than seconds before she managed to fix the chain to the boat and she let herself drop into the water. Never had water felt so good, even as the salt of the water stung. She allowed herself a moment of rest as she slowly floated to the surface. She broke the surface of the water to see the townsfolk hard at work tugging at the boat. Moments after Elara had willed herself back onto the ground, the townsfolk managed to touch the boat's deck into the water. They managed to submerge much the deck under the water and released it before the water infiltrated and sunk the boat. The water sloshed about the deck, extinguishing much of the fire. When the boat finally stopped rocking, the women who were trapped in the berth of the vessel trickled out, many being supported by one another. Elara continued to lay as the citizens aided the women off the boat. She felt an unbearable pain in her hands and struggled to find the courage to look at them. She slowly raised her hands and turned her palms to meet her eyes.

Tears filled her eyes as she fought the urge to vomit.

15

It was a long and painful night for Elara. She wasn't alone. The entirety of the town hall had been converted into an emergency infirmary for the incident. Many of the girls could be heard coughing through the night. Others moaned from the pain of their burns. Elara tried to figure out what had happened, what had gone wrong, but it was unwise for them to speak openly in this venue. Even if she was inclined, the pain in Elara's hands kept her from thinking clearly. In the morning she would face many harsh truths.

The doctor in charge of her care was confident that her right hand—the hand she used to grab the chain—would recover, if with quite a bit of scarring. But Elara's left hand did not fare as well. It had remained on the hot surface of the boat longer. Luckily, she wouldn't have to lose the hand, assuming there were no complications, as they were able to treat it right away. But they were not sure how much function it would retain, if any.

A few of the Sparrows lost their lives. Many were now riddled in burns. Some minor, some major. Whatever the case, they were defeated and marked.

Ajaxx had set them up. The boat was a sacrificial lamb. He intended to end the lives of the invaders and his 'merchandise' alike. That was why it was a small boat. No need to lose a more seaworthy one.

And, to top it all off, a small group of bandits had ransacked The Drifter's Roost. They destroyed much of the interior. The inn and brewery were totaled. Worse still, Madame Cantabelle was nowhere to be found, though her office showed clear signs of a struggle.

Elara had tasted the most bitter of defeats. She had no idea what she would do next. She laid in the infirmary and cried from the intense pain in both her flesh and her in soul.

A Sort of Homecoming

1

Ivivin was struck by nostalgia as Smithton became visible on the horizon. As Ivivin approached the city, though, his nostalgia turned to worry. He was anxious about returning to Smithton and to Smith. He wasn't quite sure why. He worried that maybe no one would remember him. Or that he wasn't as important to Smith as Smith was to him. Or that Smithton would be nothing like he remembered it. He was afraid that Smith would be disappointed in him for coming back for help. Or for what he allowed to happen to Icarus.

"Where were these doubts on the weeks it took me to get here?" Ivivin scolded himself. Still, carried forth by fond memories and trusting in his bond with Smith, he continued at a steady pace. As he approached the city, Ivivin was struck by an idea and decided to circle the perimeter a way until he arrived at a familiar stable near the familiar remnants of a house scorched. Forgetting his troubles for a moment, Ivivin sprinted inside the stable once more and collapsed on the hay that remained there still, though admittedly a bit worse for wear. Ivivin grabbed Icarus, who did not share Ivivin's enthusiasm, and held him on his palm.

"Do you remember this place, Icarus? Though we met before, when you crashed into me, this is the place where we first stayed together." Icarus looked around a bit before retreating once more into himself. Ivivin was never sure if Icarus could always understand his words, but he wanted to say something, anything, to cheer his friend up. To let him know that things were going to be hard, but they'd get through it together. Ivivin wished he had studied even more with Smith as he could not find words to describe this feeling, let alone to an owl. Ivivin replayed their meeting in his head once more and found the words he sought.

"Icarus..." Ivivin stated, looking at the owl with dead seriousness. "You owe me fish. You ate my mother's salted fish here in this stable. You owe me fish." It was not often Ivivin confused Icarus—usually the opposite was true. But Icarus seemed genuinely confused by Ivivin's words as Ivivin settled down for the night, reliving the early days of his adventure.

Ivivin woke the next morning.... wet?

"What the…" Ivivin thought to himself groggily. On his chest were two soaking masses. One, a freshly killed fish, slimy and small. And the other, a sopping heap of feathers breathing heavily. Ivivin smiled and patted the owl gently with a cloth. Their eyes met. Ivivin giggled and told the bird:

"Alright buddy, we're square."

Icarus was beaming with pride as he let sleep overtake him. Ivivin sighed as he set the bird aside and began to prepare the little fish brought to him by his little friend.

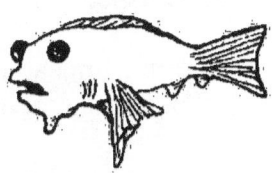

3

As he wandered into town, Ivivin could not stave off his nervousness at the prospect of seeing Smith again. But he was equally excited to show his mentor how much he had grown and to recount all his stories. Ivivin entered Smithton with high spirits that were met with an unusually gloomy air pervading the townsfolk. Sure, as Ivivin walked about he saw many of the same people doing the same things, but there was a certain uncertainty looming over the people. They didn't talk as much to one another and the market, while no less full, certainly was missing the hustle and bustle Ivivin remembered it for.

"What changed?" Ivivin thought. *"Do I just remember this place with rose-coloured spectacles?"*

Ivivin wanted to inquire and investigate, but he figured simply asking Smith would be the fastest way to get an answer. Plus, it would spare him the inevitable awkward exchanges involved.

Icarus had slumbered steadfast throughout Ivivin's roundabout stroll to Smith's forge, but the little heap of feathers sprung back to life as the familiar scent of soot and warmth that surrounds the forge reached him. Ivivin paused at the entrance. He fidgeted in the doorway for minutes before he heard a thunderous but comforting voice echo from within.

"Would you just get in here already, boy! And bring your winged rodent with you. I don't want him scaring off any customers!"

Ivivin smiled and stepped over the threshold into the forge.

4

"How did you know I was here?" Ivivin asked Smith, a bit embarrassed by his own inaction.

"How could I not sense something so antsy?" Smith said, laughing at his own joke as he finished tending to the flame and finally faced Ivivin.

Ivivin was struck by Smith's appearance. He was still large, burly, and muscular, sure, but he was gaunt and weariness was all too apparent in his eyes.

"I have a bit of work to finish up here before I can enjoy a chat with you, Ivivin. How about you do me a favour and go to the baker's and get some sweetrolls—three of them. Pick up some tea while you are at it, from Minerva just a few stores down. She owes me some tea for fixing up her equipment. Got that boy?"

Ivivin nodded, took some change from Smith's hand, and set forth back towards the market. He had been back in the forge for mere minutes, but already he felt as if he had never left. Of course, Ivivin was curious about what seemed to be worrying Smith and the town at large, but he reasoned that Smith would open up to him again in due time. Ivivin picked up the tea before headed to the familiar baker's. Ivivin was giddy, excited to see the baker-woman who was always so kind and had helped him out in the past. Instead, though, there was a young man, even younger than Ivivin, manning the store.

"Hmm, that's odd." Ivivin thought. *"I don't think I've ever known her to take a day off. Didn't trust even her family to handle everything without her around."*

The young man seemed just as tired and unwell as Smith. Ivivin didn't want to trouble him with unnecessary questions, so he purchased his sweetrolls without making a fuss and made his way back to Smith's forge.

"That was fast. Did you skip all the way there?" Smith heckled Ivivin upon his return.

"Ah, sorry. I was just excited to have some of the baker's bread and to come back and catch up with you." Ivivin responded earnestly.

"Aye, I suppose it has been a long time." Smith said, setting down his tools and joining Ivivin in the kitchen. Smith gave Ivivin an unexpected hug and, while Ivivin was still much shorter than him, Smith seemed shorter than he remembered, too.

"It is good to see you, boy. How is your journey going? Making any progress?" Smith asked Ivivin as he sat down at the table and gestured for Ivivin to do the same.

Ivivin recounted to Smith all of his adventures since he left, trying not to leave out a detail. Smith grew more and more impressed by Ivivin's tales, almost to the point of incredulity. They chatted about all manners of things while sipping on tea and munching on sweetrolls. After what seemed like hours, Ivivin had long finished his sweetroll but couldn't help but notice Smith hadn't even eaten half of his.

"Smith...what has—"

Ivivin was cut off by Smith.

"So, Ivivin, what brings you back here exactly?"

"Oh, well, my armour didn't fit anymore so I am in need of a new set. I couldn't bring myself to risk fixing up the set myself."

"I see. That's good... In fact, I think this works out well for the two of us. Ivivin, I will make you a new set of armour and show you more about how to alter and maintain it. But nothing is free, you know, even for you. I need to leave town for a little while and would appreciate you looking after the forge while I am gone. Does that sound like a good deal?"

Ivivin was taken aback. Both by the frankness and abruptness of the proposal, but that Smith still trusted him with the forge after all this time. Ivivin looked at Smith again and saw the weariness in his face once more.

"I think getting out of town for a while would be good for him" Ivivin thought.

"Sure, Smith. If you think I can handle it."

6

Smith wasted no time in bringing Ivivin back up to speed and expanding his knowledge. Indeed, Ivivin seldom left the forge. Smith seemed to want to cram all the knowledge he could into Ivivin as fast as he could.

"Man, Smith must really want to take his vacation." Ivivin thought.

But, even though he hadn't been able to reconnect with the people of Smithton as he would have liked, he did gather pieces of current events while he was dealing with customers now and again. There was, apparently, a plague of sorts that had started to make its way to Smithton and, though it had not become an epidemic quite yet, it worried the townsfolk terribly. Tension and uncertainty permeated many interactions between the citizens. Like many people his age, Ivivin wasn't terribly worried for his own health. But he could understand why people who all made their living so close together might be worried. In fact, hearing of all this made Ivivin worry about his parents back near Gemi. He tried to push the thought from his head and focus on Smith's teachings.

He found his old skills returned to him easily and that he could more easily handle the tools of the trade. He could wield hammer with ease and tong with precision. It helped that Smith was a good, if harsh, teacher. Ivivin could tell the real reason, though. He was no more prepared or astute than he was when he had first left the forge. Rather, he was stronger and that seemed to make a world of difference. Smith himself took note of this and pushed Ivivin even harder than he had the first time around, making sure to include flexing of the mind as well as the muscles. Smith tasked Ivivin with recording his work as he did it and with reading daily. The art of reading and writing did not return quite so easily to Ivivin, but he tried his best nonetheless. And so Ivivin's training would continue. Ivivin would work both his mind and his body to its limits every day in preparation for Smith's departure.

After what seemed like both an incredibly long time and an incredibly short one, Smith sat Ivivin down and let him know he planned to leave at the next full moon, in about a week. Ivivin was startled, not because it was particularly soon, but because Smith had yet to forge him new armour. Ivivin trusted Smith to uphold his end of the deal either way, but Smith was the sort of character that pays his due up-front. Not once had Ivivin seen or heard of Smith being in debt with another person.

"Smith, not to sound accusatory..." Ivivin started, "...but are you going to make my armour before you leave? It doesn't seem like enough time."

Smith smiled. "No Ivivin. I won't. You will make your own armour while I am gone. If you are unhappy with the product, I will touch it up for you when I return. Use whatever materials you wish, but waste none. This will be the final task of your apprenticeship. Do well, and I will grant you the title of Blacksmith."

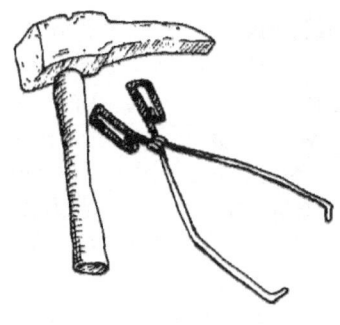

7

Ivivin was both excited and frightened by the prospect of completing his apprenticeship in Smith's absence. Ivivin had been reassured that he was under no obligation to practice smithing if he successfully completed this task. Rather, it was a ceremonial gesture. It was Smith's way of acknowledging Ivivin's growth and skill.

"Knowing Smith though..." Ivivin thought *"he won't take it easy on me. I will really have to impress him."*

Smith made his expectations of Ivivin clear. Ivivin was to take on no more work than he himself could finish in the mornings. In the afternoons, he was to develop his own armour and to clean the forge. And, in the evenings, Ivivin was to read or write. Smith had offered up any book in his study for Ivivin to read. Any profits turned were to be used first and foremost for the upkeep of Ivivin's health and body, then for the upkeep of the forge and Smith's home. Anything else was Ivivin's to keep.

Inevitably, the day of Smith's departure arrived. Ivivin didn't really know why, but the departure felt awfully like the day Ivivin left Smithton with the travelling merchants. The whole ordeal seemed overly ceremonial and sentimental for a vacation. As was their little tradition, the owl, the smith, and the boy shared sweet rolls over a worn table before goodbyes and farewells were said. When Smith had made his way into the distance, Ivivin returned to the forge. With a soot-filled sigh, Ivivin walked around the forge, both inspecting it and basking in his new responsibility.

8

Ivivin quickly fell into a routine. It reminded him of his time at home, working the land. But, rather than viewing the work as tedious and necessary, Ivivin felt more at ease when working in the forge. Within a day or two of Smith's departure, Ivivin already felt confident at the helm of Smith's smithy. He anticipated that more difficult jobs yet to come would challenge that confidence but, for now, he basked in the sense of worth he got from running things.

"Maybe...if this whole knight thing doesn't work out...being a smith wouldn't be so bad." Ivivin often thought.

There were a few things that weighed on Ivivin's mind, though. Icarus, while in decent spirits, didn't seem to be recovering from this assault. Ivivin made sure to set Icarus in a variety high places often, which seemed to help the small bird stay cheerful. But it was not hard to notice Icarus staring wistfully, almost hungrily, at the sky. Ivivin's other big problem was reading every night. The size and scope of Smith's collection intimidated Ivivin. He recalled specifically the difficulty of the book he had given Elara. He was, honestly, frightened he would try a book and get nowhere with it. After all, books are under no obligation to make sense to you. You must make sense of the book. Or, at least, that is what Smith told Ivivin. Presently, Ivivin was re-reading the book of constellations that Elara had given him but, in truth, Ivivin knew he should be reading something else. But the comfort and familiarity (as well as ease and pretty pictures) of the gifted book made it too easy to pick up time and time again. The fourth night after Smith's departure, Ivivin spent the entire evening too paralyzed to read. He almost just decided at random, but figured that was no good either. Before he had realized it, the moon was high in the sky and he had read nothing. The solution to both of these problems came to Ivivin as he lay to bed—ask for help. He would find a falconer to check on Icarus and he would ask the baker woman Isabella, with whom he wanted to catch up with anyways, for a book recommendation.

9

    The following day, Ivivin resolved to head into the market for the guidance he needed. But he had also promised Smith that the afternoon be dedicated to working on his armour. Ivivin had thus far been experimenting with creating specific contours to fit his body. But Ivivin justified the afternoon trip by making a shopping list of materials to restock on, including a large parchment to try and draw out a simple plan for his armour. After a busy morning, Ivivin scooped up a sleepy Icarus and headed to the market to find someone specialized in the avian arts.

    Ivivin knew some hunters that routinely made their way to the market to sell pelts and meats. He figured they would be the best people to ask about a falconer. As Ivivin made his way to the hunter's hub, he noted the same pervasive worry permeating the town. People were abundant, but guarded.

    "How strange…" Ivivin thought. *"It's not as though whatever illness has made its way here. I have hardly seen a sickly person since I've been back."*

    Ivivin gathered from the hunters that there was an old hunter who used all manners of birds of prey who lived not too far from the outskirts of town. He retired both his birds and himself, with his children now providing for him.

"Sounds promising, huh, Icarus?" Ivivin prodded the owl en route to the bird-man's home. Icarus was despondent and refused to meet eyes with Ivivin. Ivivin's heart hurt fresh for the fallen flier. He hastened his pace, hoping that there would be something he could do for his feathered friend.

10

"You'll know it when you see it, ehh?" Ivivin recalled his conversation with the hunters as he wandered an unfamiliar bloc of Smithton. *"I wonder what they mean—"*

Ivivin's thought was cut off by a house coated with birds of all manners. There were as many varieties of birds as Ivivin knew words, casually hanging about the building. Amidst the sea of plumage was a single gentleman, sitting on a hand-fashioned bench with a tiny sparrow on his finger. As Ivivin approached, the bird army scattered. The man turned and stared daggers at Ivivin. Ivivin hadn't felt so intimidated since he had faced the Shaa'Id up north. The man certainly looked to be a hunter—even in his old age he towered above Ivivin and was swollen with muscle, even if it surrounded a swollen belly. He stood up and marched towards Ivivin, opened his mouth to let Ivivin have it, and even had his scolding finger locked and loaded on Ivivin. However, just before Ivivin felt the bird-man's wrath, he noticed the owl on Ivivin's shoulder.

Never had Ivivin noticed such a rapid change in someone's disposition. One moment, the man looked ready to end Ivivin for some unforgivable transgression and the next he was a looking at Icarus like a doting father his toddler daughter. He scooped Icarus up and began a little dance with the bird, complete with face snuggles. Ivivin couldn't make out all the sweet nothings and baby talk, but they were plentiful. The man resumed his seat, Icarus in hand, and gestured for Ivivin to join him. As Ivivin joined the bird-man, the birds that had scattered began to flood back to the haven. Ivivin looked on as the birds drank from plentiful pans of water and fed on a variety of seed.

After a few moments, the man turned to Ivivin and smiled.

"The name is Kranich, though the birds call me *sudden, loud, and awkward squawking sounds.* Pleased to make the acquaintance of a fellow bird lover."

Ivivin was, understandably, taken back. "Ni-nice to meet you too…" Ivivin managed.

"Should I be worried for Icarus?" Ivivin wondered as the man continued to stroke the wee owl. Suddenly serious, the man faced Ivivin.

"So, this fellow here was bullied something fierce, eh?" Ivivin nodded. The man sighed.

"Birdkind should just all get along, don'tcha think? Of course you do! Well little fella, let me take a look at you." The man started probing Icarus all over, causing the little imp of a bird to twitch uncomfortably.

"Can't fly, can you buddy?" The man asked Icarus upon the completion of his inspection. Icarus tried to squirm away from the man's grasp, but Kranich yielded nothing.

"Woah there, feisty fella. Gonna hurt yourself. There is no reason for you to delude yourself and pretend you're fine."

Icarus continued to struggle, but relented when the bird-fiend would not allow him to so much as budge.

"Looking at him, I don't think he'll be flying anytime soon, if ever again." Ivivin's heart broke. It wasn't so important to Ivivin that Icarus could fly, but Icarus was important to Ivivin and it was important to Icarus that he could fly.

"It's best that you and he both come to accept it." Kranich told Ivivin, handing him Icarus. The small bird refused still to look at Ivivin, who could feel fresh tears welling up in his eyes.

"Wait here a mo…" Kranich said as he went into his home.

"I should have never come here." Ivivin thought desperately. *"He probably doesn't even know what he is talking about. He just wants to hurt us. To take Icarus' hope away. To—"*

Ivivin's thoughts interrupted by Kranich tapping his shoulder. Kranich was standing with a large falcon perched on his forearm.

"This is Felix. Say hello Felix!"

The bird of prey screeched loudly.

"Felix was my partner for many years."

Ivivin's dismay was starting to become anger.

"What is he doing!?" Ivivin thought, his rage escalating.

Just as Ivivin was about to have an outburst, Felix spread its wings, revealing a gaping hole in one of them.

11

Ivivin composed himself as he walked back towards the market area, towards the baker.

"I didn't expect him to show me anything like that." Ivivin thought. While he was still immensely sad about Icarus' low chances of flying again, something else had been burnt brightly into his mind during that encounter—something he couldn't get out of his head and something that was somehow comforting to him.

"Felix...looked very happy." Ivivin reflected. *"Even though he could no longer fly—could no longer hunt—Felix seemed very, very satisfied."* Ivivin looked at the mopey owl in his hand and smiled, if sadly.

"That's why Kranich brought him out then, huh?" Ivivin thought as he came to peace with the situation. *"It'll be hard on Icarus, sure, but that doesn't mean he can't be happy."*

"Icarus!" Ivivin shouted, startling the bird. "We are headed to see our old friend the baker woman! I am craving a sweet roll. Wanna split one?"

Icarus perked up slightly as Ivivin placed him on his shoulder.

12

Ivivin cheerfully entered the bakery, only to be met with the same somber fellow from his previous trip.

"Huh, maybe Isabella is in the back?" Ivivin thought.

"Excuse me?" Ivivin said, getting the fellow's attention.

"Yes sir. How may I help you?" The young man recited flatly.

"I'll take a sweetroll and a loaf of whatever is freshest." Ivivin said, handing the man coins to pay for his indulgence. The transaction completed, Ivivin followed up with the young man.

"Is Isabella here? I had something I'd like to ask her." Ivivin asked cheerfully.

The man looked offended, which faded to again to a somber expression. "I guess you haven't heard, then. Isabella, my aunt, she passed away quite a few moons ago."

Perhaps it was because Ivivin had already been emotionally on edge all afternoon, but he started crying immediately. Clearly unsure how to handle the situation, the young baker patted Ivivin awkwardly on the shoulder and waited for him to get it all out.

"Ho—how did she...?" Ivivin managed after a few minutes.

The baker sighed solemnly and uttered just one word.

"Crumbleheart."

13

Ivivin paced around Smith's dwelling, reeling with so many emotions.

"This explains Smith's gauntness." Ivivin realized. *"He and Isabella were close friends. And he lost her to the same disease he lost his wife to. I'd want to get out of town for a while, too, if I were him."*

After some time, Ivivin composed himself enough to resolve to enter Smith's study once more and face his challenge. Once there, though, Ivivin could not focus on the books. Instead, his mind wandered to the tragedy of Wayland and Grandia.

"Crumbleheart, huh? Sounds like such a horrid ailment." Ivivin thought to himself as he sat at Smith's desk. *"Is that the plague that has everyone so on edge? I thought it was only something that you caught down south? How did Isabella get it?"*

Ivivin's mind raced with questions. While Ivivin recounted Smith's story to himself time and time again, he remembered that Grandia had written a book, finished by dictation on her deathbed by Smith.

"That's...that's the book I'll read." Ivivin decided. *"But...where can I find it? I don't even know what it's called or what it looks like..."*

Ivivin looked around at all the books on the bookshelves.

"I don't think that Smith would unceremoniously keep it with all his other books. Nor do I think he'd risk it getting damaged by taking it with him out of town. So, if I were Smith...where would I keep that book?" Ivivin pondered. He recalled the book Elara had given him and how he always liked to keep it close. And that he often read it at night, just before bed. Ivivin forged an idea and went into Smith's chambers, somewhere implicitly forbidden, and, on the bed, there laid a single book, bound with a deep green cover.

Ivivin cautiously retrieved the book and brought it back to the study. He wasn't particularly excited to read it, but, rather, felt compelled to, as if possessed. However, on this, the first night, Ivivin made it only to the first sentence of the first page before retiring for the evening:

Dedicated to my flower picking troll. I love you, always.

Recovering

1

Elara sat alone at the docks, as she often did. She was hungry, as was usual these days, and her hands and heart alike ached and stung just as fresh as the day of the Sparrows' catastrophic failure. It had been only a month, but that month felt like an eternity. Madame Cantabelle's business had essentially been shut down by both the destruction of the property and a sluggish investigation of the premises. The result was that many of the workers were now suddenly, if not permanently, jobless. Elara likely could have found work elsewhere, but the burns on her hands prevented her from doing much besides staring at the ocean and brooding. Moreover, Ajaxx and his associates had slowly been tightening their grip on the town. Honest enforcers of the law were gradually replaced with thugs. Trafficking of ill-gotten goods and people continued more brazenly than before. People were afraid to even mention Ajaxx's existence and pretended as if everything was as it were, as it should be. Slowly, like a serpent, this man who few had even seen was squeezing virtue and honesty from this city and turning it to profit.

Elara was disgusted with the state of affairs in Rumi. She often stared out into the waters and wondered why she hadn't yet just left. She figured she had two main motivations for staying. Firstly, she had given all her money to the doctor to help with her recovery. While she had yet to see any benefit from the visits, she hoped that they would figure out a solution together soon. Her doctor, Dr. Sandra Buckley, was an honest woman and a skilled doctor, so she was hopeful. Secondly, Elara had become obsessed with revenge. She stared onto the sea and often imagined throwing Ajaxx in to sink to the bottom, alone and afraid. Other times, she looked at the sandy beach below her and imagined the fiend buried alive and left to the tides. Still other times, she looked at her hands or at the faces and bodies of the other women and imagined setting him ablaze. The worst of it was that Elara had no clue to what this man actually looked like, so her image of him became more hideous and awful with each iteration of her ever-swelling fantasies of revenge.

"Yes..." Elara thought. *"My hands will be healed and then I will return our suffering ten-fold onto that husk of a human."*

Elara sat at the beach, staring at her feet and the waves all night, sleeplessly. She would see the doctor in the morning.

All she had to do was wait.

All she had to do was wait.

All she had to do was wait.

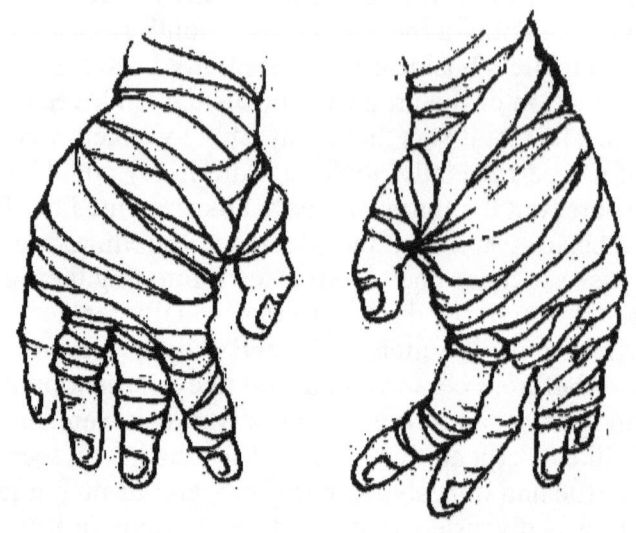

2

With heavy eyes, Elara made her way to her doctor's building. She was a little early, sure, but Elara was also sure Dr. Buckley would understand. And, if the good doctor was too busy, Elara would just wait until she was free: no harm, no foul. As Elara approached the building, though, two large men exited, sweating and laughing with one another.

"How strange..." Elara thought. *"I haven't seen them at the clinic before..."* Elara suspected something was off and made her way to the clinic. She was met by a disheveled Dr. Buckley. The doctor's hair was strewn about every which direction. Her face was glowing red and she was gripping her stomach and sides tightly. It was apparent by the swelling of her eyes that she had been in tears just moments prior to Elara's arrival. Elara stared at the doctor and the doctor at her.

"Dr. Buckley...Sandra...what happen—" Elara was cut off.

"Elara, please leave. There is nothing more I can do for you. There is nothing more I can do for any of you burn victims." The doctor said, glancing everywhere but at Elara.

"But, Doctor...!" Elara tried to object.

"Leave! Now! And don't come back! I'm sorry! Just...I'm sorry." The doctor said as she closed the door in Elara's face, tears trickling down both their faces.

3

Elara was furious with the doctor, first, and then with the men who were there just before her.

"They must be Ajaxx's men, sent to intimidate Dr. Buckley so she'd stop helping us. Coward. He fears retribution." Elara thought scathingly. Elara's rage was fed by a newfound hopelessness—she no longer had any means of helping her hands heal. And, no hands meant no revenge. Elara paced around, anger overwhelming any sense of purpose she may have had. She heard women of the Sparrows crying as she marched town furiously. They, too, had their care discontinued. Some of these women had horrid burns on their faces which threatened more than their self-image—it threatened their sight and their lives. Eventually, Elara's random walk brought her to a tavern. She had gone a few days without food and hunger had finally pushed her rage aside for a moment. Elara sucked up her pride and entered. She would beg for scraps.

Naturally, the tavern was loud and boisterous. Elara walked up to the proprietor and begged her for some food. The proprietor, a stern looking and spectacled woman, said she would bring her out some food but that Elara was to take it and leave. Naturally, Elara agreed, though internally hurt she was already being treated as subhuman. Elara waited for the owner to return and, to pass the time, was inspecting the cutlery that had been laid out for washing. Elara was tempted to steal the cutlery and peddle it for food, but her conscience would not let her. Elara refused to steal from someone kind enough to feed her, even if it would be her end otherwise. The woman returned with a plate of scraps. It was a generous portion, though. The woman handed Elara the plate and asked her to return the plate in the morning, when all the patrons were gone, and then walked away. Elara had difficulty holding the plate and set it down for just a moment to get a cloth to wrap the plate in so that she might carry it with just her good hand. Elara looked down to untie the hip scarf given to her by Petil and, reluctantly, use it to carry her meal.

Crash. The sound of a plate slamming to the ground. Elara could see her meal now splattered on the floor. She slowly raised her head to see two figures standing near her, laughing and facing away.

They were the men from the doctor's office.

Elara's fury reached a head and her reason gave way to instinct. Elara grabbed a knife from the pile of nearby cutlery and gripped the handle so hard she began to bleed fresh. She raised her arm with intent and...

With a flash of red, Elara was suddenly pulled away, out of the tavern, forcefully.

Elara struggled and squirmed, eventually shaking off whatever had removed her. She felt her assailant fall to the ground. It was Bennu. She had stopped Elara.

"Come Elara. Let us return to the cellar of The Roost. I have a meal for you there."

Elara fell to her knees and let the tension, the knife, blood, and tears leave her.

4

Bennu led Elara back to The Drifter's Roost and into the Sparrow's hideout. It was the only place left undiscovered and undamaged by Ajaxx's men. Bennu provided Elara a modest meal, explaining that they had been using all their assets to try and care for those affected by the incident. They were struggling to get care for the most severely injured girls who were kept at the hideout for safety.

"All of a sudden, the few doctors left in this town started to refuse to see us." Bennu explained.

After her meal and Bennu's explanation, Elara stared at her and asked Bennu a question, sternly and resolutely.

"So. When is it?"

"I don't know what you mean, Elara." Bennu replied, a bit confused.

"Our revenge plans. When are we getting revenge?" Elara nearly shouted.

Bennu looked at Elara seriously. "There will be no revenge. The Madame is gone. Others have fled or are dead. We have people to care for here. That is how we will use our limited resources."

"But!" Elara objected

"No buts! You almost threw your life away there in the tavern. I know it hurts, but you've let the hurt change you. Who have you become, Elara? Look at yourself!"

Elara furrowed her brow and was about to scream in protest, but caught a glance of herself in the reflection of a goblet. She saw herself and trembled.

"Bennu…" Elara managed. "Please… help me?"

5

Life changed slowly for Elara. Bennu and the other remaining Sparrows helped each other. Elara was no exception. If nothing else, Elara had a place to eat and lay her head to rest. Still, she could barely use her hands to do anything and was plagued by a sense of worthlessness exaggerated further by the knowledge that the Sparrows' resources were quite finite. Moreover, it was not as if Bennu had given Elara a magic remedy to get over her obsession with revenge. Elara could still feel the festering hatred for Ajaxx and his men stewing within her. It was incredibly difficult for Elara to go even an hour without thinking cruel thoughts about the man. After all, the pain of her hands as she struggled to do anything was a constant reminder. Bennu had simply pulled Elara back from the brink.

On particularly bad nights, Elara would find herself walking the beach, kicking the sand as hard as she could sporadically along the way. She glued her eyes to the floor and kicked and kicked and kicked until she could kick no more. Never had Elara felt such anger and never, even under the thumb of her divine fate, did she feel like such a victim. Days passed in this way, with Elara barely scraping by.

Then, things changed.

If you asked her, she couldn't tell you what happened or why. Just that, one night, she stopped looking out to the waves or down at the sand. She looked upwards, at the stars, as she used to do. And they made her feel ok.

"Sometimes, it's better not to question it." Elara thought, perplexed by her own calm. As she stared at the stars, though, she came to a revelation that was so obvious and yet so obscured to her.

"The stars look different here! The constellations are a bit off and nothing is quite where it should be!" Elara realized, mouth agape as she scanned the heavens above her.

"I had heard that the cycle of the stars was different in faraway places. I can't believe I didn't notice it sooner."

Elara managed a small smile for the first time in a long while.

"I really have made it far."

6

With a new handle on her life, Elara tried her best to do anything she could to support herself and the Sparrows. Even though they had a small reservoir of money and goods, Elara wanted to make what they had last as long as she could. So, she started off begging. She panhandled on the streets in the day. The town's generosity had certainly diminished in the recent months, but anything she could manage could be a meal or new dressings for one of the injured Sparrows. At night, however, Elara focused on her own recovery. Using parchment and ink scavenged from the disaster that was Madame Cantabelle's office, Elara had been trying to chart the stars above her. It hurt to write and it was hard to steady herself. The first two nights Elara attempted this, she, unimaginably frustrated, threw the materials and swore at the very skies she hoped to catalog. With time, though, she improved and developed the patience to deal with her new handicap, which got a little better each day she charted.

At one point, about a week and a half into her new routine, she began to ache for proper purpose—for a job that could allow her to more effectively help both the Sparrows and herself. Inspiration came with a glance at her hip scarf. Her hands had not yet recovered to do any labour, sure, but she could try and be like the graceful Petil. So, rather than simply panhandle, Elara became a street performer. She danced. She hardly made more than as a beggar, at first. But her pittance slowly grew as her dancing did. Elara found this incredibly satisfying. Even if she wasn't making a lot, the fact that her effort and improvement yielded tangible growth in the amount she brought home each day was motivating. Eventually, some other street performers—musicians—asked her to dance to their music and that they'd split the money. Their small little troupe, called the Sagehens and led by a fellow named Cecil, didn't explode in popularity. But they had garnered enough attention to be allowed to perform at a few local taverns a few times a week.

One night, after working on her charts, which, she admitted, were rough imitations of the ones from her book, Elara stood tall and proud on the beach. Her hands ached as she opened and closed them, but she was grateful for that ache because her hands moved. She began humming and dancing about the beach until her legs were worn from the weight of sand. She let herself fall to the sand and giggled as she looked back up at the stars. In this crusty and corrupt town, with her damaged heart and hands, Elara had managed to create, from only the sound of music and the feel of pen on paper, just a little bit of happiness.

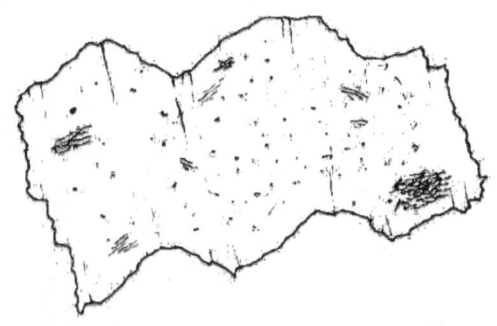

7

Of course, even though Elara had forged some happiness and peace in Rumi, despite all that had happened, she was faced still with lingering problems, both internal and external. Her awareness of these issues came to a head one fateful evening while the Sagehens performed at a tavern on the edge of town. There was no stage in this dusty and rough tavern, just a little bit of cleared space for their simple and honest performance. Elara and the Sagehens didn't command the attention of the whole building, but nor were they entirely ignored. Those who looked closely saw the faint beauty of artistic expression in the dim corner and saw themselves in it. Some just enjoyed the sound of music over a hard drink at the end of a long day. Others still were indifferent, the music and dance simply a backdrop in their lives as they chatted with others or thought about the happenings of the day.

When Elara and the Sagehens finished their performance, the last call for drinks was announced. The remaining patrons were already nice and buzzed, if not outright drunk and rowdy. As Elara headed to the exit, no desire to spend a moment longer in the musk of excess, she overheard the Madame's name. At the corner of the bar were some rough gentlemen, known goons working for Ajaxx. One of the three men was notably drunk.

"I tell ya, I couldn't stand working up in 'dem towers. I know the boss pays ya better if you hang about there, but it is sooooo boring. A total sausage fest, ya catch me? The only woman there not to entertain 'da boss is off limits. Not that it matters—she's more beast than woman anyways. That 'Madame' wasn't much to look at to start, let alone now that she's stewed in her own piss for months. So, when even she started to look good, I knew I needed to get back here and get my hands on some of the goods." The drunk continued rambling and rambling. His two compatriots half-heartedly tried to get him to cease, though they seemed more annoyed at the man's persistent rambling than they were of him spilling secrets.

Elara was filled with intense and passionate feelings once more.

"Those scumbags don't even care if they're found out. They know they've already gotten away with it! I can't stand how they're corroding this town. Moreover, they're holding Madame Cantabelle at the old castle? To what end?" Elara hurried from the tavern to the shore, as she feared that she would let hate and revenge seep into her heart once more and consume her—bring her back to the brink of losing herself, who she had just barely put back together. Elara looked to the stars, exhausted from her work. The feelings did not fade, but morphed. Elara recollected the time she first met the Madame and how her presence was so heavy, yet motherly. The urge for revenge was transfigured, now replaced by the urge to hear that woman dote and prattle on once more. Elara resolved herself to action once more: this time out of love, not hatred.

For all her desire to rescue the Madame, Elara had to admit to herself that she didn't really have a plan, really, or even know how to go about making one.

"If only I had some more information. Like how many people were in the castle, or even what it looked like."

In a moment of clarity, Elara decided not to try and shoulder this alone. She would trust the Sparrows once more, even if the reminder of failure yet ached fresh on her palms.

"Bennu is my best bet, I will share with her my intent."

9

Bennu met Elara warmly, though she was caught off guard by Elara's earnest and straightforward explanation of the Madame's whereabouts and her desire to rescue her. Bennu set down the papers she was holding—she had been attempting to reestablish trade and commerce with the Madame's old business partners, but with no success. She wasn't even receiving proper responses in return. Just silence.

"I am happy to hear that the Madame is alive and well. I feared the worst for her. Perhaps it would be more fruitful to try and recover her than to send messages to these ghosts of merchants. I take it you came to me for a plan then, Elara?"

Elara nodded.

"Well, I am just as clueless as you. But I can fix that. If we want to rescue the Madame, I suppose we need to know at least two things: How many people Ajaxx has in that monster's castle and how that castle is laid out. That is where we start." Bennu informed Elara.

"I am small, agile and experienced, Elara. I will go to the tower and I will try and ascertain the number of inhabitants by the coming and going of men and supplies. I leave the matter of learning the structure of the castle to you. I know that the town council sent architects to map out the castle after Ojasa was driven from it. Records such as those are kept in the city planning section of the town's library." spouted Bennu.

Again, Elara nodded.

"Lastly, let us meet back here in a week, at midnight. If I have not returned by that morning, assume me captured or killed. I entrust the girls to you in the meantime." Bennu finished.

They had a plan.

10

The very day Bennu left to begin her reconnaissance, Elara went to the town's library. She would not be allowed to leave the building with the structural investigation, as that privilege was reserved only for officials, but Elara brought supplies to copy the document the best she could. She wouldn't want to take the plans from the building, anyways, lest she alert Ajaxx to her scheme. Elara spent the first day simply acquainting herself with the building and its organization. It was surprisingly large and well-maintained, especially considering Ajaxx was now effectively the leader of this port-city.

When Elara returned the next day, however, she was shocked and livid to find no such records on file. In fact, many of the documents seemed to be missing. In addition to the castle, the layout of the docks, the city hall, and even the Drifter's Roost were all inexplicably absent. Elara asked the librarian if any of those materials had been checked out. The librarian checked and responded that the materials were not checked out and Elara must be looking in the wrong places. Elara checked and scoured the entire building looking for her goal, but it was nowhere to be found. Although dejected, she vowed to look again the next day, if not for the plans themselves, then anything that could be of use to her.

When Elara returned the third day, the materials were, again, nowhere to be found.

"Ajaxx must have worried about something like this and covered his own arse. He may be a crooked man but, just as the Madame said, he is as clever as a fox."

Unsure of how to proceed, Elara wandered the library, simply enjoying it for what it was for the first time since she arrived. She stumbled upon a section of folk-lore: History of Rumi and its citizens contained in some tomes and volumes. Intrigued, Elara began to read from the books. It was hard to tell how much of what was contained in these books was truth and how much was parables. Elara's interest was piqued when she discovered the tale that the storyteller Koza had told her was recounted in one of the dusty tomes, though in vivid detail. And it was in this book, Elara found what she was looking for. The was not made by Ojasa. He was just a single man after all. Just like Ajaxx, he had happened upon it and abused it for his own gain. The castle was the defunct castle of the royalty from the time of the wolf-princess of Sanai. The location of the castle had been perfect for defending against siege and the like, but was largely abandoned when the country of Vasilios was unified. There was no more need for the upkeep of such a structure, no royalty to inhabit it, and it was inconveniently far away from the shore for the leadership of a port-town to occupy. It made perfect sense to Elara. She unearthed, in these worn relics of the past, a schematic of the castle as it was when Rumi was a part of the kingdom of Sanai.

Elara set to work copying what she would need. Somehow, the ache of her hands was unusually dull and her pen-strokes quick and precise. She smiled, a silent celebration of her first victory over Ajaxx, and returned the book to its proper home.

Elisabeth and the Troll

1

After discovering the nature of the plague weighing on the minds of the Smithton residents, Ivivin had fallen back into the routine he and Smith had worked out. Each morning, he'd wake and tend to the forge, servicing as many people as he could in the morning. At noontime, he'd switch gears and experiment with armour making techniques and try to design what he wanted his armour to be. After supper, Ivivin would take Icarus on a stroll, trying to show the owl as many new places as he could each day, and return to the forge by sundown. He'd sit and write a short reflection on the day's happenings, often in the form of letters. He had jokingly addressed each one to Icarus.

"Imagine if anyone found these!" Ivivin thought, snickering. *"They'd think me a loon!"*

And, at the end of each night, Ivivin would approach Grandia's book. It was dense, but at a level Ivivin could read if he really focused. That meant his progress each night was limited. Ivivin had also decided he would surprise Smith when he returned. Ivivin could only imagine how important this book was to Smith and how devastated he'd be if anything happened to it. So Ivivin had begun copying the book in its entirety. Ivivin often had to read pages several times before he fully grasped the contents anyway, so taking the time to transpose each page really didn't slow him down terribly. If anything, it helped him focus.

Each night, Ivivin would think to himself *"Smith will be so happy when he gets back. He can take this copy with him next time he ventures out of Smithton! It won't be as good as the real thing, but, still!"*

Of course, all this spoke to the routine Ivivin followed each day. But the book and its contents deeply moved Ivivin, captivating his attention each and every night. Grandia's writing reflected well her life as a traveler. Ivivin certainly was not well-read, nor was he a critic of books, but, to him, Grandia's most captivating passages were surely her immaculate, yet artful descriptions of surroundings—be they out in nature or in the dwellings of man. Indeed, she would often spend pages detailing the environment of the protagonist, a travelling young woman named Elisabeth. Each setting was described in such detail that Ivivin could see it clearly in his mind's eye. She could make each riverbank, each dusty tavern, and each sunset seem unique and vivid. The story itself was captivating, too. From what Ivivin could tell, this was an account of the young woman's life and her travels. It started off in her home village, where (much to Ivivin's excitement) she worked as a farmer. From the very first sentence on the very first page, Ivivin fell prey to this lexical spell of Grandia's vision.

2

One day, while tending the land, Elisabeth spotted a figure in a far-off field of jonquils to the south. Intrigued and, admittedly, bored, she went to investigate the figure. There, in the field, amoungst all the petite yellow flowers, stood a rough and rugged troll, disheveled from head to toe. It took a while for the strange troll to notice the young woman—it was too engrossed with the sea of flowers that surrounded it. When it finally broke free of the flowery hypnosis, the troll was startled by the Elisabeth's presence. Its peaceful lumber was replaced by a frantic looking-about before it vanished into thin air.

Curious and bewildered, Elisabeth asked the people of her village about the bemusing creature. She was told many a frightening tale about the troll, who had been seen all over the countryside. Rather than be frightened by the tales, though, Elisabeth was inspired by it. If such creatures truly existed, imagine what else lay out there in the world, just waiting to be discovered! How truly grand the world must be! Her interaction with the troll had given the young farmer an uncontrollable and incurable case of wanderlust.

Stricken by this once-dormant urge to travel and see the world, Elisabeth began preparing for her journey, little by little. She had no idea where she would go or how best to get there. She often drew inspiration from the troll, wondering where it had been, what it had seen, and the things it had experienced. She began spending her spare time wandering the field of flowers where she had first seen the troll, both to indulge in the floral paradise and in hopes of glimpsing the troll once more. She continued preparing day after day, bit by bit, always making time to wander the field of flowers to envision ever more fantastic adventures.

Finally, the day came. She was to leave her home this day to see the world and test herself. She still hadn't a destination in mind, but, as fall would soon be upon the land, south, towards warmth, would be her best bet. She figured that one last trip to the flowers was in order as, even if she stayed, they would likely wilt in just a few short weeks.

Rather than pace about the flowers, imagining her grand adventure, Elisabeth was struck by the revelation that, this time, she was actually setting out for her dreams. She set down her gear and frolicked about, indulging in one final trivial act before she began her adventure proper. Tired and breathing heavily, she let herself fall into the sea of flowers. Elisabeth laid there, staring at clouds as they passed by. She began to doze, but jolted awake upon hearing footsteps. She burst to her feet and clutched her gear, expecting bandits or vagabonds come to pillage her supplies. Instead, it was the troll, again looking at the patch of jonquils. Moreover, it seemed to be trimming and weeding the surrounding plain. Elisabeth approached the troll from behind, wanting to get a close look at the figure, who was easily a few heads larger than her. Elisabeth got close enough to see the troll's back, which bore scars from both burns and lashes. She also thought she could hear the strange being hum, if coarsely. She reached out, entranced by the markings and song in equal measure, and touched the oddity. Startled, the troll swung around, nearly taking off Elisabeth's head with its arm in the process. It, again, looked panicked. Elisabeth tried to calm the upset troll, reaching out to touch it reassuringly. When she touched him, though, she felt herself whisked away in the strangest whirlwind of colour and scent.

4

Elisabeth could hear something strange. A strange rumbling and pounding, rhythmic in its action, with crashes coming at regular intervals. The air was somehow heavy and she could feel the salt of sweat on her skin despite her laze. Elisabeth opened her eyes and found herself in again in a patch of flowers, but not the large field of jonquils by her farmland. Instead, she was surrounded by sunflowers, small and large. Elisabeth climbed slowly and cautiously to her feet.

Water.

Elisabeth faced the shimmering waves of this unfathomably colossal body, mouth agape and very much confused. Elisabeth managed to break her gaze from the majesty of the sea to examine her surroundings. As confused as she was, she couldn't help but absorb the beauty of the landscape to which she had been spirited away. There was a small community not far from here. It wasn't exactly how Elisabeth expected to start her adventure, but she couldn't help but be giddy that it started with such a mystery. Excited, Elisabeth made her way to the nearby settlement.

5

The village and its people were incredibly kind to Elisabeth, but she was likely an unusual case. As Elisabeth had learned from the denizens of this quaint fishing village named Bien Hoa, she wasn't just whisked away to the seaside. Rather, Elisabeth had found herself on an island, surrounded by water. The villagers were intrigued by Elisabeth and entertained her story seriously, as neither of the two boatmen who crossed the waters regularly to sell the island's goods had ever seen her, let alone ferry her across the vast blue. Add to that preexisting rumours about a strange figure having been seen on the island, vanishing just as quickly as it came, and the villagers were surprisingly willing to believe her.

And so, Elisabeth started her adventure, here on this island. She felt no rush to hurry back to the mainland and earned her keep on the island by learning to fish and helping with odd jobs as needed. The pace of island life was slow and steady, allowing Elisabeth plenty of time to explore the small island and get to know its every nook and cranny. The young woman took great pleasure in leisurely strolls and was often caught staring at scenery, as if she was trying to capture its most base essence in her mind's eye.

Eventually, Elisabeth decided she would leave the island and continue to see the world. The day she was to board a small vessel and head to the mainland, the village had planned a small banquet to celebrate her having dropped into their lives. They insisted that Elisabeth need not help prepare, so she gathered her things and went for one last walk around the island, stopping again at the patch of sunflowers she had awoken upon her first day. Just over the top of the flowers, she could make out a lopsided and fleshy orb dusted with unkempt and stringy hairs. She recognized it as the troll who frequented the jonquils. Though he was anything but approachable, Elisabeth approached the troll. The troll jumped and was knocked off balance by its own surprise. It went to great lengths to avoid falling on and crushing the flowers. This resulted in the clumsiest of movements that Elisabeth had ever seen. She could not fight the urge to laugh at the troll's misfortune. This sound of laughter struck the troll hard. It had been many years since he had heard it. Rather than run away once more, the troll rose and laughed along with Elisabeth.

When the chuckles died down, Elisabeth knew it was time to return to the village for the banquet. She gestured for the troll to follow along, telling him there would be plenty of food and friendly faces. The troll's smile faded as he shook his head and began to retreat to the center of the sunflowers. Elisabeth quickly followed, grabbing the troll's swollen arm in an attempt to persuade it to join. At this distance, Elisabeth could see clearly the reason for the troll's resistance. Scars adorned the trolls body, head to toe. Elisabeth knew not the history of this troll, but the scars were numerous and obviously from varied sources and distinct events. Burns and lashes and lacerations were stories told by the skin of this florally inclined troll.

The troll could see the sudden and pointed pity in Elisabeth's eyes and allowed himself to soften once more. The troll reached down, picked a small sunflower, and put it in the hair of the woman who ached at the sight of his pain. Elisabeth remained there woebegone, pensive and still. The troll, preferring the laugh and smile of the gentle flower in front of him, picked a second, much larger sunflower. He stuck it behind his own ear and made a face at

Elisabeth, who, even in her empathetic trance, could not refrain from giggling at the absurd figure in front of her.

"You're less like a troll and more like the old men in Bien Hoa!" Elisabeth managed between chuckles. "Do you have a name?" Elisabeth inquired, wiping the tears of excess laughter from her eyes.

The troll shook his head.

"Then I will call you Oldman. My name is Elisabeth. Nice to meet you." Elisabeth said, extending her hand expectantly.

The troll nodded once more, shook hands with Elisabeth, and smiled a goofy smile as it returned to the center of the flowers and vanished

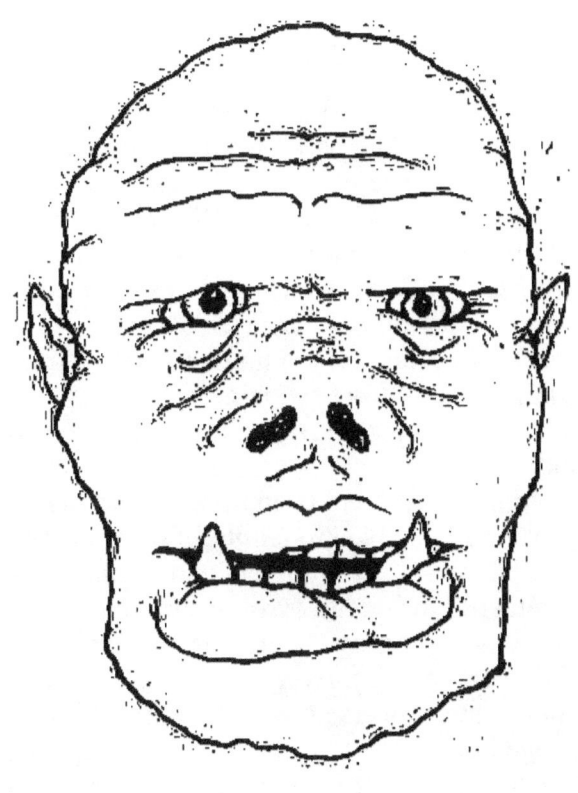

6

Elisabeth continued her adventure to see the world. The sunflower given to her by Oldman was still neatly tucked in her hair, somehow succumbing rot. While traveling itself certainly wasn't quite exciting as she had expected, she appreciated every moment and every step. Elisabeth would walk from town to town, doing whatever she needed to get by. She struggled, for a time, though. She met so many incredible people on her journey that were so talented, but she felt she lacked a such vocation or calling. She wanted to somehow share a piece of her and her travels with those she encountered along the way. She yearned for expression and attempted to learn from those she encountered.

First was the musician, who helped Elisabeth realized she couldn't carry a tune nor hold a beat. Next was the dancer, who complimented Elisabeth on the force of her stomp. The woodworker who lauded how quickly she recovered from cuts. The sculptor reassured her that her vase didn't need to hold water to be pretty. The calligrapher acknowledged the uniqueness of her script. The poet reminded her that words could invoke feelings and that nausea was *technically* a feeling. The paper folder let Elisabeth know how lovely her scrunched up face was while focusing on her folds. The weaver was impressed by how much of Elisabeth's hair found its way into her loom. The glassblower claimed she had never seen glass broken into such unique shapes, and in such quantity no less! It was not until she met the oil painter Frida Morisot in a backwoods village at the base of a grand mountain that she found the medium for her expression. Elisabeth's first painting was the view of the sea from the patch of sunflowers on Bien Hao, reconstructed from the eye of her mind.

Armed with oils and paints and brushes and knives, Elisabeth resumed her journey. She loved to paint. Selling her works was both a way of sharing her voyage with others and of making sure she could support herself. During her travels, she saw many festivals and murals and people. And, during her travels, she would often stop at large fields of flowers to paint. Every so often, she'd run into Oldman, tending to the flowers as he always did. When fortune brought them together in this way, they'd never linger excessively, but simply enjoyed each other's company for a while. Indeed, Elisabeth had even made a habit of painting wonderful patches of flowers and leaving the work in the center for Oldman to stumble upon next time he fancied that field. The thought of the troll's goofy grin alone kept that habit alive and well for quite some time.

As Elisabeth's adventures continued, she came to realize how little of the world she had seen, despite her travels. Even more striking was the realization of how little of the world she would actually ever be able to see, no matter how hard she tried—it was simply too vast. While this did not deter Elisabeth on her travels, it was a little disheartening to think about all the places she was going to miss by no demerit of her own. Still, she loved her travels and the things she derived from them. Not a day passed that she regretted leaving home.

All good things, though, must come to an end and Elisabeth's journey came to an abrupt halt. While she was passing through a large, bustling city, she felt her legs become suddenly enfeebled. She would have difficulty standing, much less walking, during these now-recurrent fits. She visited physicians there in the city, hoping one of them could help. None of them could even identify what ailment was taking away her legs' strength, let alone help her manage her blight. They could only recommend she go home, wherever that may be, as it was likely she would soon lose her mobility entirely. The still-young woman was burdened by the weight of her condition and knew she could not make it to the farm she once called home. So, instead, Elisabeth left the city, hoping to find a peaceful patch of flowers to paint. She managed to make it to a smaller farm community, surrounded by lilies of varied colours. The trek had taken its toll on her, but she sat on a rock and painted nonetheless. She painted and painted and painted until her sadness was the blue of the sky, her anger the red of petals, and her confusion the hazy backdrop. She tried to stand to place the painting in the flowers, as she oft did, but was met with legs of lead that refused cooperation. Frustrated, Elisabeth tossed the painting into the flowers. She laid on the rock and resigned to her fate, that she might die amoung the beauty of the flowers. A peaceful sleep overtook her.

Of course, a single nap does not death make. Elisabeth inevitably woke. She tested her legs. They would bear her weight, but only just. She heard the nostalgic rustling of grass and flowers. In the middle of the flowers pranced Oldman the Troll, complete with his goofy grin, admiring the petite petals. Elisabeth whistled and waved to the troll, who returned the gesture. For the first time, though, Elisabeth gestured for the troll to join her as she resumed her seat on the rock. The troll, surprised by this novel scenario, lumbered over cautiously.

"Oldman..." Elisabeth weakly started "I have a favour to ask of you."

8

Elisabeth dusted off the old lantern in her old farm house and laid upon her old bed. Over the years she was gone, no one had meddled with her things— a welcome surprise. Though once quite restrictive and suffocating, home held a new level of comfort and familiarity after her travels. It was cozy and safe. She would not need to manage anything more than what she needed to eat and stay warm for the winters. She could survive here and even be happy.

She could be happy here at home.

Elisabeth smiled weakly, holding the wall as she made her way to her bed. As she passed her window, she looked out the window and saw the grand patch of jonquils nearby. She paused, her smile inverted as her eyes welled up. The illusion she had tried to conjure and convince herself of gave way. Tears poured ceaselessly down her face. Elisabeth's heart roared:

"I want to see the world!"

9

The next day, Elisabeth sat in front of her home to paint the jonquils from a distance. It was a struggle that took her a frustrating amount of time. As she brooded and painted, she was surprised to see Oldman appear. He seldom visited the same flower patch in such quick succession. Her surprise only intensified when she realized the troll was headed straight for her home. As Oldman approached, Elisabeth began to drown in thoughts of her own worthlessness, upset she could no longer keep pace with the globetrotting troll. Oldman stood in front of Elisabeth, who would not meet his eyes. Instead, her turned head allowed the sunflower in her to meet the troll's gaze. Oldman reached out his hand, like Elisabeth had once done for him amidst the field of sunflowers. Elisabeth did not let her hand know his. Dejected, the troll did what any reasonable and sapient creature would do—he scooped her up in his arms and carried her to the patch of jonquils. Once there, he spirited them somewhere she had never been before. He brought her to a bed of irises beside a tall and mighty lighthouse. And, at the sun's slumber, he brought her back home to the field of jonquils.

Oldman would do this each and every day with Elisabeth, until it became a ritual. He would come in the morning from the field of jonquils, scoop her up, and be her legs as they travelled to far-off and exotic lands. Day after day, they saw the sunrise over new mountains and the sunset over new waters. Deserts and creeks and plateaus and archipelagos reflected in their eyes. If they found a place particularly lovely, they would return. On occasion, when Elisabeth was feeling well, Oldman would take her to the edge of a town before the townsfolk woke and leave her there to socialize. More and more often, Elisabeth would try and get the troll to stay with her, thinking that her presence would assure people he was no danger or threat. But each and every time, Oldman shook his head, waved, and left before anyone could see him.

Elisabeth thought that people would understand if they just spent a little time around Oldman—after all, a troll who picks and admires the flowers is hardly a troll at all. The issue was clear to Elisabeth, though. Oldman had come to see himself as horrid and putrid and ugly and unnatural and undeserving of life, just as those who had wounded him in the past. They had left scars on his body, but they were dull in comparison to the ones left on his soul. Elisabeth could not help but notice that Oldman only really smiled to reassure her. It saddened her immensely that she could not bring joy to his day in quite the same way as he did hers.

Their days continued in this manner for years and years. Though the sunflower residing in it was as fresh as the day Oldman picked it, Elisabeth's hair had greyed. Her legs were no longer the only feeble thing about her. Her skin was wrinkled and discoloured (though Elisabeth wore this as a badge of honour—a record of the hours and hours she spent in nature). Her eyesight had worsened, but she turned the blurriness of her sight into an artistic style incorporated seamlessly into her paintings. Age had certainly changed her, but Elisabeth liked to think she aged gracefully. Oldman didn't seem to age at all—at least, as far as Elisabeth could tell. Despite her age and disability, Elisabeth and Oldman yet ventured out into the world each and every day.

Time passes and changes everything, regardless of its merit and beauty. Wondrous spectacles and locales known to Elisabeth in her youth had become uncomely or even outright unattractive, while wastelands, given time and care, had metamorphosed into near paradise. People are no exception to the incessant march of time. Elisabeth could handle the rigours of the world less and less each day, so the pair departed from and returned earlier to Elisabeth's home each day.

One day, in early autumn, Elisabeth woke and awaited Oldman's arrival, as was their ceremony. She saw in the reflection of her window, a sunflower in the hair of an old woman, as was the truth of these days. But today, nearly a lifetime after it was plucked, the ancient flower had begun to wilt. She sighed deeply and patiently waited for Oldman to come. And, as always, he rapped gently on the door before letting himself in. When he saw Elisabeth sitting in bed with the wilting sunflower in her hair, his eyes moistened and the blood rushed from his face. Trembling, Oldman picked up Elisabeth, who, as she always did, met him with a gentle smile. Usually, Oldman would whisk them away to somewhere Elisabeth had never been—she never did figure out if there was a pattern to his fancy. But today, as they started towards the jonquils, Elisabeth made a request.

"Oldman..." Elisabeth called out to her silent chariot. "You've been to my home many, many times, but I have never gone to yours. Could you bring me to the place you go each night? The place you call home?"

Oldman stopped. He hesitated for a minute or two before striding out to the middle of the flowers. And, just as always, a whirlwind of colour and fragrance swept them away. Elisabeth took note of her surroundings. They were near an ocean or sea—the smell and feel of salt in the air was almost overwhelming. But they were not at a sandy shore. Rather, this was a rocky cove. The flowers that brought them here, cosmos from the looks of it, were planted in barrels strewn about. On one end of the cove was a tall cliffside looming overhead. At its base was a cave, separated from the main inlet by a gauntlet of sharp and slippery stone. All but the most hardened of human adventurers would experience great difficulty in reaching the opening. But Oldman carried Elisabeth through the rocks expertly, as though thoroughly and properly rehearsed. A few minutes later, Elisabeth found herself at the mouth of the coastal cave Oldman called home.

11

The entrance of the cave was like many others she had seen. The ocean had made the stone chill as ice and she shivered slightly. As they voyaged deeper into the cave, though, warm resumed the air. Elisabeth could see small bursts of water bubbling from the ground, steaming. These little geysers heated the interior to a cozy temperature. A little further in, Oldman's residence came properly into view. The first thing she noticed was that Oldman had a bed, though it looked rather shabby and worn. She had never supposed to ask how he slept. What ultimately caught her eye and took her breath from her was the wall opposite Oldman's bed.

In this drab cave of greys, this wall was colour.

Every single painting of flowers Elisabeth had ever left for Oldman was on full display. Vibrant colours from literal decades past were preserved and mounted on this mural to Elisabeth's work. Hot tears streamed down her face as the magnitude of her life's journey and the expression of her soul was laid bare before her, framed whole in a perspective she could never have imagined.

Elisabeth's sunflower drooped further under its own weight.

12

Weary from sudden and overwhelming burst of emotion, Elisabeth rested awhile in Oldman's abode, napping in the face of years of her work. When she found the strength to carry on, Oldman scooped up the feather of a woman. The troll's arms quivered though bearing her weight was easier than it had ever been before. They headed back towards the potted flowers. Elisabeth figured that she could make another request of Oldman—after all, he didn't ever really seem to have a preference.

"Oldman, can you take us to the place where I first gave you your name? Bien Hao: the shore with the sunflowers?"

Oldman obliged and, in less than an instant, they found themselves in a nostalgic field of sunflowers. Oldman set Elisabeth on top of the small bump of a hill, from which both the sea of water and the sea of sunflowers were visible.

"Oldman, I know it has been a while, but I'd like to paint today. Could I bother you to fetch me my tools? You know the case well by now, I'm sure. I'd appreciate it. Oh, and no peeking inside, ok?" Elisabeth gently teased the giant.

Oldman was gone only minutes and returned before the sun had even reached noon overhead. He gingerly handed Elisabeth her painting supplies, neatly packed in a well-worn leather bag. And so, just as they used to, Elisabeth painted while Oldman tended and admired the flowers, though the troll stole more glances at her than he ever had in the past. The foot of the sun was barely touching the horizon when Elisabeth finished her painting. She wrapped it gingerly in a plain grey cloth and held it to her chest as she weakly called for Oldman, who nearly sprinted to her side.

"It's time. Shall we, my Oldman?" Elisabeth spoke, no louder than a whisper.

13

Elisabeth and Oldman found themselves amidst the jonquils of her home once more. Oldman barely took a step toward her home before Elisabeth objected.

"Here is fine, Oldman. It's where my adventure truly began. I'd like it to end here, too."

Indescribable is the face of someone forced to accept a harsh and terrible truth delivered to them by one held fondly in their heart. The troll stared at the fragile woman in his arms with a truly pained expression.

"Don't look at me in that way, Oldman. We both knew today was coming. Honestly, it is much, much later than I thought it would come to pass. I blame that on you." Elisabeth cackled a bit at her own joke.

"Anyways, I have a gift for you, so you should smile. It isn't every day a beautiful young flower like myself gives away something so precious. Lean me against that stone over there so I can watch you open it, if you would."

Oldman glanced at the sunflower in her hair. It had nearly withered away entirely. Trembling once more, he obeyed and leaned the brittle flower against the stone. He took the cloth-wrapped painting into his unsteady hands. Slowly, Oldman undid the binding and gazed upon the painting by the light of sunset.

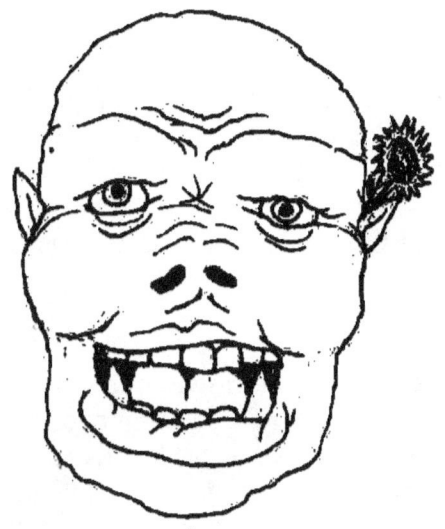

It was a painting of him, adorned with a flower behind his ear. His features, his scars, and, frankly, his ugliness were all represented flawlessly in the painting. But Elisabeth had somehow made Oldman beautiful, despite all of it. There was an aura of peace and kindness that exuded from his portrait. The troll seemed approachable and gentle, for all his faults and wounds. Perhaps most strikingly of all, this representation of Oldman was smiling a true and sincere smile from the very bottom of his heart. Oldman turned the painting around and saw, scrawled on the interior of the canvas, a note from Elisabeth.

I'm not sure if you can read or not, my Oldman. I suppose I never bothered to ask. Sorry about that. But I have a feeling my words will still reach you whatever the case. Regardless, this painting is for you, my flower picking troll. It is my dearest wish that you come to see yourself as I have come to see you. Thank you.

~E~

An unexpected gust blew past the troll, who then tore his eyes from the gift to check on Elisabeth. She was gone, vanished, nowhere to be seen. Where she last settled there was now a large sunflower: tall, proud, and vibrant. Next to it lay Elisabeth's painting tools, packed neatly away in her bag. After loosing literal puddles from his eyes, Oldman grabbed the supplies and sat in front of the sunflower a while. Eventually, the troll returned the bag and its contents to her home. He returned to the lone sunflower, which stood far above all the jonquils. It was even far taller than Elisabeth had been, but it still only reached to Oldman's chest. He patted the top of sunflower lovingly, Elisabeth's final painting tucked gingerly under his arm. And then, just as suddenly as he had stumbled his way into Elisabeth's life, he was gone.

On a rock near a lone sunflower in a sea of jonquils, they say there is a mural of sorts—the only painting ever done by a troll. Though it looks like the work of a child, there is charm in its roughness. On this stone, in paint that never fades, reposes a young woman with a sunflower in her hair, a brilliant smile, and a hand outreached.

14

It had taken Ivivin quite some time to finish reading Grandia's book. However, he related greatly to the story of this adventurous woman and all his waking free time was spent reading and transcribing it. Finally, he had reached the conclusion—the passing of Elisabeth. The last page, which detailed her passing and Oldman the troll's monument, was clearly written by a different person. He recalled that Smith had scribed the last of the book for Grandia on her deathbed. Smith's script was noticeably shakier and more uneven than on any of the documents Ivivin had ever handled from him—a clear reflection of his state of mind. Ivivin turned the last page and encountered Smith's handwriting on the binding on the book once more. In stark contrast to the conclusion, these words were written as resolutely and firmly as usual.

The source of the unnatural plague lies in Giganta Valley.

Ivivin stared at the note, trying to discern it's meaning. It slowly dawned on Ivivin. Smith hadn't left on vacation. He had gone to try put an end to Crumbleheart.

"One week." Ivivin said to himself. "I'll finish my armour in just one week. Then I shall give him chase."

Operation Big Bird

1

Bennu returned from her reconnaissance mission at Ajaxx's tower without complication—she was an expert, after all. She met Elara to discuss their plan to free the Madame, a mission they lovingly called 'Operation Big Bird'.

"There are somewhere between twenty-five and forty of Ajaxx's goons staying at their stronghold at any given time. It sounds like a lot, but given that the whole of the castle is much larger than the small area Ojasa had occupied, they are pretty spread out. It certainly won't be easy to infiltrate undetected, but not as impossible or impenetrable as I had thought." Bennu told Elara while examining the castle's plans from the old book of lore.

"So..." Elara started. "Any idea of how we can get in and find the Madame?"

Bennu smiled slyly.

"Yeah. You see, the grunts at the castle have a taste for women—one they have a hard time satisfying way out there. A few local women have taken to making the journey out there and keeping them company, for a steep price."

It took Elara a moment to realize to what Bennu was alluding. Once understanding finally crept to Elara's face, Bennu continued.

"If we want in, that's our best bet. A little of the art of seduction—an act of sorts to be granted entrance." Bennu proposed.

Elara had never once looked down on those who traded in sexual acts. In fact, many of the Sparrows were at one time willingly involved in that sort of business. Elara tried to imagine such a life and taking such actions for herself. It felt wrong for her, no matter the end for which it was the means.

"No, Bennu. I will think of another way."

Bennu shrugged.

"Let's hear it, then."

2

It took Elara the better part of an evening to decide on a plan she both felt could work and that she was at peace with. She pitched it to Bennu, who, while skeptical, decided to have faith in Elara's plan. There was not much required for the plan and they set themselves to work almost immediately. Each day they were more prepared and, with each day, they felt more and more like their plan could work. Confidence in herself and her abilities slowly returned to Elara.

When the day to enact Operation Big Bird arrived, Elara was a bit excited, despite the danger. Mobility on this day would be key, so she donned only thin leather armour. She armed herself with lancea and dagger. A few hours after the sun's down, the two made their way to Ajaxx's fortress, hopeful that their preparations would lead to their victory. After making their final adjustments, the duo acted.

3

Fire, as fierce as the one on the boat, erupted in the shrubbery around the castle. Bennu, hidden well behind a small boulder, banged all manners of drum and cymbal as loudly as she could muster. Between the smoke and the noise, some of Ajaxx's men arrived on the scene to investigate. Just as Elara had hoped, they did not wait for the men on the further ends of the castle to arrive before they stepped out into Elara's domain. It was not long before the first henchman fell to the floor, screaming in pain. He had stepped onto a modest sized leg trap. Elara had become familiar with these when trapping beavers and smaller deer in the north. Men who stumbled into these traps were likely to survive and keep their leg, but they would certainly be left in no condition to fight. They were the right size for the job at hand. The fire blazed along the frequented and familiar path, forcing Ajaxx's men to wander into less familiar terrain. Now warier of traps, they walked slowly and cautiously. The bright light of the fire made it hard for their strained eyes to focus on the shadows.

Elara waited for her opportunity and, when a goon wandered close enough, she charged him with the flat end of her lancea and knocked him into a cleverly planted pitfall. Bennu, small and agile as she was, focused on moving swiftly about the landscape and creating noise to manipulate the movement of the trickling flow of Ajaxx's henchmen. Between the hunting traps, pitfalls, and the element of surprise, they had incapacitated well over a dozen men in a matter of minutes. As the fire began to die down, though, Elara knew it was time to make the next move. When the brazen flames turned to smoldering cinder, she used the fresh blackness of night to enter the castle. She could hear Bennu retreating with the drums lower down the mountain, as they had planned. While Bennu was fast and full of guile, she would not be able to fight anyone if cornered. But Elara...

Elara could fight.

4

Elara quickly found a safe nook with vantage to take account of her surroundings and her person. She glanced quickly at her hands. She had only pushed a handful of unsuspecting goons into pitfalls, but already faint traces of blood could be seen through her bandages.

"I need to minimize my encounters." Elara noted, pulling out her map of the area for one final reference. Bennu had marked up the map with potential locations where Elara might find the Madame, along with ones she would be better off avoiding. She sighed and went on the move again.

"I am sure Ajaxx will have some body guards that never leave his person. I would do better to not bump into them." Elara thought as she headed to the dungeons. *"I suppose this makes sense—keep your prisoner in the prison, right?"*

As she approached the dungeon, she could hear two men talking to one another.

"This is good." Elara thought. *"Guards mean there is something here worth guarding!"*

Elara readied her polearm and her mind. She attempted to ambush the men, hoping to have caught them on the unaware. Unfortunately, they were more than just well-prepared—they had been waiting for her. One man sported a flail and the other a tremendous two-handed sword.

"This is bad!" Elara thought, just managing to avoid being struck by the menacing duo. *"Even if my hands were 100%, I don't think the lancea itself could handle a direct strike from these fellows."*

She reminded herself of the nearby structure of the castle and retreated as fast as she could to a nearby staircase. She would attempt to funnel the scoundrels and deal with them one at a time. Elara would have to create every advantage she could.

The pair followed her and found themselves single file, just as Elara had planned. What's more, Elara was further up the staircase, giving her lancea the advantage.

"It's over henchmen!" Elara yelled at the pair, hoping to deter them. "I have the high ground!"

Unfazed, the wielder of the broadsword wound up for a monstrous maneuver and yelled as loud as a bear does roar:

"You underestimate my power!"

Elara flinched, but held her ground. Just as Elara had hoped, the corridor was too narrow and the man's sword scraped along the walls, slowing the strike and allowing her to parry. With a few quick jabs to the shoulders, the man dropped his weapon, fell to his knees, and screamed in agony, as if set ablaze by the fire of betrayal. Elara deftly kicked the man in the chest, sending him tumbling into the flail wielder. Using the resultant and carefully synthesized turmoil, Elara charged the flail weirder and struck him, too, about the shoulders. Though her hands now dripped blood, she had managed to defeat two able fighters. Elara's confidence burgeoned once more as she made her way back to the dungeon. She searched all the cells and found…

Nothing.

The Madame was nowhere to be found, though from what Elara could tell, there was someone there recently.

"Damn." Elara thought. *"The sleaze played me and Bennu both for fools. He knew we'd look here first!"*

5

Elara hadn't anticipated Ajaxx to be prepared for such an invasion. She deliberated a while, trying to decide her next course of action.

"If he outsmarted Bennu then I don't think there is much use in following the predictions she laid out on my map. In fact…"

Elara was struck by an idea. She opened her sketched map and looked at it carefully.

"Maybe the best thing to do is the worst thing to do. I will go to where Bennu thought Ajaxx might reside—the very place she said I should avoid."

Elara bit her lip and decided to execute this risky gambit. She made her way towards Ajaxx's quarters, just barely managing to avoid detection by a few patrolling goons. She arrived at a large, heavy door. The wood was well finished, but looked ancient and was reinforced by fresh iron. Elara expected such a barricade to be locked tight but, to her surprise, it swung open with relative ease. It was dark, save a starving lantern in the corner in the room. Elara squinted and tried to focus on a large object slightly illuminated by the lantern. Her heart skipped and then fell when she realized it was the Madame.

Madame Cantabelle was, simply put, in bad shape. Her body was coated in cuts and bruises, though her face remained surprisingly untouched. Her large limbs were all bound together by heavy steel chains. A blindfold prevented the even minuscule bit of light of the room from entering her eyes. Her ears were covered by thick layers of fabric, muting her external environment and she herself was muted by a cloth gag. Elara creeped closer to the Madame. The closer she got, the more apparent it was that the Madame was malnourished. She was as gaunt as a woman of her stature could be and her skin was sickly pale. It had been months since the failed mission and it seemed that the Madame had paid a terrible price for her failure since that day.

Elara dropped her lancea and rushed over to try and loose the chains.

"No good!" Elara thought, noticing that the shackles required a key. *"I can't move her like this. Let's see if the Madame knows anything that could help."*

Elara reached out to remove the blindfold when she heard the heavy door behind her slam shut, cutting off another source of precious light. Elara scrambled to resume her weapon, but it was gone. Moments later, she felt a devastating blow to her stomach that left her reeling on the ground, gasping for breath. She stared as, one by one, lanterns on the wall illuminated her surroundings.

6

When Elara's vision finally came back into focus, she met eyes with the perpetrator of the obscene blow. He was a tall, fit, and conventionally attractive man. If not for the boldly serpentine look deep in his eyes, Elara might have found him quite handsome—well, the eyes and the fact that he had just leveled her with a swift kick.

"Not exactly the rat I expected, but vermin nonetheless. But I do laud you for making it here so soon: I almost didn't have time to prepare. Almost. I suppose introductions are in order. I am Ajaxx. And from your broach, I suppose you are one of the Sparrows."

Elara struggled to catch her breath as she thought to herself. *"This is Ajaxx? I expected a gross and decrepit old man…"*

She had iterated his vice so many times in her head that she expected evil and sin embodied.

"He will be tough to bring down." Elara thought as she managed to stand. Ajaxx had orchestrated both the location and the situation. Elara struggled for inspiration—anything that could create an advantage for her. She had found herself in Ajaxx's quarters. It was more ornate and elegant than any other part of the castle Elara had seen, but it was also simple. There was the door she had entered through and another almost exactly across the way. A ludicrously large bed and unnecessarily girthsome desk resided in the room. There were a few trinkets and novelties strewn about, but nothing stood out to Elara in particular. There was little she could use to her advantage here. She considered trying to flee but, as if reading her mind, Ajaxx positioned himself between Elara and the door, backing slowly towards it. He pulled out a ring of keys from his person and locked the door. Elara looked around, hoping to find a weapon. Her lancea was nowhere to be found, presumably removed from the room while Elara fussed with the chains. The dagger she carried, hidden, came to mind, but that was her ace in the hole—she would use it only to get her out of a tight scenario. She'd never touch this man with its blade if she brandished it brazenly. She would have to fight him the old-fashioned way.

7

Elara clenched her fists. Pain shot through her arms from her wounds. She winced a moment before collecting herself.

"He can't be any worse than the Shaa'Id and his cult. I do not welcome this handicap, but I won't let it stand in my way."

Elara assumed a fighter's pose, much to Ajaxx's amusement.

"How absolutely absurd!" Ajaxx cackled. "You stand as if we are to fight as equals!" His humour faded. "Let me assure you, little girl: We are not." Ajaxx proclaimed and threw a punch at Elara. She dodged, easier than she thought she would.

"Oh? Better than I thought, but I'll have you learn your place, just as I did with that mass in the corner—that heap that has the audacity to call herself woman."

The two combatants boxed for a moment, each feeling the other out. Elara had managed to avoid his blows and even land a couple of her own.

"But... " Elara noticed *"my blows don't seem to do much. He is resilient. And I seem to be wearing myself out faster, too. I must end this! I can't linger and play his game. If he lands another blow as severe as his last, I'm a goner!"*

Elara glanced back—there was still an unknown there. The door across from the entrance was an option.

"Even if it doesn't lead anywhere or is locked, I can use the wall to my advantage." She returned her glance to the fight. Though Elara had turned only for an instant, a fist was already hurling towards her face. She threw her arms up to block the blow, which knocked her backwards to the floor regardless. Dazed and with aching arms, she wasted no time and scrambled from the floor to the door.

Locked.

Elara turned to face Ajaxx, who was slowly approaching her.

"I'll use the walls and this door. If I dodge his blows, he will bust up his hands. He'll have to be cautious about the force behind each one. I'll wait and strike when the time is right!" Elara resolved, assuming a fighting pose once more.

8

Ajaxx strode towards Elara menacingly. When he was within striking range, Elara instinctively threw a hook as hard as she could. She sound of hand on jaw was loud and echoed throughout the chamber.

But Ajaxx absorbed the blow. It had left his face swollen, but he did not stop. He grabbed Elara by the throat and pressed her against the wall.

"You throw punches at me as if this were sport, woman. This is no game." His grip on Elara's throat tightened. "Mankind... we are beasts. All of us. We take what we want at the expense of others.

That's not cruelty. That's law. And what I want is for you to struggle. Struggle as I ruin you."

Ajaxx delivered a brutal knee to her abdomen.

Elara met eyes with Ajaxx and felt a new fear. She recognized something primal and unrestrained in his eyes. Civility was a tool to him, only to be used when necessary, just as women were goods to be traded. He looked at her and she saw no person in the reflection of his eyes. Elara had felt the fear of an endangered life and the fear of the loss of loved ones. But this fear was different and eroded a different part of her. She screamed and struggled and fought as Ajaxx continued to rough her up against the wall. Eventually, she managed to get him to release his grip on her throat with a well-placed bite. She dropped, wheezing, to the floor.

Visceral panic had set in. Elara crawled to the nearby door, hoping to escape even though she had already discovered it was locked. Ajaxx thrust himself on top of her. Elara struggled, but her strength and energy were failing. Her resistance was supplanted by tears and disbelief as Ajaxx forced her body to his will. Her mind and body both were dazed and tired, almost blank. She stared at this beast and his face burned into every recess of her mind.

Then, a gentle melody, just barely audible behind the door, calmed Elara and brought her back to her senses. She loosed her dagger deep into his thigh. The beast rolled over, off of Elara, and gripped his leg, yelping like a dog disciplined.

Though she now had the upper hand, Elara trembled at the sight of the man, her stomach begging to be emptied. The ring of keys had been flung to the side during their scuffle. Elara weakly grabbed the ring and walked over to the Madame. Her shaking prolonged the Madame's restraint, but she managed to undo the shackles and bindings. Madame Cantabelle swung fiercely at Elara, who just barely managed to avoid it. Upon seeing the sniveling figure rolling about on the floor and the pained and confused look on Elara's face, everything snapped into place. The Madame embraced Elara tightly and, though she stank something awful, her bosom was the most welcoming place in the world.

9

Elara didn't recall much after her defeat of Ajaxx. The Madame had restrained the fallen man and instructed Elara to lock herself in the room until her return. Strangely numb, Elara sat in the corner, head buried in her knees, and waited. After a couple of hours, Elara was so tired of being trapped in her own head, she decided to investigate the room. She looked took the door across the entrance and recalled the music that had snapped her back to reality, allowing her to mount a defense. She suddenly became obsessed with unveiling the source of the melody. She grabbed the keyring and tried the keys one by one to see if she could unlock the door. After a minute or two of chicken between her and the door, it gave in and opened for her.

Treasure, everywhere.

The room looked to be a study once upon a time, but it had been repurposed into a sort of personal treasury for Ajaxx. There were all manners of currency packed into the room, as well as all manners of valuable objects (some of which Elara recognized from Madame Cantabelle's office). She looked around desperately for some manner of music box from which the tune might've come, but to no avail. Frustration mounted as the weight of the evening's happenings returned to Elara. She desperately longed to be held by her mother or to hear the soothing voice of her sister. Her heart wanted nothing more at that moment and, at that moment, music began to fill the room once more. Elara looked down at her feet and could not believe it. There was a stone from which the sound was coming. It was patterned strangely but was otherwise quite plain. She picked the stone up, held it close, and let the music comfort her as she gave herself to sleep.

Elara was jolted awake by gentle rapping at the still locked entrance to Ajaxx's chambers. Elara made her way over, but hesitated to open it. Elara struggled with lumps in her throat, vainly trying to call out to identify the knocker.

"My sweetest little hummingbird, it's me. Take as much time as you need. I'll be waiting right here." came the Madame's voice, unprompted.

Elara took a moment to try and compose herself before unlocking the door for the Madame. The large woman opened the door much more slowly than necessary for one of her stature. Once the Madame entered the room, Elara could see a whole swathe of other members of the Sparrows lined up behind her, including an exhausted, but thankfully safe Bennu.

"Come Elara, my sleepy grebe..." cooed the Madame "I will return with you to town—to the hideout—so you might get some rest. I have much to say to you, including an ocean of 'thank yous' and a heap of apologies."

Elara managed to nod and left the castle to the rest of the Sparrows, pocketing the stone from the treasure room. It took only a few steps down the mountain for Elara to realize her body wasn't going to hold up for the trip down. She was too bruised and worn. Her legs trembled at the thought of taking one step more. The Madame took notice of this and bent over, gesturing for Elara to climb her back. Elara looked at the Madame once more. She was debatably in worse shape than Elara was.

"But Madame..." Elara started.

"I will hear none of your 'buts' my weary dunlin. Climb on or I will sweep you off your little webbed feet!"

Too tired to protest further, Elara relented. She climbed onto the Madame's back.

"Thank you, Elara. I cannot thank you enough for freeing me and bringing down the filth soiling the city I call home. Bennu told me much and I am sure it was not even the half of it. When you are ready, I would like to hear your story. But, for now, let me tell you mine and assure you that, tonight, you have made a difference."

11

As the pair wobbled down back to the city, The Madame recounted the events of the failed mission from her perspective. As everyone suspected, she had been ambushed and kidnapped that same night by Ajaxx's men. For a while, though, Ajaxx had treated the Madame as more of a guest—one that was not permitted to leave the grounds, sure, but a guest nonetheless. As long as the Madame complied with Ajaxx's requests, he vowed leave be the remnants of the Sparrows, including the Madame herself. Ajaxx coerced the Madame into fulfilling many of her own trade deals in Ajaxx's name (they had arranged for all post to be intercepted before even leaving the city, explaining Bennu's lack of response from the Madame's routine partners). It was not until Ajaxx started pressing her for information concerning the Sparrows directly involved in the failed mission that the Madame resisted. She refused to give out such information, going so far as to spit in the man's face. With this simple defiance, his civil facade evaporated, leading to heinous torture in a cesspool of inhumane conditions. This also prompted Ajaxx to intimidate the doctors in town to cease care for any known Sparrow.

The good news was, as the Madame informed Elara, that Ajaxx had been taken into custody by folk she trusted. It would be announced that Ajaxx had been captured and a ledger of his payroll found (whether or not such a document actually existed was beside the point). They reasoned that should lead to a mass exodus of villains from the city. Moreover, the Madame had exercised a bit of manifest destiny on Ajaxx's castle, which was currently being occupied and fortified by the other Sparrows.

Elara struggled desperately to stay awake until they returned to the hideout. She managed, but only just. If the Madame had smelt any less, Elara might've given in to her weariness. Just moments after Elara hit the bed, merciful sleep gripped her once more.

12

Elara would soon yearn for the ease of sleep that came with utter exhaustion as, in the days following, sleep largely evaded her. Even when she could sleep, nightmares ensured it wasn't for long. It had been a week since Ajaxx had been brought down and the fallout was pretty well what the Madame had predicted. It seemed like a significant portion of the town vanished overnight. An emergency council was assembled to deal with the restructuring of the city and handling the aftermath of Operation Big Bird. But Elara had little interest in such matters. She was struggling to handle the trauma she had endured since arriving here in Rumi. Some horrible things had befallen her during her tenure here—things she feared would haunt her mind for the rest of her life. Yet she couldn't come to hate the city and its inhabitants. As much as she wanted to villainize the city and use it as a scapegoat for all her suffering, fond memories would slip in and shatter her attempts. It left her mind in shambles as she failed to reconcile the contrary feelings she had for the location. She couldn't help but blame herself for the way her assault on Ajaxx's castle had progressed.

"If only I had been stronger or braver or smarter, none of that would have happened. He wouldn't have even had a chance to try and..." Elara pushed the thought from her mind.

"It's my fault, I know it is."

After a few more days, Bennu had noticed that Elara was not recovering from the incident well. Rather than get better in any noticeable way, she seemed to be getting worse. She wouldn't eat and often had to be consoled in the middle of the night. Bennu approached Elara and asked if she wouldn't grant her a favour. Elara agreed, hoping that maybe the task would wear her out enough to sleep.

"Could you meet me by the city building at midday tomorrow?" Bennu asked simply.

13

Elara managed to get herself to the city building, letting the prospect of being useful guide her legs. To her surprise, Madame Cantabelle, who had been exceptionally busy since their return, accompanied Bennu.

"Elara, my resilient hawk, I am so glad you made it. I have been worried sick about you." greeted the Madame.

"I suppose you must be wondering what favour I have to ask of you, Elara. I need help helping you. Can you help me help you?" Bennu riddled.

"Huh?" Elara was too tired to follow Bennu's wording closely.

"How about some tea, first, and talk later my darling ducks?" The Madame intervened.

They went to a nearby tea-shop, recently opened by an associate of the Madame who had once resided in the Drifter's Roost. The Madame could not stop raving about the foreign tea that they had managed to get their hands on. As the tea steeped, the Madame raved.

"In my youth, while I was still a sailor, I had some of this tea. The locals called it yerba, a fitting name I think. It is the most invigourating brew I have tasted in all my years."

The three enjoyed a hot cup of this yerba. Elara found herself more refreshed and awake than she had been since Operation Big Bird.

"So…" Elara prompted "What did you need from me, Bennu?"

Bennu sighed. "Well, I am not quite sure. You see, the Madame and I have reached an impasse of sorts. She and I both have noticed that you are haunted, in a way, from something that happened to you the night you felled Ajaxx."

Elara winced instinctively.

"Can we please not—" Elara began.

"Please, hear me out, it is important." Bennu interrupted.

Elara's resumed silence prompted Bennu to continue.

"You see, the Madame and I both encounter a lot of women who have drawn sorry lots in life. Like the ones we…saved…from the trap boat the night of the fire. They often come to us wounded and scarred in unique ways."

Elara stared at her hands and held them out demonstrably. Bennu had to forcefully restrain a chuckle.

"No, Elara, I am sure you know what I mean. The scar is internal, from their mistreatment. Their ache is not that of flesh, but that of the soul, caused from being treated as less than human. The Madame mistook you for one such woman when you first met her. In any case, we have always tried to help those who have been hurt in this way—so much so that we have gotten quite good at helping them help themselves. But each person is different, as is their road to recovery. Usually, the Madame and I agree on which course to pursue, but for you…we disagree."

220

Elara lashed out.

"Nothing happened! So I don't need your help! Leave it be!"

This time, the Madame spoke up. "I am afraid we can't do that, my pained chickadee. You see, you are very important to us. What's more, it's our fault you had to endure so many traumas."

Silence.

"No, it's not. It's my fault, all of it. I deserved it. I deserved it all."

Tears formed in the Madame's eyes as she suddenly embraced Elara, making a bit of a scene in the tea house.

"I am so sorry you feel that way, my dearest sparrow. I am so, so sorry. It's not your fault at all. It is not, so please don't feel such things."

Stunned, Elara liberated pain from her eyes for the first time since that night.

Chasing Smith

1

In what could be described as a montage of a week, Ivivin powered through the design and fabrication of his armour. Ivivin himself was surprised that he managed to complete a set in such a short time. It reminded him of how Smith had likewise made Ivivin's sword in such a short period of time.

"The feats of men on a mission are truly incredible." Ivivin thought each day, examining his own incredible progress. Of course, something had to give. Ivivin could not manage all the tasks and achieve this goal. He forwent his nightly reading and did only the absolute minimum amount of work in the forge, wrapping up current orders and accepting no new ones.

"I'm sure Smith will be sore about the loss of business and that I went after him instead of keeping my obligation here, but…" Ivivin remembered how Grandia's death to Crumbleheart nearly ruined Smith. *"I don't want to lose Smith to that dreadful disease. I will convince him to return!"*

Ivivin held up his handiwork—his new armour. It was far from perfection, but the fact that Ivivin could see these imperfections in his work spoke volumes about how far he had come. Moreover, these were imperfections he was more than willing to accept. Each slight dent or mildly jagged end had a story and Ivivin was proud nonetheless. Just as before, it was chain based with a single pauldron. However, he had added some steel plates he could take on and off as necessary. The tradeoff was that the armour would not be as durable, but Ivivin adored the flexibility of the idea. The last, new addition to Ivivin's set were gauntlets. They were fashioned from both leather and steel. Due to Ivivin's unfamiliarity with leatherwork, they were more than a little rough, but Ivivin was mighty proud of the metalwork. The protective plates delicately followed the contours of Ivivin's hands and they were surprisingly comfortable to wear. Ivivin donned the armour, noting that it was heavier than before.

"But, that's ok." Ivivin thought, inspecting himself in the mirror. *"I can bear the weight and walk forward on these legs of mine."*

2

Ivivin prepared to follow Smith. Since the south was the subject of gossip as it was, it was not difficult for Ivivin to ascertain the best way to get to Giganta Valley. It was a straightforward journey, if you had the right supplies. By now, though, Ivivin felt travel was an old hat trick for him. There was one task he was not looking forward to, though, and that was figuring out whether Icarus was going to be joining him on this endeavour. On one hand, Ivivin knew travel with the scamp along would be so much more enjoyable for both of them. On the other hand, Ivivin worried about Icarus' safety. He doubted his own ability to protect the owl. After hours of not coming to an answer, Ivivin realized the choice didn't really lie with him. He scooped Icarus out of a tree near the forge, where he had left him earlier, and brought him inside.

"Icarus…" Ivivin started. "…you can understand me, more or less, right? It seems to be the case, but sometimes I wonder if I imagine it."

Icarus looked at Ivivin skeptically.

"Yeah, ok, that's about what I thought." Ivivin continued. "It's just, well, this is a big deal. You must know by now that I intend to set after Smith. I am at odds with myself as to whether or not to bring you. It's not that I doubt you, my feathery friend, but we can't pretend that you'll be as safe travelling with me with the state that you're in. I am sure you could stay with Kranich and he would watch you, treat you well until my return. Whatever the case, though, I must leave tomorrow. Time is of the essence."

Icarus did not gesture obviously as to what he would be doing. Instead, he stared out into space pensively. Ivivin set him on the windowsill and continued his preparations for his departure. He packed absolutely everything he would need, including his copy of Grandia's book, and laid his head to rest earlier than usual. He would away at first light, just donning his armour, grabbing his pack, and leaving. Icarus would need to decide by such time—there would be no dallying.

3

Ivivin woke at first light. He hadn't slept terribly well, but there would be time to remedy that on the road. The first thing he noticed was that Icarus was nowhere to be found, though a freshly ejected pellet sat on the sill where Icarus sat long after Ivivin had fallen asleep. Ceremoniously, Ivivin slowly assembled and equipped his armour. He set his pack upon his shoulders. He considered just leaving. Indeed, he had made it to the door before his sentimentality and doubt caused him to turn around and call for Icarus.

"Icarus! Are you here!?" Ivivin shouted into the unusually still forge. "If you are, I would hear your answer!"

Nothing.

"Icarus, I'm leaving! It's your last chance, my friend!"

Nothing.

"Alright, Icarus, I will stop by the crazy bird man's home and ask him to come care for you. Please, please be safe my friend. I will be back, that is my promise!"

Ivivin stood in the doorway for several more minutes, realizing now that he had been hoping the whole time that Icarus would come.

Tears welled in Ivivin's eyes as he locked the door behind him.

4

Leaving Icarus behind weighed on Ivivin's mind and in his eyes, but he had to trust the owl's judgement and press on. Ivivin didn't want to lose Smith and, maybe more pressingly, he didn't want Smith to lose himself. Ivivin had perfectly planned his trip, but he knew the journey would be long—far longer than he would like. It would be hard, if not impossible, to catch up to Smith on foot. So Ivivin was headed first to the stables to see about getting his hands on a horse. Then, he would stop at Kranich's home and ask him for the favour.

Before Ivivin knew it, he stood in front of the stables. Yet he could not bring himself to enter to haggle with the owner within. His feet remained planted as if set in stone.

"Did I really make the right call with Icarus? Leaving him behind because he cannot fly... it must have hurt him something awful." The conflict he had thought settled again found life in Ivivin's heart and mind. After turning the issue over in his head again and again and again, he realized how much time he was

wasting—Smith could be in trouble, after all. This thought, though, brought Ivivin to a new one.

"How can I expect to protect Smith if I can't even protect Icarus?"

Ivivin about faced, poised to return to the forge and find Icarus. Just as Ivivin was about to take his first step back, he felt a nibbling on his ear. Icarus had crawled out from Ivivin's pack and was chewing at Ivivin's ear, presumably telling him to get a move on.

"Icarus?" Ivivin said in disbelief. He reached to grab the owl, who promptly returned to Ivivin's bag, refusing to leave.

"Stubborn little imp..." Ivivin said frustrated at the owl's refusal to face him. Then, gently, Ivivin whispered.

"I'm glad to have you along, Icarus."

The duo entered the stables in hopes of starting this, their next grand adventure.

5

"Are you crazy, boy! Rent you a horse to take to another country!? How absurd! Horses aren't for rent, so scram!" The stable hand responded to Ivivin's request. Just as Ivivin was about to leave, though, the stable hand caught sight of the ring bearing Smith's emblem hanging around Ivivin's neck.

"Hold now, child. You are the apprentice of Smith? I thought he had stopped taking apprentices after Wayland..." The stable hand inquired of Ivivin.

"I am." Ivivin answered simply. "Did you know Wayland? You seem shaken."

"Yes, he used to come here to spend time with the horses. They all loved him so. He was such a gentle soul. Things got quiet here after his passing. I tell you what, boy, I still cannot lend you any of these horses. But there is one I can part with. A real scoundrel of a horse. Young and strong, but stubborn as can be."

"Great!" Ivivin said optimistically. "I will take whatever help I can get. Where is he?"

"She..." the stable hand corrected "isn't here. In fact, I don't exactly know where she is. You see, she bucked off a prospective owner and ran off, saddle and all, into the hills just south of here. She's young, so I doubt she wandered too far, but I can't spare the time to go wrangle her. If you can catch her, she is yours to take down south. Heck, if you can ride her, you can keep her. But I want that saddle back!"

Ivivin weighed his options in his head. Ivivin could waste a lot of time chasing this horse. But, if he did manage to catch her, it would more than make up for it.

"If only Icarus could still fly..." Ivivin began to think before stopping himself. *"Nonono, no good can come from entertaining that which is not. But, perhaps..."*

Ivivin had an idea.

"Come Icarus," Ivivin said, scritching the owl's head "we are going to pay Kranich a visit after all."

6

Ivivin marched with purpose to Kranich's home. This time, though, the birds did not flee upon Ivivin's arrival. Just as before, the loon sat amoung loons and other such birds in the middle of his land. Ivivin approached Kranich, who immediately assumed Ivivin was there to leave Icarus. Kranich seemed pleasantly surprised when Ivivin corrected him and asked for his help finding the horse.

"Sure thing! Just wait here a mo! Clea should do the trick!" The man took a few steps away from the heap of birds and whistled. A falcon landed deftly on his arm. Kranich spent some minutes doting on the bird, as if she were the most adorable thing he had ever set his eye upon, before remembering the task at hand.

"Oh, yes, that's right! Clea, be a dear and help this poor boy and his owl out, will ya? They're looking for a horse out south."

Clea the falcon looked unenthused.

"Oh, come now Clea, don't be such a sourpuss. How's this, you help these fellas and I'll give you a bath when you get back!" Kranich bargained

Clea perked up.

"And I'll throw in some scritches too, you greedy, greedy bird." Kranich relented.

Clea took flight and circled above Ivivin. Kranich handed Ivivin a falconer's glove and told him to put it on. When he did, Clea immediately descended and perched upon Ivivin's arm. Her talons were nothing all that fierce, but seeing her beak up close rather worried Ivivin.

"Take her out for a spin, Ivivin. Carry her out to the southern outskirts of town and she'll do the rest. When she's done, give her that glove and she'll find her way back to me. Got it?"

Ivivin nodded and headed south, dual wielding birds of prey.

7

Ivivin had never really spent much time in the plains to the south of Smithton. He had noticed them when he traveled southeast to Rumi, but only from a distance and only for a short while. But Clea, it seemed, knew the landscape in and out. She departed Ivivin and flew off into the distance. Less than an hour later, the falcon returned. After a brief rest, it took flight once more and, this time, Ivivin followed. Sure enough, the falcon Clea lead Ivivin and Icarus straight the escaped horse. Ivivin removed the plating from his armour to reduce both weight and sound. He snuck up behind the horse and jumped on it. Ivivin remembered how easily horse-riding had come to him when returning to Crosstown from the fort. He recalled how, even though he was in a rush, it was strangely natural and relaxing.

This could not be further from the case now.

The horse bucked and bucked. Ivivin held on more because of instinct and reaction than any actual desire to stay atop the wild beast. At some point, though, Ivivin accepted the horse's challenge and resolved to outlast her. The horse ran and ran and bucked and bucked, but Ivivin persevered. When the escaped horse finally wore itself down, it assumed a resting posture in the grass. Ivivin hopped off and met eyes with the tired animal.

"Your owner has given me to you, but I need you only for one journey. Bring me south, to Olympia, so that I may help a dear friend. After that, you can have freedom, true and honest." Ivivin panted at the horse. They had earned each other's respect and managed to come to an agreement in just that short glance.

"Let's see here, do you have a name?" Ivivin said, inspecting the gear on the horse. As far as Ivivin could tell, this was top quality gear. He could see why the stable hand would want it returned to him. On the saddle, there was a name burnt in the leather.

"Alright then, Lili. Let's head back to the owl and the falcon. We can stop back in town and get you a treat before we head out. That sound alright?" Ivivin asked, worried that the horse would get up and book it the first chance she had. Lili stood slowly and the two returned to the birds together.

8

With sugar cubes in hand, the new crew was ready to head to Olympia. Ivivin and Icarus rode atop Lili and journeyed southwest. At first, Ivivin found the scenery reminiscent of his trip to the Wolfelaw Caverns and Rumi. But very quickly, that changed. After a time, the earth adopted a red tint that Ivivin had not ever seen before. Standing on it felt different. It was sturdy, sure, but he had never stood upon earth that felt flexible. Still, it was easy on Lili's hooves and they made even better time! Later on, though, they weren't so lucky. Ivivin and company stumbled upon a grand forest, one they would need to cross. There was a path, sure, but the branches of the trees also hung quite low, preventing Ivivin from adding his height to Lili's.

The canopy in this forest was thick—so thick that Ivivin could not see the sky. He could hear all sorts of critters, mostly bugs and frogs, jittering about. As the sun began to set, it became clear to Ivivin that they needed to stop and prep camp right away, as there would be no moonlight permeating the thick membrane of the treetops. Ivivin and company laid down for the evening. In earnest, this place scared Ivivin. The noises of the night only intensified and he felt their campfire, as modest as it was, only drew attention to them in the pitch black of the night. Ivivin struggled to sleep, scared by the heavy abyss encompassing him.

9

"What's wrong with me!? I've dealt with much worse than this before!" Ivivin thought, frustrated. The dark of night and the enclosure of the forest had brought to the surface of Ivivin's mind his experience in Wolfelaw caverns. Specifically, he began to remember being trapped within his own head, accompanied only by overwhelming fear and anxiety. Recollection of this morphed his childish fear of the dark into something much more sinister and unsettling. Ivivin tried to do what the wise fellow in the cave had suggested. Ivivin tried to remind himself of the vastness of the world, but it just made him feel even smaller here in this forest. Ivivin thought of trust and so many people he trusted flashed through his mind's eye. His parents, the celestial sisters and their foster mother, Smith, the innkeeper in Winter's Fort—so many people he felt he could trust passed through his head.

But none of them were here to help him.

Ivivin struggled to catch his breath. He was tensing up and sweating a cold sweat.

"Blast!" Ivivin thought. *"What else did he say I should think of...?"*

Icarus, recognizing the special agony Ivivin was in once again, nibbled on Ivivin's fingers, which grounded Ivivin, even if only temporarily. Ivivin reached into his pack and pulled out the book of constellations given to him by Elara. Both her and this book held a fond place in his heart. The book was comfortable and familiar, presenting Ivivin with a task to occupy his mind. Finally starting to relax, Ivivin opened the book, using the magic of the tear to supplement the light of their now dying fire. He stared upwards, eager to find Elara's favourite constellation, Lupus.

Darkness.

Ivivin had forgotten, for a moment, that he was ensnared and surrounded by trees. He could no more easily see the stars here than in Wolfelaw itself! Trembling in both terror and frustration, Ivivin held the book to his chest tightly, as if trying to squeeze out by force the potential positivity it held. For hours that felt like years, Ivivin sat awake, fighting a losing battle against his own fears, terror, and anxieties.

10

Eventually, the sun broke the horizon and traces of it trickled through the thick canopy. Ivivin sighed, relieved that the night had finally given way to the dawn. His heavy eyes and achy body told him to just let sleep wash over him. And he almost did, but forced himself to his feet, not wanting Icarus or Lili to see how the night had tormented him. He shook off his weariness and attempted to leave fear behind with the campsite.

The trio made their way through the forest, trekking at a steady pace.

"Can't be more than half a day to the other end of the forest!" Ivivin bargained. Noon came and left, though, and the forest did not seem to be thinning.

"That's ok, we just got off to a slow start is all. It'll open up any time now."

The adventurers continued, though Ivivin had quickened the pace to the limits of what could still be considered a walk. As hours inevitably marched onwards, Ivivin began to fidget.

"Should I... should I climb a tree and see if we are near the end? No, no that's a waste of time and energy. But...what if we got turned around?"

He looked for the direction of light.

"The sun...which way does it rise again? Has it been on the same side this whole time?"

Ivivin shook himself back to his senses.

"Calm down, Ivivin, you're not scared. Let's just keep at it. No need to fiddle here."

Ivivin slowed his pace to a reasonable walk for a while, trying to elude a calm demeanour. His charade ended when the sun's light was tinted freshly with the colour of sunset. Panic overcame Ivivin and his walk erupted into a full-blown sprint, startling his passenger owl and his horse follower. It was only a few minutes before Ivivin tripped on a tree's root and fell to the ground. His ankle burned with pain. He quickly inspected it. It was only a sprain, it seemed. Ivivin tried to put weight on it and walk on, but it would not bear his weight readily. Ivivin was not one to swear, but curses lined the air as Ivivin reluctantly gathered material for a small fire.

Anticipation of the coming of night was nearly as bad as the night itself.

Nearly.

11

Ivivin was exhausted, but his mind would not let him rest. Worse still, Ivivin was sure his overtired brain was playing tricks on him. He heard unnatural sounds and saw impossible shimmers in the woods. Ivivin was gripped by the now uncomfortably familiar feeling of his chest tightening and his mind clouding with disparate, nonsensical thoughts. The fit came to pass, leaving Ivivin trembling on his knees and gasping for breath.

"How many times is that now? More importantly, how many times more must I endure this?" Ivivin struggled to recount his fits and gave up entirely.

"Isn't there some way I can do away with all of this? These woods? Burn them to the ground so no man be cursed to step foot in here again?" Ivivin yelled in frustration, waking Lili.

"Or, maybe... I could just do away with myself." Ivivin thought.

He immediately caught himself.

"Did I just...no, I don't mean that, but the thought did cross my mind. But I'd never..."

Ivivin chased his thoughts in circles, too tired to coherently reach a resolution.

Ivivin faced another night of fear and torture. Holding the book of constellations and cuddling next to Icarus and Lili lessened his anxiety, but did not eliminate it. He dealt with fits and cold sweats and tears all night until the sun mercifully pierced the horizon.

Ivivin gathered his things and left. His body was unsteady and weary from lack of sleep. Ivivin had been exhausted before—it seemed every time he faced a new foe, he had worked himself to exhaustion and sleep took him against his will. This time, though, sleep would not have him and Ivivin would not have another night in this wood. Ivivin stumbled, doing his best to ignore the pain of his ankle, and continued to flee the woods. It was no more than an hour or two later when Ivivin reached the clearing. The trees ended abruptly, as if they were presenting themselves rank and file for the wide open plain before them. Only a few steps out of the woods, Ivivin dropped his things and fell to the floor. He laughed and laughed and laughed.

"Somehow, I had forgotten how human I was. I am just as frail and weak as the next person. The simple dark of night drove me to be the mess than I am now! How funny!" Ivivin thought.

"Isn't that right Icarus!?" Ivivin shouted to the owl. "Isn't it funny!?"

Just before sleep forgave him and accepted him with open arms, Ivivin could have sworn that he heard the tiny owl whisper in a deep, bassy baritone to Lili the horse

"I think the human has finally lost it."

12

Ivivin slept nearly the whole day away. He woke periodically to gulp down some water or when Icarus pecked at his nose to ensure Ivivin was still of this world, but otherwise he dozed, fading in and out as he pleased. When Ivivin finally sat up with the intent of continuing his adventure, he realized the sun was already setting. Icarus and Lili looked a strange combination of concerned and annoyed.

"Sorry about that, you two." Ivivin said, showing them each some affection. "I'm actually kind of surprised you didn't run off on me, Lili." Ivivin joked, nodding to himself. "Yeah, thanks for sticking by me, guys. I'm sorry."

He looked back towards the forest, which seemed so serene and wondrous from this vantage, and was tempted to write off the entire nightmare as just his imagination. After all, how could he be scared by something so natural and basic when he had fended off bandits and monsters and demons? He shook his head and turned to stare out towards the sunset.

"I was scared. So, so scared." Ivivin admitted to the animals and to himself. "The darkness strangled me and there was nothing I could do about it. So, sorry and thanks. I'll get a fire going."

That night, Ivivin was at peace. He read Elara's book and delighted in finding the constellations in the sky. He noticed that they looked different than they usually did.

"Oh yeah, that's right! This book was made up north and was meant for the north. I don't really get it, but I guess the patterns of the stars change a bit as you travel, just as they do with the change of the seasons. Everything changes, after all. Even the stars." Ivivin mused.

Ivivin chuckled "It was getting a little too easy to find the patterns, anyways."

Ivivin fell asleep, book laid open on his chest and a tiny dusty owl to his right. The woods lingered still in the background, but weighed not on Ivivin this night.

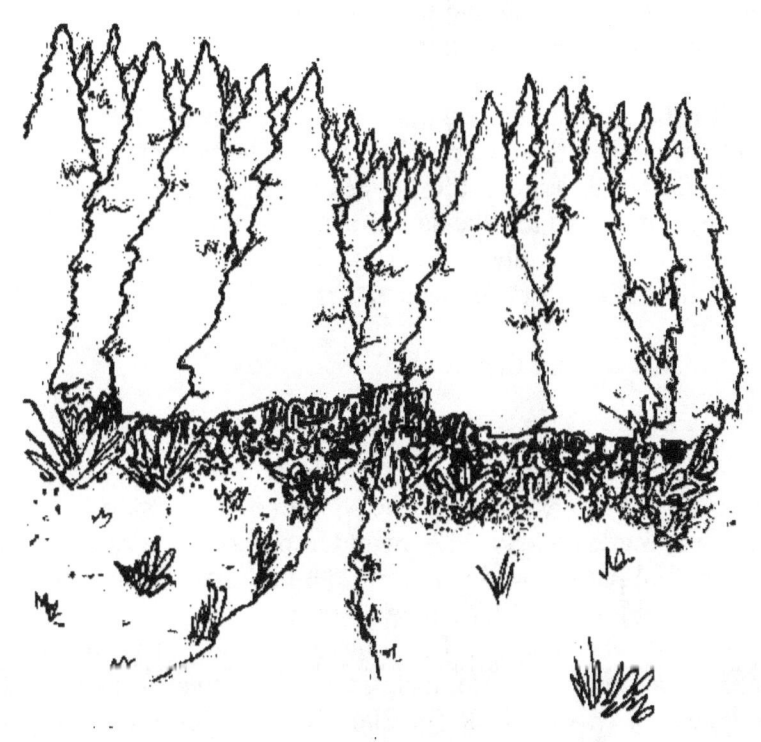

Walking On

1

Since the night at Ajaxx's castle, Elara had not so much as touched her gear. It laid in a pathetic heap in a damp corner of the Sparrow's basement. Everything that had been at the castle that night, Elara would not even look at—including the mysterious stone of music. It had all been quarantined, tainted by Elara's recollection of that night. Today, though, Elara would make good on something she had agreed to do at the tea house with the Madame and Bennu. The Madame and Bennu had a disagreement and Elara resolved it. The Madame thought that Elara should face Ajaxx, who sat firmly behind bars. Bennu thought that there would be nothing for Elara to gain from such an encounter and would only prolong her time to recovery. Elara, feeling the caring support from each of them, had boldly decided to face Ajaxx. Ever since that day, though, Elara had regretted her decision and had been dreading the arrival of this day. But the Madame believed in her, even if she didn't believe in herself, and that was enough to get her out of bed.

For the first time since that night, Elara made her way to the dusty pile of gear in the corner. She saw the leather armour and thought to don it, to add another layer of separation between herself and the beast in the cage. She saw the lancea and thought to bring it, to make her feel strong and dangerous. In the end, though, Elara grabbed only her dancer's hip scarf, dirty and worn.

Why?

It made her feel like herself.

2

Even with the support of the Madame, every step felt as if her feet were made of lead. She meandered about in a random walk whose eventual path would led her to the jailhouse. Out front was a very concerned looking Madame and an impatient looking Bennu. Elara knew she was late, but didn't have it in her to care this day. She approached the jailhouse, trying to make herself look confident and collected. It wasn't working. Elara felt the blood fall from her face. Her stomach objected violently to the mere idea of taking a single step into that building. The trio stood at attention for a few minutes before Bennu shattered the silence.

"So... how are we doing this?" Bennu threw out there.

"What...do you mean?" Elara asked, genuinely confused.

"Well, Elara, my boisterous little turkey, we are here for you. For support. But what that means is up to you. If you'd like, we can just wait out here for you. Or, if you like, we can be at your side the whole time. Or anything in-between. It's up to you and what you think you can get out of this."

Elara hadn't considered any of this yet. She had tried not to think too much about the details of this day, as the very abstract thought of what she was to do alone made her queasy. It was the first time Elara considered what the benefits of this meeting could be, that she might even be able to recover from it if she played her cards right. Eager to face and defeat her demons, she decided that she would go in alone, but, as she went to tell Bennu and the Madame this, her tongue betrayed her. She quivered and muttered nonsense. Elara was afraid, after all. She wanted the Madame there. Bennu too. But she also wanted to face him alone.

"What was that dear?" The Madame prodded.

Elara sighed.

"I don't know. I want to face him alone, but I do not think I can do it without you two next to me. I just don't know." Elara found herself flustered by her own circular thinking.

"How about this, my troubled woodpecker. We will stand just outside the room, within earshot if you call for us. We will be just mere feet apart, but you will be facing him alone." Madame Cantabelle proposed.

Elara considered the proposition. It was not a completely satisfying solution to her circular dilemma, but she could imagine no better approach. Elara agreed and the trio entered the jailhouse.

3

The jailhouse was more orderly and well-maintained than Elara had imagined. It certainly was not a comfortable place to be, but it was not the dingy cesspool she had imagined—even hoped—it would be. The Madame had obviously made previous arrangements with those tending the building and it's less-than-willing occupants. After a few words were mutedly exchanged, Elara found herself being led through a door and down some stairs. This part of the jailhouse was a little dingier, made of old stone walls. But it was also pleasantly cool and damp. The Madame and Bennu stopped abruptly in front of a particular door and turned to Elara.

"This is where we leave you." whispered Bennu.

"But we aren't really leaving! We'll be right here." corrected Madame Cantabelle.

Elara took a deep breath and reached for the door. It was heavy, much like the ones in Ajaxx's castle. The thought of the castle and that night already had permeated her thoughts anew and were wreaking havoc on what little confidence she had managed to muster. Her whole body trembled like a seismic wave had passed through her. She turned and faced her cheerleaders, using their presence to summon the strength to enter the room.

Something strange happened when she passed the threshold. Her trembling stopped and her heart slowed almost back to its normal rate. She was still fearful and nervous. Nothing appealed to her about the situation in the least, but something about taking the first step over that insurmountable threshold had imbued her with a temporary surge of capacity. Not two steps in, the door shut behind her. She turned right slowly and found herself face to face with the usurper of her inner peace.

4

It took Ajaxx some moments to even register Elara's presence. He laid in a small bunk, staring at the ceiling. He had been reciting something when Elara entered and continued until he met eyes with her. It was only for a moment, but anger flashed through the man's eyes before the glossy sheen of feigned civility suppressed it. He said nothing, but faced Elara squarely. If he were not behind bars, Elara might have imagined that they were there to discuss business over tea. When it became clear Elara would not break her silence, Ajaxx sighed in frustration.

"Get on with it. I haven't all day, despite what you think." Ajaxx stated with tones of exasperation.

Startled by the insistence and thrown from her delicate balance, Elara blurted out the first thing she could think to say.

"What were you telling yourself, just now?"

"What a strange creature you are." Ajaxx mused. "It is really none of your business. Though, as long as you are here, I suppose there is chance for enjoyment or, at least, a break in the monotony. So, I will answer. It was a passage from a book. One I enjoy very much."

Still unable to shift the conversation's direction, Elara queried further.

"Which book is that?"

Ajaxx snorted softly. "I doubt you have ever heard of it. It is a classic and not exactly suitable in scope for one such as yourself.

Elara could tell he was prodding her—that he was trying to work her up with a bombardment of small insults, so that she would break herself and save him the effort. And it was working, despite her knowledge of his plan.

"Try me. Perhaps you'll be surprised." Elara shot back at him.

"It is a passage from the story of the first king. In particular, it comes from a philosophical discussion about the nature of rule. Of course, the self-righteous king-to-be argued that he who would best represent the will of the people is best suited to rule. And he raised some fair points. But even he acknowledged that some men were more suited to lead. Perhaps, then, those who can control the masses best are who should lead, no?"

Elara couldn't believe it, nor did she know what to say or do next. She knew the book and passage well. It was a story contained in the tome gifted to her by Ivivin. The discussion in question occurred between the man who would become the first king and his brother, who would have untimely death. It would be the first king, his own kin, that would fell the brother years after this discussion during a failed coup not moments after the first king took the throne.

Elara took a breath and a moment to respond.

"The hand that fells you is not my own. I would sooner die than harm my dear brother. No, this hand belongs to the people."

5

Elara stared at the man, proud of her retort. To her surprise, Ajaxx smiled and laughed.

"How fascinating! You have read it! That is quite a feat, I laud you and your efforts. It can't have been a simple task. So, did you come just to discuss books with me? Are we starting a little reading club? How quaint!"

Elara realized in that moment what she was attempting to do. She, for some unknown and ungodly reason, was trying to win the respect of this man. And now she realized the futility. Just like on that night, he did not see her as a person. No number of daggers to the thigh or quotes from literature would change that. Still, though, she could not help but take note of how normal and civilized he appeared. Even in this cage, meant to protect others from the danger he posed, he seemed to belong in society. The air of assault did not linger around him. The face burned into Elara's memories and haunting her dreams was not the face he wore here. As horrid as Elara found this man, she also couldn't reliably distinguish his bestial nature from that of any other stranger. He wore the veil of civility well and masqueraded as a citizen. There were brief moments, sure, where Elara could see flashes of his true self, but the flashes never lasted long enough for her to be sure they weren't imagined. As far as she could tell, he was just a man. It was both a reassuring and terrifying revelation.

"I don't think... I shall be returning to this place. I'll leave you to your business." Elara remarked flatly.

"Aww! Done already? Stopped just short of a good time once again! What sour luck I'm having these days!"

Elara could hear Ajaxx ramble as she opened the door to exit. The words hurt worse than daggers, worse than hot coals, and worse than bitter cold. But Elara left the room without turning to face the slinger of words. She crossed the threshold and closed the door behind her. The trembling and racing heart she had left with the Madame and Bennu returned to her in full. Her shaking legs could bear her weight no longer and she fell to her knees. The two Sparrows aided her to her feet and, when Elara was sure he could hear her no more, she allowed her pain to show. She sobbed deeply into the Madame's sleeve. Still, in the back of her mind, Elara felt a semblance of pride at having faced her nightmare head on.

It was just a seed but, perhaps with time, it could bloom.

6

The Madame and Bennu were both hesitant to ask or comment on the events that transpired in the room. It was obvious, though, that Elara hadn't gotten true closure. It was also obvious, though, that no one expected her to. It was just a single step in a single day, after all. Still, Elara enjoyed spending the rest of the afternoon with the two of them. They had such a pleasant afternoon that she forgot her troubles for a while. But, as is often the case, the solitude of night allowed the thoughts to flood back. Elara did not fight them. She took up her normal spot on the beach by the port. It wasn't that she hated everything about this city. There was plenty that was nice. Her time with the Sagehens, the Sparrows, and nights she spent looking up at the stars with sand between her toes were all invaluable. At the same time, she was scarred, both in the flesh and in her soul. Elara held her hands to her face. They were disfigured, but functional. They were not quite healed, but her and the apologetic Dr. Sandra Buckley were both hopeful about what she could expect.

They hurt, though. They hurt and they hurt to look at, these scars. She did notice something, though, with her arms outreached. She had another scar. It was from the wound she earned when she rushed off to save Idalia from the Shaa'illi—just before Ivivin found her. That laceration, too, had left her scarred. And yet, that one never hurt. Not her flesh nor her soul. Perhaps it was because she took the blow in passionate pursuit of her dearest sister that she never gave the brand the time of day. It was certainly not an aesthetically pleasing mark, either. It was curious to Elara that the wounds she gained here in Rumi would impact her so much more. Then again, perhaps it wasn't so curious after all.

Elara was still struggling to accept that these hands were hers now. They did not match who she felt she was. Bennu had acknowledged that her wounds should pain her. Bennu also posited, however, that Elara should also think of them as a badge of honour—that she should treat them as a matter of great pride. A sign that she tried something grand, even if she failed, and that she got up and achieved greatness despite it. Elara could recognize some truth in those words, but she didn't feel that truth herself. Unsettled and unable to resolve her own discord, Elara lowered her hands to her side and watched the moon's reflection shimmer in the ocean.

After an hour or two alone, she returned to the Sparrow's hideout. Bennu had fallen asleep at the desk not far from Elara's own bunk. Elara draped a blanket over her and laid down. Surrounded by people, she relaxed and let sleep wash over her. She had not solved all her problems, perhaps, but she was rewarded for her progress in the form of an all-too-rare good night's sleep.

7

The next morning, Elara walked about town. Even she wasn't sure what led her to the decision, exactly, but by the time Elara returned to the Sparrow's hideout, she had decided she wanted to leave Rumi. She had been here so long already. Moreover, despite her fond memories here, there were too many memories that fueled her nightmares. Elara felt that she had to leave this place, if not forever, then for a while, to even begin to recover properly. At least, that is what she thought this morning. It wasn't like this was the first time she considered leaving this place since Ajaxx was subdued. But she had often convinced herself that leaving now was essentially running away. It was an admission of defeat. It was accepting that she wasn't good enough, strong enough, or smart enough to make it through. Today, though, she felt grounded and confident. She wanted to share the decision with the Madame as soon as she could to obligate herself to the plan, so that, even if doubt seeped through and took back over, it would already be done.

The Madame was saddened, but not entirely shocked, when Elara told her of her decision to leave Rumi.

"Of course, my terse tern. I understand. Tell me, when do you plan on leaving?"

Elara pondered this a moment. "Before the week's end, I will leave, I think."

The Madame chuckled. "So hasty! That was a sort of trick question, Elara. Recall that you'll need to pass through Wolfelaw caverns if you wish escape from this little corner of the map. You'll need to wait for a group or find a guide, no?"

Elara felt her face flush with embarrassment. She had indeed forgotten this in her sudden, if not desperate, desire to leave Rumi behind.

Elara, as always, was incredibly easy to read.

"It's quite alright, my hasty cuckoo. If I recall correctly, I have an acquaintance leaving Rumi in a week. Or, if that's too soon, I think the next fellows looking to leave will be doing so in three weeks. I'll arrange for the former, but do not feel obligated to go so soon." Madame Cantabelle offered.

Elara responded flatly. "Thank you, Madame, but I am sure I will leave as soon as I can."

The Madame sighed. "Of course, you are quite the wandering duck, aren't you? This brings me to my next point. Your reward, as it were."

"My...reward?" Elara was genuinely baffled.

"I know that, to you, your efforts do not feel like a victory. They may never feel like a victory. But to the people of this town, to the people who you've talked to and danced for, to the girls you saved and the ones you couldn't, to Bennu and I... you are a hero. You saved a city with which you had no history, with a problem that you stumbled into. You can demerit your own accomplishments, Elara, but we are truly thankful. Not just for what you've done, but for who you've been. If not a reward, a gift."

8

The Madame took the time to explain to Elara the logistics of what Rumi had decided on regarding Ajaxx and the damage he caused. The leadership of the city was being reworked from scratch. Madame Cantabelle was a key member of the committee, but she certainly did not just go and fill the vacuum of power left in Ajaxx's wake. Though, through some clever lobbying and sleek business sleight of hand, The Madame had managed to secure ownership of the castle. The Sparrows had begun their occupation of it the same night Ajaxx was torn from it. Now, though, they formally had the right to reside and set up base there. The Drifter's Roost could then be repaired and reopened, since there would not be inhabitants in its cellar.

Additionally, the Madame had managed to secure a large portion of Ajaxx's accumulated wealth in various forms. Some was allocated to her personally, as restitution for her suffering. Some of it was given to her business, to rebuilt it. Some of it was given to the Sparrows to pay for their continuing medical bills and to support their future investigations into human trafficking. When all was said and done, the Madame found herself sitting on quite the golden egg.

"Of course, dear, the reward I mentioned includes financial compensation." The Madame smiled and handed Elara a hefty bag of coin. Elara opened it and panicked the moment she did. There was more money in this pouch than Elara had ever held in her life cumulatively.

"Madame Cantabelle...there's no way I can—" Elara was cut off.

"Think nothing of it, my young swan! It may seem like quite a lot, and I suppose it is for one person, especially at your age, but it really is only a fraction of what we recovered from the castle. Of course, there are some assets we didn't liquidate that you can have a look at and pick a thing or two from. Anything you think might help you on your travels. I insist."

9

Though not eager to accept anything more from the Madame, especially anything that was the result of Ajaxx's profiteering, Elara decided to at least check it out.

"After all, I found that wondrous music stone from the room full of Ajaxx's private treasure. Speaking of, I must remember to give that another look over, I haven't touched it since that night. Who knows what else he had there!" Elara thought, her curiosity finally outweighing her reluctance.

The Madame and Bennu led Elara to a room in the castle full of all manners of goods. They had been organized, though roughly. The clear majority of the items were weapons and armour.

"A lot of what Ajaxx had, my awestruck albatross, were goods that were easy for us to liquidate. The town needed the money more than the goods themselves. There are other things that are harder to find buyers for and other things that are harder still to find honourable buyers for. Weapons and armour are such items, though there are plenty of other odd curiosities lying about as well."

Elara immediately thought that she didn't need a new weapon, that she had the sword she's owned since she was young. And, failing that, she was sure Bennu or the Madame would allow her to keep the lancea she used. However, Elara reminded herself of the pain of wielding such weapons with the state of her hands.

"Perhaps there is something here that would be easier for me to wield." Elara thought, hopefully.

"Alright, Madame Cantabelle, I will look around and see if there is anything I might be able to use. Thank you."

"Of course, my chipper chicken. I have business to attend to, but Bennu will be here to help you if you need anything!" The Madame called back to Elara, already half out the door.

Elara inspected the weapons for quite some time. She was really only trained with spears and one-handed swords, which limited her choices. She would test the hilt and hold of weapons she thought might be less painful to wield, but failed to find any that were any less painful than the one's she already had. Elara sighed.

"So much for that." she mumbled.

"Not find anything you like?" Bennu inquired, hoping to help.

"No, if they are all going to hurt, then I'd just the same stick with my sword from home."

"I see, you are looking for something that is a little more comfortable to wield, given the state of your hands…" Bennu thought a moment. "Ah! Perhaps you are looking in the wrong place! Come with me!"

10

Bennu led Elara away from the weaponry and towards the armour. Elara was visibly confused, but Bennu indeed knew what she was doing. She led Elara to a full suit of armour. It did not look like anything Elara had seen in this country. It was chain, sure enough, but an embellished sort. It was a bronze-gold and seemed thin and light. There were two small plates that covered the area on each side of the sternum. More interestingly, though, were the gauntlets. They were thicker and heartier than the rest of the armour and sported some manner of adjustable hardware on the top. The display mannequin wore the armour well, even holding a blade, albeit an odd looking one, and a small shield. It was truly a fine and exotic decorative piece that was probably worth a small fortune.

"Is this the blade? It doesn't look any different." Elara prompted Bennu.

Bennu smiled. "Well, Sometimes, you just need to look closer." She said as she removed a gauntlet from the figure. To Elara's surprise, the blade came with it. Upon closer inspection, Elara realized that the blade was built into the gauntlet itself. Rumi handed it to Elara and strapped it on. There was a handle that ran perpendicular the blade inside the gauntlet for her to grab, not unlike the structure of push daggers. Elara held her arm up and swung the blade about. It was shorter than her sword, sure, but it was thick and heavy. There was still pain from holding the handle, but the slashes and stabs seemed to put more pressure on her wrist and forearm than her hand proper.

Elara turned to Bennu, remarking. "What a strange weapon."

"Strange to you, yes, but better, is it not?" Bennu replied, giddy at Elara's fascination.

"It certainly is! But I have never seen such weaponry. Where did this even come from?" Elara wondered aloud.

"Well, I don't know about those specifically, but they were not uncommon in the land I was born in. In fact, the ship that... brought me to these lands had a fellow or two sporting these. I hadn't seen any in ages. They are difficult to craft, so I hear. You must have talent in making both armour and weaponry. This piece looks exceptionally well made, as it seems you can use the hardware to stow the blade along the length of your forearm." Bennu fiddled with the pieces and demonstrated the mobile nature of the blade to Elara.

"Wow, this is incredible!" Elara remarked. "It is like a fine tool!"

"It's all yours Elara, though you should probably take the other gauntlet for good measure." Bennu remarked, equipping Elara with the second gauntlet. Just as with the blade, the second gauntlet had a small shield built in. It was so small, in fact, that if Elara didn't know better, she would have thought it to be a true part of the gauntlet. It was elongated and came to a point, if a dull one. The metal was thick and heavy. Elara was sure it could handle a blow. Moreover, it seemed to have been built with the intent of using it to strike, as well.

"Are you sure?" Elara asked Bennu.

"Absolutely. Take them with you as you journey. Protect yourself well, my sister." Bennu replied.

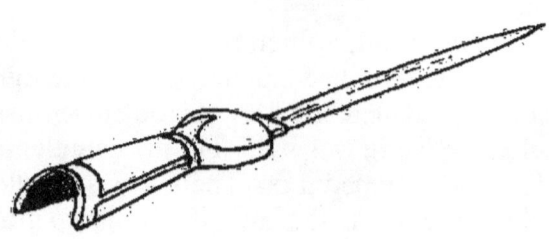

11

Elara did not find anything else she particularly wanted from the treasures harvested from Ajaxx, but did accept the strange gauntlets from Bennu. Although Bennu did not know the true name for the weapon, she jokingly called the shield Elara's beak and the blade, her talon. Elara liked these names for them, even if her curiosity compelled her to know what they were truly called. In any case, the new gear seemed to imbue Elara with a fresh burst of confidence. She managed to gather everything she would need for her trip without dwelling too much on the idea of leaving. Before she knew it, she was ready to leave. In fact, she had gotten ready so fast, that she realized she had several days to do nothing.

"Let's see, if I am to meet the merchant caravan at Wolfelaw, I would need to leave here by midday three days from now. I'll leave in the morning that day, just to be safe." Elara planned. Still, the rest of the day drug on. Now that she was not busy and not occupied with the task at hand, negativity had returned to seep into her mind. The next few idle days were hard, but Elara managed to hang on until the day before she was to depart. She faced some awkwardness and anxiety, though, as she wasn't sure how to say goodbye to the Sparrows.

"Maybe I should just leave tonight and not tell anyone. I'm sure I've caused them enough trouble." Elara moped. *"I think it might be better that way. I don't really belong with them anyways. I'll just leave Madame Cantabelle a note saying thank you and be on my way."* Elara decided.

So, just as the sun was setting, Elara gathered her things. She carefully wrapped her cleaned and patched dancer's hip scarf around her otherwise plain attire. She had decided to forgo armour of any sort as it would just encumber her. She donned her Beak and Talon, strapped on her bag, and made her way towards the outskirts of town.

Suddenly, Elara was grabbed from behind. Startled, and ready to fight, Elara turned to face her assailant. Instead, she was greeted by a smiling Madame Cantabelle.

"Oh, my fussy little lovebird. As always, you are too easy to read! You didn't think I'd let you leave without saying good-bye, did you!? Come, come!" The Madame pulled Elara by the hand to a nearby pub.

Inside the pub were the Sparrows, even some that had left Rumi after the boat incident. When Elara walked in, a tsunami of cheers spewed into the air. Elara hadn't been close to many of these girls, but she did care for them. And now, Elara could finally tell that they cared for her too, as different as they seemed to be from each other. Elara smiled and let loose with the others. They drank and celebrated, leaving Elara unusually merry and sociable. The other members of the now defunct Sagehens even made an appearance. Elara once more had the honour of dancing to their music. Even in a drunken stupor, Elara knew that many challenges and problems lay still before her. But, she also knew that, in this room full of passionate people and good vibes, she could make it to tomorrow.

The next dawn, Elara woke uncertain of where she was or how she got there. The sunlight trickling in from the window split her head in two. Elara, like many of the bar's patrons that night, had passed out. The Madame arranged for them to sleep there, paying a pretty coin for the privilege. Elara had planned to leave at dawn for Wolfelaw caves. She stared at the ceiling before covering her face with a blanket that had found its way to her the night prior.

"The morning is overrated anyways." Elara grumbled before drifting off once more.

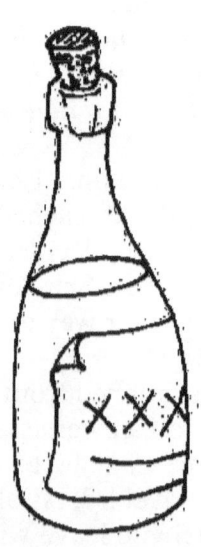

12

Elara left the pub after nearly a pitcher of water and a greasy breakfast. It was quite unceremonious. There was no crowd of people to see her off. Everyone had gone and went about their day. Though she was already a bit behind schedule, Elara found herself wandering back to the docks and beach clear across town. She had spent a long time here. She had enjoyed pleasant and weathered horrid times here, on this beach. It wasn't often she paid that much attention to it in the day—it was a nighttime sort of place for her. In the light of day, Elara didn't find it all that particularly special. It was just a place, even if it was one where she had spent a lot of time. It was just a place, even if it was one that would frequent her nightmares. It was just a place, but it held a unique place in Elara's heart. She would never forget dancing carefree on the beach. She would never forget the smell of her own searing flesh on the metal of the boat. It was certainly with mixed feelings she left this place.

Stuck with an idea, Elara went and purchased a small jar of blueberry jam and some bread. She devoured both and washed the jar of jam out in the sea. The air dried it as she let the waves pour over her feet. She filled the small jar with sand from the beach, sealed it, and placed it in her bag.

She would carry this place with her.

The Valley

1

As Ivivin and his duo of animal partners continued, they began to anticipate arriving at the border of a new country, Olympia. With each day that passed, Ivivin began to worry what crossing the border would entail—what sort of trial he would have to undergo. After quite some time without seeing civilization, Ivivin saw signs of humanity on the horizon. He set Lili's course towards the location, hoping to get an idea of how much further south he had to go before he reached Olympia, as well as what he would need to do to cross. As he approached the settlement, he noted that some of the buildings were a little strange and there seemed to be many stone sculptures sprinkled about. After leaving Lili at the stables and paying for her maintenance, Ivivin stepped into town, hoping to find someone to inform him.

"Well..." Ivivin thought. *"I've had pretty good luck with innkeepers. Might as well give one here a try!"*

Ivivin looked about for an inn, noting that people were coming and going quickly. This was a busy city indeed! Looking more closely, Ivivin saw that the people of this land had a thing for sandals. Moreover, many people were dressed in a fashion that Ivivin was familiar with, but others wore strange draped cloths, wrapped and fastened in clever fashions. Ivivin entered what seemed to be an inn. He looked around for the innkeeper but was instead met by dozens of bunked beds with many people chatting throughout.

Finding his brave, Ivivin approached one of the men.

"Excuse me, what is this place?" Ivivin meekly asked the gentleman.

"Ah! A traveler! And a young one at that! Unusual these days. This here, my lad, is a taberna. Are you from Vasilos, young man?"

Ivivin nodded.

"I see. Well, I don't know if it is exactly the same, but you can think of this place like a hostel from your land. It's like an inn, but for far more people. We have several here in the capital."

Ivivin was overwhelmed by questions, the first and most obvious of which was inspired by the man's response.

"Wait, you asked if Vasilos was my land as if it were not yours. Where am I? Surely not in Olympia?" Ivivin asked, unsure of himself.

"Indeed you are! And not just anywhere! This is the capital... hmm... well, you can think of it as being like the Castletown of your homeland. Welcome!"

Ivivin could not believe it. "But...I didn't cross the border, I don't think. I mean, I didn't see any guards or see any fencing or anything of the like."

The helpful gentleman could not help but laugh a bit at Ivivin's expense. "Sorry for that. It is just that you seem a seasoned traveler, by the feel of you. But now that I look closely, you're also still just a boy. Yes, I assure you that you are in Olympia. There are a few military outposts along the merchant trails, but I assume you didn't take one of them. You can't honestly expect Olympia to line its entire Vasilos border with a wall, can you? That'd be ridiculous and a waste of public funds to boot! Truly a testament to the arrogance of man! Only a fear-mongering megalomaniac would seriously consider it! Anyway, young man. I must away to the capitol. My name is Xerxes. What is yours, if you do not mind me asking?"

"Ivivin, sir." Ivivin stated, trying to be both confident and respectful.

"Ivivin. Alright then, Ivivin, you'll want to enter the building from the other side. A woman named Ari runs this place. Tell her that Xerxes offered to pay for your stay tonight. It's the least I can do for a rare visitor to these parts. Perhaps I shall see you this night!" The man gathered a number of parchments and hurried out of the taberna, leaving Ivivin to check and settle in. He laid on his bunk for just a moment, remembering his naivete during his encounter with Xerxes. He buried his flush cheeks in his hands.

2

Ivivin was not eager to leave his belongings behind in the huge sea of people staying in the taberna, but didn't much feel like hauling around all his belongings either. He compromised and took his coin, his ring, his books, both tears, and Icarus with him— everything valuable that could not easily be replaced. He had originally planned to gather information here, but Ivivin was quickly swept up in the uniqueness of the city. There were elements of Vasilos culture here, sure, but the Olympia culture was very different and juxtaposed strangely next to the former. He found himself in a large building full of art of all different mediums. There were sculptures, like the one lining the streets, but there were also paintings of all sorts. Ivivin had never been surrounded by this much art all at once. There were fields of flowers and rocky shores. There were abstract figures and whimsical scenes. It invoked a strange emotional state in Ivivin. He was overwhelmed, especially by the paintings of obviously real places. He presumed them to be here, in Olympia someplace. They were wondrous locales that Ivivin had not even imagined, despite his traveling ways. He thought back to the story of Elisabeth and the Troll, when Elisabeth was surrounded by her art and how she felt. Ivivin was struck with a similar sentiment and understood the story just a bit better now. Though there was also a twinge of envy towards the artists who captured these scenes, both in the form of wishing he had been there himself and in their ability to capture such scenes and conjure such emotion. Recalling the story, however, also reminded Ivivin of his purpose here. He was here to find Smith and prevent him from falling victim to the same blight that felled Grandia.

3

Ivivin found that the people of the Capital were quite willing to help, if only for a moment here or there. It seemed like everyone had somewhere to be! Through his patchwork investigation, Ivivin found out that this place was not only the capital of the country, but it was also called 'Capital'. That was the actual name of the city! Moreover, Capital housed the capitol of Olympia. And Ivivin thought Smithton was a lame name!

Ivivin was also educated in the structure of government here. Unlike in Vasilos, there was no king. There were periodically elected rulers. There are many senators who consult in the making and enforcement of laws, but there were also two other figures of individual importance. One person was elected to oversee domestic affairs and another in military affairs. They worked together with the senators to ensure peace and stability in the land. The senators hailed from all over the country and they would meet here, in the capitol, every so often to take account of the country and vote on appropriate changes. When the senate is not in session, the country is ruled by the other two leaders. From what Ivivin gathered, there was a special session of the senators happening now, no doubt to address the Crumbleheart outbreak. The taberna that Ivivin occupied was actually very popular for visiting senators. Usually, very few others were allowed to stay there when the Senate was in session. Ivivin was lucky Xerxes had vouched for him. In any case, Ivivin had few things to guide him: the note in the back of Grandia's book about the valley, his knowledge of Smith's mannerisms, and the fact that he was staying in the same place as the politicians discussing the very plague that brought him here. Ivivin headed back to the taberna to await Xerxes' return, hoping to get directions to Giganta Valley and further insight into the nature of Crumbleheart.

4

It was obvious to Ivivin that Xerxes was very worn after his day in the capitol proper. Ivivin considered being considerate, considering the consideration Xerxes had shown him, but Ivivin considered that he likely did not have time to consider such considerate considerations further. He approached Xerxes and explained his mission to the tired senator. The gentleman was quiet, but nodded knowingly at appropriate intervals. When Ivivin finished explaining his situation, the man sighed.

"Ivivin, my lad. I feel for you and your quest. But it is not safe for me to discuss these matters here with you." Xerxes stated bluntly.

"There's nothing you can tell me?" Ivivin nearly pleaded.

"I didn't say that. Hrm..." Xerxes contemplated silently for a moment. "Yes, I do believe that will work. Can you read and write, lad?"

Ivivin nodded.

"Very good! That makes things far easier! Come with me tomorrow to the capitol. You shall be my attendant. In exchange for your help taking notes and the like, you will be granted attendance to our discussions on the matter. Does that sound agreeable?"

Ivivin wasn't sure if this was the best use of his time, but he didn't really have any other leads. He did not want to risk going to the valley unprepared.

"Yes, thank you very much, Senator Xerxes. I'll do my best!"

"That a lad. Now, if you excuse me, I must be off to the land of dreams. Hopefully, with your help, I can be far less tired tomorrow and enjoy some spirits in the evening! We leave at dawn, Ivivin. Be ready!"

5

Ivivin and a groggy Icarus followed Xerxes closely, carrying his things and trying not to lose sight of the senator. There were a lot of odd and, frankly, useless meetings that started the day off. Ivivin had never been so bored as when he took notes here. After what seemed like days of bureaucratic babbling, all the politicians finally gathered together in a grand hall to discuss the plague. Ivivin followed Xerxes into the intricate and artful hall, trying not to stick out too much. Ivivin noted that all the senators were seated in a semi-circle surrounding two seats in the middle. Ivivin presumed correctly that they were for the military leader and the domestic leader. It took a full half of an hour for the room to quiet and for the meeting to begin. It was a long, mind numbing briefing. If Ivivin did not desperately need the information, he might have dozed through the whole thing. The military leader and the domestic leader were conflicted on what course of action they would take. The domestic leader, Brutus, wanted to quarantine the county. He wanted no one to leave and no one to enter until the plague passed. Brutus also theorized that Crumbleheart was only getting worse than it had been because people were bringing a new type of it from outside of the country. However, Arastoo, the military leader, was in favour of keeping the borders open and using their resources to investigate potential causes within their own border. Yesterday, they asked the senators to vote on a course of action and they were split. Today, they were to hear arguments from proponents of each side and vote again at day's end. Ivivin sat through the hearings diligently. By the end of it all, he sided with Arastoo, as did Xerxes. However, the vote at the end of the day was still quite evenly split. Another day of deliberation was scheduled for tomorrow and they were adjourned.

After Ivivin's long and boring day, he had learned a few things. Firstly, that, if the government closed the borders, he would likely be told to leave the country or face jail time—he would need to find Smith before that happened. Secondly, it didn't seem like the officials knew anything about the potential source of the Crumbleheart outbreak that Ivivin had learned from the note in Grandia's book. Giganta Valley was not mentioned at all, so Smith must have discerned that information himself. And, lastly, Ivivin learned the most important lesson of the day—that he never wanted to be a politician.

6

Just outside of the capitol building, Xerxes was stopped by a messenger. After reading the message, he sighed. "Come, Ivivin, it seems we are not done yet."

Ivivin's heart sank, thinking longingly of his bunk back at the taberna. "What do you mean? Is everything alright?"

"Yes, yes. Arastoo just invited me to dinner with him and a few others. It is not exactly an offer I can refuse. Incidentally, I'd like you along so that I have an excuse to excuse myself early. He already has my vote and I have no intent of changing it, so there is no need for him to schmooze and, thus, no need for me to be there. Let's away, Ivivin."

The pair headed to a small hall towards the edge of town. Ivivin had expected the meal to be in a more grandiose location.

And, judging by the look on Arastoo's face, he did as well. They entered to find themselves at an intimate gathering of people. Arastoo sat at the head of the table with a boy at his side. Other than that, there were only a handful of other people.

"Ah! Welcome Xerxes! I hope you found this place easily enough. It is a little out of the way, I suppose. But you know how places fill while the Senate is in session." Arastoo caught sight of Ivivin. "Well now, I saw you and thought you a grown man, but I can tell you are still a youngling. I take it he is your assistant, Xerxes?"

Xerxes nodded.

"He doesn't look to be from these parts, but if you trust in him, I will too. My advisors tell me you are a man to be trusted, after all! I am glad we have the occasion to sit down and know each other, even if it is under troubling circumstances." Arastoo's gaze turned again to Ivivin.

"You, my young lad! What is your name?"

Ivivin did his best to sound confident, though he could tell his nerves were well represented in his voice.

"Ivivin, sir."

"Ivivin, eh? Well, how about you and Xerxes come take a seat near my boy and me. It has been a while since he's made a new friend!"

Ivivin and Xerxes looked at each other and shrugged, before joining Arastoo and his son near the helm of the table.

7

Ivivin was promptly introduced to Belen, the son of Arastoo. He could not have been much younger than Ivivin was when he first set off on his journey, but he certainly appeared more prepared for such an endeavour than Ivivin was. Belen was tall and fit in a way that was clearly the result of dedicated training.

"I suppose that is the result of his father's occupation." Ivivin thought. *"The same reason I know how to till fields is the reason he looks like he could tear a book in two."*

Belen, as Ivivin would find over the course of the evening, was still very much a child, despite his appearance. He found Ivivin's story intriguing and prompted him to tell more and more of it. It reminded Ivivin of the children up in the north he would tell stories to. Everyone had a jovial evening. Ivivin was surprised by how relaxed and informal everyone was being. It was the closest he had felt to having a family dinner since he left home or, perhaps, Elara and Idalia's home. He allowed himself to bask in the warmth of it, which made him both quite happy and a little homesick. Icarus was the life of the party, hopping around on the table from person to person. Apparently, the variety of owl to Icarus belonged did not reside in these lands, so he was new and exciting for them.

Eventually, something had to give. And it did, when Arastoo called attention to those in the room in a serious manner.

"Friends, pardon the interruption. It has truly been a stellar time. However, before it gets any later, I must address the issue I wanted to discuss with you all today. The matter of Crumbleheart. I wanted to further discuss it with you, those who I think I can trust, if you will indulge me for just a moment." His commanding voice easily captured the room. "I have been elected our military's leader for years and years now. Not because I am a lover of war and conflict, but because I am a lover of peace. Still, the nature of my position has led me to see heinous things. Crumbleheart has always dwelled in this land, but is spreading faster than ever. It is a horrible ailment, but it is, in my experience, far from as bad as some travesties man has inflicted on one another. Perhaps Brutus is right—perhaps shutting our borders would help quell the disease. Though it doesn't seem to be spread from person to person, I truly do not know of its true nature. But what I do know is that boundaries and barriers lead to animosity, both between our neighbors and within ourselves. This animosity will mature into conflict and conflict will not help us cure this blight." He paused for a moment to allow the words to permeate his audience fully.

"But, I acknowledge my ignorance. This is an issue so complicated that Brutus and I are both involved. I, just as he is, am out of my depth in many ways. So, I wanted to ask you all for your advice, as I know you will not see my seeking help as weakness but, rather, wisdom. Please, speak if you can fathom alternatives to the plans being voted on or if you have any information to volunteer."

There was mumbling as people racked their brains, trying to solve the problem at hand. Ivivin thought of Smith's note.

"Should I say something?" Ivivin thought, conflicted. Ivivin himself did not understand the nature of the note nor could he elaborate on its meaning. Moreover, he wasn't sure if this

information was meant for these people. It wasn't even really meant for him!

When it became clear to Arastoo that no one had anything new to contribute, he called everyone's attention once more.

"Thank you all for your time. You have my deep and sincere apologies for discussing such unpleasant matters. Let us enjoy the evening once—"

Arastoo paused, noticing that Ivivin had sprung from his seat and was raising his hand, though his eyes were fixed firmly on the floor. Ivivin would trust this man who exuded such a hospitable warmth.

8

"Speak up, young Ivivin." Arastoo gestured. "You have the floor."

Ivivin was nervous, but explained who Smith was, the note he left, and why. Naturally, this led to Ivivin's purpose here in Olympia.

"Hmm…" Arastoo deliberated. "I am sorry, young Ivivin, I cannot yet send troops to investigate the valley. Such an expedition would take much time and many resources to prepare. It could be done, but not while we are in session. I cannot act now, as it will appear as if I am defying the system and acting out against Brutus and those who side with him. And I doubt your evidence would be taken seriously, given its scarce and dubious nature. I believe you; they will not. But you seem set on your mission, so how about we do each other a favour. Go investigate Giganta Valley and report to me your findings. In exchange, I will have my some of my men inquire about the whereabouts of your master. Who knows, it is not unlikely you will find him yourself. But it is also possible you made it here first. In any case, does this sound agreeable, young Ivivin?"

It took only a second for Ivivin to agree.

"*I was going to go anyways. So at least this way, I can search for Smith in several places at once!*" Ivivin reasoned.

"Very good. If there is nothing else, fellows, I suggest we get back to having a jovial time." Arastoo announced.

Ivivin, though, was done. It was enjoyable, but he wanted to sleep so he could set off at first light. Ivivin said goodbye to the disappointed Belen and went to give his thanks to Arastoo. The commander pulled Ivivin close, handed Ivivin a map, and whispered:

"Good luck lad. Be careful out there. Remember, you are not resistant to the disease. Eat only what you bring with you and drink as little as possible. We don't know how it spreads, yet."

9

Ivivin and Icarus mounted a freshly pampered Lili early the next morning. Giganta Valley was further southwest still, according to the map given to him by Arastoo. So, they set their course and travelled as much as they could each day. Ivivin took note as the terrain became more rocky and arid. Fields of grass were supplanted by shrubbery. The earth beneath them became more red. It felt almost like a desert, though the heat was not as extreme as Ivivin remembered. Moreover, there was no sand like the one near Crosstown. Still, Ivivin figured that, if they didn't arrive at the valley today, they would travel instead at night.

As luck would have it though, Ivivin saw the earth open on the horizon just a short while later. It seemed like a modest hole, from a distance. However, as our heroes approached it, Giganta Valley revealed itself to be a massive rift in the earth. It went on as far as Ivivin could see. He dismounted Lili and approached the edge. It was immensely deep and, if there was a way to safely get to the bottom, it'd be steep and difficult. At the bottom, Ivivin could make out water flowing. Suddenly, Ivivin was hit with a bout of vertigo and threw himself away from the edge. His knees were weak and wobbly just from glancing down.

"I'll find a way down there somehow." Ivivin thought *"but only after I check the perimeter. As long as this valley is, it is not particularly wide. I can see pretty clearly across, so I think I can get away with only surveying this side."*

Ivivin, Lili, and Icarus set about the perimeter, each hoping that they would find something so they wouldn't need to descend into the treacherous wound.

10

"What terrible decisions in my life have led me to this point?" Ivivin thought as he scaled down the Valley wall,

desperately fighting the urge to look down. The trio's investigation of the valley perimeter bore no fruit. They had arrived at an unbelievably steep cliff from which the water in the Valley fell to the land below and fanned out in a delta. Upon encountering this roadblock, Ivivin knew he must investigate the interior of the rift. Ivivin instructed Lili to slowly keep pace with them from above, if she could. Ivivin also wasn't confident the horse understood or cared enough to actually do so but, hey, he tried. Icarus, despite having flown his whole life, seemed quite scared of the path that lay before them. There were definite segments where Ivivin could just walk carefully down, but there were also stretches, like the one he found himself on now, that he would need to climb down. Ivivin wasn't particularly afraid of heights before, but he could feel that he was fostering the conditions for such a fear inside himself now.

After long, grueling minutes climbing down, Ivivin touched his feet back to stable and walkable footing. He walked as far as possible before needing to scale down the wall a way. He did this again and again and again, all day before he reached what could be considered the bottom. There were boulders and other loose rocks all over, leading Ivivin to believe that they had fallen from above and that he should keep an eye out for falling debris. Ivivin was on the southernmost end of the Valley. Ivivin watched as the water fell from the valley out to the ground below. The sound of the water was thunderous—much louder than Ivivin had expected. He took a moment to look around and realized that his surroundings were strangely familiar. Eventually, Ivivin realized that he had seen this locale from this perspective in a painting on display in Capital. Ivivin also took note that the shadows cast by the walls of the valley were going to bring darkness earlier than he had anticipated. He would take Icarus and march back towards the northeast for an hour and then he would rest. He found himself more excited than he thought he'd be—after all, this place was a natural marvel that very few people would likely ever have seen or ever would see. As Ivivin tried to find constellations in the narrow band of stars visible to him, he couldn't help but wonder if Elisabeth and Oldman had visited this place on their flowery outings. Yawning, Ivivin ordered Icarus to keep an eye out for trolls as the flowing of water lulled him to sleep.

Ivivin and Icarus got a late start the following day—the sunlight did not stir them until later in the morning. Further, Ivivin's aches from climbing held him fast to the realm of dreams. When they did finally get on their way, Ivivin had to catch himself from stopping and drinking from the river. He had water still and would expend that first before risking the river. They resumed their walk back to the northeast end of the valley. In clear sunlight, Ivivin marveled at the beauty that resided down here. Although nothing seemed to flourish directly by the river, the area along the walls of the valley were lined with strange and exotic plants. Ivivin smiled as he and Icarus passed a small patch of flowers.

He was a little conflicted. He knew he should hurry as to conserve his water and to maximize his chances of learning about the plague. On the other hand, the valley air was cool and it was a marvelous sight to behold. Also, reaching the other end of the valley meant Ivivin would have to scale the walls—a task he was not looking forward to. *"I have had Lili for so long now that I had almost forgotten how long it takes to walk."* Ivivin thought. The resolution of his conflict was a compromise: a fast pace, but with many short breaks intermittently to admire his surroundings.

Ivivin and Icarus had cleared most of the valley quickly. As the sun went down, Ivivin guessed that they were only a few hours away from the other end. He sighed as he tossed rocks into the river.

"I can't believe we came down here for nothing." Ivivin told his owl compatriot. He looked around at the natural wonder surrounding him.

"Well, maybe not for nothing."

Ivivin smiled and laid down, eagerly awaiting the stars' arrival. Once darkness replaced the sundown, Ivivin noticed something in the distance. Ivivin squinted at the dancing light.

It was a fire. A campfire.

Ivivin grabbed Icarus and his things and set out towards the flame. He used the small tear to provide a little extra light to ensure their safe arrival. Sure enough, when Ivivin and Icarus arrived at the campfire, there was Smith, reading by the fireside.

12

It was so surreal, Ivivin seeing Smith outside of Smithton. It was like the man gained a whole other dimension in Ivivin's mind by the simple act of existing somewhere other than from where Ivivin knew him. Smith did a double and then a triple take when he saw Ivivin. He couldn't believe his eyes, either. It didn't take him long to piece together how Ivivin had found him.

"I take it you read Grandia's book then?" Smith asked, not even bothering with formalities.

Ivivin just nodded.

"I would have thought you to have enough respect not to be prying about in my personal things while I was gone. I'm a little disappointed in you, Ivivin. Especially since you're here, instead of keeping your word." Smith grumbled.

Ivivin was a little hurt by Smith's words, but defended himself. "One's word is valuable, yes, and I value mine dearly. But I think there are some things more important than my word. Like you, Smith."

"None of that now. You are here now, anyways, I suppose. What exactly brings you here, lad?" Smith inquired.

Ivivin told Smith about his journey to Olympia, his time in the Senate, and the deal he had made with Arastoo.

"That's all well and good, boy, but that doesn't really answer my question. Why did you come here in the first place?" Smith pressed.

"I came to bring you back, Smith. Please, don't risk your life for this. I beg you. Grandia wouldn't—"

"You have no clue what she'd want!" Ivivin was cut off by an agitated Smith.

The two sat silent for a while, by the campfire. Eventually, Smith sighed.

"Sorry, Ivivin. It's been rough. For what it's worth, I think you're right. She probably wouldn't want me to be out here, doing this. But I don't live just for Grandia's ghost. I make my own choices too. Grandia isn't the only reason I am out here."

Ivivin realized what Smith meant.

"Isabella, the baker woman." Ivivin managed grimly.

"Aye. She was my closest friend, you know? Besides that winged rat of yours, perhaps. Speaking of, hand him over, will ya?"

Ivivin handed Icarus to Smith, who pet the ragged bird delicately as he told Ivivin his story.

The baker woman, Isabella, had gone south to the border to trade with some merchants from Olympia before the current epidemic had spread as far as it had. It was part business venture and part adventure. She traded with them there for a number of Olympia's regional specialties. Naturally, she returned home, both consuming and selling the goods. Not too long after, she contracted Crumbleheart. Smith had recognized her illness immediately and obsessively began to probe the around for answers. He was able to confirm that everyone who bought Olympian goods from her also contracted Crumbleheart. Smith let Isabella know what was going on with her and the other townsfolk. The knowledge that she had sealed the fate of so many others haunted her until she turned hollow. Smith was present for her last words. Although she had not felt or even said a word for days leading up to her death, she looked at Smith just moments before she died. Her face and voice lacked emotion, but she told Smith weakly

"The merchants...south of the great valley."

13

Upon receiving the last words of Isabella the baker, Smith became a man possessed. He paid top dollar for any information he could get about the south, which eventually led him into the possession of a map. There was a city, Pompeii, that was directly south of Giganta Valley. Smith, again, would ask desperately for any information he could get his hands on. Eventually, a traveler from the South—an envoy from the Capital to the king of Vasilos—stopped in Smithton. He had actually made his way to Smith's forge for some routine repairs to his equipment. Smith was not keen on working on armour or weapons, but volunteered his services for free in exchange for news of Pompeii. The envoy was shocked at Smith's proposition—not because it was outrageous, but because Pompeii was the reason that he was headed to see the king in the first place. Pompeii and nearly all of its citizens had gotten sick and died from Crumbleheart. Since then, small isolated waves of it had been appearing all over the country. The envoy was to inform the king of the happenings and gather as much information as he could to bring back. Smith told him about the outbreak in Smithton, fixed his gear, and wished him luck on his journey.

"And then you came here?" Ivivin asked.

"Not quite. Obviously, you came along and gave me the peace of mind to leave. From there, though, I headed straight to Pompeii and some other settlements near it. There weren't many left, but those who had avoided the disease or were not quite felled by it seemed convinced that the disease was the work of a demon in a foreigner's flesh. After much convincing, they let me look at their libraries. There, I found something interesting about the disease. There is a natural amount of the disease that exists all the time for reasons no one knows. That is what I imagine happened to my dear wife. But there were tales of magical beings conjuring outbreaks of the disease to punish those who opposed them. It seemed to match the pattern of the sporadic outbreaks. And if whole towns were being hit, then it made the most sense to me that the source was water. The water in the goods Isabella brought back. The water that the residents of this country drink. And I found that no major outbreak had yet to happen upriver of this Giganta Valley. I arrived here not long ago to investigate. Then, a strange boy and an even stranger owl showed up and started giving me a hard time." Smith finished, smiling at his own little jest.

"I don't suppose there is any way I could convince you to leave and come home to Smithton with me?" Ivivin said, still serious.

"No, I don't suppose there is." Smith replied, poking at the campfire.

Ivivin allowed his expression to ease.

"Well then, I guess I will just have to help you out, then. And then we can go back together."

Smith laughed.

"I don't suppose there is any way I could convince you to go back without me?"

"No, I don't suppose there is."

A Fresh Start

1

Elara had made her way, uneasily, with a group of merchants through Wolfelaw once more. Being in the dark with strangers made her quite uncomfortable, which Elara felt was strange, considering she didn't have an issue with it before. Luckily, there was a very friendly family traveling with the merchants as well. The mother Able and the father Abraham decided that they were going to move their two daughters, Hope and Grace, to Smithton. The wanted to get a fresh start, as they had lost a lot during Ajaxx's rule over Rumi. The sisters were excited and energetic the whole way. They were young, 5 and 7 years old respectively. Hearing their strange and nonsensical imaginings and musings made Elara fondly recall all the times she played with her sister. Although reluctant at first, she allowed herself to be roped into the siblings' hijinks before long. When the caravan had stopped at the halfway point to rest for a few hours, Elara showed the young girls some of the dancing motions Petil had shown her. At first, they lacked coordination and balance (which was adorable and extremely endearing). Elara was surprised by how quickly they picked it up, though. Moves that had taken her hours of practicing seemed to come to them much easier.

"Huh, I suppose I also learned very quickly when I was young." Elara thought as she watched the girls frolic about.

Elara was still filled with a torrent of different emotions and sentiments, but watching these little ones dance about carefree warmed Elara's heart and brought her peace, for a while. She chatted with the parents, who had sold their home to go live with the Able's sister in Smithton. When they reached the exit of Wolfelaw, Elara said her goodbyes to the young girls who had grown quite fond of Elara.

Elara didn't really have a plan for where she was going, but she wanted to explore aimlessly for a while. She had always had a mission, destination, or a goal in her mind. For once, though, she was unbound beyond her general aspiration of seeing the world.

2

Elara set out due west of the Wolfelaw caverns. Today, she just wanted to keep moving. Her legs felt strong and she was proud of each step she took. Her strength, it seemed, had returned to her when she was back on the road. Elara wasn't even sure how long she had been in Rumi. She didn't keep track. She certainly felt older, though. As the sun started to set, Elara decided to call it a day early. The march through Wolfelaw had worn her out and she was in no hurry to get anywhere. She felt a peaceful weariness start to wash over her the moment she laid down. Elara had to stop herself from getting excited at how easily sleep was coming to her. She drifted off without incident.

Faces flashed. Scenes melded together in a distorted fashion. The sound of heavy breathing intensified and resounded in Elara's mind over and over and over. A raw fear, unprocessed by the lens of reason, invaded Elara's being. Finally, a disfigured face of a man with beastly features snuffed out all her other senses and consumed her.

Elara awoke, unable to breathe and with a searing pain in her chest. Her stomach quivered with unease and her world was spinning. Elara wanted to stand and breathe, but felt any movement would cause her to vacate her stomach. Trembling, she wiped her face of the coldest of sweats. The salty expressions stung her sensitive hands. After what felt to Elara an eternity, she had recomposed herself. Tears welled up in the corner of her eyes, but did not fall. She was disappointed in herself and shocked at how quickly her state of mind could go from at peace to being in shambles. She laid awake, alone, until the sun broke the horizon.

3

Elara packed her things and, less than eagerly, continued marching due west. She was tired and feeling numb. Lethargy stripped her of all motivation to walk within just the first few hours of travel. So, she stopped. Usually, Elara greatly enjoyed lazy days. Lounging around and relaxing were her favourite ways to spend a day while traveling. Today was different, though. She stopped with the intent of relaxing, but felt anxious and restless, despite having no motivation to be productive and continue her travel. She didn't have an appetite, so eating or gathering food both sounded like unbearable chores. A vague and nebulous unease was knocking upon her psyche. She picked up the book of the tale of the first king to re-read some of her favourite passages, but they would not capture her attention, let alone her imagination. Frustrated at her own disinterest and inability to relax, as well as the amorphous cause of her fidgeting, Elara grabbed her things and set out in a huff.

Frustration had sprinkled some motivation into Elara's well, but that well ran dry again within another hour of walking. And Elara repeated the cycle again and again, becoming more upset with each iteration. It was not until she noticed the sun nearing the end of its daily slog that the cycle was broken. Elara's frustration was replaced with dread of the coming night. She convinced herself that things would be different, this time, and set up camp. Acting for only herself, she pretended she was chipper and excited to rest for the evening. As soon as her preparations were complete, though, the facade failed. She was back to feeling terrible. Inspired briefly, Elara got out some of her charting paper and tried to take account of some of the stars in the sky. It was literal seconds before the excitement faded. She realized that her enthusiasm was for the prospect that charting the stars would help, rather than for the charting itself. She laid down, her body and mind tired both from the lack of sleep and from the emotional turmoil of the day.

Nightmares invaded Elara's sleeping mind once more. As she fought to hold herself together upon waking, Elara had never felt so alone—so lonely. The solitude that was once peaceful and natural felt to her a curse laid onto her as punishment for her own weaknesses. However, time and weariness eventually served as an anesthesia and she managed to sleep, for a while.

4

Elara could feel herself wasting away. She knew something was wrong with her, but knowing didn't help her combat it. She forced herself to eat and drink from time to time, but derived no enjoyment or satisfaction from it. Moreover, Elara traveled very little these days and actually found herself walking in circles some days. The nightmares were not an everyday occurrence, but they had a way of infecting her dreams anytime she managed to build a little motivation. Days that were nightmare-free instead left Elara in an analgesic state. She would lay about all day, feeling both pain and numbness in unpredictable and alternating fashions. Most days, she didn't even bother to unpack her bag and there were contents therein that had not seen the light of day in nearly a week.

What made all this even worse, to Elara, is that she knew it was not normal. She knew that something was wrong. She felt stupid and weak-willed for not being able to address and overcome this obstacle that lay directly in front of her. Still, Elara was a sensible young woman. When she happened upon a pristine and comfortable location near a creek, she decided she would stay there until she sorted herself out. She could scavenge to feed herself easily here and try to conquer the demons inside playing her for a puppet. Honestly, Elara didn't see an end to these tiresome and miserable days. She still had no clue how she would deal with herself. But she knew that, if she didn't try, she was going to lose herself. This was as good a place and as good a time as any to try. As a sign of her resolve to stay her until she fixed herself, Elara unpacked all her belongings, making a sort of abode under a large elm tree by the creek.

5

Things had not improved much in the days immediately following Elara's decision to stop near the creek. She continued to be lethargic and unmotivated. Her nightmares continued. They weren't always compilations of her experience in Ajaxx's castle. Other times, they were of the night the boat burnt. Sometimes she saw the women that were burnt terribly blaming her for not coming to help them sooner. Yet other times, though, and more and more often, Elara would just dream of non-specific locales and people in Rumi, but the association of that place with her anxieties and fear caused those to feel like nightmares too.

On this particular night, Elara woke from a nightmare in which she relived a hellish version of her confrontation of Ajaxx in his prison cell. The bars could not contain him as he became a noxious mist that surrounded and invaded Elara. She tried to get to the Madame and Bennu behind the door, but they were gone. She woke and released bile from her empty stomach. Weak, tired, and afraid, Elara went to her belongings to get her book and try and calm down by reading. She wished that she had the constellation book that she had given Ivivin. She missed reading it.

No, that wasn't quite it.

She missed reading it and staring at the stars with her sister. She missed her sister terribly.

"If Idalia were here, I think I'd be ok." Elara thought as she stopped paused with her hand still in her bag. In this moment, Elara yearned desperately to not be alone. She desperately wanted somebody, anybody, to hold her. She especially wanted to hold her sister and looks at the stars and sing silly ditties. Elara was losing herself to her pain and longing. But then, a tune broke the silence of the night. A soft, simple, and familiar melody echoed in the air. Elara remembered the stone that she had taken from Ajaxx's castle and dug in her bag to find it. From the very bottom of her belongings, she pulled out the small stone. Sure enough, it was the source of the music.

Elara listened to the tune closely and nostalgia hit her like an ox. It was, roughly, the lullaby that her mother sung to her when she was young and that, in turn, Elara would sing to Idalia. Maybe it was just wishful thinking, but Elara swore the tone and timbre of the notes were the same as Idalia's own lovely voice. Warm tears flowed from her face as she leaned against the tree. With the music continuing to penetrate the night, Elara managed to fall into a restful slumber.

6

Elara woke the next day. She did not feel any less insensate towards doing, well, anything at all really. She was tempted to just lay like a log all day. But she forced herself to her feet. She forced herself to eat. She forced herself to dance. She forced herself to practice with her new weapons. She forced herself to read. She found no pleasure in any of these things this day and in this place. But she did them anyways. And, when the sun fell and the stars came out of their hiding place, Elara forced herself to add to her charts, too. She felt nothing for the activity other than the twinges of pain still lingering in her bad hand. But she did it anyways. She hadn't figured out how the stone worked or why, but she held it tight to her chest as she went to bed. There was no music tonight. Elara left from and returned to the waking world many times throughout the night. But when morning came, Elara rose all the same. And, again, she forced herself to eat. To dance. To practice. To read. To chart. She would teach herself to feel like herself again, slowly. Her only encouragement was the idea that things couldn't get worse so, if she could just hold on, they would have to get better.

And so, day by day, Elara desperately held on. There were nights where she felt strongly. These days every sad thought or occurrence brought her to tears and felt like the end of the world. On these days, the smallest, most inconsequential fond memory would carry her through the day. Other days, she felt little. Apathy dominated her being and Elara existed and persisted simply out of routine and habit. Some days, the music stone would sing to her heart. Some days, the song would help Elara reach peace and ward off her nightmares. On others, they still seeped into her mind despite the sweet melody. Some days, the stone was still as, well, stone. And on some of these days, her terrors dictated her dreams. But on others, her mind was as clear and still as the night.

Little by little, Elara felt more and more like herself. And, for no reason in particular, she decided to leave her spot by the creek. It wasn't that she felt one-hundred percent or even that she was confident that she would be ok. It was that Elara realized she could not conquer these problems by sheer force of will. But she could bear them. She could bear them and try to thrive despite them. She knew she was alone and that she was lonely, but came to realize she didn't have to be. She thought of the little girls, Grace and Hope, and the sorts feelings they and their parents brought to the surface.

"Maybe I, too, need a fresh start." Elara said to no one. And so, step by step, Elara headed nearly due north, towards Smithton— towards her fresh start.

7

Elara's journey to Smithton was a lot like her time at the creek. There were days where she was eager and excited to be starting the next chapter of her adventure. She was even hopeful, at times, that she could find happiness. Other days, her legs felt like lead and the days felt like they would never end. But she slogged on regardless. And, while she was walking, she had time to reflect. She might not be able to conquer herself with force of will, but getting to the heart of some of what haunted her might help her mitigate the damage. It was difficult, as Elara had always felt as if she was responsible for her life and what happened in it. Previously, her pains and sorrows, as few as they had been, were always a result of her choices and pretty obviously so. So, she often felt that the failure of the Sparrows, the way that Ajaxx saw her, and all the pain that came after were all her fault too. This made her feel like she was just too ignorant and incapable to even find know why she deserved these wounds, but she felt certain that she did indeed deserve them. Even as she told herself that there were things in this world and in her life beyond her control—that she could never control—she never could fully bring herself to believe it. Even when she thought back to things like the Shaa'Ra and the circumstance of her own birth— things she knew predated her very existence—she couldn't bring herself to detach responsibility from it. Still, she was aware of it and that was better than nothing, right?

Elara spent her days journeying to Smithton in this way, with habits slowly returning to hobbies and introspection both helping and harming her. After what felt like both a long time and no time at all, Elara arrived at Smithton. She entered town from the west side, passing some burnt down buildings and a shoddy barn. She considered resting inside a while but, upon second glance, she decided she would have to be extremely desperate to sleep in such a dingy place. She'd sooner sleep on the hard earth. At least then she'd be under the stars. Still, she allowed herself to marvel at her accomplishment for just a moment before taking her first steps into Smithton—her first steps to a fresh start.

8

The novelty of Smithton did not endure nearly as long as Rumi. It was not nearly as large or impressive, nor was there a vast sea and beach for her to lounge about. Elara had money, plenty of it, from the reward given to her by Rumi. She lived comfortably and kept up with her routine, save the reading. She had finished the tale of the first king. Though she had really enjoyed it, she grew tired of rereading passages from it. But even if she spent a few hours a day reading, it would not be enough fill her time. She spent much of the day idly wandering around. Often, she found that while she was in town, she yearned for the wilderness. But no sooner than she left, she found herself wanting to interact with people in town. It was a frustrating and contradictory duality.

Elara found it hard to make friends in Smithton. Not because the people seemed unfriendly. They were nice enough, though some seemed a little uneasy to be talking to an out-of-towner. No, Elara was just unsure how to go about opening up to and connecting with people. It didn't help, either, that her self-worth wasn't particularly high—she did not feel deserving of friends. So, most of Elara's interaction with people were short exchanges while shopping or the occasional over-friendly person over-sharing.

She felt like, at best, being here so idly had stalled her growth and recovery. At worst, Elara feared that she would slip up and give in to herself once more.

Elara sighed.

"As much as I love my lazy days, I think it's time I looked for work."

9

Elara's job hunt bore fruit, but not the sort she wanted to eat. She had funds to sustain herself for quite some time, so she felt no need to accept whatever job she was offered first. She inquired at the local taverns about positions similar to those she worked at in Rumi. She even worked a few evenings at one. But the work reminded her too much of her time in Rumi—a sentiment further amplified by the gaze of drunk and careless men. So, she left that job, apologizing profusely to the owner, but regretting nothing. Elara did not see herself above working some laborious jobs that she happened upon, but the tools she'd need to use would cause her hands a great deal of pain. Elara was at a loss for what she could do and it made her feel a bit worthless. It was not until Elara saw an older woman struggling to carry her things in the market that things started to change for the better.

Elara saw the woman and quickly asked if the woman she could help. The woman smiled and agreed, allowing Elara to ease her burden. They caught each other's eyes for a moment. Elara saw a lot of her mother in this woman. And, much like her mother, Elara felt this woman could see right through her.

"Thank you, dear. I hate to bother you further, but if you're not busy, could I trouble you to come with me to one or two more places?" The older woman asked Elara in raspy, but gentle tone.

Elara nodded.

"Excellent! Thank you so very much. My name is Minerva. May I have yours?"

"My name is Elara. It is a pleasure to meet you Minerva. So, shall we get going?"

Elara accompanied Minerva on her last two errands. First, Elara went with her to meet a hunter. Elara thought she might be getting meat from him, but instead found herself carrying snakeskins and an assortment of feathers. It was certainly strange. But Elara really didn't mind. Minerva was a charming old woman. She masterfully held a conversation with Elara, choosing topics that resonated with them both, all while weaving in subtle jokes in seamlessly. Elara just enjoyed her time walking around town with Minerva.

Their second stop was not to pick something up—it was to drop something off. Minerva asked Elara to wait for her just a moment outside of someone's home. Minerva handed a small glass vial to the fellow who answered the door. His face had been gaunt and it was easy to tell he had been losing sleep—something Elara knew and recognized all too well. But when Minerva handed him the vial, he perked up and shook her hand profusely, even bowing to her a little. They parted with a wave, the whole exchange taking no more than a minute or two. Minerva rejoined Elara and they set off towards Minerva's own store.

"Aren't you going to ask me what that was about? You seem like you are dying to know." Minerva asked Elara.

Elara was caught off guard.

"Umm, well yes, I am curious, but it is none of my business and I didn't want to upset you." Elara managed, flustered.

"Oh, you won't upset me dear Elara. When you are curious, ask questions. It's the best way to learn, you know. Come, my tea shop is just a little way from here."

Elara blushed, but followed Minerva nonetheless.

10

Minerva's teashop was pungent. It wasn't necessarily an offensive fragrance, but it's presence was certainly overwhelming. For the most part, the front of the shop was filled to the brim with different tea leaves available to purchase and make yourself.

However, in the corner there was a small table with two seats, which Elara took to mean you could get a hot cup made for you here, too.

"I'll have to come have some tea here sometime and chat with Minerva some more." Elara thought.

"Come, come dear. Here in the back, if you would. Thank you so much." Minerva said, leading Elara through a small doorway leading to the back. This part of the building seemed to be Minerva's living quarters. There was an area for cooking and an area for sleeping. But, other than that, Elara couldn't make out many features of the house—not because it was bare. No, she couldn't make out the features because it was horribly cluttered and full of a variety of things. It honestly reminded her a bit of the Madame's office...after it was destroyed.

"Just put it anywhere, dear." Minerva said, dropping the things she was carrying haphazardly and suddenly. "I'll put them away later."

It felt wrong, but Minerva kept staring at Elara expectantly, so she awkwardly dropped her encumbrances.

"WHAT ARE YOU DOING!?" Minerva yelled, making Elara jump. Minerva then started giggling. "Sorry dear, sorry. It was just too tempting to resist. Give me a moment and I will meet you in the shop. Feel free to look around a bit while you wait."

Elara obeyed and walked about the shop, looking at the variety of teas, roots, and herbs on display. Elara read small labels on top of different jars and cases. Some things, she had heard of. She even found the same tea she shared with Bennu and Madame Cantabelle in Rumi. Others, though, were strange, and she wasn't even sure how to make the proper sounds to pronounce them. There was one that caught her eye.

"H-I-B-I-S-C-U-S" Elara spelled out, looking intently at what looked to be dried flower petals.

"Oh, you can read then?" Minerva said, causing Elara to jump yet again. "Sorry, sorry. You're awfully excitable, you know that?" Elara shook off her alarm and responded.

"Yes, I can. My mother taught me. You remind me a lot of her." Elara said, reminiscing. She brought herself back and asked Minerva about the hibiscus. "Can you really make tea out of these? They look like flowers, not leaves."

"Yes, you can. And they are flowers indeed. I find them beautiful in all stages of being: When they are small and simple seeds, like a newborn; when they're fresh and live, like you; when they're dry and wrinkled, like myself; and when they are seeped and lay buried under red waters. How about I give you some to take with you, as thanks for today?"

Minerva pulled a small pouch out and filled it with hibiscus. Elara tried to object, but Minerva insisted. Elara looked down at the gift and felt incredibly touched. She had really enjoyed her day with Minerva. She felt safe. She felt useful. And she felt wanted. And, now that she had finished the errands and even gotten a token of gratitude, she felt like she was expected to leave. And she wasn't ready.

Minerva, the experienced and worldly woman she was, read Elara like a book.

"You know, I could use someone as young and strong as you around the shop this afternoon. I'll pay you what I can for your time, of course, though it isn't much more than a pittance. I need some things moved while I work on some things. We can chat while we work. What do you say, Elara? Could you help me out a little longer?"

Elara accepted, almost ashamed at her own eagerness, and put on an apron Minerva handed her.

11

Elara was charged, over the course of couple of days, with organizing some of the larger containers and cleaning up the shop. Lifting pained Elara's hands, but she didn't want to disappoint Minerva, so she dealt with it. All the while, Minerva prodded Elara to tell her about herself and Elara felt unnaturally inclined to reveal things about herself. She did not mention anything about Jupiter, of course, but she told Minerva all about her life so far. She started with how she and her sister were orphans, adopted by their foster mother. She told her numerous stories about her time as a sort of unofficial guardian of her hometown and how it felt good to help people. She told her an abridged and redacted version of her confrontation with the Shaa'Illi. She told her about Ivivin and his mangy owl. She told her about setting forth on her own journey, of crossing a sandy desert and seeing a giant water-lizard with an island on its back. She told her of meeting Petil and her bear. She told her the legend of the Wolfelaw Caverns. But, when it came time in her story to talk about

Rumi, Elara stopped talking about her life altogether and focused entirely on her work.

Shrewd and attentive, Minerva finished the page of a book she was reading intently. It's not that she didn't trust Elara. To her, she seemed like a trustworthy gal. But the stories she told were a bit fantastic. She knew of magic and of creatures, but Minerva had a hard time believing that the sweet young girl in front of her had taken out a cult. However, this pause in her story intrigued and worried Minerva. It lent credence to Elara's tale, if only because Minerva could tell that Elara had reached a painful point in her recollection. Minerva closed her book, marking it with a dried flower, and walked over to the store's front door and locked it. Given that it was in the middle of the day, Elara was naturally a bit alarmed at this.

"What's wrong, Minerva?" Elara said, finally looking up from the floor she was sweeping.

"Nothing, dear. Nothing. I just thought we might have a seat and chat a while." Minerva said, gesturing to the small table in the corner of the shop. They both sat and enduring a rare silence before Minerva prompted Elara.

"I'd love to hear the rest of your story, Elara, and wanted to give it the attention it merits."

"No, you wouldn't want to hear about it. It's nothing, really. A really boring time." Elara defended.

"Nonsense, deary. You've done such a good job. Don't stop now that it's gotten hard." Minerva met Elara's eyes.

"You can do it."

Elara's lip quivered as she tried to fight the urge to cry. She couldn't believe how transparent she was.

"Now there, Elara. Just because I can see your scars doesn't mean you're weaker for the wound. I am listening."

Elara burst open like a floodgate. She told Minerva of the wonder she had when she arrived in Rumi. About the beach. About the water. About the Sparrows. About Ajaxx. About the fire. About the Sagehens. About the hate that nearly consumed her. About Operation Blue Bird. About the nightmares that plagued her. About her trip to and time thusly in Smithton. She told her everything. By the time she finished, several waves of tears had already washed her face and the sun had already begun to kiss the horizon.

Minerva grabbed Elara's wrists and had her open her hands. Minerva saw fresh rawness and blisters forming on the scars of her wound and cried a little herself.

"I am so sorry I had you do all that moving. I didn't know."

"It's ok, its ok. I wanted to, really." Elara tried to assure the kind woman.

"I know, deary. I know. Wait right here. I have something that can help." Minerva said, headed back to her home. She reemerged with a small bowl of a light green paste.

"Put this on your hands. It will help." Minerva said, setting the bowl in front of Elara. Elara obliged and gingerly put the paste on her hands. Instantly, the pain in her hands eased. Elara looked at the paste on her hand and saw it was glowing faintly. After a few seconds, the paste had become white and dry. It crumbled off Elara's hands. They were healed! Well, not *healed* healed, but they were in the best condition they had been since the incident with the burning ship.

"How...?" Elara stated, startled.

Minerva snickered.

"Deary, I must have lived nearly five of your lives. You aren't the only one with an interesting story. You see, before I sold tea, I was an apothecary and potion maker. Even spent some time in the castle, I did. I do not mean to change the topic too much but, as I have a proposition for you, I fear it is unavoidable. You see, in a way, I have come out of retirement. And I'd like your help."

12

"Elara, the reason many of this town are uneasy, especially around strangers, is the recent spread of a disease from our neighbor, Olympia. Usually, very few cases happen at all, let alone up this far north. But there were recent outbreaks all around down there and as far north as here, in Smithton. The exact cause of the disease is unknown, though many have come to suspect it is transmitted via food or water, so everyone is a little cautious and on edge. There are even those who are pushing for us to close our borders with Olympia altogether. The disease is devastating and it'd be worth seeking a treatment for that alone, but I'd also hate to see our countries pushed to conflict over something like this. That is why I am, once more, seeking a cure." Minerva explained to Elara.

"What is the disease like?" Elara asked, morbidly curious. She imagined all manners of rotting flesh or bloody excrements must be the reason everyone is on edge.

Minerva sighed sadly.

"The disease is amoung the most horrid of ailments man has ever come to face and there is little else like it in this world. It makes explaining it quite difficult. It is both a disease of the body and of the soul, though which gives out first depends on the individual. The heart—the one in your chest—is slowly weakened and eroded away. Usually, the cause of death is that the heart falls apart under the pressure of its own beat."

Elara clenched at her own chest, the description enough to cause her own heart to feel pained and feeble.

"That sounds horrid." Elara remarked.

"As far as deaths go, that isn't so bad. Not great, mind you. But there is far worse." Minerva continued. "But that is only half the story. You see, Crumbleheart also assaults your spiritual heart. Those ill-fated enough to contract the disease will slowly lose themselves. They'll be unable to feel any joy, any love, any happiness. As the disease progresses still, they'll even lose the bittersweet sensations of homesickness and longing. Eventually, even the sorrowful feelings of man are lost to them. They become numb and insensate. They become truly and entirely cold." Minerva's voice trembled a little as she finished.

Elara was horrified by the disease's description, but her horror evolved into panic when she found notes of the disease's progression in what she had been battling with recently.

"Minerva, I… Do I have Crumbleheart?" Elara asked, breathing heavily.

Minerva stared at Elara a moment, filled with compassion and pity at Elara's struggle.

"No, deary, I do not think you do. Your struggles and turmoil seem to be of a natural sort, even as intense and terrible as they are."

Elara was not so sure. The onset of a disease like that would explain how weak she felt she had become. It would explain how she found it hard to derive joy, her unrest, and the numbness she often felt.

"Are you sure?" Elara almost begged. She wasn't sure if she'd be happier if her pain was caused by a disease or not, but the thought now bounced around inside her incessantly.

The old apothecary saw clearly the tension rising within Elara. "I am sorry, my gentle girl. I, perhaps, spoke too soon or too frankly of the ailment and I can see that my words have left you confused and panicked. I hinted before how this is not to be my first attempt at curing the disease. Last I tried, I failed to save the woman I desperately fought for. But I had invented, at least, a way to test for the disease. It has never once failed. Would you like to undergo it?" Minerva offered.

Elara was conflicted. Surprisingly, she felt she could deal with either outcome of the test. The larger issue was a matter of pride. Elara feared that even the act of taking the test would be conceding and admitting she was weak. Whether it was the disease or her own sorrows she could not conquer did not matter. Elara felt she needed to face them alone. Still, she wanted the test. She wanted to know. She wanted something resembling help. After some moments of silence, Minerva again pipped up.

"Elara, dear, just as I said before about learning and asking questions, it is ok to ask for help. I will not condescend you and tell you that asking for help is an act of strength. That trope is as old and worn as I am. And I know it doesn't feel like an empowering option. But there certainly is not weakness or shame in it. It is just you and I here, people all the same. So, did you want me to fetch the test? Peace of mind is a powerful thing." Minerva replied.

Elara nodded, thankful for Minerva's words.

13

After some rustling and the sound of broken glassware came from the back, Minerva emerged with a vial of scarlet, a small stone cup and a tall, narrow stone vessel. Minerva set herself back down at the table and poured some liquid from the vessel into the cup. Watching the liquid flow was entrancing. The liquid seemed to form thin silver threads as it fell into the cup but, after settling a moment, formed a single clear pool in the cup. In fact, the liquid was so clear, it was only in movement that Elara could tell there was anything in the cup at all.

"I am sorry, deary, but I must prick your finger for some blood. I know it will hurt more for you than for others, but please bear it." Minerva said, grabbing a needle from her pocket and holding out her hand for Elara's.

Elara held out her hand for Minerva. As she went to prick Elara's finger, Elara was strongly reminded of her mother once more and of the test for Jupiter's tear. She recalled the scene as Minerva pricked her finger. Rather than wince or moan or cry, as Minerva expected, Elara burst into laughter as her blood fell into the cup. Elara had remembered that Ivivin's mangy owl was the reincarnation of a divine being! How could she have forgotten that absurdity for even a moment?

Elara gathered her senses and returned to the serious matter at hand. She joined Minerva in staring as her blood sank to the bottom of the cup, knowing she would need to explain the outburst later. Slowly, the blood was broken apart and simply became part of the clear fluid.

"What's that mean?" Elara asked the wise woman.

"You have not the disease, Elara. I have here a vial of blood taken from a woman who fell to the disease many years ago, when I last fought against it. I will show you what would happen if you had the disease."

Carefully, Minerva let some drops of blood flow from the vial into the cup. The liquid formed cold crystals along the side of the cup. The area right around them had gotten noticeably cold. Lastly, small black flecks were released and floated to the surface of the liquid as the blood was broken apart. After a few moments more, the flecks, too, dissolved and brought the liquid to a soft boil in the process. A minute later, the reaction had ceased and Minerva packed her supplies away, returning them to the back. Elara was left to marvel in the phenomenon she had just witnessed. It was surely a thing of magic!

When Minerva again resumed her spot at the table, Elara could not help but blurt out: "You're a wizard, Minerva!" Minerva got a chuckle out of Elara's frankness.

"No dear, not quite. While it's true there is magic weaved into some of my concoctions, I far from command it. Instead, I just take the magic found in the world around us and try to bring it out in useful ways. Of course, not everything has a cure and not everything is magic."

Elara's heart sank. She had allowed herself to hope, even for just a moment, that Minerva would have something that could help her ward off her internal pain.

"I do think I have something that will help you feel better, though, now that I know your story. I'll go fetch it, should be about done by now." Minerva said gently to Elara.

Minerva once more went into the back and once more came out with stone cups. This time, they were filled with a creamy brown liquid concoction. Minerva handed Elara one of the cups. "Here, deary, drink this. Be careful, it's hot!"

Minerva handed the potion to Elara, smiling. Elara sipped the liquid. It was as creamy as it looked and sweet to boot! The elixir began to spread throughout Elara's body. She looked at Minerva and thought of her kindness and how grateful she was for the time they had gotten to spend together over the course of just a few days. Warmth and comfort spread throughout her body. She relaxed. As she kept sipping on the magical draught, she decided that it was alright to ask Minerva about the fantastic brew.

"Minerva, what is this brilliant liquid salve? What magic is it made of?" Elara asked.

"Oh? Is it working?" Minerva responded.

Elara nodded.

"Why, my deary, that is tea. Chai, to be exact. Served with plenty of cream and sugar. It, combined with each other's company, is pretty magical, no?" Minerva revealed before sipping from her own cup.

14

Not wanting to taint their evening, Minerva dropped the topic of the cure and the two of them just chatted about silly nothings. After many laughs and stories, Minerva yawned.

"Sorry, deary. These old bones aren't meant for this hour. Please, come back by tomorrow. I have something to discuss with you."

Elara nodded and the two went their separate ways. Elara found it hard not to skip along with her heart all the way back to the inn she was staying at. Unease crept its way into Elara's mind when she laid in bed, but she did not allow it to strangle out the positive feelings and thoughts of the day. She slept peacefully, despite the thoughts lurking in the back of her mind.

15

When Elara returned to Minerva's tea shop the following day, Minerva took her to the back and revealed a small stairway leading to a basement. There, Minerva had all manners of equipment and materials. Unlike her home, everything was neatly organized and tucked away. There were even strange ducts above some of the equipment as way for smoke or fumes to escape.

"What is this place?" Elara wondered aloud.

"Well, it's my workspace. A laboratory, some would call it." Minerva elucidated. "Let me get to the point, Elara. Before, when I first tried to cure the disease, I was old but still quite capable. I could go out and find materials for my trials on my own. Now, though, I find myself quite unable and I fear I cannot find everything I need readily or affordably in town. So, dear Elara, I'd like you to journey out in my stead. Of course, I cannot pay you lavishly, but there will be a small salary in it for you. Plus, I'll even teach you some of my tricks. There is not enough time in my years left on this world to make you a master, but I can get you started, if you'd like."

Elara had never considered this sort of work before, but it seemed right up her alley. As it was, she had found herself paradoxically both drawn to and pushed away from town. At least now, her coming and going would have purpose. Elara agreed to help Minerva, but a question formed in the back of her mind.

"Minerva, I am excited to help. But I can't help but notice how somber you become when you mentioned when you last tried to do away with the disease. What happened?" Elara inquired.

"Ah, I see. You are not the only one that's easy to read, hmm? Yes, I shall tell you. The woman who I keep alluding to was a woman named Grandia. She was a wild spirit and wonderful woman. Keen and clever and kind. I knew her well, as she'd often come ask me about my life and share a cup of tea with me, not unlike you and me. She loved to sing, though the gods certainly did not bless her with the voice for it. More than that, though, she loved to travel, to read, and to write. She contracted the disease while visiting the south during a fit of wanderlust. Her husband was desperate and distraught and sought many avenues to find a cure, some of which ended tragically themselves. He knew of me through stories from his wife and came to me, pleading for me to help develop a cure. He brought with him a book his wife had brought back for me in Olympia. It was an encyclopedia of flora and fauna she thought I might find useful." Minerva paused for a moment to sip some tea before continuing. "Well, to be frank, I didn't much care for the man. He was large, brutish, and lacked the sophistication that I felt Grandia deserved. But, I knew her love for him and I could see his love for her. My heart would have been stone itself had I declined. So, I agreed and poured my everything into curing her. She...passed before I found one, though I earnestly was likely nowhere close. She was a good friend and a young mother. I wanted quite badly to save her, but could not. After she passed, I abandoned the idea of a cure and, not long after, abandoned my craft in favour of running this teashop." Minerva finished.

"Such a tragic story for all involved." Elara thought before reaffirming her decision with Minerva.

"I am happy to help however I can."

"I am happy to hear that, Elara. Then, I will be sending you away quite soon. I have a list here for you. I am glad you can read, it makes all this much easier!" Minerva said, handing Elara a well-organized list.

Elara looked the list over. At best, she knew what half of these things were and, at best, had seen just half of that half.

"I am sorry Minerva, but I truly do not think I can find all these for you. I don't even know how to say some of these, let alone what they are."

Minerva smiled. "Yes deary, that makes sense. It takes a lifetime of being out in the wilds to characterize and commit to memory that which exists there. However, I have one of man's greatest inventions that should help you on your way."

Minerva handed Elara a book. It was the encyclopedia of flora and fauna that Grandia had gifted to her. The corners were a bit dog-eared and the cover stained by the sun. It was easy for Elara to tell that Minerva had brought this out on many an excursion.

So, Elara left the town of Smithton in search of ingredients. As she walked, she opened the book to gather clues on where she should head first. On the very first page, in very proper and, frankly, artful handwriting, was a note to Minerva.

To Minerva, my dear friend.
You have helped many more than you have ever hurt. You are wonderful. Forgive yourself and, while you're at it, forgive me for being so blunt and forward.
Thank you for sharing your passion and your life's tale with me. I hope this book helps you pass that passion on to others still.
Your friend, now and always,
—Grandia

Mars

1

Ivivin and Smith woke early alongside the sun. They were going to further investigate the valley. Smith had started on the same end that Ivivin had, but had taken his time to thoroughly inspect the details. They planned to investigate this end of the valley with equal scrutiny. Icarus sat perched on Smith's shoulder, excited for some time with the surprisingly soft-hearted smith. They had saved the area around the great waterfall that continued the river for last. They had done so in hopes that they'd find clues before facing the torrent of water. Unfortunately, they had no such luck. They cautiously approached the wall to inspect it. Ivivin found nothing, though he couldn't get as close as he had wanted. But when Smith went to double check, still sporting a soggy Icarus, the waterfall parted around them, revealing a cavern. Smith backed away and the waterfall closed the cavern shut again. He stepped forward and it opened once more. Smith did this several more times, fascinated by the strange phenomenon. After a few dozen times, Ivivin's patience wore a bit thin and he called out to Smith to cut it out.

Ivivin went to grab Icarus so he could protect his feathered friend from any potential dangers that lay within. In grabbing Icarus, he moved the bird slightly further away from the waterfall. At the same time, the waterfall sealed the cavern once more. Smith and Ivivin looked at each other and then at the owl, who was preening himself in Ivivin's hands. Ivivin held Icarus out, parting the water and opening the cavern again. He brought the owl to his chest and it closed. He repeated this a dozen or more times before Smith coughed loudly and deliberately. Ivivin snapped to and the trio decided to enter the cavern.

As the young Ivivin took his first step into the cavern, Icarus in hand, he couldn't help but think:

"I'm getting too old for this."

2

The trio proceeded down the dark cavern carefully. While small amounts of light penetrated the thick wall of water behind them, it did not stretch nearly enough to light their way. They decided to follow a small stream of water that was trickling out of the cave and into the river. Ivivin used the tear to illuminate the path the best it could, though Ivivin couldn't help but be a smidge frustrated.

"For being a magical artifact, it sure puts out an underwhelming amount of light." Ivivin thought while he and Smith stumbled and stubbed their toes repeatedly. They reached a wall that responded to Icarus' presence and glowed with the symbol of Jupiter, the same that Idalia embroidered on the medicinal pack she had gifted Ivivin. The wall became translucent and ethereal. Cautiously, the trio walked through it, revealing a grand chamber not unlike the one Ivivin and Icarus had found themselves in during their encounter with the Shaa'Id.

There was a small fountain of water that surrounded a small altar, made of the same white and polished material Ivivin had encountered in the Capital. On it laid a small stone that seemed to be emitting a fair amount of heat. The fountain leaked the water that formed the stream that led out of the cave. Lit torches lined the walls of the cavern, eliminating the need for Ivivin to continue the use of the tear. Still, Ivivin felt something was off. He couldn't put his finger on it. He looked to Smith who seemed to share in Ivivin's unease. It dawned on Ivivin and a sense of dread washed over him.

"Smith...who lit all these torches?"

3

"I was wondering what manner of rats were skittering about this place." came a voice from where Ivivin and Smith had entered the chamber. It was assuredly a woman's, though it seemed to be forced deeper than its natural pitch. Ivivin and Smith turned to face the source of the voice. There, near the entrance, stood one of the most beautiful women Ivivin had ever seen. She was perhaps just a few years into adulthood and was absolutely stunning. However, it seemed to Ivivin that this woman did not care for her own beauty. She tried to obfuscate it by burying her body under ill-fitting clothing. Her face was plastered with war paint in gritty design. Her hair, though sleek and alluring, was kept unusually short for a woman of these parts. Ivivin did not understand why she rejected it so, but it was a testament to her innate physical beauty that it still shone through her attempts at banishing it. The ethereal entrance behind her glowed with a ♂ behind her. Ivivin knew not what the symbol meant, but, given that Icarus caused the door to glow with the symbol of Jupiter, he could only assume this person was also the reincarnation of some deity's child. The woman walked towards them. The symbol faded and the wall returned to its corporeal form.

Ivivin felt Icarus trembling on his shoulder as the woman approached. Maintaining her forced voice, the woman addressed the bird.

"Well, if it isn't another testament to the cruelty of the fates. The son of Jupiter, the proud and skilled Ganymede, reborn as a runt of a bird. And one that cannot even fly, by the looks of it. We may have not fought for the same cause, my fellow celestial being, but I feel your suffering deeply. Come, I shall rid you of that flesh. Who knows if you'll be reborn, be given passage back to the stars, or be cast to oblivion—but all those options sound better than being stuck as such a pitiable creature." The woman approached Ivivin and Icarus, drawing an iron dagger en route.

Ivivin drew his sword.

"Stay away. Icarus is my friend and I shan't let further harm come to him."

The woman stopped, clearly annoyed by Ivivin's words and actions.

"His life is a curse and I will not have one of my kind bear such an indignity. Even my own is hardly acceptable." The woman replied, her intentionally raspy voice starting to strain. Ivivin stood his ground and replied.

"Who are you? And...is your voice ok?" Ivivin couldn't help but quip.

The woman bit her lip in anger, seemingly on the edge of screaming at Ivivin. She took a deep breath and calmed herself before responding. This time, though, the woman spoke with a melodic and especially sultry voice. Ivivin was sure she could have won anyone over with her voice alone.

"Who am I? I am leagues above you, mortal, so I would appreciate you treat me with respect. Though, given this...form, I do not blame you for your ignorant disrespect. I am Mars, deity of war and virility, infuriatingly reincarnated into this comely exhibition of man's lust, so weak and ill-suited for battle."

"Though I know of the celestial spirits, I know not of you in particular. But I do know this: Deity or not, I will not allow harm to come to this bird." Ivivin said, shield raised defensively. Smith decided to intervene before things further complicated and escalated into violence.

"Young woman..." Smith started, but stopped when she leered at him. "Mars, I insist you tell us what you are up to."

Mars turned to Smith, seething.

"You all make this so much worse, you know that? You condescend and dismiss me simply because of this form and its apparent daintiness. But that is a mistake, and one you will pay for with your life. I may not have much power elsewhere but here, a place where the sky touches the earth, I have more than enough power to deal with the likes you!"

4

The earth beneath Smith and Ivivin trembled and the stone of the ground shifted and manipulated itself into the form of wolves. There were only three, but they were fierce and, well, made of animated stone. Ivivin and Smith both were unsettled and unsure how to proceed. Smith had only a small hand axe with which to defend himself, so Ivivin tossed him the cross shield. Ivivin struck one of the stone beasts at the nape, but his blow rebounded and left his arms shaky and pained. The stone wolf was shaken, but hardly harmed. Ivivin sensed a presence behind him and only just managed to avoid getting stabbed by Mars and her iron dagger. Mars quickly recovered and assaulted again, leaving Ivivin open to attack by one of the wolves. Ivivin could not dodge the heavy claws of the wolf entirely, but limited the wound to a nick. Smith pushed his way towards Ivivin. "Boy, focus on taking down the girl. We stand no chance against these stone monsters. But if you fell her, I am sure they, too, will fall. I will keep them off you the best I can." Smith called, parrying the wolves with Ivivin's shield.

Ivivin went to engage Mars in combat. Ivivin would not underestimate her, given how intense his prior experience with this business had been. Still, he had no wish to end her life. Mars, however, did not share in that compassion and lunged at Ivivin with killing intent again and again. Although she seemed harmless in appearance, Mars was skilled. Far more skilled than Ivivin, in fact. He recognized the disparity in their skill almost immediately and it took nearly all he had to avoid the fang of her dagger, let alone land a blow of his own. Meanwhile, Ivivin could hear Smith's breathing becoming more and more laboured. He would not be able to hold the stone creatures off much longer. Ivivin knew he was out of time. He dropped his sword and charged Mars, tackling her. Ivivin felt a pain in his leg. He glanced and saw the dagger sticking from his leg, but just barely. He had somehow managed to avoid the brunt of the vicious strike. He had Mars pinned down and applied pressure to her throat with his forearm. Ivivin could not look at her as she gasped and struggled for air. Instead, he looked at Smith fighting the wolves and held fast. The moment the wolves crumbled apart, Ivivin released the pressure and was relieved to hear coughing and breathing from underneath him.

Smith approached them both, catching his breath. He pointed his axe towards her. "Tell us, Mars. What business have you here!" Smith demanded.

5

Mars struggled a moment under Ivivin's weight, but relented when he would not be budged.

"What was I doing here? My divine purpose." Mars sneered. Just then, the stone on the pedestal began to glow brighter and hotter. From it oozed a black liquid that poured into the fountain rapidly, turning the small stream of water leading out of the cave into a more sizable one. Ivivin and Smith looked at Mars, expecting an explanation.

"I am seeding war, friends. This world is far too peaceful. Man and spirits alike have grown feeble and weak-willed. War is terror, but it also forces men from laze to valour. I may not have power to will conflict like I once had but, luckily, even lowly humans are capable of cleverness. Since the day I learned of my true heritage, I have searched for a relic of the gods. I had hoped for my spear, but I could not sense it in this world. Instead, I happened upon the Tear of one of Jupiter's children, Ganymede. It is a weak relic— he was the weakest of Jupiter's children, after all. He could not even hold a candle to my own sons, Phobos and Deimos. But, when I learned what it could do, I found a way to corrupt it to my design. That liquid? That is water tainted heavily with Crumbleheart. To even touch it at this potency would insure you contract it a thousand times over. The disease steals warmth and strength from the hearts of men, but that warmth needs somewhere to go. Ganymede's empathetic and moral ways made his tear the perfect candidate. Man's warmth is converted to literal warmth in that stone and so it made a perfect tool for propagating my design." Mars explained. The heat grew more intense and the black ooze poured at a higher rate each moment.

"So you would poison all of man!? To what end?" Smith barked.

"No, you mistake my intentions, you foolish mortal." Mars retorted. "It is true that this is many times more the natural amount of this ailment that lingers yet from the war of the stars and earth. But it is still quite a small amount when it is diluted into the rivers. I do not intend to end the lives of men or continue to enfeeble their hearts forever. No, I wish to spark war! War between the city-states of Olympia! War between Vasilos and Olympia! And this is only the start! I will seed conflict elsewhere. And I will die in the grand battle I have created, even without my divine powers, like an honourable warrior. That is my goal. Of course, even if you kill me now, it is too late. The die is cast and the cruel fates have been defied." cackled Mars.

Ivivin leapt from the ground. Smith already was en route to the tear, carefully avoiding the ooze. The heat had gotten so intense, though, that Smith could not even get close to the tear. Ivivin thought of Grandia and the pain that Crumbleheart had inflicted on Smith. He wanted more than anything to spare others from that fate. Ivivin set Icarus on the ground and rushed towards the stone. Like Smith, the still-intensifying and immense heat prevented him from getting close. Ivivin looked at the water that was nearing torrential levels, clouded with black. He took a deep breath and submerged himself completely in the water, knowing what such an action meant. He emerged, absolutely soaked to the bone. Smith rushed towards him, but Ivivin yelled at him to stay away. Smith stopped in his tracks as Ivivin rushed towards the stone. The poison water shielded him against the heat of the stone and Ivivin knocked it from the pedestal. All at once, the fountain ceased to flow, the heat dissipated, and the ooze coagulated before vanishing from the water entirely.

6

Mars looked at Ivivin incredulously. "Why? You know you've doomed yourself, right? It matters not that the curse no longer persists in the waters—it safely harbours itself in anyone it infects."

Ivivin shrugged. "I didn't really think about it, I guess. I suppose I am in for a rough time, huh?" The knowledge of what the disease entailed lingered in the back of Ivivin's mind, but he had not the time now to worry on it.

Ivivin and Smith both cornered Mars. Without a weapon, she struck Smith repeatedly, but the blows were without much impact. She was hardly half Ivivin's size, after all. And Smith was larger still. Still she pounded at his chest in frustration. Ivivin looked into her eyes and saw suffering. It was a suffering he couldn't understand, but it was there in her eyes, plain as day, if he looked closely. He was reminded of Idalia and Elara's mother's words to them concerning their status as divine incarnations. She had told them that this life was their life now and they did not need to bear the weight of their heritage. Of course, there was still the matter of Jupiter's tear (which, in hindsight, Ivivin was glad he left in his bag at Smith's campsite. Who knew the havoc Mars could have caused with it in hand). It seemed, though, that Mars...no, this girl who is the reincarnation of Mars, never took such a lesson to heart.

"What's your name?" Ivivin asked the now crying woman.

"Mars, you dullard." She replied.

"I won't be one to tell you that's wrong. But, tell me, what name were you given at birth?" Ivivin asked, sincerely interested.

Mars, shocked by the nature of the question, stopped both the strikes and the tears coming from her. "I was given the name Rebeca. And I lived as her for years before realizing who I really was."

Ivivin nodded.

"I think I understand..." he started.

Mars was livid at that utterance.

"You say those words but they are hollow. What do you know of hating who you are, not by any choices you made, but by the circumstance of your birth? To be unhappy and uncomfortable in your very skin. I do not feel like a woman and yet I am trapped as one. And not just any woman, but a near caricature of one at that! I feel lust and love not for men, but for those that share my form. You know not the frustration of needing to lay with a woman and not being able to do so in a way you find satisfying! You don't know how it feels to be gifted in ways that you cannot and never will utilize fully simply because of your lot in life! People see me so very differently than I see myself and it is maddening." Mars erupted, tears welling freshly in her eyes.

Ivivin paused and considered his words carefully. She was right, Ivivin truly did not understand. When he spoke before, he merely meant that he had figured out what the source of her suffering was, not that he understood it. Ivivin had nearly always felt comfortable with who he was. It seemed natural and, even when he wasn't satisfied with some aspect of his life, it was nothing immutable. He attempted to fathom, to emulate a scenario in his head where he was trapped in another's body, perhaps even the body of the woman before him. It wasn't that he found the idea of being a woman beneath him, but the idea of being trapped as someone he clearly wasn't sounded torturous. And he was sure his brief imaginings were not nearly as poignant as having that as a waking reality. Ivivin didn't understand, truly, and didn't think he was capable.

"Mars… no. I won't call you that any longer." Ivivin started. "Nor will I call you Rebeca, since you seem to hate that name. What would you like to be called?"

The young woman in front of him looked at Ivivin, puzzled. She thought for a moment before responding.

"Lance."

Smith was growing impatient, but indulged Ivivin who seemed unusually serious.

"Lance…" Ivivin resumed. "Why did you do this all, really? Why did you assume the mantle of Mars? I know others like you and they seemed happy to cast aside their divine history."

"The truth? It's petty. But I suppose this is where my life ends anyway. My disgrace will be short-lived, at least. I searched for a relic that could reshape my form. But I learned that such a magic does not exist, not even with the tears. I learned this from a library in Capital and it broke me. I knew I was not obligated to follow the path of Mars and I truly had no desire to see the lands at war. But, if I was going to live a lie, the one of a god scorned seemed more respectable than a foolish girl, unhappy with her body. I chose the path of Mars, rather than facing the harsh path of Sappho."

Ivivin's heart ached for Lance. But before he could find the words of comfort he sought, Smith cut them both off.

"I don't care what your reasoning. The fact is, you caused the deaths of a great many people, including a dear friend..."

Smith glanced at Ivivin.

"...dear friends." he corrected himself. "And you remain a danger yet to others. Here, I strike you down. Goodbye, Mars."

Ivivin reacted quickly and used his gauntlets to deflect Smith's axe, preventing it from hitting its mark. It was painful, but the armour held. Smith roared at Ivivin.

"What are you doing boy?! She is heinous! She took so many people! She has taken you!"

"I am still here, Smith. I am not taken yet." Ivivin retorted.

"We haven't time to argue, boy. Move aside. Don't you see her foul deeds far outweigh her suffering? It's an excuse. A clever ploy for her life!"

Ivivin recalled the look in Lance's eyes.

"Smith, I agree. I don't know if these deeds could ever be undone. Many lives have ended because of this and some will still end. I agree with you, but, I don't feel like it's right to strike them down."

"My patience is wearing thin, Ivivin! If we fail to end her now and she resumes her villainy, that blood is on our hands too, not just hers!" Smith exclaimed.

Ivivin was, honestly, terrified of Smith. He was his mentor and a sizable man. But Ivivin held his ground. Eventually, they became so engrossed in their argument that the subject of debate had escaped. It was only when Icarus let loose a pellet that either of them broke from their quibbling long enough to notice.

7

Smith attempted to give chase to their adversary, but Ivivin remained in the cavern with Icarus. Smith returned briefly to grab a torch from the wall before hurrying away once more. Ivivin took a moment to consider the situation he had put himself in. He was now afflicted with the same disease he had tried to save Smith from. He didn't regret his decision, per se. He knew he had likely saved many people. That being said, he was becoming acutely aware that he had lit a fuse on his own life and the explosion would be something awful. If Ivivin had just barely allowed himself a flickering thought of taking his own life in the woods, it was a serious consideration now. Ivivin picked up the dagger left behind by Lance and trembled as he debated lodging it through himself. Ivivin did not think himself strong enough to endure the fate he had wrought upon himself, nor did he want to prolong his tragedy. Icarus tugged at Ivivin's boots, wanting to be picked up. Ivivin shook away his thoughts and pocketed the dagger. He lifted his friend and set him upon his shoulder, where the little ruffian nibbled at Ivivin's ear.

Ivivin walked over to Ganymede's tear and lifted it from the water. Icarus looked upon the stone with a look of owl-nostalgia, almost somber in its expression. The tear activated in Ivivin's palm. It emanated a gentle and comforting warm—a far cry from the overwhelming heat that radiated from it before. It wasn't just the intensity of the heat, either. Ivivin felt the heat from the stone now felt somehow different. It didn't rid him of his negative thoughts, but it did reassure him and embolden him to leave the cavern. He would sort out his feelings later.

Ivivin and Icarus went to join Smith at the cavern's exit, the tears both leading the way.

8

Ivivin found Smith kneeling at the waterfall, still inside the cavern. Without Icarus, Smith could not leave the cave. When Ivivin approached him, the waterfall parted and the trio exited the cave. Lance was nowhere to be seen. It was unlikely that they had managed to escape the valley, but Ivivin was not motivated to give chase. Instead, he just sat down at their campsite and kicked off his boots. Smith twitched and paced for a while, unsure at what he should do. It wasn't until Ivivin called to him that he sat down and joined Ivivin.

"Smith, what do you want to eat? I don't have a whole lot left, do you? Don't mean to bum off of you, but I am starving."

Smith stared at Ivivin's nonchalance. "Are you—?" Smith started.

Ivivin held up his hand.

"Hey Smith, I am more than willing to talk to you about what just happened. But not right now, alright? Let's at least get some warm food in our stomachs first."

"Sure, boy. I have some fish. I'll get it started." Smith indulged Ivivin in his request.

They enjoyed an ordinary meal by the campfire and, somehow, it made Ivivin feel much better. Besides his imminent illness, though, Ivivin and Smith still knew they had other matters to discuss. After they both apologized for how they acted in the cave, they had to address the issue of what to do about Lance.

"I understand we can't leave everything as it is." Ivivin started. "But I still think there must be a solution other than cutting Lance down."

Smith replied. "I don't think leaving Mars alive is wise. But even if we entertained the idea of bringing her to custody, there is no way we could detain her and ascend out from this valley."

They both remained at this impasse for quite some time. Smith began to get a bit impatient.

"Ivivin, I understand your hesitance. I really do. But every moment we spend deliberating, the more likely it is that she finds a way from here. I will not be deadlocked into inaction. I am open to ideas, but given the options we have in front of us, I think we need to find her and kill her. I won't make you do it and I won't make you help. But, unless we come up with an alternative, I won't allow you to get in my way."

Ivivin thought about the issue. It's true that he couldn't know or even really trust that Lance would not return here with a new relic and cause some other manner of havoc. But, perhaps, Lance wasn't the problem. Much like the Tear of Jupiter, this place was likely very dangerous if the wrong person stumbled upon it. And, now that he knew there were more people like Elara and Idalia (and Icarus) in the world, it was no longer proper to ignore that possibility.

"Smith...what if Lance isn't the problem?" Ivivin posed.

"Oh, for god's sake, of course Mars is the problem. You saw what she did! She did it to you!" Smith countered.

"Hear me out, Smith. I don't think Lance is the only one who could abuse this place and its power. So, instead of hunting them, why don't we make it so that no one can use this place again?" Ivivin posited.

"Hmm...that is an interesting and disturbing thought. I am not keen on destroying that place, though. I imagine there must be a proper reason for its existence beyond its potential for abuse." Smith put forward.

Ivivin had not thought about that. Just like in all things, their actions would have consequences. Still, Ivivin was averse to ending the life of another needlessly and there was another option, even if the consequence was unknown. Ivivin felt strongly that he'd rather face the unknown than give in to a known evil.

"Who knows." Ivivin responded. "It's true that we have no idea what will happen if we destroy this place. But we know exactly what will come of bringing your axe upon Lance." Ivivin stood his ground against his mentor.

Smith looked at the young man, so adamant in his ideal, and decided that if they could come up with a plan, he would do as Ivivin wished.

"Fine, boy, you win. But only if we can think of a way to destroy this place. Come, and grab the owl, too. Let's appraise the structure." Smith led the way to the area by the cavern.

The formation of the cave seemed unnatural. At least, that's what Smith thought. Ivivin, truthfully, had no clue. He chose to trust Smith and his judgement. Smith determined that the structure was certainly not a naturally formed cavern. But, he was able to identify the structures that gave the cave it's unusual amount of durability. He told Ivivin that destruction of these pillars would almost assuredly cause a cave in. But they struggled with how to go about it. They certainly didn't want to be inside the cave when it collapsed, so they would need some way of causing damage remotely.

"Smith, I have an idea!" Ivivin said, recalling his time in Wolfelaw. "Why don't we use some oil? I found that lighting a barrel of it causes quite the impactful force. If we had a few, I think we could bring the whole place down."

"How would we get the oil down here? A barrel won't survive that drop, even into the water." Smith opposed.

"Arastoo. He believed and trusted me. He tasked me with investigating this place. He could send men. I'm sure they could help." Ivivin proposed.

"I suppose they could. Given the grandness of their buildings, I imagine they have some advanced methods of construction. But we cannot leave this place unguarded, lest Mars returns. You go. I shall wait for you here."

That plan didn't sit particularly well with Ivivin. He knew Smith was sincere in this moment about not hunting Lance down, but solitude and time can lead people to dark places.

"No, Smith. You go in my stead. I will guard this place." Ivivin said.

"No offense, boy, but I am still larger and stronger than you yet. This place is too important to let Mars return." Smith replied.

"You're right, you are better suited to protect than I. That's why you will go and you will take the tears with you. Without them, this place is useless to Mars...Lance. I can keep an eye on things here." Ivivin said.

Smith hesitated to admit it, but he knew Ivivin was right. It was probably better that he be the one who leave.

"Alright then, what do I need to do?" Smith asked, impressed a bit by Ivivin's adherence to his stance.

"I will write you a note to Arastoo. The senator Xerxes has notes I took for him if they want to compare handwriting. Take Icarus with you and keep him safe. I don't know exactly how to use these tears in a way I could describe to you. But Icarus seems to have a knack for it. He can demonstrate the stone's power. I have a horse, Lili, that should be waiting for us up above. Icarus should be able to help you score a ride." Ivivin explained.

Smith agreed and left as soon as Ivivin had given him the note. He wasted no time, knowing that the sooner they put this business behind them, the sooner they could try and address Ivivin's new sickness.

9

And, just like that, Ivivin was completely alone, owl friend and all, for the first time in a long time. The knowledge that he had Crumbleheart weighed on him, but he was also not terribly concerned. There was nothing he could do about it at the moment, after all. He was almost in denial about it as a result. He didn't wander terribly far from the cavern entrance at any given time—he had a feeling Lance might try to return and, without Icarus, he couldn't follow them into the chamber.

This feeling proved correct. But, rather than trying to enter the cavern, Ivivin found Lance sitting at his campsite after he had gone fishing further downriver. Ivivin saw Lance sitting there, unconcerned with Ivivin's approach. It seemed like Lance meant no harm to Ivivin, so he took a seat next to them. An awkward and uncertain silence hung around as Ivivin cooked his lunch. This silence was broken when Ivivin offered Lance a bit of fish.

"Hey, Lance, you hungry? I got a bit I can spare. You'll have to catch your own if you're still hungry after that, but it's better than nothing." Ivivin asked.

Lance was surprised by the offer, but accepted nonetheless. While they ate, Ivivin addressed the elephant in the room.

"Why'd you come back here, Lance?" Ivivin asked.

"I was watching you. This small body has a few benefits, I suppose. I noticed that the larger one of you left and took Ganyme...er... your owl with him. I honestly don't know why I came over. I am pretty confused about a lot of things. But you seemed pretty against killing me, so I felt safe, at least."

"I see. Well, you are welcome to stay here as long as you'd like, as long as you promise not to slit my throat." Ivivin joked. "Oh. And I think you should probably leave before Smith returns. That'll be a few days at minimum, though."

Lance sat there in disbelief, unable to believe the casual and accepting air with which Ivivin spoke.

"You know, I tried to kill you not too long ago. And because of me—" Lance started, but Ivivin interrupted.

"I know what happened. You are not without blame. But, in my mind, that was Mars. And you are Lance. Maybe it's ignorant. Maybe I am not even close to understanding. All I know is that the look in your eyes is different. For now, at least, I don't harbour ill will for you." Ivivin said, realizing the truth in his own words as he spoke them.

And so, Lance and Ivivin spent some days together. Ivivin showed Lance how to find the constellations in the stars above. Lance gave Ivivin some swordplay advice. They shared with each other parts of their life's story. They were cautious and hesitant but, considering the circumstances, they grew close.

10

It was the night before Lance had planned to leave the valley. Lance and Ivivin were sitting around the campfire, making jokes at Icarus' expense. It felt a little cruel, but it was in good fun. They both felt a serious conversation on the horizon, but they wanted to enjoy a bit more of the jovial chitter chatter they had gotten accustomed to. Of course, nothing lasts forever and Ivivin confronted Lance.

"Lance. What will you do now?"

"I am still not sure. I still feel hate deep in my heart."

"Do you not feel any remorse for what you did? I know you said you were living a lie, but that doesn't excuse you."

"I... regret it, yes. I especially regret... what I did to you, Ivivin."

"Do not steer the subject away." Ivivin warned.

"I am remorseful. At the same time, I feel as if the path I set down is not one from which I can turn back. I have gone too far. I need to either follow it to the end or... terminate it prematurely."

"You don't think you can change? You aren't even going to try and make up for it?" Ivivin accosted.

Lance got defensive.

"I can't make up for all that I've done! Are you kidding me?"

Ivivin raised his voice as well. "And you are not even going to try? I can't believe you're such a coward."

Ivivin felt a sharp hook to his chin that knocked him to the ground. The two fought for a few minutes before they were both worn out.

"This damned body." Lance lamented, panting. "If only I were a man, you wouldn't be getting up right now."

"Man or not, you'd still be a damned coward for giving up." Ivivin spat, also struggling to catch his breath. Ivivin's nose leaked blood and pained dreadfully. He was sure it was broken, adding further to his difficulty catching his breath. He looked over at Lance, whose hyper-feminine face now sported a fresh black eye and a few small lacerations.

The pair caught their breath before resuming their seats around the campfire. Ivivin knew of the horrible things Lance had done, but he felt that if they turned over a new leaf, they could use their talents to help a lot of people. Ivivin didn't know if that made up for anything or if there was even a scorecard. But surely that'd be better than Lance being put down or left to rot. Ivivin tried desperately to think of anything he could do or say to help Lance. But Ivivin really couldn't understand the turmoil that consumed them. How could he help someone he didn't even really understand?

"Lance…" Ivivin stated. "Is there anything I can do to help you?"

"Again with that patronizing…" Lance started before detecting the sincerity in Ivivin's tone.

"No, Ivivin. I think you've already done enough. I don't think I have ever come as close to feeling like myself as the time I've spent with you. I am still not happy or comfortable, but the way you treat me makes me forget sometimes, even if it's only for a short time."

"You still feel guilty about what happened to me because of you, right?" Ivivin asked.

"Of course. Especially now, after these last few days." Lance replied.

"Then you don't get the luxury of giving up. I am going to die because of you. So, the least you can do is live and do the good I would have." Ivivin asserted.

"Ivivin, I… It's not that simple."

"Of course it is. You chose before. And you will choose again. In fact…" Ivivin said, struck by inspiration. "You are going to choose right now."

Ivivin got up and rummaged through his bag. He couldn't believe he hadn't thought of this earlier. He returned to the campfire holding a different item in each hand.

"I still have the dagger you, as Mars, tried to kill me with. It is rightfully yours. But, you have another option. You see, it's a fine dagger and I have grown fond of it. I will trade you it for this armlet."

Ivivin held out both of his hands to Lance. In his right was the dagger and in his left was Ojasa's bracelet. Ivivin had held onto it all this time, hoping it might suffice for the king's request. Ivivin continued.

"I will not tell you what the armlet does, not until you chose. But should you choose the armlet over the blade, you must promise me you shall never again take up the mantle of Mars. Any unease with who you are, any pain you feel, and any choices you make are your own, Lance, and you shall own them."

Lance took several minutes to decide. Reflection, it seemed, came slowly. But it was not until Lance met Ivivin's eyes and saw earnest compassion and faith that they made their decision. Lance reached for the bracelet took it from Ivivin.

"You have my word, friend. I am Mars no more."

11

Ivivin was so relieved he almost dropped the dagger. He inspected his new weapon, the result of a strange trade. It was well crafted and certainly a worthy weapon. It was plain, with the symbol of Mars engraved at the base of the blade. However, it paled in comparison to Smith's work, if he was being honest. It certainly would not be a grand treasure he could present to the king, but he was glad that it was his nonetheless, if only because it meant it was no longer in Lance's hands.

Ivivin put away the dagger and embraced Lance. This embrace reminded them both of the reality Lance faced, but also that, at least to each other, it didn't matter.

"Alright Lance. Let me tell you about your new bracelet. At the start of my journey, I was tasked with felling a great and terrible beast Ojasa. He was larger than a house and was even more fearsome than you."

"And you defeated such a monster?" Lance asked, impressed.

"Well, yes and no. You see, Ojasa was no monster at all. He was an old and portly man. He used that bracelet to appear as a monster to extort wealth and favours from the townsfolk. The bracelet cannot transfigure reality. It could not make him a beast any more than I could. Instead, its magic caused people to see him as something he was not. He was able hide who he really was behind an illusion. It is my hope, then, that you can use it to help others see you for how you are, so that who you really are is not hidden behind an illusion." Ivivin concluded.

"And you trust me with such a powerful item?"

"I do now. Besides, I know not how to cast magic. It isn't much use to me in any case."

Lance put the bracelet on. After a few minutes of concentrating and fiddling about with the bracelet, Lance elicited a reaction from the tool. In front of Ivivin's eyes, Lance was replaced with a real man's man. He was tall, rugged, and muscular. However, he interacted quite unnaturally with his surroundings. It was quite obvious to Ivivin that this was an illusion. Ivivin was reminded how Ojasa avoided interacting with anything directly to preserve his illusion, even conjuring up illusionary victims of his assault. Lance seemed to notice this limitation, too, and returned to normal.

"I see…" Lance said, a little disappointed. "I cannot alter who I am and I cannot alter what I look like too drastically, else the magic fails to be convincing."

"I truly am sorry it cannot do more. Like everything, there is a limit to what it can do." Ivivin apologized.

"That's alright, I never have seriously considered what I'd want to look like if becoming a man were actually attainable. But, now that I tried on the look, I don't think going from one caricature to another would be satisfying."

Lance looked at the bracelet and then to Ivivin. Lance turned to Ivivin and smiled, tears starting to fall from their eyes.

"Thank you, it's incredible."

Ivivin did his best to ignore how feminine Lance was and tried not to let it influence how he treated them. It was hard, honestly. Thoughts of how beautiful they were snuck their way into his mind from time to time. After all, Ivivin still didn't really understand. Perhaps that is why it was so easy for him to give up the trinket that, to Lance, was the treasure of a lifetime. But in this moment, when their eyes met and without an illusion, he knew he saw Lance and the real Lance only.

12

In the morning, Lance parted ways with Ivivin, not wanting to get caught by Smith. It would take some time for Lance to master the magic of the armlet enough to hold the illusion for longer than a few minutes, but considering that an old and feeble man had cast it on an entire mountainside, Ivivin was confident that Lance could learn to sustain it permanently. Their parting ways was unexceptional, just as Ivivin wanted it.

No longer than a few hours after Lance had left, Smith returned. He had with him an assembly of men, including Arastoo's son, Belen. They assembled a machine—a large pulley not unlike that Ivivin had used to draw water from the well at his home. Using it, they began to lower barrels of oil and people into the valley. By the time they had finished, though, it was dark. No one wanted to attempt such a sensitive task in the dark, so they put the mission off until morning. Smith had joined Ivivin back at their campsite, a little way from where the other men had set up. Ivivin did not wish to lie to Smith and so he told him of his time with Lance. At the end of the recount, Smith just sighed and ruffled Ivivin's hair.

"You're too soft, but if you can forgive and trust her, then I can start to, as well. I'm sure that is what Grandia and Isabella both would have wanted." Smith told Ivivin. Smith smiled and pulled from his bag three sweet rolls.

"They're not as good as Isabella's, but they'll do. Let's just enjoy ourselves until we get back to Smithton, Ivivin. We can worry about everything there. I know someone who might be able to help."

Ivivin, Icarus, and Smith all enjoyed their little ritual and, for the first time, did so under the stars. When the light first broke the horizon, a sleepy Ivivin and Icarus escorted the Olympian men into the cavern to set their oil charges. A few minutes after they had all evacuated the cave, explosions erupted from inside and the thunderous crashing of rock continued for several minutes. When all settled, Ivivin and Icarus approached the waterfall once more, but this time it did not part. The chamber was destroyed. Ivivin and the others used the pulley to ascend out of the valley. Ivivin mounted an annoyed Lili and they all began their voyage back to the Capital. Belen eagerly clung to Ivivin, eager to hear more about his travels. Ivivin obliged, asking Belen all about his country in the process.

13

Ivivin, Smith, and the demolition crew were greeted by a cheering crowd. Both senators and citizens alike had come out to celebrate their arrival. Arastoo and Brutus had made the announcement the source of the epidemic had been located and eliminated, though they left out specifics. Ivivin was again invited to a small dinner with Arastoo and a few others. Ivivin thought about skipping town, but Smith seemed to need a day to recuperate from all the travel and the emotional strain he had been under, so Ivivin obliged.

"Ivivin! You have my thanks! Brutus', too, though he has already left to set about renovation of the affected areas. But I can see in your face it was not without cost. I suspect I know the steepness, but I shan't force you to of speak it to me. Instead, I'd like you to tell me what I can do to begin to repay you."

Ivivin had been continuously putting his newfound illness from his mind, but he allowed himself to consider it now. He knew little about the disease or how long he had before he felt its effects. Ivivin tried to take account of the things he needed to take care of before that happened. He struggled at first, as the list was bogged down with things he wanted to do. No, the need-to-do list was much shorter. Ivivin needed to become a knight, both for his own personal ambition, but also to deposit the Tear of Jupiter within the castle. To become a knight, he still needed a squire. Moreover, he needed to learn more about the tears he held. The innkeeper had told him that Olympia was the place for such knowledge. With any hope, he could find a way to seal away the Tear of Jupiter so that Elara and Idalia could live their own lives and finally sever their connection to a past that is not theirs. Minimally, Ivivin needed these things. His heart sunk as he made tactile the abstraction of his own mortality. But in doing so, he now had a list of things he could ask this powerful man for.

"Sir Arastoo, I apologize if I ask too much, but I have many things I wish to ask of you." Ivivin responded. He explained how he needed someone or something that could help him with the tears and that he was in search of a squire.

"Is that all?" Arastoo bellowed. "These are modest and easy tasks, Ivivin. Here, I shall grant you permission to enter the university. Ask the librarians there for the knowledge you seek. As for the squire, my son has been pestering me non-stop about voyaging out into the world. He seems quite fond of you and I can trust his life in your hands. I wish to hold him here a few months more, but I will write you a note guaranteeing my son as your squire and I will give you an heirloom of my family as proof of its legitimacy. When he ascends beyond his squiredom, then I ask that you return it to him as a symbol of his growth."

And, just like that, Ivivin was much closer to his goals, though he was sure it was not worth the price.

Ivivin went to the library at the university, as Arastoo had suggested. They expected him and met him with open arms. Between the scholars and the books there, a truly vast amount of information was available to Ivivin. He couldn't help but brood as he realized that he no longer had the time to become such a scholar. He didn't even want to be a scholar, yet knowing that the option had been stripped from him upset Ivivin. Still, he focused on the task at hand. According to the scholars, Lance was correct in the assessment that the tear being used to spread Crumbleheart was indeed Ganymede's. Furthermore, they determined that the tear that Ivivin had gotten from the shopkeeper up north belonged to Europa. The scholars agreed to have a scribe copy the book containing the information they used to answer Ivivin's question for him, but it would take a few days, even on rush order.

"Europa huh? Elara..." Ivivin thought to himself. He really wished he could see her again. Idalia too. He wanted to return to the Flor festival and see the children grown. Ivivin wished to see all manners of people. And the notion that he would never be able to, it broke his heart. Ivivin returned to the taberna and buried his head in a pillow. He cried hot and messy tears, trying to muffle his pain and keep it silent. He cried and cried until he fell asleep.

The next day, Ivivin awoke to a sticky mess of dried mucus and tears on his face. He hurried to get water to wash it away before anyone saw. Already his mood was sullied. The scholars had provided him information about which Moon's tear he held, but they knew nothing of how to seal away Jupiter's Tear. Ivivin had an idea, though. Elara and Idalia's seer mother might be able to make use of that book and determine how to seal away Jupiter's tear. At the very least, she was better suited to the task than Ivivin was. Ivivin was excited at the prospect of seeing the sisters again before reality came bearing down on him once more.

"That land is far away. I don't know if I will make it that far and back to the Castletown before Crumbleheart saps me of my strength" Ivivin reminded himself.

Instead, Ivivin sought an audience with Arastoo once more and requested a messenger take the book and Ganymede's stone to Idalia's and Elara's mother in the north. His request was granted. He suggested Ivivin leave everything he wanted to send there with the scholars before he left the next day.

That night, Ivivin could not find rest. Lonely and under the same moon and stars he once shared with the two sisters, Ivivin decided to write each of the three residents of that house a letter. He wrote late into the night and into the early morning. He was filled past the brim with emotion. He poured the overflow and more into each note. He sealed the letters and left them with the scholars, along with Ganymede's tear. Tired, but satisfied with his work, Ivivin left Olympia with Smith. Ivivin knew there was a long and difficult road ahead of him. But, for now, he was just happy to be leaving this place with Smith.

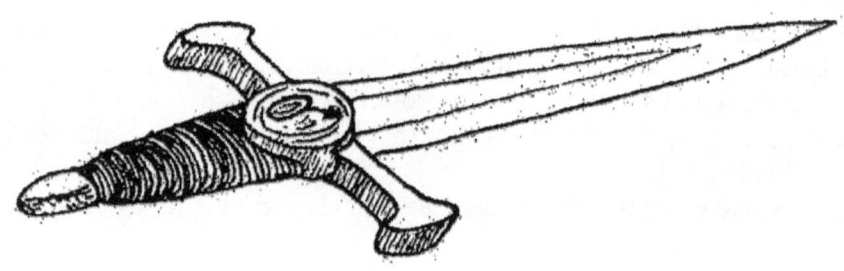

Gathering

1

Elara had settled into the routine her and Minerva had laid forth, despite still struggling with much internally. Elara would go out into the field to collect specimens for Minerva. Grandia's guide of flora and fauna certainly helped, but there were times where Elara could not seem to find all of what Minerva requested. Still, Elara took great pride in her ability to rustle up the majority of Minerva wanted. And when she returned to Minerva with the materials, she watched as Minerva experimented. Although much of the process went over Elara's head, she certainly learned while watching Minerva. On occasion, Minerva would show Elara how to make basic medicine and ointments, too. She recognized the very first, very simple recipe as the same one Idalia had used to assemble Ivivin's medicinal pouch. Although she was satisfied with watching, Minerva often insisted that Elara garner some hands-on experience in addition to the gathering of materials. So, Elara slowly learned the basics. In particular, Minerva showed her how to make a pain-easing ointment. It would not heal her hands but she could use it to set aside the pain to carry out important or painful tasks. Minerva's version of this ointment completely numbed the pain, but Elara only managed to make it dull. Still, she couldn't help but be proud of that, too.

Despite what she learned in the lab, though, Elara loved the other part of her job much more. She had come to enjoy and appreciate the players in nature, what each of their roles were naturally, and how they lived their lives. From flowers, to rodents, to trees, to birds, Elara had really taken to identifying and studying nature. She brought the book with her everywhere, reading it casually, even while not out fetching materials for Minerva. Elara found she had a soft spot in her heart for one creature in particular, though she was embarrassed to admit it, even to Minerva:

Toads.

Elara saw the wrinkle-prone and warty hoppers and could not help but find them adorable. She found their chubby bodies, rude croaking, and silly eyes incredibly endearing. More than once on her ventures into the wild did she drop the task at hand to follow their raspy and belchy songs. They were easy to catch and hold, which is more than Elara could say for a lot of what she was sent into the wilds to get. Furthermore, they didn't seem to mind too terribly much that she held them, though perhaps they were just resigned to their fates at the hand of a giant. So, on or just after drizzly days, Elara would prod Minerva to send her out in hopes of stumbling upon some. Minerva was suspicious at Elara's insistence, but never questioned it. In any case, Elara was learning much, though she wasn't sure how much progress Minerva was making. They spent their days in this routine and, so, Elara was a little unprepared for what awaited her during her next venture into the wild.

2

Elara was out collecting materials for Minerva, just as she always did. When she heard the croaking of toads in the distance, she followed the sound, elated by the chance to see her pudgy little friends. As she got closer, though, the sound of the toads became mingled with the sound of human voices and children crying. Elara hurriedly approached the scene, hiding in some tall and swampy grass amoung her toads to investigate. Elara caught sight of three wagons, drawn by horses, stopped along a narrow pathway. Looking more closely, Elara realized that two of the wagons were worn and occupied by rough looking fellows, a few of which were hassling the occupants of the third. It seemed to be a family. Elara looked closer still and recognized the family as the same that traveled with her in Wolfelaw—Able, Abraham, Hope, and Grace! She almost didn't recognize the children, she had forgotten how quickly children changed! Elara watched as the bandits unloaded possessions from the wagon and loaded it into theirs.

Elara wanted to help and even applied the pain-killing ointment she made to her hands in preparation. However, there were a few things keeping Elara from action. First was experience. She had dealt with some ruffians back north. As long the family followed their orders, it was likely that the bandits would let them leave with their lives. Terrible as it may be, it is better to live than to die for your things. But if Elara intervened, violence was likely. Which led to the second inhibiting factor: Numbers. Elara knew not how many bandits there were. She could see one at the helm of each wagon, plus two threatening the family. But, for all she knew, the bandit wagons were laden with reinforcements. And, finally, the last thing keeping Elara in place was, as much as it pained her to admit, fear.

She saw the men and could not help but relive the night at Ajaxx's castle in her mind's eye again and again, to the point where she was heaving and sweating ice just looking at the scene. Despite this, though, Elara prepared herself the best she could. She readied her Beak and Talon, manipulating the hardware for battle and donning them. It seemed like the family was being cooperative. If all went well, she could approach the family after the bandits left and help them get back to Smithton.

A woman's scream shattered that fanciful hope.

3

Elara's eyes darted to the source of the shrill and continued scream. The bandits seemed to have finished pillaging their wagon. Instead, one of the bandits was dragging a flailing Able back towards their wagon. Instinct kicked in as Elara charged towards the bandits. She was a decent distance away, so the element of surprise was lost well before she arrived. This was to be Elara's first battle with the Beak and Talon. The motions of traditional swordplay skill came naturally to Elara, despite the strange and quirky weapons. But when Elara met steel with the first bandit's blade, she could immediately feel the difference. The weapons shifted the impact further up her arms. This was great for her hands, but it also caused each clash to rebound her more. She barely recovered from her own strike in time to block the assault of the bandit. The two bandits at the helm of the wagon had not yet been incited to action, likely underestimating the threat that Elara posed. The fourth bandit was still dragging Able away, undeterred. Abraham was standing in front of his children, willing to throw his life down to protect them, even as he glowered at the bandit that was abducting his wife.

Elara knew she must act while the situation still favoured her. She lowered her hips and waited for the bandit to strike. She deftly parried the blow and spilt scarlet onto the grass of the surrounding plain.

That got the others' attention.

Though the one bandit had his handful with Able, the other two began to scramble about their wagon seats for their weapons. Elara wasted no time and rushed front-most wagon. Rather than attempt to scale the wagon and assault the bandit, who had just reached his weapon, Elara charged the horse. She struck it hard with her shield, sending the beast into a frenzy and bucking the wagon about. The bandit lost his balance while attempting to dismount the unstable wagon and fell hard to the ground, forcing the air from his lungs. Elara stood above the bandit and stomped on his hands repeatedly, ending the exchange with a sweeping kick to the bandit's head, knocking him unconscious. She still found her weapons unwieldy and they did not suit her traditional swordplay well, but it was not easy (nor did she have the time) to remove them in favour of one of the bandits' weapons. She turned to face the driver of the other, now dismounted and closing in on her. As she engaged the bandit, she could hear Able still resisting being placed in the wagon. The bandit shoving her yelled.

"Boss! Boss! We got trouble!"

Distracted by the scene, Elara had taken her eyes off her opened, resulting in her getting nicked in the arm. If she had reacted an instant later, the battle would have been over. Instead, the bandit had overextended and fell prey to an uppercut with the dull edge of Elara's shield. She heard the crunching of bone as the bandit fell to the floor, rolling in agony and clenching his jaw. A voice from the wagon, weightier than the others, commanded.

"Let the woman run. We can catch her on horseback, fool. Let's deal with the pesky rat. And don't think you're getting off easy for waking me from my nap, just because you dimwits couldn't handle yourselves."

The voice became embodied, as a muscular figure emerged from the wagon. He was tall, slim, and fit. The way he just carried his weapon, a moderately sized one-handed sword paired with a buckler, alerted Elara to the fact he was on another level than the goons she had dispatched. She cursed her luck as the only two bandits remaining approached her.

4

Retreat was immediately in Elara's mind—she knew the land and area well enough that she felt she could get away from at least one of the bandits, splitting them up. But she couldn't leave that family behind. There was always the possibility that the bandits would cut their losses and kill the family, or worse. Elara did not approach the pair, using their transit to recover her breath.

"Get away from here. Take your wife and children and run!"
She yelled to Abraham.

Abraham's pride caused him to hesitate, but the look of terror
on his children's faces paired with the gruesome scene convinced
him to cast aside his pride. He carried both his daughters as he and
his wife ran in the general direction of Smithton.

"All right." Elara thought. *"I just need to give them enough
time that, even on horseback, these fellows won't find them. Then I
will flee myself. I do not think this is a fight easily won."*

Elara looked at her opponents. The would-be abductor
approached her with extreme caution and detectable fear. The other
man walked confidently towards her, ready, but not concerned. She
became fixated on the man. She fought her anxieties the best she
could, but still, the night in Ajaxx's castle unnerved her. Her arms
felt weak, suddenly, and her blade abnormally heavy. Her clear state
of mind became hazy and thoughts turned her legs to stone. Her
confidence that she could win was nil and she even began to doubt
her ability to escape. Despite being in a very open field, she felt
trapped.

The boss bandit stopped just out of her reach and glared at
his companion. "So much for a rat! This one's hardly a mouse, and a
trembling one at that!" he declared.

His underling saw Elara's progressing unease and became
reassured himself and approached Elara more confidently, though
neither men let their guard down. As the first blade was cast at her,
instinct kicked in, temporarily overriding her paralysis. Elara
endured an onslaught of blows from the two men, attacking in sync.
The henchman was obviously taking risks and attacking viciously,
but the boss was more cautious and guarded, though his blows still
carried a heavy weight. It was only seconds before Elara felt the
burning of her muscles. Defending the blows took all Elara had!
Each block rebounded her arms far more than when she wielded her
usual weaponry. It took extra effort to keep up her guard and
maintain her stance.

Sensing her weariness, the henchman let loose a vicious
strike. Elara met her blade with his in time, but the force of the
rebound caused her to twist about the waist, her torso alone unable to
bear the brunt of the strike. Elara caught a glimpse of the boss' face
that recognized the opportunity.

"I must dodge, I must move!"

The positioning of her body and the urgency of the situation caused muscle memory to kick in. A movement practiced near daily and not one intended for combat came to her. Elara rode the momentum of the goon's vicious strike into a graceful twirl that allowed her blade passage deep into his triceps. This same twirl caused the boss' opportunistic strike to hit only the air where Elara once stood.

The goon fell to the floor, trying to contain his blood while yelling in pain. The boss took a cautious step away from Elara. Her unintentional strike had looked very practiced and deliberate to him. Elara herself was astonished at how natural the technique felt. She waited for the boss to approach her once more. She backed up and circled, hoping to get a sense of how far the family had made it. She could see only a single figure, Abraham, running back towards her, though it would be minutes before he arrived.

"That damn proud fool!" Elara thought. *"If he had just stayed away, I could have escaped from this man."*

She continued to back away from the bandit leader, trying to allow her body time to recover. But the longer she removed herself from the battle, the more fear and doubt began to creep into her mind. She realized that her thoughts would defeat her if she did not act soon and engaged the man once more. His swordplay was on point. Elara struggled to defend herself, much less create an opening.

Desperate, she recalled the feeling of her dance-strike. The motions she had spent so much time developing, from when she first met Petil onward, came now to her, almost as readily as her swordplay. She danced between his blade and let herself flow into an assault. The unusual pattern of attack put the man on the defensive, which only increased the rate of Elara's attack. Every time she struck his buckler, she used the bounce of her strike to land another. The bandit began to grow accustomed to Elara's relentless and graceful assault. He predicted her next motion and stabbed. Elara changed quickly to a more traditional maneuver, rotating her shield to direct his blade away. She slashed across the man's chest diagonally, catching the bulk of his abdomen in the process. He stumbled backwards and fell.

Despite her victory, the sound of his gurgling pain brought her back, once more, to Ajaxx's castle, where her dagger had elicited a like reaction. Without a battle to distract her, these memories overwhelmed her. She removed her gauntlets as quickly as she could. Blood smeared on her now bare hands and its odor sickened her. She fell to her knees and loosed her own painful howl. Her chest grew more and more tight and her vision blurred. No matter how hard she breathed or how many breaths she took, it wasn't enough.

Abraham in her peripherals, Elara fainted.

5

Elara awoke, terrified and unaware of where she was. Her hands and feet were bound. Panicked and fearful she had been captured, Elara furiously fidgeted. She was in the back of a wagon, which stopped in response to her fumbling about. Elara readied herself as a figure parted the cloth to enter. She lunged at and bit the hand that found its way inside the wagon. The man yelped, only for Elara to recognize the voice. She released her fanged clench to find Abraham, now nursing a gently bleeding hand.

"Wha...?" Elara stammered.

"Good gods, I am glad I tied you up! Who knows what you would have done to me otherwise!" Abraham explained. "If you promise you won't bite, I will cut you free."

Elara nodded, a bit confused by the whole scenario. Once the ropes were cut, Elara asked Abraham why she was tied in the first place. Abraham would not meet her eyes and answered meekly.

"...I was afraid of you. I thought you might hurt me in a frenzy, too."

Elara was shocked that a grown man would be afraid of her, but when she looked and saw her bloodstained hands and garments, she understood. Elara had killed before and for reasons no better than this. But something had changed in her since then. The wounds she inflicted on those men, she felt them on her soul. Flashes of what happened replayed in her head, including the way Hope and Grace had been looking at her before they fled. Behind their father's sheltering arms, they saw her and they saw her kill. She was chilled and shivering. Abraham looked at her concernedly, her reaction allowing him to cast aside his fear.

"She's just a girl, after all." Abraham thought, tears welling up in the corner of his own eyes. He reached out towards her, but she flinched away.

Abraham nodded slowly and left her be.

A few minutes later, Able entered the still stationary wagon. She was obviously very shaken herself, but sat next to Elara and presented herself calmly. Elara allowed herself to hold the mother and cry a while. Able said nothing and just caressed Elara gingerly.

When Elara had shed all her tears, Able whispered into Elara's ear.

"Thank you."

Reassured by this simple gesture that she was not a monster or, at least, that Able did not see her as one, Elara calmed down and collected herself.

"Abraham has taken the girls a little way down the road to give us a moment together. They want to see you, Elara. But... well, I didn't think you wanted to be seen this way, nor did we think the girls should see you this way." Able told Elara, who was reminded that she was still coated in blood. She looked at the woman beside her and realized that her clothes were now blood-stained too.

"I'm sorry." Elara said, trying to distance herself from Able, who just pulled her closer in.

"It's ok, it's ok. We are stopped by a stream. I don't have any trousers or other such fitted garments that will fit you—a blasted result of pregnancy, I'm afraid."

Elara was caught off guard by the statement, but, looking closely, she could tell that Able was indeed with child. Awestruck, Elara continued to stare at Able's belly until she heard Able giggle.

"Sorry, sorry. I you just looked so innocent and cute I couldn't help it." Able said before continuing. "Like I said, I don't have anything like you are wearing that will fit you, but I have a few dresses. Let's clean ourselves in the stream and you can pick whichever you find suits you best. After, I am sure the girls would be ecstatic to see you."

6

Elara and Able washed themselves in the stream by the wagon. Elara could not help but stare at Able's protruding stomach. It seemed paradoxical to her. It looked both extremely unnatural and like the most natural thing in the world. Elara knew full well her own womanhood. She had been reminded of it more and more recently with each travesty that befell her and each hungry man that looked upon her. Elara had never resented being born a girl, but it had

312

begun to feel like a prohibitive liability as of late. But looking at Able reassured Elara. She did not know if she wanted to bear children—it was a thought that still seemed foreign to her. However, Able reminded her that people, Elara included, could do more than destroy and hurt. As they washed, Elara heard nearby toads croaking to and fro. It further calmed Elara. Able presented Elara with a multitude of dresses. Save for an extra floofy one she wore, on occasion, to dance with the Sagehens in Rumi, it had been quite some time since Elara had worn a dress. There were only a few options, but she became nervous at the prospect of picking one. None of them stood out to her and she didn't feel like any of them would suit her. It was a silly problem, but very real to Elara in this state. Able noticed panic starting to grow in Elara and snuffed it out by pointing at one.

"Oh, Elara, I think this one would suit you so!"

Elara, relieved that the decision was made for her, quickly put it on. It was a not-quite-brown-not-quite-red colour. It was lighter than her hair, but much darker than the hip scarf she got from Petil. Able, who seemed to know colours far better than Elara, told her it was terracotta. Elara had never heard of such a colour, but she liked it nonetheless. It was earthy. It wasn't drab, but it also didn't call attention to itself. Able could see how smitten Elara was with

313

the dress. It didn't fit her quite properly, but Able could fix that. She dressed herself quickly.

"Come here, Elara!" Able called, accidentally speaking to the young woman as if she were one of her small girls.

Elara noticed this, but found it charming and let it slide without comment.

"Here, let me make some adjustments." Able said, taking a thread and needle to the dress. Elara stood frozen, terrified of moving.

"Able, there's no need. This is your dress, after all." Elara tried to say while staying still as stone.

"Oh, well, it suited you so well, I figured I would just let you have it." Able replied, working diligently. Elara mumbled a small 'thank you', but was secretly quite happy.

After far longer than they had anticipated, Elara and Able went to meet Abraham, Hope, and Grace just a little way down the road. The girls, both a few inches taller than last she saw, greeted Elara warmly. They had remembered her from the caverns. While they were idling in boredom, they had made a small circlet of wildflowers that they now placed on Elara's head. They played together a while before Abraham and Able explained to Elara that they were relocating once more. Their sister's home was already a bit cramped and, with a third child on the way, they had taken the opportunity to move once more. By way of inheritance, they had come into possession of a small plot of land that was perfect for tilling. They could supplement their income with Able's skills as a seamstress, if they needed to. So, in addition to their lives, Elara had saved their livelihood as the wagon had all manners of tools and seed that they would need to get started. They asked Elara to watch the girls while they went and repacked their wagon. She agreed and took great enjoyment in the girls as they frolicked about. Elara started teaching them the names of the flowers and birds around them. Then, a mischievous thought came over her. She snuck over to the ground and captured a toad, hiding in her palms. She called the girls close before opening her hands. Grace was scared and creeped out by the toad and recoiled. But Hope reached out and pat it on the head, eliciting long croak from the toad.

Abraham and Able returned. They thanked Elara profusely before parting ways. Elara contemplated returning to Smithton, but did not want to let Minerva down, no matter how tired and beaten she was, inside and out. Elara still had not resolved all her feelings about this last encounter, but, unlike what all happened in Rumi, she wasn't worried about these feelings. All Elara had to do was recall the bump of Able's belly and the smiling faces of the girls to know she had done the right thing. In her new dress and covered in flowers, Elara washed the blood from her weapon before continuing on her way.

7

As determined as Elara was to return to Minerva with everything she had requested, Elara returned early without having quite fetched it all. Her hands had taken a beating and her body was tired. She managed to get the bulk of the request for her teacher, though, and knew that Minerva did not expect perfection every trip.

Elara returned to the teashop, her pack brimming with different ingredients. Minerva was nowhere to be found. Elara presumed Minerva to be in her lab and entered silently, as not to disturb her. Elara saw her mentor, head against the table and hands in her hair. Minerva tugged at her hair and roared in vexation. Elara had never seen Minerva this way. She didn't know if she should leave or make her presence known. Instead, she just watched as Minerva stood and grabbed a nearby cauldron. She yelled again as she threw the container with all her might against the stone wall. Minerva looked upon the object of her frustration with rage and contempt, huffing heavily from both the toss itself and from her boiling emotion. She caught sight of Elara from the corner of her eyes and allowed herself to calm.

"Well, this is a bit embarrassing, isn't it deary? I wasn't exactly acting my age just now." Minerva said, pacing the room back and forth.

Elara fully entered the basement.

"You don't have to pretend with me. I don't get exactly what you're doing, but it seems much, much harder than anything you have shown me. I don't blame you for getting frustrated, no matter how...young you are." Elara attempted a compliment.

"Is that so? Well then, I suppose you won't mind if I do this!" Minerva exclaimed, just before kicking the already broken cauldron across the floor.

After Elara finished bandaging Minerva's toes, she took to tidying the lab and emptying the spoils of her trip. Elara desperately wished to talk to Minerva about what happened this last trip, but could tell that Minerva needed some time to focus on her own issues. Elara had faith that, after she cooled, Minerva would be more than willing to hear her out. Elara picked up the broken cauldron to inspect the damage. There was a sizable crack from the rim downward, but nothing that could not be repaired by a smith.

"Minerva, how about I take this cauldron to be repaired and bring us back a treat to enjoy over tea? Then, you can get back at it!" Elara proposed, hoping Minerva would be agreeable.

"Don't bother..." Minerva started. "...with the cauldron that is. My smith is out of town and even his apprentice seems to be playing hooky, too. Took off a few weeks ago. I am...quite the loyal customer. No one else will do. I have another container that will suffice until he returns."

Minerva clenched her fist tighter as she spoke. Eventually, she shook away whatever enigmatic thought was tensing her.

"How about you and me both go on a little walk to grab our treat? The fresh air will do these old bones good!" Minerva proposed.

Elara agreed and the pair left the store together.

8

Elara told Minerva all about her encounter with the bandits over tea and cake. Minerva's eyes grew wide as Elara recounted the tale. Elara maintained a surprising amount of composure throughout, until Minerva asked what became of the men. Elara became gaunt and somber when she answered.

"At least two of them died as a result of my actions. Though the other three were gone when I returned to grab my things, I suspect at least one other was fighting for his life and the other two...I don't know if they'll ever recover fully."

"Are you well dear?" Minerva asked.

"Yes, I am fine. Bruised, nicked, and sore as can be but, otherwise, they didn't hurt me." Elara responded.

"That is not what I meant." Minerva prodded sternly.

Elara sighed.

"I think so. It shook up some memories, the encounter. And my heart aches from what I did. I know now, especially after my time in Rumi, that not everyone is a criminal out of scorn or malevolence. Some just need to eat. Some just need to feed their families. Some know nothing else. I don't know who they were. I didn't even learn their names. But I put an end to their lives. But I think I did the right thing, so it hasn't scarred me like I thought it would." Elara elaborated.

"What makes you feel that way?" Minerva asked, genuinely curious.

Elara concluded her story, focusing especially on Able and her children.

"I don't know if what I did was right. I don't know if more people will suffer than I saved. And that is hard. But I don't think it's wrong for trying to just help those in front of me. I want to believe that I can make a difference without having some grand goal. I think I need to believe that." Elara thoughtfully remarked.

Minerva nodded.

"I think that's wise, coming from such a spring chicken. I think I need to keep that in mind myself, sometimes. Thank you for the reminder. Come, let us head back to the lab. I'll give you a little lesson today."

9

Weeks passed and Elara only grew more and more fond of her work for Minerva. Though the work in the lab still did not come easily to her, Elara was proud of her amateurish skills. Moreover, Elara started to pick up on her own tricks in the field. She often noticed some plants tended to occur in pairs, for instance. Or that some insects tended to be found in softer earths. Elara scribbled these observations down, when she thought to. Minerva did not seem to be making any progress with a cure, but they did their best to stay in high spirits. More cases of Crumbleheart had come to light recently, so every day they held the notion that they were helping. But, every night, they had to struggle with the worry they were not helping enough.

Elara returned from her most recent outing and made her way to the teashop early in the morning. Minerva was unusually energetic—a mixture of excited and anxious, by the looks of it. The pair of women had gotten to know each other well enough that this did not go unnoticed by Elara.

"What has you so animated this day?" She asked.

"Oh, I am just relieved. My smith and his apprentice returned from their trip a few days ago and I only just got word today. They are coming here later, in fact. He is a little difficult and crass, but I am happy he has returned. I feared..."

Minerva almost said too much.

"Never you mind that, now. I suppose I have been doing you a disservice, Elara... If that scoundrel could open up and accept an apprentice, I suppose it is only right I make you mine, formally, too."

Elara was struck by the offer. She enjoyed working for Minerva, but she never really thought about how long she would be here. Elara always assumed she wouldn't be here that long but, when she thought about it, she didn't really have any inclination to leave. She still wanted to see more of the country, but she felt calm and happy here. She was healing. Still, the idea of chains binding her here was less than appealing.

"Are...you sure?" Elara asked.

Minerva laughed heartily.

"Of course I am sure! Worry you not, deary. I don't expect you to stay here forever. You can leave whenever you want. As long as you know and understand that, I am happy to have you as my apprentice. So, how about it?"

Elara nodded. She didn't realize it until it now, but Elara really looked up to Minerva. Her acknowledgement meant a great deal to Elara.

"Alright then, I will have you run an errand for me then." Minerva said, scrawling a note on a scrap of paper. "Take this to Smith the smith. Tell him I need it by tonight."

Elara took the note and headed to the door.

"One more thing!" Minerva called Elara back. "Might as well take that leaky cauldron with you, too."

Elara nodded and went to the basement to retrieve the small cauldron. She, again, went to the door to leave, but was called back by Minerva.

"One more thing! Tell that ruffian Smith to wash up before he comes. He's always so sooty and I can't have it getting in my tea!"

Elara nodded and opened the door.

Again, Minerva called to Elara.

"One more thing!"

Elara closed the door and faced the old woman. Despite her best effort, Elara's exasperation showed slightly on her face.

Minerva grinned slyly.

"I hear Smith's apprentice is about your age. Handsome, too. Be careful not to fall too hard for him." Minerva teased.

Elara's face burned a deep red at the suggestion. She scurried out of the store, flustered in a way she had not been flustered in quite some time, leaving behind a cackling Minerva.

10

Ivivin sighed as he hammered away. He had nearly forgotten how hot the forge could be. When he and Smith returned just a few days ago, he had presented Smith with his armour properly, hoping his craftsmanship would please the picky smith. Smith looked at the armour and evaluated it.

"These gauntlets aren't bad. Makes sense you were able to deflect my axe with them." Smith complemented. "And removable plates were a good idea, especially for you. It's almost a shame to fail you."

Ivivin's heart sank. He thought that, perhaps, after what happened in the Valley, Smith would be softer with him.

"This isn't the best you can do, boy. You rushed. It's so easy to tell."

Ivivin was about to object when Smith brought down his hammer onto one of the plates, which cracked cleanly in two.

"Salvage what you can and start over. The design is fine, just needs better implementation. Take your time." Smith told Ivivin, leaving to tend a customer.

Though Ivivin was sad, at first, that he had not passed, he knew Smith was right. He had rushed—no excuse changed that. He was even a bit happy that Smith had not treated him any differently despite his condition.

So Ivivin found himself back at it. He worked on his armour in the afternoons and would alternate between his swordplay and reading in the evenings. But in the mornings, he would help Smith with his business, just as he did now. While Smith tried his best not to treat Ivivin any differently, it was not as if they could ignore the problem indefinitely. Smith told Ivivin of a woman who had attempted to cure Grandia when she had the ailment. Smith had arranged for them to visit her tonight.

Ivivin set down his tools and wiped the sweat from his brow. He looked over to Smith, who was taking inventory of materials.

"I wonder where Mrs. Jenkins is? She said she'd be here to pick up her spade's head first thing this morning. It must be nearly noon!"

Just then, Ivivin faintly heard an old woman's voice from the front of the store. Smith called to him.

"Boy! Take care of them!"

Ivivin, thinking it was Mrs. Jenkins, grabbed the spade's head and rushed to the front. When he arrived, though, there was no one at the counter. Thinking that Mrs. Jenkins had gotten impatient and left, Ivivin hurried to the door to catch her before she got too far. He swung open the door and rushed into the street. Or, he would have, had he not run into someone about to knock on the door. Luckily, they both captured their balance and did not fall. But, when Ivivin looked at his victim to apologize, his jaw, on the other hand, did fall.

11

Elara couldn't believe she had forgotten to ask Minerva where Smith's shop was! She wasn't in the mood to talk to strangers for directions. She was still brooding over Minerva's teasing. To avoid returning to the gabbling old hag and interacting with strangers, Elara decided she would just ask the fellow at the nearby bakery. Perhaps she'd get herself a sweet roll or something while she was there to lighten her mood. She indulged her compulsion and got directions from the baker.

"He seems to be in better spirits than usual!" Elara said to herself, munching on her sweet roll as she walked the street towards the blacksmith's forge.

"I lucked out, it's not too far. I was going to be livid if it were back near the teashop."

Elara approached the smith's shop and suddenly got quite self-conscious.

"That damn hag, she got in my head." Elara swore to herself as she attempted to tidy herself up. She scarfed down the rest of the sweetroll and approached the counter. She called for assistance, but her throat was dry from the rapidly consumed roll. She barely made a sound. The sound she did manage sounded like it came from an old lady. She waited a moment before deciding they probably just couldn't hear her. Banging on the counter seemed like a rude thing to do, so Elara made her way to the door and checked herself over once more before raising her hand to pound at the door. Suddenly, the door flung open and a man barreled into her. Her reflexes and balance allowed her to recover without falling. Still, she boiled to anger. She looked at her assailant to let him taste her disdain. She almost lost her balance from the sight alone.

Ivivin.

12

"Elara? Is that you?" Ivivin asked, looking upon the young woman he had nearly run over. She certainly looked like Elara, but was not quite the girl he left in the north.

"But, it has been a long time." Ivivin reminded himself.

Elara did not answer the question, instead, she posed her own that was lacking in subtlety.

"What are you doing here!?" Elara had to admit, Ivivin had grown and matured, at least in appearance. She'd even say that Minerva's assessment that he was handsome was fair, if debatable. Still, she recognized a silly, almost dorky, aura about him.

The pair stared at each other for a moment, as if trying to ensure the other wasn't an illusion. It was Ivivin who decided to trust his eyes first and went to embrace Elara friendlily. Elara, having wanted to see anyone familiar for a long time and having longed for fond contact for quite some time, allowed Ivivin to enclose her with his arms. But, the moment that Ivivin's arms touched her back, Elara filled suddenly and dramatically with apprehension and unease, first flinching at his touch and then pushing him away forcefully.

The act of shoving Ivivin made Elara wince, too. She looked to her pained hands and then to a pained Ivivin. She tucked her hands under her armpits, hiding them from view. Elara did not understand herself at this moment. She had stopped feeling so self-conscious about the scarring on her hands, at least here in Smithton, so why did she feel fresh the urge to hide them? Why did she feel panic when he embraced her? Moreover, this was not the panic of a skipped heartbeat or an unexpected act. No. She was scared Why was she scared of him?

Ivivin was a little hurt. He certainly wasn't good at reading people, but he had thought she was welcoming the hug.

"I suppose I didn't really know her all that long. It must be like getting hugged by a stranger. I bet she scarcely thought of me once I left." Ivivin considered. *"Now is not the time to be hurt, though! I am on duty and clearly she came for something."*

"So, Elara…uh...what can I do for you?" Ivivin said, fumbling over his own words.

Elara jolted to attention. "Oh, uhh...I have something for, um, the smith? Smith?"

Ivivin chuckled. "I know, it's weird, right? Smith the smith. Got me too. I do work here. I could help you, you know."

Elara shook her head vehemently.

"Minerva was adamant that it goes to Smith." Elara told Ivivin, recognizing there was only partial truth in her words.

Ivivin nodded.

"Sure, sure. He's in the back. I'll go grab him." Ivivin headed to Smith, who was busy moving some ingots from storage to the forge.

"What's got you so red in the face, boy? Mrs. Jenkins try and seduce you? She's a sly one, I'll admit, for being nearly 80 years old." Smith laughed at his own joke.

Ivivin shook his head. "No—nothing like that. There's a customer, insists on speaking to you directly."

Smith was a bit irritated at this explanation.

"Boy, what'd I say about bugging me about every single person that comes to see me personally? I'd never get a thing done. Should have just taken their request and got on with it." Smith barked.

Ivivin just looked at his own feet.

"Well, too late now. Take these to the forge boy. Careful, they're a tad heavy." Smith said, handing Ivivin the metal heaps before headed to the front.

Ivivin waddled his way with the ingots to tuck them away for later use. Smith approached the counter.

"Well now, I can see why the boy was flustered. Not often a girl his age comes by here."

"How can I help you?" Smith asked Elara.

Elara looked nervously behind Smith for Ivivin before proceeding. She handed him the cauldron and the note from Minerva.

"I'd like this cauldron repaired. Oh, and this is from Minerva. She says to wash up properly for tonight." Elara meekly told the gargantuan man. Smith immediately caught sight of Elara's scarred hands during the hand-off, but tried not to stare.

"That old, dusty hag! Always acting like she is my mother! I mean, look at me, I'm fine right?" Smith put Elara on the spot, smiling and trying to look presentable.

"Oh ye—" Elara almost managed her lie, but the soot on Smith's teeth prevented her from completing it. Instead, she giggled at the sight. Smith shook his head.

"Fine, fine. Tell her I'll clean up. Haven't even been back a week and already she's leaning into me."

Smith then read the note.

"Oh, that's a surprise. Well, then, tell her it'll be ready by tonight then. I suppose I really will have to clean up." Smith told Elara, as he headed back into the forge. Elara just remained at the counter. Smith caught sight of her just before reentering the forge.

"You are all set! We'll bring it by tonight!" Smith yelled to her. Elara, jolted again to attention and scrambled away from the counter. As Smith approached Ivivin, still stacking ingots, they heard Elara call from the front.

"I'll see you later, Ivivin!"

Ivivin went to the front to say good-bye, but Elara was already gone. Still, Ivivin returned to the forge with a little smile.

13

"Oh? You know her, boy? I don't recall giving you time to go out and flirt." Smith continued to tease.

"No! I mean yes, but not from here. Do you recall the sister's I told you about? The ones I met up north? She is the older sister, Elara. I was just caught off guard. Never thought I'd see her here of all places." Ivivin explained.

"Oh? Is that so? In that case..." Smith put his hand to his chin in thought. "Boy! What have you still to do this morning?"

"I need to sharpen the sickles and make that axe head for Mr. Rutherford. And I was hoping to get a head start on those carpentry nails for Logos. He seemed pressed for time." Ivivin recounted.

"Never mind that, then. I have another task for you. We might have to put off your armour for today, but that's fine. A special occasion and all. I expect you to put your all into this, do you understand me? Especially since I'll be doing your share today!" Smith commanded.

"Naturally." Ivivin was taken aback by Smith's eagerness, but was confident he could handle whatever Smith threw his way.

"What would you have me do?" Ivivin asked.

"First thing's first, take care of that cauldron. I'll get things ready while you do." Smith called, himself now hustling about. A little while later, Ivivin had repaired the cauldron and Smith called him over.

"Here, boy. Take a gander at this note." Smith said, showing Ivivin the now slightly smudgy note. "You think you can handle it?" Ivivin was struck by nerves.

"I—I don't know." he stammered.

"What's that boy? Hardly can call yourself a blacksmith if you can't manage a task like this. At this rate, you'll be here for years!" Smith egged Ivivin on.

Ivivin slapped his cheeks with both hands and tried to envision a plan. Nerves turned to inspiration turned to excitement.

"Yeah, got an idea. I can do it." Ivivin confidently asserted to Smith.

"Good. I'll be around if you need me. Don't need me." Smith said as he returned to work. Ivivin got out paper and began to sketch out his next project. He hadn't been this focused or determined since he resolved to finish his armour and go after Smith. It made him feel alive and well, clearing his thoughts and removing the haze over his emotion.

An afternoon later, Ivivin presented the fruit of his effort to Smith. "Aye, boy. Fine work, indeed." Smith gave Ivivin a rare compliment. Smith recalled the morning's happenings and furrowed his brow.

"Hey, lad, why don't you put this on a chain?" Smith suggested.

Ivivin thought about it. "You're right. She doesn't seem like the type to wear something like this, after all." He said, headed back to see what he could do.

"So that's how it is, huh?" Smith thought to himself. *"Best for me not to intervene."*

"Youth..." He sighed and said to himself gently before yelling at Ivivin. "Boy, there's no time to dawdle! We are expected there within the hour! Get the chain and clean yourself up. There's a basin of water already in the back. Hop to!"

14

Ivivin made sure he was presentable. Usually, Ivivin didn't care much for his appearance. He was a pretty haggard traveler, after all. But tonight was a special occasion and he could not keep himself from double and triple checking himself from every angle he could manage. He grabbed Icarus and scratched under the bugger's beak.

"Hey buddy! Sorry I was so busy today. You wouldn't believe what happened. In any case, how'd you like to see Elara tonight?" Ivivin asked the owl, who perked up and looked at Ivivin like he must have hit his head.

"I know, right? I had the same reaction when I saw her here, too. But I assure you she is the real deal. I don't think she remembers our time together quite as fondly as I do, but she remembered me nonetheless. I suppose that'll happen when you seal away an ancient and unstoppable evil together to subvert a grand prophecy, huh?" Ivivin rambled away at the owl nervously. "In any case, tonight is a special night for her, so make sure you congratulate her, ok?"

Ivivin picked Icarus up, grinning.

"Geez, you didn't even make yourself look presentable to see your own sister." He teased the owl, who spent the whole walk to the teahouse preening himself proper, a little upset he wasn't given more notice.

The men and owl rapped on the door of the teashop. Elara opened the door. Minerva had told her she, too, needed to be presentable this night. Elara tried to get away with her usual attire, but Minerva insisted on the dress she had gotten from Able. Elara relented, but wore her trousers as well. Minerva saw she was wearing the leather gloves Elara often wore when picking thorny plants in the field. Instinctively, she almost shrilly told Elara to remove them, but was reminded of the young woman's pain. Elara had been doing so well recently that she had almost forgotten she had many wounds yet. Minerva still had a hard time believing Elara knew Smith's apprentice and that he was the fellow who helped her and her sister up north.

"Elara hasn't been terribly shy about her hands… I mean, she doesn't go around talking about them or anything, but this is the first I've seen her hide them. But…I suppose this is different. She knew him before, after all." Minerva reasoned.

However, as Elara had paced around anxiously in the minutes leading up to their arrival, Minerva saw, too, a flicker of youth in her actions.

Elara stood at the entranceway and invited the trio in. Ivivin had never seen Elara in a dress. Seeing her there reminded Ivivin of when he first met her. The scene replayed in his head and Ivivin realized, much to his embarrassment, that he had seen her much barer in the cave where he met her.

"Why am I thinking of that now!?" Ivivin thought, trying to shake away the memory.

Ivivin and Smith entered as invited. Ivivin looked around at the teashop. Perhaps it was having spent all day breathing hot air and soot, but the teashop was not as fragrant as he had expected. He looked to Elara, who had just returned from calling Minerva from her lab, and approached her. He handed her a slightly-less-dusty-than-usual bundle of ragged feathers.

"Your brother missed you!" he teased her. His joke came at the cost of a slightly-harder-than-playful punch to the arm. And, just like that, any tension was gone. Minerva came out and the four of them sat at the too small table and enjoyed a cup of tea together.

After some time spent on jovial nothings, Elara asked Smith a question.

"Not to be rude, but I wonder what brings you here tonight? Other than to return the cauldron, of course." Elara had taken it from Smith at the door and was impressed at the repair. If she didn't know where to look, she wouldn't have been able to tell it was cracked in the first place. Minerva sighed.

"Such an impatient child. I suppose we can get started, then." Minerva said, pushing back her chair and standing. She held her teacup high in the air and tapped on it with a spoon.

"Tonight, we are here to honour Elara, whom today I formally accepted as an apprentice! She has already done more than enough to justify such a title and it would be simply disrespectful to deny her it a moment longer!"

Elara retreated into her chair, very aware that all attention was on her.

"So, deary, I present you with this token. With it, you represent me. Everyone will see you and know that I am your mentor and you, my apprentice." Minerva smiled and handed Elara a ring on a chain. The band was heavy, like steel, but did not quite look it. Elara inspected the ring. On two ends, across from each other, the ring was elevated. A small plate on each end was finely engraved. Elara had to look closely to tell what the engraving was, but recognized it as a hibiscus flower protruding from a mortar and pestle. Elara had never cared for jewelry but the meaning of the gift, plus the sheer artisanship, made her giddy at its receipt. She turned to Smith.

"You made this? It's incredible, the steel looks unique somehow and the engraving must have taken ages! Thank you!" Elara told Smith.

"Me? No, no, young lady. I didn't touch the thing. That's my apprentice's handiwork in your hands." Smith gestured with his head towards Ivivin, who was now taking his turn to bashfully retreat into his own seat.

"Wha—? Really?" Elara said, flustered that her compliments belonged now to Ivivin.

Ivivin nodded.

"The metal is a blend. Didn't have a lot we could spare, but it is steel with just a bit of silver folded in. I had to put those little bands on, with the flower on it, afterwards. It took me nearly a dozen times to get the damned thing right." Ivivin explained.

Elara was genuinely surprised at Ivivin's talent. "Well, thank you, then Ivivin. It really is good." Her compliment was followed by a silence from all parties. It was not until Ivivin, willing to do anything to escape from this awkward hellscape, decided to show Elara his apprentice ring that conversation returned to normal.

"I guess we are both apprentices now, Elara! See, here's my ring." Ivivin blurted. Elara saw and recognized the ring from when she met Ivivin in her hometown.

"He's been a smith's apprentice all this time, then?" Elara thought to herself. "I suppose there is a lot I don't know about him."

"Actually, boy. About that…" Smith said, standing up and clearing his voice.

"You are my apprentice no longer."

15

Ivivin's heart sank. "What did I do wrong? Why did Smith decide to be rid of me?" Ivivin struggled with his own thoughts.

"Is it because I took too long to finish the armour? But it is almost done!" Ivivin racked his head for answers.

Smith saw the strife in Ivivin.

"Ah, no boy. I think you have the wrong idea. Though you haven't been with me long, in the grand scheme of things, I have no qualm vouching for your abilities. This ring was enough for me to see that you're ready, armour or no. Unlike Helmschmied, Tubal, Cain, and even myself… I don't think you were made to forge tools of war. Not that you don't have the skill. No, I think you are more like Wayland...my son. Your skill shines brightest when you craft tools of peace. It was my folly as your master to try and assess you in the way I did, but it is clear as day to me now that you are deserving of the title Blacksmith. From now onwards, you are my apprentice no longer. You still have much to learn—not as my student, but as my equal. Congratulations, boy. Don't let it go to your head."

Ivivin didn't make it through the speech: He was crying tears of happy disbelief the moment Smith compared him to his son. Ivivin hadn't realized how highly he thought of Smith or how much his approval meant to him until this moment. Ivivin had a father of his own, one who he missed dearly and thought of often. But Smith had treated him as a son, too. And Ivivin held him as dear to his heart as a father, too.

"Now, now, boy. None of that." Smith said, trying to maintain his hard exterior. Minerva smirked as she saw tears form in the corner of Smith's own eyes. Minerva spoke.

"Well, this calls for celebration. Spirits, if you will. Elara, if you would be a dear and grab some of the wine I have in the back?"

Elara nodded and left. Minerva turned to Smith and Ivivin.

"I am sorry to switch the topic to something so bitter, so abruptly, but we have strayed far from the original intent of the night. I am sure you know full well who I am, Ivivin?"

Ivivin's elation faded as the gravity of his reality set back in. He nodded.

"Quick, then. While Elara's gone, I must bleed you. We need not discuss the matter further on this night nor with Elara, but time is our sworn enemy in this." Minerva asserted, pulling a vial from her sleeve. "Hold out your hand."

Ivivin obeyed, but refused to look as Minerva drew the blood. It stung, much more than a prick alone should. By the time Elara had returned with the wine, the trio were already laughing and celebrating anew, with Ivivin's blood safely tucked away in Minerva's sleeve.

16

The moon rose and passed well overhead. Smith and Minerva had begun drunken chatter that led to emotional stories about the late Grandia. Ivivin and Elara had paced themselves a bit better, though Icarus lay drunk in an empty teacup. In the middle of Smith's story about the time Grandia had left him tied to a tree naked as the day he was born, Minerva paused him with a raised finger.

"Just a moment, I'll let you finish. After all, I love any story that has you painted the fool. But…" She turned to Elara and Ivivin. "I just realized I needed something from the out in the field."

"Sure, I can leave first thing in the morning. What do you need?" Elara answered dutifully.

"Nonononono. No. I need it ASAP. You and Ivivin go get it now." Minerva drunkenly insisted.

"What could you possibly need at this hour?" Elara said, not yet seeing Minerva's game.

"Ohhh, I don't know…" Minerva put her hand to her chin and stroked, struggling to think of a proper excuse. "Oh! How about one of those toads! They always seem to put you in such a chipper mood, Elara!"

Elara shushed the old woman hurriedly.

"Fine, fine. I'll go get one. Enough of that." She grabbed a small pouch and headed out the door. Minerva and Smith bellowed in laughter until Minerva noticed Ivivin yet sat before them.

"What are you doing, you daft child!? Hurry up and go! And take this with you!" Minerva screeched at Ivivin, pushing a bottle of wine into his hand and forcing him out the door.

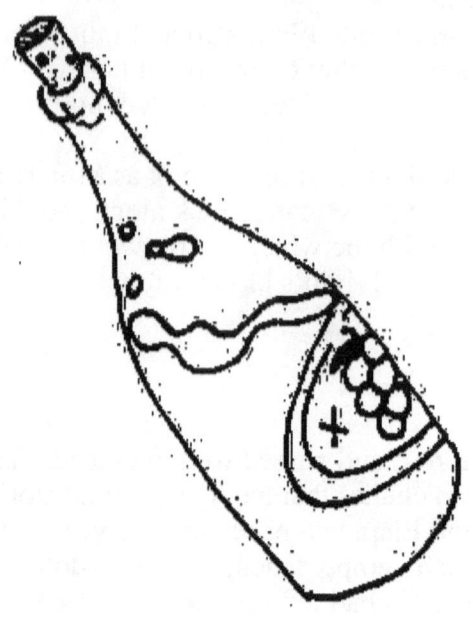

The Duel

1

Ivivin caught up to Elara, who had already made it an admirable distance down the street in a huff.

"Oh, you're coming along then, Ivivin? What's with the wine—"

Elara had figured it out mid-sentence.

"That nosey woman!" She thought frustrated and embarrassed. *"Still...It has been a while since I've seen Ivivin. Perhaps this is a good chance to catch up."*

Elara led Ivivin to one of her favourite spots on the outskirts of town. It was just far enough to be rid of the lingering lights of late night loners in Smithton, but not quite so far to have a tremendous walk back if you got tired. There were, of course, toads, croaking gently in the distance. Elara sat down and looked upwards, to her stars. Ivivin stood there, bottle of wine in hard, befuddled.

"Uh, Elara. Aren't we going to get a toad for Minerva? I think I hear some over that way."

Elara couldn't help but laugh at how dense Ivivin was. Not that she was much better. Took the bottle of wine for her to realize, too, that the toad was a ruse.

"Never mind that, Ivivin. There will be toad time to come. For now, just sit down and let's chat and look at the stars, just as we did that one night with Idalia." Elara said, eyes still affixed to the sky overhead.

The stars were especially bright this night—perfect for stargazing. Ivivin shrugged and sat next to Elara, not exceptionally close, but not far either. Elara turned to him as he began to squat, looking to start a conversation. Instead, his closeness and the desolation of this location struck a familiar, primal fear in Elara. She felt a desperate need to get Ivivin away from her. She fought the urge to shove him away and, instead, as Ivivin touched the ground, she rose from it. Ivivin looked at her confused, unable to resolve her face well in the night lighting. Elara took a few steps away from him and sat anew, still struggling to compose herself.

"Damn, he isn't going to hurt me. I know this! The dense boy didn't even realize what Minerva had intentioned. So why am I still so damn scared!? So maddeningly weak and unable to control

myself!? I was doing so well... " Elara thought, looking at her hands, shaking from both anger and anxiety.

"Even at this distance, I can't relax. What is wrong with me?" Elara brooded.

The silence that fed Elara's turmoil was broken when, out of nowhere, Ivivin pointed to the sky.

"Lupus." he said, briefly pausing. "That is your favorite constellation." He finished with a grin.

Elara recalled their night on the roof together and laughed, albeit weakly.

"That's right. Do you remember what it is?"

"A wolf." Ivivin said, proudly.

"Someone's been reading, then? Good, I am glad my book didn't go to waste on a helpless case." Elara teased.

"Of course I have, I must have read it dozens of times on my travels!" Ivivin said, eagerly pointing to the sky. "There's Orion! And the Northern Cross, just barely! And Virgo!" Ivivin declared, hand flailing about the sky.

"Ok, ok. I believe you, I believe you." Elara voiced, Ivivin's childishness bringing her some ease. "So, what's your favourite constellation then? You know mine, it's only fair you tell me yours."

"Hmm…" Ivivin hummed deep in thought. "I never really thought about it, to tell you the truth."

Elara scoffed.

"How can you have read that book again and again and not have a favourite constellation? You strange, strange creature. Probably stranger than your dingy little owl, to boot."

"Shhh! I'm thinking, ok?" Ivivin pondered a moment as the pair looked to the stars. "Aquila, I think, by a large margin." Ivivin decided.

"The wolf and the eagle, huh? Sounds about right." Elara remarked, with just a hint of sadness in her voice. "So, Ivivin, where have you been? What have you been doing besides, apparently, becoming a blacksmith?"

"Oh! I suppose you wouldn't have heard, being here and all!" Ivivin pulled out his moon's tear.

"Check this out." Ivivin said, before illuminating the area around them with a faint light. Elara was amazed, not just by the tear and its power, but, again, by how much Ivivin had appeared to have matured. He was no longer baby-faced and she could tell he shaved regularly, if poorly. Unfortunately, this returned unease to Elara's gut.

"Put that out!" Elara snapped at Ivivin.

"Oh, sorry did it hurt your eyes?" Ivivin asked apologetically, letting the stone lose its light.

"Anyway, that's not the important part…" Ivivin started, before explaining everything he had learned about the tears. He detailed to an attentive and interested Elara, his journey thus far. He even powered through the part about Icarus' injury. Then he reached the part about giving chase to Smith and felt heavy lumps form in both his throat and his chest. He uneasily shifted the conversation into Elara's court, rather than finishing his own tale.

"Never mind the rest of the story, for now. What about you, Elara? Why did you leave home?" Ivivin asked, genuine in his interest.

Elara began eagerly, just as Ivivin did, put tapered off when she reached the point where she arrived in Rumi. Though it was dark and she wore gloves, Elara still tucked her hands under her armpits.

"I think…that's enough storytelling tonight, don't you?" Elara proposed. She had never before wanted to both share and hide something so much.

"Even if he would listen, tonight is the night he became a blacksmith. I won't sully it." Elara justified to herself.

"Mhm… perhaps you're right, Elara." Ivivin said pensively. He did not wish to hide his ailment from her, but was fearful she might treat him differently if she knew.

"Even if she assured me, tonight is the night she became an apprentice. I won't sully it." Ivivin justified to himself.

The pair was surprised when dawn touched the horizon. The last time either had stayed up so late to be exposed to the morning's first light, it was due to nightmares and strife. But, for the first time in a while, it was due to the acceleration of time in good company. Ivivin stood and patted down his legs. He walked over and offered a hand to Elara to help her stand. She almost took it, too, but the sight of Ivivin standing over her caused her fear to return to her. She sprung to her feet on her own and stared to the horizon, listening to the toads sing their little song. Ivivin stood a few arm lengths away and joined her in watching the sun crawl above the horizon.

Elara eventually yawned.

"Shall we?" Ivivin asked, falling prey to the contagion himself.

"Yes, yes. Just a moment, though. Almost forgot something." Elara said with a mischievous smile.

The pair returned to the teashop. Ivivin waved good-bye to Elara as he woke and supported a groggy and drunk Smith back to the forge. Elara returned to her room in the nearby inn, tired, but smirking.

2

The day's light broke into Minerva's bedroom and disturbed the weary and still-drunk woman. She rolled over to ease the burden and found herself face to face with the biggest, most warty toad she had ever laid eyes on. Her heart jumped, but weariness won the battle. As she drifted back out of consciousness, a single thought entered her mind:

"Eh, I've gone to bed with worse."

Ivivin carried the drunk smith and the inexplicably drunk owl back to the shop, with Smith managing to aid Ivivin just enough for them to make the trip. Ivivin guided Smith to bed and laid him there. He was about to take Icarus with him back to his room, but an idea struck Ivivin. He set the tipsy talon-bearer in Smith's hands and moved them near his face.

"That'll be a pleasant surprise for the both of them." Ivivin laughed softly. Ivivin left the room, his soft laughter turning to gut-busting by the drowsy, dreaming musings of Smith.

"Oh, darling, you look so beautiful tonight. Especially your hair." Smith mumbled, his hands combing through Icarus' feathers.

4

It was well after noon when Minerva roused herself. She fed the toad some fresh insect parts and let it out her window before entering the teashop. To her surprise, the shop was open and doing business. At the helm was a very drowsy and disheveled Elara who, nonetheless, was taking care of things. Minerva smiled at Elara's kindness and approached her.

"Oh, thank you deary. How about I take over from here? You can take a nice nap in my room, if you'd like." Minerva offered. Elara was already halfway to the bed by the time Minerva finished.

Elara slept heavily. So heavily, in fact, that Minerva was worried when she accidentally dropped and broke a jar, but Elara was unfazed and unmoved. Minerva went to check on her. She was alive and well, but Minerva could not help but chuckle at her napping apprentice. Elara lay, limbs strewn about most ungraciously. Her hair went every direction, including into her own mouth. Elara was not a tiny woman by any means, but Minerva had quite a luxurious and generously sized bed. Elara seemed determined, even in her deep slumber, to occupy every inch of that bed.

Minerva sat and watched the young woman sleep for a moment, trying to commit the scene to memory. While she found it endearing and precious to see this young woman, who she had grown to be fond and proud of, resting comfortably and relaxed in her home, she mostly wanted to etch the image into her mind to tease Elara at a later juncture.

"I suppose she'll be out for a while still. I suppose I can close up shop and take care of my... unpleasant business." Minerva thought.

Minerva went to her basement lab, vial of Ivivin's blood in hand, and sighed heavily as she set to work prepping what she would need to detect and confirm the ailment. In her heart, she knew that the test was necessary. Not she, nor Smith, nor Ivivin could bring themselves to truly accept reality until it was confirmed. Still, she thought of the smiles and laughter of the previous evening. She thought of the young man, so warm and full of energy, growing cold and feeble. She thought of Elara, who seemed to enjoy his company. She thought of Smith, who had already lost so much to this loathsome disease. She thought of her dear friend Grandia, who she thought of as the daughter she never had, and the fate that befell her. These thoughts unsettled Minerva. Her burdensome work was prolonged by an emotional tremble.

"Perhaps we shouldn't..." Minerva found herself thinking. *"Maybe he can live life a little more wholly if we don't know for sure."*

She was conflicted. The kind thing, in her mind, was to lie or to refuse to administer the test. Perhaps then he would still be moved to continue his life. Sure, the disease would come down on him eventually, but it could be months or even a few years before it claimed his life. Minerva had lost confidence in her ability to cure the disease. Weeks and weeks of effort led nowhere, even with Elara's help. She had readied the test, but sat at the bench as seconds turned to minutes turned to hours. All she need do was add Ivivin's blood, but she was paralyzed by indecision. She thought much of Grandia during this time.

"Grandia, that kind soul, didn't deserve her premature ending." Minerva thought again and again, fruitlessly, until a new thought finally pierced her mind and ended the cycle.

"She deserved not her fate, sure, but she had spent every moment she could making the most of her life, even post-diagnosis. She believed in knowledge and in art and in love. I can't deny the boy this knowledge. I can only encourage him to act on it in a meaningful way."

Minerva steadied her hand and her heart and added to the assay, Ivivin's blood.

It reacted just as it had for Grandia's blood. It was strange. Minerva was a well-read and wise woman. She tried her best to understand the natural world and how it works. She knew there was great strength in knowledge. She believed that truth and fact were inherently good. Perhaps that is precisely why she felt so betrayed. Why she felt that truth had failed her. That it tore at her soul viciously and with deliberate contempt. She knew the world and the truth cared not what Minerva wanted. But she had become so accustomed to having a say, to having strength in her knowledge, that her own powerlessness was a crippling realization she had before and would have time and time again.

Elara stood at the entrance of the lab as she saw Minerva cry hot and heavy tears while pounding on her bench. Elara knew not what had happened, but she could tell that her mentor was hurting this night, likely frustrated at the difficulty of the problem in front of her. Elara could not easily express herself with her words. Instead, she started a fire, put the tea on, returned to the basement, and hugged her precious friend and mentor from behind.

5

Elara and Minerva sat upstairs in the shop at the small table in the dusty corner. They sipped on tea—Elara's own assemblage.

"You know, this is probably my favourite thing you've shown me how to do since I came to work here." Elara joked, taking another swig of her over-sweet and over-creamy tea. Minerva couldn't help but smile when she looked at her apprentice.

"I'll save the sleep teasing for later." Minerva decided. *"Besides, I have other ammunition."* She thought, remembering her mischief from the night before.

"So, deary, I saw you brought me back a lovely toad, just as I asked. How was having Ivivin along?" Minerva asked.

Elara withdrew into herself, looking away from her and turning red.

"Oh, she's embarrassed! She must like the boy after all." Minerva judged internally.

"So, what did you two talk abo—" Minerva cut herself off, getting a closer look at Elara. Her redness was not of embarrassment, but of shame and conflict. She looked away to hide away the tears forming in the corners of her eyes. The blood fell from Minerva's face as she feared the worst. She couldn't fathom such sweet boy would have hurt her but, perhaps…

"He didn't hurt you, did he!?" Minerva said, anger bubbling in her quickly.

Elara seemed startled by the accusation.

"No, no! He didn't do anything to me all. I don't even know that he realized what your plan was, the dense child." Elara responded. "It's just...." Elara's voice raised from a near whisper to a modest shout.

"I was just so afraid of him. He did nothing. That awful, haunting look wasn't even in his eyes. But he made me fearful and anxious and distrustful. He's grown so much...I am so weak! To let my base instincts win and conquer what I know to be true and how I feel about my friend. I am broken!"

Minerva's heart broke for Elara. She had never considered that Ivivin would trigger her so. Worse yet was Elara's fondness for the boy—he was not her enemy and considered her a friend. There was no villain or tragedy to share in the blame or to direct the pain towards. Just Elara and her feelings. Minerva could not imagine how much that ate at Elara. That every fond and youthful feeling for Ivivin was coupled with something nasty and repulsive.

Minerva moved her seat closer to Elara and returned the embrace she received earlier.

"You are not broken, my dear child. Don't say such putrid things about yourself." Minerva whispered softly to Elara.

The words drew not comfort, but anger, out of the distressed Elara. She moved quickly away from Minerva, forcing herself away from the embrace. Minerva had allowed herself to believe she could help Elara with positivity and pretty words, so she let the hurt of rejection show on her face, just for an instant. She realized what she was doing and remedied it, but it was too late—an instant was all it took for Elara to see.

"You see, even you!" Elara loosed.

"Elara, dear…" Minerva stopped herself. She was about to offer shallow banalities once more. She took an all-important moment to consider her words before proceeding.

"Elara. Know that I do not say this lightly. I think of you as my own daughter, just...just as I did Grandia. You are wounded. You are hurt. But you are not broken. And until you come to believe that yourself, you will be forced into this corner of hurt again and again.

And it breaks my heart to see you...so intelligent, so kind, and so very, very strong...it hurts me to see you doubt yourself so. I know why, though I can't understand. I'm as sure as I can be that you've made mistakes. But I'm also as sure as I can be that you don't deserve this misery, either. It pains me that you can't see yourself as I see you—as a wonderful young woman who has much to be proud of, much to look forward to, and... much to leave behind." Minerva finished her heartfelt speech.

Elara returned to Minerva's arms.

"It's just... it feels like every time I feel like I am getting better, that I am moving on, I am drug back. It's like none of the 'lessons' I've learned mean anything. They feel like false epiphanies that just give me the illusion of recovery. Every time I find a new secret to being happy and build a foundation on it, something comes and proves it a lie! I'm so tired of it. I'm so tired of crying. And I'm just so tired and I'm so tired of being so tired." Elara called into Minerva's shoulder.

Minerva knew not what to say. All she could do was sit there, lend this girl her shoulder, and try to understand. Tears, like all things, cannot last forever. Eventually, Elara lifted her head and faced Minerva once more.

"I hurt him in my actions. I'm sure of it." Elara said.

Minerva didn't know exactly what Elara had done, but she suspected it hurt Elara more than Ivivin. "If it pains you so, why not apologize? Even explain to him why? Do you think you need to hide the scars on your heart from him as you do the ones on your hands?" Minerva posited.

"I can't. What would he think of me, if he found I was broken. He has been blessed in his travels and seems unencumbered by his past trials! He would not understand and he would refuse me from his life entirely." Elara countered, tucking her hands away under her armpits.

These words stung Minerva. Just as Ivivin knew not of Elara's pains and tribulations, Elara was not privy to Ivivin's suffering. And it was not her place to tell her. Still, she could not say nothing.

"You may be surprised, Elara. Perhaps he will understand even better than you do. You only yesterday learned he was a smith's apprentice. There is still much for you two to learn of each other. You're kindred spirits, but you are not yet close friends."

Minerva offered. "I am not saying you need to tell him now. Or even all at once. Just, consider that he cares for you. I don't think his feelings are so superficial that he would reject you for your pain."

Elara nodded and sought comfort in her tea. She wanted to believe Minerva. But wanting to believe something is not the same as believing. Elara took what she could from the talk, finished her tea, and went to find her peace at the inn. She prayed that her nightmares would give her just one more night's reprieve.

6

Soon after Elara left, Minerva heard a fresh knock on her door.

"Who could it be at this hour?" Minerva thought, knowing Elara would simply have let herself in. Her question was answered when she discovered Smith at the door, Icarus in hand.

"Ah… I see." Minerva said. "Couldn't sleep then? Come to pester an old woman and spread the insomnia?"

"Couldn't wait." Smith answered. "May I come in?"

"I suppose. But I'm not brewing any tea. My apprentice gave me tea so potent and so sugary, I'll be up for days" Minerva said, gesturing to Smith that he could enter. "I suppose you've come for the boy's results?"

"Yes, I have. Though I suppose your silence today speaks volumes. He's got it then? For certain?" Smith asked.

Lumps formed in her throat and her words resisted exit as lead resists lift.

"Yes, I'm certain."

"Damn it. That impulsive boy!" Smith exclaimed, pain leaking clearly into his voice. Hope returned to him though, as he continued.

"But, surely…you are close to a cure? A treatment for this malady? It isn't as needed anymore, with the epidemic cut off at the source, but I will gladly work off the debt for the rest of my days if you can heal the boy." Smith bargained.

"Unfortunately, no. I am not closer to a cure. And all your money and all your metal won't change that. Do not fall back to being how you were with Grandia. I am sure you do not need a reminder of the price thinking in that manner entails." Minerva chided the grown man.

"You're right. But why? How, after years, are you no closer?" Smith struggled to understand.

"It is no easier for me to explain this to you than for you to teach me how you fold metals so expertly. It is my vocation. It would take me many months to teach you enough to where you could recognize and understand the immense difficulty of the problem. Still, I will offer up my best explanation, if you'll calm down and listen carefully." Minerva offered.

Smith nodded and allowed Minerva to continue.

"Everything in this world has physical properties. There are plants that contain toxins that will end human life if consumed. There are metals that are harder than steel and others more brittle than stone. These properties are available to all and would exist even if there were none around to observe them. It matters not if you know if the plant will end your life—eating it is enough to guarantee your demise. It also matters not that you eat the plant itself. If the toxins are extracted from the plant, they remain toxic and will end you all the same." Minerva started.

"I understand, what does this have to do with Crumbleheart, though?" Smith interjected.

"Your rude impatience betrays you, Smith. Listen, and do not interrupt again." Minerva snapped. "All things have physical properties. But all things also have the capacity for magic. Wood, stone, people, animals…disease. Most things never feel the touch of magic, just as most people never wield it. But, if you spend a lifetime, you can learn to sense it. I have. I can sense and, to an extent, imbue my draughts with magic. You wield magic as well, though I am sure you are unaware of it. Your metal work is superb on its own, but you have developed a sense of magic as well. Subconsciously, you imbue your creations with magic. Most of it is minor, like most magics. On occasion though, I am sure it has made a noticeable difference. Armour that does not give way when it ought. A weapon that endures weathering. Even cauldrons that resist decay. My point is, Smith, that man is both natural and magical. Most medicines work on the natural part of man. Ointment that eases and cleans a wound. A draft that soothes a pained stomach. That sort of thing. There are, of course, a few magic ailments man can get, too."

"Crumbleheart?" Smith proposed.

"No, not quite. Again, patience." Minerva answered, though more gently than Smith had expected. "There are diseases that are solely magic in nature. For sake of discussion, we can call them curses. A particular manifestation of spell. These, too, can be remedied, though the methods of doing so are known to fewer still than those who can cast them to begin with. But, in principle, it is no different than knowing the magic properties of the curse and using the magic properties of the world around you to counter them. For a toxin, an antivenom. For a curse, a counter-curse." Minerva simplified.

Smith followed her explanation well, though he was dubious of her claims that he had somehow enchanted his crafts. Still, he nodded.

"Crumbleheart... is an enigma in every sense of the word. It is hard for me to see its form, natural or magical. They are interwoven together as much as they are into the hearts of the afflicted. Crumbleheart is a curse, sure, but it is also a natural malady of man. Even if I rid a person of the magic, the natural part remains. And vice versa. It is not a long after that the curse or the sickness returns, even more potent than before." Minerva explained.

"So why not treat both at the same time?" Smith asked.

"As if I hadn't thought of a solution so obvious." Minerva responded, a bit annoyed. "They are incompatible."

"They cancel each other out?" Smith queried.

"No. Far worse." Minerva answered. "They become toxic. Or, more precisely, they enhance the extant toxicity of the disease. The heart crumbles and falls to the toxin at an accelerated rate. You will be granted levity and sentiment again, for a few moments. It is actually quite dramatic, the change, as if all the warmth one had been missing was returned all at once. People will literally glow. The formulation for this combination is quite simple. I taught it to Grandia, should she feel her time neared. You have never told me...how she passed." Minerva was hindered by her own words.

Smith realized how he had protected that memory of her and was unwilling to share with anyone...until Ivivin wrought it from him. It was a selfishness he would remedy now, for this woman who loved his wife.

"She had me make a caustic and deadly brew. She drank it and passed on, with me at her side and with Wayland in her arms." Smith confessed resolutely.

The frank forwardness of Smith's words stunned Minerva, who had known this man to monopolize his last memories with her. Moreover, it fed a curiosity in her.

"Smith...was there anything strange about her passing?" Minerva asked.

"No, she passed peacefully." Smith responded.

"No illumination?" Minerva prodded again.

Smith was losing his patience.

"No. She smiled and died in her sleep."

Both Smith and Minerva had been near tears the whole talk, but at this statement, Minerva succumbed to them.

"She was whole when she passed. She was whole last we spoke. Her body's heart had eroded but her spirit had yet to yield even an inch. She was truly an incredible woman, Grandia. She probably only used that particular draught to ensure you did not try and follow her to the beyond." Minerva realized. "I am so glad she did not suffer in that way."

Smith had not realized that this weight had lingered on his shoulders, but, upon hearing this confirmation, he felt it leave. He had instinctively trusted in his love's assurance that she was whole. But there was doubt he was unaware of—that she, in her kindness, could have lied. She could have been losing herself and wished to spare Smith the loss of her love in addition to the loss of his lover.

"She was. Truly an incredible woman." Smith managed.

7

After some moments recomposing themselves, Minerva continued with her explanation. By this point, though, it had turned into more of a rant of frustration.

"There seems to be something unavoidable and fundamental to this disease. It's inevitability flies in the face in everything I know. And with...Grandia, I thought myself to understand everything about this world. But, as I was reminded today by my apprentice...that is an arrogant notion. Perhaps every facet of humanity is not knowable. Or, at least, not to us. Not to me." Minerva trailed off.

"In any case, don't you think it's time you told me the whole story, Smith? I was in a good mood when I heard you had returned and a better mood still when you left me a note saying that the

Crumbleheart epidemic had been solved by your apprentice. What exactly happened?"

Smith explained what had happened. Minerva was shocked to learn about the existence of reincarnations of the celestial spirits. She had Smith recount the verbal exchanges with Mars again and again.

"Even those great and powerful deities…can only manipulate the ailment. Augment it. It is something intangible, but resting firmly in the domain of man. Smith, I know you want me to tell you I can cure this, that I can heal that boy who you have come to see as brother to Wayland. It is beyond me, Smith. I am sorry for ever leading you to believe otherwise. It may be understood one day. But I am old. And I am tired. I want to spend my days helping those I can, right in front of me—those I know I can help and that need me. For that, I will come out of retirement once more and for nothing else."

These words made sense to Smith. He understood her decision. It made sense. But knowing and understanding didn't stop his heart from tearing asunder. His chest ached and he felt numb. He thought of Grandia and the pain of losing her. He thought of Grandia and her strength. He thought of an idea.

"Minerva… what if you treated only the boy's body?" Smith asked.

"What do you mean? You would have him cursed to such a hollow existence?" Minerva accused Smith.

"No… let the boy fight it. Grandia did." Smith stated.

Minerva realized what Smith was implying. If the magic that left them insensate could be combated somehow without medical intervention, then treating their physical heart could at least elongate their lives.

"Perhaps. I will not act on it until I investigate further. Acting rashly out of fear or panic could cost Ivivin his life. And, even if it works, he risks being cursed to feel nothing, though his body lives on. Wait not to tell him of his illness, Smith. But do wait to tell him about this possibility we stumbled upon this night." Minerva concluded. Smith wanted to protest, but could see seriousness in Minerva's eyes.

"Right. As you wish." Smith agreed, scooping up Icarus, who had fallen asleep during Minerva's lengthy explanation. He gingerly scritched the snoozing owl, noting that he had gotten tubby.

"Well, that weight of that conversation might have passed, but not the weight commanding my eyes to close." Minerva said, standing. She looked at Smith directly and, with her usual sarcasm and sass, yelled at Smith.

"Get out of my house, you vagabond! And take that mangy and cursed imp with you!"

8

It was difficult, but the following morning Smith informed Ivivin of his diagnosis while hiding the potential for treatment from him. Ivivin was shocked at his own nonchalance at the news and went about work. He and Smith had agreed that Ivivin would stay here a little while longer. While Smith had granted Ivivin the title of blacksmith, it did not change the fact that Ivivin needed quality armour before he set forth again. If Ivivin helped, he was free to stay and complete the armour. Ivivin felt numb to the news, as if it applied to some other fellow named Ivivin. And he continued his day as if nothing had happened.

It was not until later, when Ivivin found himself making plans for far in the future, that he realized why he was acting so casual about the news. It was simple. He didn't believe it. He did not accept that this...thing… was actually going to kill him. His justification changed from moment to moment. Sometimes, just the fact he did not feel ill was enough to convince Ivivin he was well. At other times, he believed that Minerva would find a cure and he would be fine. Other times still, Ivivin figured that he was different. That he was somehow special and that, because he didn't deserve the disease, it wasn't going make him sick.

Minerva had sent a note to Ivivin with the symptoms and how they develop, as well as an assurance that she would tell no one, not even Elara, of his condition. She had made sure to tell Ivivin that the human body is an incredible thing. She had seen symptoms start and vanish a few times before finally firmly taking hold. Some of the early symptoms just included general fatigue and shortness of breath during exercise, but also included sharp pain in the chest. This led Ivivin to work vigorously each day to prove to himself he wasn't sick. With each stroke, his stamina improved, not worsened. Sometimes, it wasn't enough, though. Sometimes he was compelled to prove it even further and would strain himself training with his sword, shield, and some cheap armour he hobbled together. Soon, though, that wasn't enough either. Ivivin thought back to the times he was most exhausted in life. He didn't have a mountain he could nearly freeze to death while ascending nearby, so that left him with the exhaustion of combat. For the first time, Ivivin was hungry for conflict. He was hankering for a fight. It left him on edge and aggressive. And the worst of it? Ivivin didn't even realize it was affecting him so drastically. He'd entertain thoughts of starting tussles in the local taverns, just for a chance to fight. He refused to act on them, of course, but they became less and less abhorrent to Ivivin each time it passed through his head.

In short, Ivivin was desperately trying to prove to he was not sick at all. And his denial, it had infected him.

9

Elara had resumed her daily life with Minerva. She had done her best to internalize Minerva's words. But, no matter how hard she tried, they fell flat. Elara learned by doing. That's what made her such a quick study out in the field. But even that had become tainted by her replaying the events of the last couple of days over and over in her head. She found it less enjoyable and blamed her own inability to handle her emotions. She felt herself becoming numb, like she once was. If she were not set in routine, she would have stopped getting out of bed in the morning. Even her numbness didn't last, though. She had a nightmare, like so many others. This one tormented her in a new and devastating way. This night's terror starred Ivivin, perverted with a venomous look in eyes not his own. Yes, that simulacrum was enough for numb to give way to anger.

Anger at herself for being weak.

Anger at the world.

Anger at people with whom she found it hard to connect.

She was sure that Ivivin, in his gentleness, would not want such an angry person to associate with him. And that thought fed her negativity. She wanted more than anything to be stronger. She wanted to be able to conquer her feelings. She wanted to be able to conquer her numbness. She wanted to be able to conquer her anger. If she could be strong enough to eliminate everything plaguing her, she thought she could be happy. And this led Elara to a conclusion:

If she could be rid of her fear, especially the illogical fear she felt in Ivivin's presence, she could find the strength to conquer herself.

Elara told Minerva she was headed to the field and offered no explanation. Minerva saw resolve in Elara's eyes. She knew not if it was directed well, but Minerva knew she could not control the stubborn girl. She just urged Elara to stay safe. Elara intended to ask Ivivin to spend the week with her. She would face him, cling to him if she needed, to forcefully rid herself of her fear. She was willing to do anything, even lay herself bare, if it meant driving it all from her. A woman possessed marched to Smith's shop.

10

Elara bossily called out to Ivivin from the counter, but he and Smith were nowhere to be found. Impatient and undeterred, Elara climbed over and into the forge. The fires were not blazing full throttle, but Elara could still feel the heat of the room. In particular, her glove-covered hands burned at the familiarity. Already, the heat of the room alone had reminded Elara of the burning ship in Rumi. Frustrated by how quickly she had already let thoughts leading to fear invade her, she quickened her pace and searched the forge. Near the back, she heard grunting and heavy breathing. Through Ivivin's window, she could see him swinging his sword wildly. He was focused and intense. The sight of him acting so violently sent fearful shivers down her spine, further infuriating Elara who knew he was only training. She exited the shop and went around back. She wasted no time in calling out to Ivivin, who ignored her at first. When she sent daggers his way with her eyes, though, he relented and put his things down to see what she wanted.

"Ivivin. How are you?" Elara politely asked.

"Fine. What do you need?" Ivivin responded coldly.
His tone hurt Elara, but she had already decided on her own that Ivivin would not deal with a person as broken as she, so it was not surprising to her.

"Ivivin, I must go to the field. I was hoping you would come with me. We'd only be gone a week or so." Elara proposed.

"Can't. Gotta work. No way Smith will let me off for a whole week." Ivivin answered. He began to walk back to his training gear.

"Wait!" Elara called, unable to prevent some desperation from leaking into her voice.

"What is it?" Ivivin returned, impatiently.

"Just come with me one day. Today. We can stay near town and you can be back first thing in the morning." Elara nearly pleaded.

The plea fell on deaf ears.

"You don't need me. I don't have time to waste right now, sorry." Ivivin retorted.

He was aware of how mean he just was, but figured an apology later would suffice. He was in the zone and would not allow anything to get between him and validation.

Elara panicked and grew desperate. She hadn't considered lying to Ivivin, but one came to the forefront of her mind and she blurted it without second thought.

"Please? There are rumours of bandits in the area and I could really use the second set of eyes." Elara fibbed. In truth, the bandits that escaped and lived had made an urban legend of Elara, just as she had made an example of them. They had been steering clear of the area surrounding Smithton out of fear of the woman whose arm was itself blade. Ivivin almost refused once more. But, with a moment's pause, he realized that he could fight a bandit. Really fight, not just swing his sword around. He remembered his battles. How much effort they made him exert. How much they made him feel alive.

"Sure, Elara. I will go with you. I don't know for how long I will stay, but at least for today, I shall go. Let me assemble my pack. Where shall I meet you?" Ivivin agreed. His demeanour and tone towards Elara had lightened significantly.

"Oh! How about the nearest exit to town? I think it's to the west, right? Meet there in an hour or so?" Elara pitched, ecstatic she had convinced Ivivin, who nodded in concurrence. As Elara walked away to kill an hour, guilt settled in her gut. She felt horrible for misleading him, but she would tell him the truth later and apologize. For now, though, she needed him to come. No matter the cost.

An hour later, Elara and Ivivin left town together, but so very far away from one another.

11

Ivivin didn't think he was expecting to find bandits right away, but with every step they took without one in his sight, he grew more irritated and annoyed. Elara walked unnaturally close to him—

their packs occasionally bumping together. She looked at him constantly, too, though Ivivin seemed to her too preoccupied to notice.

"Perhaps he is too worried about bandits to let his attention waver even a moment?" Elara thought, again feeling immense guilt at her manipulation.

Ivivin noticed Elara's proximity and attention to him. He figured she wanted to talk about something, perhaps the missing chapter of her story from the other night. He felt selfish and like a poor friend for neglecting her, which only fed his desire to find these bandits. If he could just fight one, then he would be at peace enough to be there for Elara and do more than just hear her words, but to truly listen with a calm mind.

Their internal torrents would soon combine to form the perfect storm.

12

In the mid-afternoon, Elara insisted that they stop and take a break before she looked around for the materials she was looking for. Ivivin grunted in reluctant agreement. Elara's guilt mounted. She felt worse and worse for lying to Ivivin each moment and his continued focus, even during their time of rest, made Elara feel terrible. Ivivin fidgeted, tapping his foot up and down while continuing to scope out the surroundings.

"Damn, nothing. How long must I wait? It is driving me mad!"

Elara rose. Her plan had been to use the night, when she feared Ivivin the most, as her arena. She would go pretend to look for ingredients she didn't need for a while and come back here when the sun began to set. Then, she would force herself to closeness with him. As Elara took her first step, though, she realized she couldn't do it. She couldn't lie to him further. It was too late for him to return to Smithton this night—she could still try and conquer her fears. But she could not lie to him a moment more. She would discard her charade, even if it meant ultimately discarding their friendship. She looked at the agitated Ivivin. She found it difficult to start her confession, but momentum carried her words to completion.

"Ivivin...there are no bandits. I lied about the rumour. Please, relax a little. I am sorry." Elara confessed.

Ivivin was furious. He trusted Elara. He trusted her so much, in fact, that her lie did not hurt him terribly. He trusted she would only lie if it was necessary. And he felt horrible that he was so unapproachable and unfriendly that Elara felt she had to lie to him to get him to listen to her. Still, the call to violence...to strength...to health persisted in him. An idea, innocent in conception, rose to the surface of his muddled mind. He had seen firsthand how fierce and skilled Elara was. Even wounded, she felled many men at unimaginable speeds. Keeping up in a sparring bout with Elara would be just as difficult as any battle he'd ever been in.

"It's ok, Elara. I'm sorry I've neglected you this trip. But I really need a good workout today. Smith's orders are that I train my body and my mind each and every day. So, since we're here and have the time, how bout we spar a little?" Ivivin requested.

Elara was surprised—both at Ivivin's quick forgiveness of her deception and his subsequent request. She saw Ivivin equip his gauntlets, blade, and shield and her fear, the fear she had come here to conquer, came back.

She was trembling and uneasy, but that's exactly what she wanted.

"Ivivin has traveled the world and done a great number of heroic feats. If I can conquer him, then I will fear him no more." Elara reasoned.

"Sure. Just, give me a moment to ready myself away from here." Elara responded. She would need to remove her gloves to wield her Beak and Talons. She did not want Ivivin to see her weakness. If nothing else, he might take it easy on her. She would not waste this chance.

Once both parties were ready, they faced each other in this empty field. In their minds, they knew it was just a friendly bout—a training exercise. But as they faced each other, their bodies reacted as they had in so many battles before. Elara's fear took back seat to clarity of mind, as it had for a time during her most recent scuffle with the bandits. Ivivin's pulse pounded, reassuring him of his strong heart. This was to be far more than a simple sparring match.

13

Elara and Ivivin started out gently enough. They tapped their blades together slowly, courteously, and predictably. Ivivin took notice of Elara's strange weapons and decided to test them. He increased the force of his strikes. Elara staggered more than he had expected. But she seemed unfazed and recovered her stance quickly. Rather than endure heavy strikes, Elara took aim with several small strikes, directed at Ivivin's shield, to test his skill in wielding it. Elara could tell Ivivin had improved since they met, but he was still rough. She had a childhood full of training and she could tell the disparity in their skill easily.

"*I can win.*" Elara thought, only briefly considering it strange that she considered this friendly bout a competition to be won.

Ivivin blocked Elara's strikes with the shield he had gotten from Crosstown. The shield he had gotten as proof for defeating a great bandit king. He wasn't going to get sick, and he would prove it. Though they were methodical and flawless, Ivivin withstood Elara's test of his defense. Moreover, he was not even close to winded from the endeavour.

"*I can win.*" Ivivin thought, only briefly considering it strange that he considered this friendly bout a competition to be won.

14

As Elara and Ivivin each pressed, the other returned the pressure in full. Their bout had quickly escalated. They were no longer thinking as they exchanged blows and they were each only vaguely aware of the danger they posed to each other. Ivivin swung heavier and heavier blows until they were his full effort. Elara began to move deftly, opting to dodge more and more and to block less and less. Ivivin, frustrated that he could not make contact, bashed at her with his shield, staggering her. He went to repeat the feat, but found himself swept off his feet by a low sweeping kick. He rolled away and regained his standing. Frustration continued to mount in Ivivin. He engaged Elara again, this time focusing on her agile movements. They were impressive, just as Ivivin expected, but they could be predicted, just like any combative motion. He brought down his sword, prompting Elara to dodge. Ivivin followed with a knee, which Elara just barely managed to catch with her shield. Ivivin's knee was certainly bruised, but that he had predicted her motion gave him confidence to keep the pressure on. He used every motion he had practiced in every combination he could. Elara was forced to block more and more of the blows. She felt weak under his blows. She worried she would face defeat if things continued in this manner. So, when Ivivin came down with another powerful blow, Elara used the rebound and her dance motions to go on the offensive. Ivivin, just as the bandit boss, did not expect such unconventional movements from such an unconventional weapon to come from such a conventional fighter. Ivivin struggled to keep up. He threw an occasional blow her way, but she transitioned to her stellar traditional form whenever she needed and used the momentum of his strikes against him. His heart was pounding hard. He was truly tired and knew that he should stop her, that he should concede and call off the duel. She clearly outshone him. But it wasn't Elara Ivivin was fighting. It was his own body. He wanted to push a bit further. He wanted affirmation that his body wasn't going to give out on him. So, he persisted. He took more chances and advanced on Elara.

Elara mistook Ivivin's weariness for him holding back. As much as she wanted to win, it meant nothing to her if he didn't give it his all. And she could not believe that she was better than him. She had built him up as a formidable and insurmountable wall. She wanted to win, but didn't believe she could.

"I will force him to give me everything!" Elara resolved, letting loose the full extent of her abilities. The blows rained down on Ivivin one after another. He could not keep up. Each blow dodged came closer to carving him. Each blow blocked brought his shield up a little more slowly.

"Just a little longer" Ivivin told himself. *"Just last a little longer, I can go just a little longer. I can go just a li—"*

Ivivin's thought was ended abruptly by the sight of scarlet and a horrified Elara. Ivivin dropped his sword and his shield and reached to his chest, which he just recognized as having made contact with the cold steel of Elara's blade. He felt his exposed flesh and held his trembling hands to his face. They were doused with blood. Ivivin looked at Elara and blamed only himself. His vision began to fade to black. He managed just a few words before he fainted and fell to the grass below.

"That's not good."

15

Elara shoved thoughts of panic and guilt from her mind—she hadn't the time for such things. She turned Ivivin onto his back and inspected the wound. She was no doctor, but perhaps it was not as bad as it seemed. Perhaps she just needed to bind the wound and he'd be fine!

Nope.

It was pretty bad. She was queasy just looking at the sheared flesh, but she needed to look closer to figure out what she could do. She sighed in relief when she realized she did not cut as deeply as she could have. The wound stretched from the upper left of his chest down to just below the right side of his ribcage.

"Still, I must do something... he will bleed out this way."

She bound the wound the best she could without constricting his airflow. Still, blood seeped out of his body.

"Damn! The chest isn't so bad but the part near his abdomen...he'll die if this keeps up..."

Elara struggled to determine her next course of action. She reached for her pain-relief ointment. It wouldn't do him much good, especially since he was unconscious. But it was thick and goopy. Perhaps it could restrict the escape of blood while she figured out what to do next. Elara applied it. It certainly helped, but not much. Elara saw the pouch on Ivivin's leg, the one that Idalia had prepped for him with the embroidered little owl on it. It was a medicinal kit! Elara opened it and found it was largely used up.

"Damn it, you stupid boy. You're supposed to restock this sort of thing. Damn, damn, damn!" Elara shouted to nobody.

There is no way Elara could carry Ivivin all the way back to town. Shock would claim him. And, even if she sprinted as fast as she could for help, they would likely not make it back until nearly morning. That left Elara with one choice.

"I'll be back, Ivivin. I promise." Elara called, running to find something—anything—she could make a medicine out of. She desperately tried to recall her lessons with Minerva...they were all so complicated! Elara never thought she'd have to make anything this sophisticated, let alone in the field.

"It's no use, I can't remember everything I need." Elara cursed.

"But I must try something!" Elara thought. She looked around her and tried to think about the properties of the wildlife around her. She saw some grasses she once saw a sickly deer eat before galloping away heartily. She harvested them. She stumbled upon a deposit of clay and took that, too. She found root of liquorice and some coneflowers. She knew she had to hurry. She would likely not be able to do much with these things—she was not deceiving herself. But she time was of the essence. She ran back to where Ivivin laid. Leaning over him was a horse, licking his face. Elara knew not what this strange horse was doing here, but it was lucky it was here and so docile too.

The horse's tongue roused Ivivin for a moment. He looked at the horse.

"Lili?" Ivivin asked before trying to move.

Pain shot through him.

"Oh yeah...Elara got me good. Ha-ha." Ivivin said before relaxing.

"You're a good horse, Lili. Don't let anyone tell you any different." he mumbled before losing consciousness once more.

Elara cautiously approached the horse.

"Lili? That's your name? I need your help, Lili. We need to get Ivivin to Smithton as fast as we can." Elara begged, hoping the horse would understand the desperation in her voice. Lili the horse was reluctant, but leaned down so Elara could put Ivivin up on her back.

"Thank you, Lili. But if I don't do something about the gash first, he won't make it there." Elara said, getting to work. She mashed her ingredients together with the clay and some fresh water, creating a very thick paste that she applied to Ivivin's wound. It dried quickly and seemed to have largely stopped the bleeding...for now. Elara hoisted Ivivin onto the horse with all her might and hopped on herself, behind him. She stabilized him between her legs. Immediately, Elara was struck by her fears again. It was extremely uncomfortable to be this close to him and she had a hard time breathing as panic spread through her. Still, she had to endure. Ivivin's life depended on it! Lili galloped faster than any horse Elara had ever ridden.

354

They made it back to Smithton just as the sun was falling. The doctor was just locking up her clinic when she saw a horse galloping in the middle of the street, headed straight for her. She sighed, unlocked the door, and re-entered the clinic, grudgingly ready to admit the injured fellow. Elara was trembling and gasping for air as she and the doctor carefully brought Ivivin in. Elara tried to explain what happened, but the doctor stopped her.

"I don't need to know right now. In fact, I need you gone and out of here." the grumpy doctor commanded. Elara left the clinic. Lili was already nowhere to be found. She hurried as fast as she could to the teashop to get Minerva's help.

16

A few weeks had passed since Elara had brutally lacerated Ivivin in the field. Ivivin was doing well, though Smith was livid at the loss of his helping hand. He made Ivivin sit at the counter and deal with customers all day—something Ivivin loathed. Elara had recently gone back to the spot and gathered everything they had left behind. She was glad it was all still there. Since she came back, her overwhelming urge to prove she was stronger than her fear had faded. After all, she had cut Ivivin down and was still fearful of him as she delivered his limp body back to Smithton. She realized her attempt to conquer her fear was misguided.

Likewise, Ivivin admitted to himself that he was sick. It didn't matter that he didn't feel it yet. It was the truth and every bit as real as the wound across his chest. He needed to plan accordingly. His denial of the truth was a thousand times more at fault than Elara for his wound. He truly felt no ill will towards her. In fact, he desperately wanted to apologize. Especially since she obviously felt guilty. She came by to chat with Ivivin every day, even if it was only for a short time. Ivivin, too, felt guilty. Neither of them had realized it at the time, but Ivivin did manage to lay a blow on Elara as well, likely early on. He had cut her left cheek, not far below her eye. It was sure to scar and Ivivin felt terrible for it.

Still, they didn't discuss such serious matters when they chatted at the shop. In fact, the only time they mentioned the fight or the fallout thereof was when Ivivin would tease Elara for being such a savage and she would threaten to give him another wound to keep the first company. Instead, they people watched and made lighthearted jokes or invented absurd stories about the occasional passersby. The would listen to or look at the birds. Elara would tell Ivivin all about them, getting caught up in her own excitement and going on and on about the little feathered friends, not that Ivivin minded. Though one time a toad happened to hop by— that was a little much for Ivivin. They also talked more about their travels— they still left the gaping holes in their stories, but went into more detail about the other chapters of their endeavours.

Eventually, Ivivin was well enough to start working lightly in the forge again. He was a little saddened, as it meant the end of his and Elara's regular chats. To his surprise, though, she often still stopped by and Ivivin would always make time for her. Sometimes, he'd even invite her in to watch him work. After a little while, Ivivin would go to the teashop, too, during downtimes. Sometimes, Elara would be gone and in the field and he would pretend he was there to tell Minerva how he was feeling. However, when Elara was there, she would make him a sickeningly sweet and creamy tea and they would chat. The two of them began to find happiness in each other's company again. Elara still would feel uncomfortable, even fearful, if Ivivin was too close, but he seemed to have developed a good sense of how close she was comfortable with him being. She still wore her gloves everywhere, too. Likewise, the uncertainty of when Ivivin's ailment would strike in full force weighed on him heavily—the future often distracting him from the now. Still, the two became good friends, in earnest. They were such good friends in fact, that their guilt at keeping secrets changed and morphed. Instead, they both genuinely wanted to share their firmly-held secrets with each other. It was just hard to find an occasion and even harder to find the courage.

Live and 'Like'

1

Smith was happy to have Ivivin around, but he knew that the boy had aspirations beyond this place. Smith would never forgive himself if he allowed Ivivin to rot here. Hell, he was not sure he was going to be able to forgive himself for letting him come to any harm in the first place. Ivivin's wound had healed well enough to where he could travel again. But the boy was dragging his feet on finishing his armour. It had been near completion for over a week now. Smith decided he needed to speak to Ivivin. He went to Ivivin's room to talk, but did not find him there, despite the hour. Instead, he found a slightly pudgy Icarus laying on the windowsill. Smith wondered where Ivivin could be while ruffling the ruffian's feathers.

2

Ivivin and Elara headed to the wilds of town—back to where they first spent an evening together hunting for toads. Elara had asked Ivivin to go stargazing. It was a new moon, so the conditions were ripe for seeing the patterns in the sky. Ivivin agreed, thinking it might even be a good time to tell her about his trip to Olympia and his illness. Likewise, Elara had plans to tell Ivivin at least a little about Rumi this night.

"Baby steps lead to long strides." Elara had thought on her way to invite Ivivin.

Ivivin carried with him firewood and Elara had a couple of old blankets. The arrived at Elara's spot and Ivivin got to work on the fire, though Elara got frustrated at how poorly he was doing it and took over.

Ivivin walked around and mused while Elara started the fire. "We have some snacks...and some blankets...and a fire...so why do I feel like I am forgetting something...? Oh! I left Icarus! He was so looking forward to tonight!" Ivivin realized.

"Don't worry about him. He's probably having a blast with Smith, anyways. They really seem to have taken to each other. You better watch out; your mentor might steal your best friend!" Elara teased.

"You're right, you're right. *Owl* he'd probably do tonight is *hoot* and holler. *Who* needs him anyways?" Ivivin joked.

Elara rolled her eyes and groaned while bringing the fire to life. In truth, it was not so cold out that they needed a fire. But the light made it easier to see, which, these days, made Elara more comfortable around Ivivin. She got up and laid the blankets out, separate from one another, and sat down. Ivivin sat on the other one a few feet over and they looked to the sky.

Silence caused both of them to struggle internally. Were they really going to do this? Tell the other their firmly held secret? Ivivin and Elara both were happy that it was dark. Even if the fire lit up the night, at least it was not so easy to be read as it would be in the day. The pair sat in silence for what felt like hours, each of them trying to muster the courage to speak. They saw a shooting star and turned to each other to point it out, inadvertently meeting eyes.

"Hey, listen..." they said in unison.

"Ooops!" they mirrored each other again.

"Sorry, go ahead!" they each insisted.

It was Ivivin who went first, as their nearly comedic exchange had caused Elara to lose her confidence a bit. So, Ivivin told Elara about Grandia's book, how he went to Olympia to bring Smith back, about his confrontation with Lance, and, most importantly, about how he had contracted Crumbleheart. It was difficult to say, but, once he noticed how attentive to and invested Elara seemed in his words, it came easier. When Elara heard that Ivivin had the illness, so many things made sense. So many things that she could not believe she had not figured it out herself sooner. Her heart ached for Ivivin. She didn't know what to say to Ivivin. She didn't know if there was anything she could say. Before she could find her words, Ivivin continued. He told Elara about his denial of the truth, how it affected him, and how it led to their duel in the fields.

"So please, Elara, don't feel responsible. It wasn't your fault. And I am so very sorry. I hope you'll forgive me someday. You are my dearest friend and I regret my actions terribly." Ivivin finished.

Elara heard the apology and found it unnecessary, though his words helped ease the burden she felt for having cut him down, if only a little. She was still hung up on his incurable disease. But when Elara looked over at Ivivin, she could tell their scuffle had been eating at him far more than his own ailment.

Ivivin asked for forgiveness.

Though she was unsure that she'd ever really understand, she'd try. Though she didn't see anything to forgive, she forgave.

"While we're at it…" Elara found strength and momentum in Ivivin's initiative "…can I tell you what happened in Rumi?" Elara asked.

Ivivin smiled, trying to reassure an obviously uneasy Elara. "Of course."

Elara's story took much longer than Ivivin's. She felt it necessary to frame it in its entirety—why she joined the Sparrows, why she felt so strongly for their cause, and why the subsequent events haunted her. She struggled to get out her fight against Ajaxx and it brought back so many horrid memories she almost got up and ran. At the same time, confessing her fears to someone was cathartic. Though every word caused her chest to clench more and more tightly, every word also lessened the weight on her shoulders. She even told him how much she struggled in the weeks after, how she fought the bandits, how Ivivin himself illogically distressed her, how she felt like every step she took forward was accompanied by a step backwards, and, of course, how and why she lied to get him to come with her to their dueling grounds.

"I'm so sorry, Ivivin. I didn't mean to hurt you. I just wanted so badly to find the strength to get on and get over these feelings. You mean a lot to me and I shouldn't have lied to you. I just thought you wouldn't have…a broken person as a friend."

Ivivin could not process this all at once. It was hard for him to empathize with parts of Elara's story. He wanted to, he wanted to understand her pain and fear. He wondered if the way she felt was akin to how he felt in Wolfelaw or in the woods. It was impossible for him to know, but he earnestly wanted to. Elara looked at Ivivin expectantly, making Ivivin realize he had been sitting silently for a long time now, having said nothing since Elara started. Ivivin saw the desire to be understood written across Elara's face.

Elara asked for forgiveness.

Though he was unsure that he'd ever really understand, he'd try. Though he didn't see anything to forgive, he forgave.

The two looked upwards to the stars, free from, at least this night and in each other's company, the pains and sorrows shackling them.

3

Smith woke late in the night to the sound of a shutting door. Ivivin had tried to be tender with it, but he sneezed at the least fortuitous time and slammed it instead. Smith groggily went to check on the commotion. Though Smith really did not keep tabs on Ivivin's comings and goings when he was not working, he also knew it was unlike Ivivin to be out so late. Ivivin entered with Elara. Smith instinctively hid away.

"I suppose Ivivin is a young man, after all." Smith thought to himself, a little flustered and unsure how to handle the situation. *"Wayland wasn't much interested in women. I suppose I really don't know what I should do."* Smith considered.

He yawned and decided he'd sort it out in the morning.

Smith woke early in the, hoping to make some breakfast and catch a chat with Ivivin before the day got going. To his surprise, he found Ivivin sprawled out on the kitchen floor, covering himself in two grassy blankets.

"Wake up boy! Wake up!" Smith demanded, gently kicking the lad to rouse him.

Ivivin woke, acutely aware that he had not gotten enough sleep.

"What is it Smith?" Ivivin asked, his brain still warming up.

"Why in the world are you sleeping in the kitchen!?" Smith asked the sleepy fellow.

Ivivin shook himself awake and noticed the grass he had drug in.

"I'm sorry Smith, I'll get his cleaned up right away. Elara and I went stargazing last night, but she had locked herself out of her room at the inn so I let her sleep in my bed for the evening, since I just washed the bedding." Ivivin half-yawned an answer.

"So why are you here? Did something happen?" Smith asked.

"What do you mean? Where else would I be?" Ivivin countered.

Smith could not meet Ivivin's gaze.

"It seems I misunderstood. Such an innocent kid, for his age." Smith thought.

"Never mind, never mind. Get this place clean and make some breakfast for the four of us. Then, we got work to do." Smith barked before headed to prepare himself for the day.

Ivivin, Icarus, Smith and Elara all enjoyed some scrambled eggs and toast around the table.

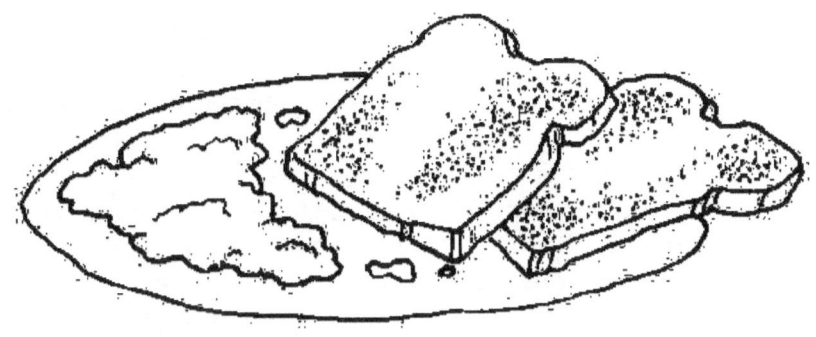

4

When Elara had left, Smith decided it was time to have the discussion he had intended to have with Ivivin the night prior.

"Ivivin, get the flames started. Then come back, I need to have a little chat with you." Smith asked of Ivivin, who obeyed. Smith paced, trying to decide how to delicately ask the boy what his plans for his life were. Minerva had yet to give him word on the feasibility of their treatment, but that doesn't mean he should stay here and let his life wilt away.

"Sorry it took so long, Smith. Had to grab some more wood from out back." said Ivivin, upon his return. Ivivin was not gone nearly long enough, in Smith's opinion. He did not feel prepared to have this talk, but he knew it needed to happen nonetheless.

"Ivivin, lad, sit down. We need to discuss your future." Smith offered a seat to Ivivin and joined at the table across from him. "I don't think it wise that we ignore your condition any longer." Smith led. Ivivin nodded slowly in agreement.

"That being said, boy, what's your plan? For the future?" Smith asked.

"I am going to be a knight." Ivivin responded, not missing a beat.

The quickness of his response worried Smith.

"Is that what you really want?" Smith asked.

Ivivin took a moment to mindfully consider what it was he actually wanted in this life.

"Well, yes and no. I still want it, but not like I used to. I used to dream of carrying the title knight. I wanted a knight to be who I am. More recently, though, I've found that I just want to do knightly things. And I think that is best facilitated by becoming a knight, so I suppose that doesn't change much, huh?" Ivivin said, walking both himself and Smith through his thought process.

"That's all well and good, Ivivin. But you do realize your days are limited, right? Surely there are other things you want? I feel like you are trapping yourself here. You haven't finished your armour and I see you working less and less on it. I love you like a son, Ivivin. But I have to ask...you have the title of blacksmith already, so why are you still here?" pressed Smith.

"I suppose I have been delaying. Thank you for pointing it out. If I think on it, I am still here, because I am having fun as a smith. It's hard but it's satisfying. And I... really like spending time with you. And Minerva. And Elara, too." Ivivin admitted. "I know it seems like I'm letting my time slip through my fingers carelessly, but I feel as if I am spending it wisely."

Smith could understand that sentiment, but the look on Ivivin's face said he was not finished.

"But...you're right, too. There is a lot I still want to do and some things I still need to do. I can spend time with you all when I am sickly, but I think I need to chase some dreams while I still can. I just worry that I will fall ill, away from you all, away from my parents and... that I'll die alone." Ivivin finished, his voice wavering.

"It's an understandable fear, Ivivin. Don't think less of yourself for it. But, if you were to die today, what would you regret most? Think carefully on it and that is what you should act on." Smith proposed.

Ivivin thought long and hard. There was plenty he wanted to do. There was plenty he felt he needed to do. But when he considered if he would regret these things on his deathbed, most of them fell away. Sure, he'd like to settle the matter with Jupiter's tear. But he also had recently been reminded of Elara's strength and intelligence. The sisters would be fine, as would Icarus. He trusted in their ability. He wanted to be a knight, sure. But he was unsure of what exactly he should offer up the king. Despite his adventures, he didn't feel like he had earned the title, nor did he think it would haunt him terribly on his deathbed. So, Ivivin thought about what he wanted most at this moment and he came to a surprising conclusion.

"I want to go home." Ivivin declared.

5

And, just like that, Ivivin was forming plans to return home. He hadn't seen his parents in quite some time. He wanted to go home and spend some time with them. He wanted to show them that their support paid off and that he had not forgotten about them. It was as simple as that. Or, it would have been. But Ivivin had a difficult time setting a date to leave. He was having a hard time figuring out his aversion to doing so. Everything he had told Smith was the truth and he couldn't think of other reasons that bound him to this place. He had accepted his illness and that staying here would not prevent it any more than juggling his owl would. His inability to commit to a date or at least know why he couldn't was uniquely aggravating. None of his usual problem-solving strategies worked. So, he decided to ask for help.

He approached Smith and explained his dilemma. Smith offered up that perhaps he was scared to know what his parents would think of him. Ivivin didn't think that was the issue, but Smith tried to reassure Ivivin that his parents would still care for him deeply. Since Smith did not have wisdom that rung true in Ivivin, he moved on.

Minerva welcomed Ivivin in. He explained how he was feeling and the crossroads he felt he was facing. Minerva cackled her usual cackle. She told Ivivin she suspected that she knew what the problem was and apologized that she could not tell him what it was. Ivivin panicked, worried that it had to do with his illness. Minerva assured him that it was very natural and suggested that he, perhaps, should seek Elara's perspective on the matter. Ivivin agreed and asked when Elara was due back from the field. Minerva assured him it would be tonight or tomorrow and to come back then.

Ivivin returned to the teashop the following day and indulged in one of Elara's now famous super-sweet tea-based atrocities. They were truly sugary testaments to the arrogance of man. Ivivin got so wrapped up in conversation and discussion with Elara that he forgot to ask her about his problem. Instead, while they joked and sipped their drinks, Ivivin forgot about his problem entirely. Ivivin realized these things as he left the teashop, almost sprinting back to the smithy as he had stayed far longer than he told Smith he would. He stopped in the middle of the road abruptly, too, as he uncovered the source of his difficulties.

"*I like Elara.*" Ivivin unearthed the truth. *"A lot."*

It was a discovery that had many implications, some of which were weighty and unkind. Ivivin knew this. Still, his sprint back to the smithy had turned into an unabashed skip.

6

Smith was surprised to see Ivivin in such a chipper mood, considering how much he had been struggling the last couple of days. Ivivin told Smith he was looking to leave in two weeks—plenty of time for him to wrap up orders with Smith and allow him to scale down his operation appropriately, as well as prepare for his journey back.

"So, you figured it out, did you?" Smith asked in response to the news.

"Mmmhm." Ivivin hummed, starting to hammer away at the forge.

"And you solved it that fast?"

Ivivin thought a moment.

"I don't suppose I solved it at all." Ivivin responded. "Though I don't know if it's something I could solve."

Smith was confused.

"Wait, what? Sorry lad, you've lost me. What was it holding you here?"

"Elara." Ivivin answered frankly, not letting his eyes wander from his work.

"What do you mean, did she ask you to stay?" Smith wondered

"No, it's just that I like her. A lot. And leaving means I won't see her anymore. That's all." Ivivin stated matter-of-factly.

Smith finally understood what Ivivin was getting at.

"Oh, so you've fallen in love with her then, have ya?" Smith teased.

At these words, Ivivin lost his composure.

"You don't have to phrase it like that. I never said that… I just said that I liked her is all."

"Ohhh?" Smith could see what was going on here. "Embarrassed of the word 'love', are we?"

"No!" Ivivin asserted.

"Well, no matter. So, what's your plan, then, Ivivin? Going to ask her to come with you? I'm sure Minerva will be sore having to let her apprentice go, but I am sure she would." Smith investigated.

"Nope. Like I said, I am going home, Smith." Ivivin answered.

"What? So, you aren't going to do anything about your feelings for the girl?"

"Not something I am planning, no." Ivivin had returned to his flat manner of speaking.

"And why in the forge's blazing fire not?" Smith asked, almost aggressively.

"I don't think she feels that way about me. Besides, I don't exactly have a whole lot of time. Even if she did care for me in that manner, I won't be around long enough. Easier this way, I think, and I get to keep her as a precious friend." Ivivin returned.

Smith was getting angry, surprising himself.

"Wow, boy. I never took you for such a coward."

Ivivin's temper was fueled by Smith's tone.

"And what would you have me do!?" He snapped at Smith.

"Live!" Smith refuted. "And don't be so afraid of rejection that your feelings die with you!"

Ivivin was reminded of Smith's persistence in courting Grandia. He was seldom so insistent or passionate about anything, especially Ivivin's choices. Ivivin clammed up and thought for a moment about his feelings.

"I… guess I will tell her then. I don't want to leave this town, much less this world, without her knowing, even if I know nothing will come of it." Ivivin stammered.

"Well, I suppose that's better than nothing, boy. I will tell Minerva of your plans and we can all get together and discuss what we should do about your illness, if anything. Now get your lovesick head out of the clouds and get back to work!" Smith barked.

Ivivin obeyed and worked hard all day, trying not to think too much about it. Later that night, Ivivin laid with Icarus in his room.

As he often did, Ivivin confided in and ranted at the bird, who he was never sure understood him completely. Ivivin engaged in this one-sided gossip and Icarus indulged him as long as Ivivin fed him first. Laying in bed, Ivivin confessed to the owl with a giddy tone:

"Hey Icarus, guess what?"

The owl turned his head in polite curiosity, despite not being terribly invested in the conversation.

"I like...I mean, I love Elara." Ivivin felt himself flush at the words and thrashed around in his bed to get the excitement out of his system.

7

Smith and Ivivin prepared to visit Minerva concerning Ivivin's imminent departure. Elara was out in the field, presumably chasing toads. This news came as both a relief and a letdown for Ivivin. Minerva had other news for Ivivin—that she had come up with a potential way of combatting the disease. She warned Ivivin that it was a not sure-fire thing. For all she knew, it may well just leave him as bad off as he'd otherwise be. Moreover, it was unlikely to prevent the disease from reaching onset; rather, it was far more likely that it would simply slow the disease's progression. Smith looked at Minerva as she concluded her explanation, expecting her to elaborate on how the medicine would treat only his physical heart. But she never did, prompting Smith to shoot her a look that screamed 'we need to talk'. Minerva duly, if exasperatedly, noted Smith's desire to chat.

In perhaps the least convincing and least enthusiastic acting ever, Minerva whined.

"Oh, no! I am parched, but my apprentice is gone—off searching the wilds for her aged master! If only there were a young, strapping lad whose name starts with the letter 'I' who would go into the kitchen and prepare this old woman some tea. Oh, if only, if only..."

Smith felt annoyance bubbling up inside of him as the Minerva put forth such a cursory effort, but, to his surprise, Ivivin laughed at the woman's lackluster dramatization and obliged her immediately. Minerva turned to Smith and told him,

"We have only a few minutes. What is so important that you would use your eyes to send daggers my way?"

"You didn't tell the boy your treatment only affects the physical heart. He will not know that he has to be vigilant to resist the degradation of his emotions, too." Smith whispered aggressively.

"Oh, I'm sorry. Are you the expert medicine maker?" Minerva snapped. "I did not tell the boy and for good reason. Telling him would oblige him to happiness and fortitude. Such obligations are counterproductive in their stress and effect. You cannot command a person to be happy, you cannot command them to be strong. The young man will either resist or he won't. It depends on how he chooses to live his life. I refuse to intervene in this regard. I won't have you doing so either."

Smith was torn. Warning people of a danger seemed the right thing to do. Moreover, it was Ivivin's life and treatment. Did they have a right to withhold information from the lad?

"I need only one assurance to seal my lips, you wordy hag." Smith refused to break eye contact. "Do you, personally, think this is the best course of action?"

"I do." Minerva responded resolutely.

"Then that is all I need." Smith resigned.

She was thrown off balance by Smith's trust in her—trust that she did not feel like she necessarily deserved.

It was touching.

But not touching enough to prevent her from teasing the man about it, and other things, in Ivivin's absence.

Ivivin returned to the room with tea to Smith defending his soiled clothing and sweaty skin. "I work in a forge, woman! Complaining about my appearance and my odor is akin to me complaining you smell like tea all the time!"

"The difference is that the smell of tea doesn't brutally assault those unlucky enough to stumble into it. It's no wonder your old apprentice is leaving. He probably couldn't put up with your stench any longer!" She quipped.

8

"So, boy, you have any questions? Basically, this medicine may give you a fighting chance. No more, no less." Minerva stated offering Ivivin a gourd canteen full of the medicine.

"What happens when I run out?" Ivivin asked, thinking to his future.

"I…hadn't thought of that." Minerva admitted, scrambling for ideas. "You are headed home now, right? Gemi, if I am not mistaken?"

Ivivin nodded.

"Well, a farm nearby there, yes."

"Hmmm…" Minerva considered. "Having you travel back and forth defeats the purpose of being home. The medicine has a decent shelf life, but certainly not long enough to send you with much more than I have given you now. I suppose it is a simple enough concoction, but you'd need the basics before you could even attempt it. And, for one already tainted by Smith's teachings, I am sure it'd take a few months to get it right… plus, I already have one apprentice to worry about. My heart couldn't take on a second." She paused as the trio heard the back door open and close.

"Speak of the devil, seems like Elara is back!"

It was clear to all in attendance that Minerva was struck by a rare inspiration. The idea that had weaseled its way into her head seemed too perfect, too satisfying, and exceeded her requirements on many fronts, some of which were less than professional.

"Elara! Set down your things and come in here, would you?"

Elara entered the dining room, sweaty and dirty. She noticed Ivivin and Smith sitting there and immediately threw her ungloved hands under her armpits, crossing her arms.

"Why didn't you tell me we had company?" Elara spoke out at her teacher. "I'd at least have washed my face."

Ivivin looked at the literally soiled and disheveled Elara, fresh from the field and felt his heart skip a beat. He had always thought she was most radiant and vibrant when she was in the field—in her element. Seeing her like this reminded him of the times he had accompanied her and indulged in her wildlife lectures. He can't believe words reflecting his perception of this managed to escape his lips.

"You look nice, Elara." Ivivin said, feeling himself turn ever more scarlet with each syllable.

Minerva cackled her signature cackle.

"See, Ivivin thinks you look fine and the dirty old man with him has no room to talk, so just come in here a moment!"

Elara relented and entered the room, but kept her hands firmly tucked.

"Elara, you see…" Minerva started. "I have developed a medicine that might help Ivivin's condition. It's not a cure or anything and I cannot promise it'll help much, if at all."

Elara's face lit up.

"That's wonderful!" she remarked.

"I am glad you are so enthusiastic, my apprentice, as you will be the one responsible for getting the medicine to him." Minerva slid in casually.

"What do you mean, Minerva?" Elara asked.

"I see. He hasn't had a chance to tell you himself. You've been in the field, after all." Minerva realized. "Ivivin has decided to spend some time at his home near Gemi. He will be leaving soon." Minerva turned to Ivivin.

"Sorry for spilling the beans, boy. Couldn't be helped."

"Oh…" Elara's lit expression faded a noticeably.

"So!" Minerva continued "You will be responsible for delivering the medicine to him and teaching him how to make it himself until you feel he can do so on his own. All this, in addition to your other duties, of course."

Elara, Ivivin, and Smith were all shocked by the announcement given by the sly woman.

"So, ready your things, deary. Ivivin leaves in just under two weeks and you will accompany him to learn the route." Minerva declared.

9

Ivivin and Elara didn't have much contact over the course of the next two weeks. Both were far too busy wrapping up their affairs and enduring low-key, nebulous panic about the coming days. In the days following their duel, Lili, the horse Ivivin technically owned, had come to take quite the liking to Elara. At the very least, Lili respected Elara in a way she did not Ivivin. Though Ivivin did not constrain her to a stable, she would show up on the outskirts for him every so often, usually to pester him for treats or a meal. But after Elara had sliced Ivivin open, Lili had started coming around more and more often. Ivivin eventually learned it was because Elara had encountered Lili a few times in her excursions out of Smithton. She had brushed and brought snacks along for the horse regularly. More importantly, Elara welcomed Lili's company without ever trying to ride her. So, Lili started frequenting the areas where she was likely to find Elara. As a result, Ivivin had ceded the horse to Elara, though a little bitter at how easily Elara seemed to win Lili over.

Ivivin said his goodbyes to Smith, promising to return knowing full well it was not a promise he could make. Smith and Icarus, too, shared a heartfelt goodbye. Ivivin sometimes wondered if Smith didn't keep Ivivin around just for the unfettered access to the mongrel. Elara left without saying a word to Minerva, having long caught onto her schemes. The trio met near the barn where Ivivin had stayed when he came first to Smithton. Waiting for them there was Lili. Elara had asked the horse to journey with them so that she might have a speedy return to Smithton, though they would go by foot on the way there. It seems the horse had agreed. She even lowered herself, inviting Elara to load her belongings onto her back as to ease her burden. Elara initially declined, until Lili repeatedly knocked Elara's bag with her muzzle. When Ivivin went to add his own bag, Lili stood tall and looked at Ivivin defiantly. It was not until Elara offered to split Ivivin's load that Lili relented and allowed Ivivin to pack some of his belongings on her back as well.

With the logistics sorted out, the quartet of adventurers set out, but it was not without reservation. Elara worried about her ability to maintain composure around Ivivin. She was embarrassed of her nightmares and still had not exposed her hands to him. Ivivin was worried that he would not be able to keep pace with Elara or that she would treat him differently because she knew of his disease. Moreover, he still had not exposed his feelings to her. Smith's words echoed in his head, pressuring him to confess them to her during this voyage. Nonetheless, they set forth, reservations and all.

More-Than-Just-A-Sort-of-Homecoming

1

It became quite obvious to both Elara and Ivivin that they had slightly different visions for how this trip should go, but they managed to compromise on the style of their travel. Elara tended to take many short breaks whenever she felt like it, whereas Ivivin enjoyed grinding out the day straight through and ending it a little earlier. So, Ivivin conceded that they should take more breaks and Elara resisted acting on every urge to do so. Of course, Elara also had work to do during their journey. She was on the lookout for items on Minerva's laundry list. Sometimes, it'd take her a few seconds to find and harvest an item. Other times, it took hours. Still, on the whole, it was an enjoyable trip. Ivivin fought his desire to push closer to Elara, wanting her to be as comfortable as possible. He purposely would distance himself from her—far away, but still in view. He also tried to fall asleep first and, if he could not sleep so easily, pretend to be asleep. He hoped this would help Elara relax and minimize the fear she felt for him.

To an extent, it worked too. Elara still would feel wary and even fearful of Ivivin more frequently than she would have liked. His actions themselves didn't do much to ease her, but the fact that he was being thoughtful and trying to ease her nerves reassured her from time to time. Likewise, Elara did her best not to think about Ivivin's illness, only entertaining it as a topic of conversation when Ivivin brought it up. She did her best to be supportive during those times, but also did her best to treat him as she did before she knew.

Something surprised both parties immensely, though, and that was how much enjoyment they got out of traveling together. They had both traveled in groups before. Even in good groups, it was hit or miss whether it was preferable to being alone, but they seldom had a dull moment together. Days passed much more quickly. Smith had refused Ivivin's gift of the copy he made of Grandia's book, insisting that Ivivin take it with him, both to enjoy the story, but also to show his parents how much he had learned. Between the book he had copied and the armour he had forged, he was sure his parents would be proud and impressed. However, he lent the book to Elara, who had long since finished the Tale of the First King and found herself wanting a book less rooted in reality Grandia's encyclopedia.

Ivivin attempted to read the Tale of the First King again. It was still difficult, but he picked up on much more of it than he had before. They often shared quiet nights reading by the fire.

Moreover, Ivivin had asked Elara to help him learn more about swordplay. Elara did not care for contact with Ivivin—it exacerbated the issues she was already struggling with. On the off-chance that they accidently bumped into each other while cooking or the like, it aggravated Elara immensely. But something about swordplay was familiar to her and that familiarity snuffed out the fears. She showed Ivivin some more fundamentals, though it sometimes frustrated her how slow of a learner he was. Still, they passed their days most enjoyably.

Not everything was perfect, of course. They still hid facets of themselves from each other. Elara would only dance when her and Ivivin were apart and never revealed her hands to him. She would have nightmares, but weather them alone or go brush Lili until she settled down. Ivivin would get sudden reminders of how real his disease was, often enhanced by paranoia about every small fluctuation in his body's function. He would get his panic attacks and weather them alone or with the still flightless Icarus clenched against his chest.

Still, despite their reservations, they had fun.

Despite their pains, they were happy.

2

Ivivin and Elara were taking a different path to Gemi than the one Ivivin had taken when he first went to Smithton. It was suggested to them by Minerva. It lengthened the total time they'd be traveling, but would allow them to stay a night or two in villages along the away. By the time they got to the first village, Ivivin and Elara had already come to greatly enjoy each other's company. Still, they had been together nearly all the time since they left Smithton, so they decided that they would spend a day apart, even staying in each of the village's two inns separately.

Ivivin spent his day doing mainly two things. First, he doted on Icarus, helping the bird clean himself and inspecting the owl for any signs of recovery. He was disappointed to find only minimal regrowth of feathers. But Icarus seemed happy just to be pampered so, which made the endeavour more than worth it to Ivivin. The rest of his day he spent writing. He had been neglecting it during their travels and didn't want to lose his ability. But he didn't have anything in particular to write, so he just wrote whatever came to mind and found it cathartic. He had a relaxing day. It wasn't that he was sick of Elara, but he was happy he was able to have such a peaceful day, even without her. He figured he'd go and get a drink at the tavern once the sun set. It was unlike Ivivin, to be truthful, but he felt inexplicably compelled to drink this night.

Elara spent her day lazily. She alternated between eating and sleeping. She picked up the story of Elisabeth and the Troll a few times, but allowed herself to doze within a page or two each time. During a trip to the tavern for a warm meal, she had asked if she could perform that night. She didn't want compensation, just wanted an audience and a stage. Luckily, there were some travelers who, though were not musicians by trade, fancied themselves talented. They offered to play and perform together, to which Elara agreed. She worried for a moment that Ivivin would see her perform, but she knew from talking to him that he didn't frequent taverns nor did he have a taste for alcohol, beyond celebrating grand events. She rehearsed just a few times with the players before she was to take stage with them and resumed her lazy day, though she eagerly anticipated the evening.

Ivivin approached the village's only tavern and heard some folk music rumbling from within. He excitedly entered the tavern and approached the bar, bobbing his head to the music. He explained to the bartender that he did not much care for the taste of alcohol, but was in the mood to drink this night. The bartender smiled and assured Ivivin he had just the thing. He poured Ivivin a large glass of beer. The sheer volume made Ivivin wince. He was unsure he could stomach all that. However, when he tried it, the sharp sting of alcohol was not there. Instead, the drink tasted of apples and honey. Enamoured, Ivivin eagerly sipped on the drink and turned his attention to the stage. There were a few musicians who seemed very passionate about their music, which augmented their honestly amateurish skills. Up on stage with them was a young woman. The way she danced seemed very familiar to Ivivin, though he couldn't put his finger on it right away. She was far from the most graceful dancer Ivivin had ever seen, but something captivated Ivivin about her movements nonetheless.

3

About halfway through the third song Ivivin had caught, he realized why the motions of the dancer seemed so familiar. They were similar to the strange style of swordplay that Elara utilized on him during their scuffle. Ivivin looked more closely and realized that the captivating dancer was Elara herself. He might not have believed it, from that distance, but two things gave her away: her orange dancer's hip scarf and her earthy brown hair.

Ivivin ordered a second drink and approached the stage to confirm. His eyes did not deceive him. As he got closer, he verified that the dancer was indeed Elara and she looked to be having a grand old time. Though Ivivin was close to the stage, she did not notice him until their final song of the night. She had just started the dance when she noticed Ivivin in the audience, causing her to stumble just a bit. She recovered by the next beat, but felt her face grow hot. She was sure it was even brighter than her hip scarf. Still, she tried her hardest to finish the dance flawlessly. When she finished, she looked back to Ivivin, who was applauding along with the other drunkards.

She helped the musicians put away their equipment in an attempt to put off interacting with Ivivin as long as she could.

"Perhaps he will have returned to his inn by the time I am done." Elara thought, not allowing her eyes to wander from the task at hand. When the musicians had finished thanking her for her help, she looked around the bar, now becoming barren with last call.

"Ah, good, he's gone." Elara thought to herself. That is, until she saw a bird pecking at a man who sat face down at the bar. Next to him were three empty tankards. Elara approached the figure and it was indeed Ivivin, with Icarus pecking him in the face as the bartender cleaned the other parts of the venue. Elara approached the bar.

"Looking for a drink, young lady? Your dancing certainly brought out a few extra customers tonight. I think you've more than earned one from me on the house. Just don't tell anyone I served you this late, I'd never hear the end of it."

It was a tempting offer, but Elara declined.

"No, I am here for him, unfortunately."

"Oh, he a friend of yours? I knew he wasn't from these parts. But neither are you, so I suppose that makes sense. I over-served him. Never thought a man his size would be brought to this state by just three drinks. I feel responsible, so I was going to take him one of the inns after I closed up here. But he's yours, is he?"

"Yeah, I'll claim him. Leave him to me. Did he pay?" Elara asked.

"Unfortunately not. I was just going to have the inn bill him for me." the bartender responded.

"No need, here."

Elara paid for Ivivin's drinks.

"Help me get him up on his feet and I'll take it from there."

"Sure thing." the bartender said, helping Elara hoist Ivivin up. The proximity unnerved Elara, but she would deal with it. She put his arm across her shoulder and walked the bumbling Ivivin back to his inn. Ivivin had enough sense about him to direct Elara to his room. When they entered the room, Elara walked Ivivin to his bed, ready to dump him off and resigned to the fact that they would likely be getting a late start. However, when Elara went to let him fall to his bed, Ivivin tightened his hold on Elara, turning the carry into a sloppy embrace.

"Thanks Elara. Your dancing was beautiful, ya'know? I mean that." Ivivin stumbled over the sentence before losing his balance and falling to the floor.

Never before had Elara felt this way. Though his touch was tainted by foul associations in Elara's mind, it was also pleasant, in a way. Moreover, she was unexpectedly overjoyed at his praise, however drunk the mouth from which it came. She looked at Ivivin, now dozing on the floor and drooling a bit.

"Eh, close enough." Elara thought as she exited, leaving Ivivin as he was.

4

Ivivin awoke to a splitting plain in his head and an inexplicably sore back. At least, it was inexplicable until Ivivin began to piece together the events of the night prior. He remembered hugging Elara and his words to her (and his falling to the floor).

That hurt far more than his back or his head. First off, it was terribly embarrassing and he was sure Elara thought him a fool. The bigger issue, though, was that Ivivin was sure he had aggravated Elara's fear of him with that act. He had met her kindness with what was, to her, a known hostile act. Ivivin swore to himself, cursing the fact that the drinks had not poisoned him. He stumbled to his feet and looked outside. The sun was already far higher in the sky than it would have been when he and Elara had decided to meet at the stable in which Lili was being cared for.

"Damn, now I am making her wait, too!" Ivivin exclaimed as he put together his things and rushed out the door. Ivivin approached the stablehand, who had a message for Ivivin from Elara.

Hey there, lightweight. I'm not feeling well, so let's take another day and relax here before moving on. Let's meet here at the same time, tomorrow.
—Elara

Ivivin, a bit queasy, saw Elara's kindness for what it was. He didn't even make it to the inn, instead opting to lay next to Lili in the stable.

5

Elara, Ivivin, Icarus, and Lili resumed their journey. Ivivin and Elara had not talked about that evening, beyond Ivivin offering Elara his thanks and payment for his drinks. Elara refused both, telling him that she couldn't leave such a sad lightweight alone. Their journey progressed much like it had been, though a new idea surged about in Ivivin's mind.

"I want to ask Elara to show me how to dance." Ivivin thought again and again.

One afternoon, they stopped early. Ivivin felt it was the right time to ask. He wouldn't be able to get the thought out of his head until he did. He awkwardly followed Elara about that afternoon, trying to work up the nerve to ask. It was only when she began getting nettled that he took the leap.

"Elara, could you show me how to dance?" He was looking for a reaction, of which Elara did not give a particularly positive one.

"You know, so I can get more balance for swordplay." He hurriedly added

"Oh… sure. It actually helped me out a lot. Maybe it will help you keep a proper stance." Elara responded. "Just give me a bit to look at the shrubbery around here to see if I can't find something I need for Minerva."

Elara began her lesson with Ivivin by having him mirror her movements. She suspected Ivivin would have a hard time, but did not expect it to be this bad. Even Grace and Hope had picked it up faster! She scolded him time and time again for being too tight.

"You needed to loosen up, Ivivin!" Elara insisted for what felt like the millionth time.

"Sorry, sorry, I'm trying. It's hard. Every time I mess up, I just get tighter and tighter." He explained.

"You care too much about what people think." Elara insisted.

"Says you, Miss I-won't-dance-in-front-of-Ivivin." Ivivin countered. His teasing was met with a light shove, destroying his already shaky balance.

After a few more attempts, the pair had taken a break and were sitting around catching their breath.

"It's just too hard." Ivivin said. "Maybe if I had music…" Elara was struck by an idea. She dug in her bag and pulled out the stone she had gotten from Ajaxx's castle. She focused and the song sprung forth, slow and simple, but very comforting as it had always been. Ivivin had heard about the stone from Elara during her tale, but was too concerned with the other, more poignant aspects of the story to worry about the stone.

"It's a tear!" Ivivin claimed.

"Oh, I suppose it is." Elara responded.

"Anyways, here is your music, Ivivin. Get dancing! Hop to!" Elara commanded.

Ivivin stood, but he was thrown off even more than usual by the slow pace of the music and found himself rushing. Elara stood up to help him, but found it hard to keep the music going while also trying to focus on Ivivin. She grabbed Icarus and forced him to hold the stone in his talons. The music again came from the stone, though it's notes were a bit purer and melodic. Furthermore, it was louder.

"Perfect." Elara thought as she approached Ivivin. She hadn't thought about it, but before she knew it she was dancing hand and hand with Ivivin, forcing him to keep rhythm. Before long, their lesson had turned into a friendly and enjoyable dance to owl-music by the fireside. It was a bit embarrassing, but Elara was not plagued by distress. They allowed themselves to get swept up in the music and the moment, just enjoying the song and dance. When the song ended because Icarus grew bored and began to fumble about in the grass in search of easy prey, the two sat again by the fireside. Elara was barely winded and had barely worked up a sweat. Ivivin, however, was gasping for air and desperately looking for anything to wipe his face with.

"That wasn't terrible." Elara evaluated Ivivin's performance. "Still too tense, though."

"Of course I was! I…" Ivivin trailed off. Besides their proximity and his ineptness at dance, one other thing stood out to Ivivin while they danced.

"Elara...why do you wear those gloves? Surely they're uncomfortable to have on all the time."

Elara sighed. She knew it would come up eventually.

"You recall how I helped put out the boat fire in Rumi, right? Well, I burned my hands pretty badly. That's why I use my Beak and Talon, too." Elara explained.

"I knew that much already, Elara. But why do you wear the gloves? I saw you without them the day Minerva announced you'd be coming with me, but you hid them beneath your arms. If you weren't wearing them then, then why do you wear them now?" Ivivin pressed.

Elara did not respond right away. She struggled with the answer herself. Ivivin already knew of her burns—she had told him as much. And she only wore them when she with him or when she was harvesting thorny plants, really. After a long, but not prolonged, silence, Elara answered, sadness in her voice.

"Because they're ugly."

Ivivin spoke up immediately.

"Who cares? It seems uncomfortable as can be! You don't have to hide them from me, Elara. You're you, scars and all."

Elara didn't know what to make of Ivivin's words. They didn't feel reassuring, but they didn't hurt either. They felt like a statement of fact and Elara didn't know how to react to it.

"That's enough, Ivivin. I don't want to talk about it anymore. I'm going to bed, I suggest you do the same." Elara said.

Ivivin nodded and awayed to his self-imposed quarantine. He spent the whole night in his head, angry at himself for upsetting Elara on such a personal matter.

"'Who cares?!' I am such an idiot. Of course she cares. Damn it, I should have chosen my words more wisely instead of blurting them out like a fool!"

Ivivin did not fall asleep until late that night, causing him to get a bit of a late start. It was not until he heard Elara packing up her gear that he got up to do the same.

Elara prepared for their departure the same she did every day. She spoke to Ivivin the same way she always did. She brushed Lili briefly while she waited for Ivivin to catch up on packing. And then they set out for the day. The normalcy of it all moved Ivivin deeply. As they moved on, Ivivin walked just behind Elara, who marched unflinchingly forward with freed and unbound hands.

6

The quartet of young adventurers arrived in Gemi in what felt like no time at all. In reality, they had taken far longer than they needed, but each day was enjoyable and so they passed Elara and Ivivin by as if a breeze. When they approached Gemi, it was still quite early in the day. Ivivin and Elara both knew they could make it to Ivivin's home before sunset. Ivivin insisted, though, on staying the rest of the day in Gemi. They settled into neighboring rooms in Gemi's only inn. It was only after they had unpacked and settled in that Elara asked Ivivin about his decision, having avoided bringing it up earlier only because she didn't want to give the air of objection. In truth, she was getting a little nervous about meeting Ivivin's family as well. Still, she was curious about Ivivin's reasoning.

"Ivivin, may I ask... why did you decide that we should stop here for the day? Surely, we could have made it there today, no?" Elara questioned Ivivin.

"I just need a day to prepare, is all." Ivivin responded succinctly, if a bit curtly.

"And what is it that you need to prepare for?" Elara prodded gently.

Ivivin's initial reaction was to clamp up and shut Elara out. But he saw her and the earnest concern in her eyes and reminded himself of how much they'd already shared with one another.

"Lots of things. First off...I don't even know if they're alive. I hadn't considered it a possibility until we got close, but I have no way of knowing that something terrible hasn't already happened. I'm scared that something happened to them while I was gone, that I was gone when they needed me..."

Ivivin trailed off.

Elara hadn't even thought of that, yet it seemed to be what was weighing most heavily on Ivivin. Her foster-mother was a seer. Elara couldn't prove it and it seemed a bit morbid to ask, but she had always suspected that her mother had foreseen her own death. This thought was only solidified by her mother's parting words with her. The point is, she had never really worried about something unexpected happening to her mother. But, when she thought now about going home only to find something horrible had happened to Idalia, it nearly made her ill. She could see why it rattled Ivivin so.

"Ivivin, I know nothing will ease your concern until you see them well and happy. But do remember that they gave you their blessing to leave, so, even if something did happen while you were gone, you still obeyed their wishes. Worrying now won't change anything, as much as you wish it would." Elara offered her advice.

Ivivin nodded.

"I know, I know. But, still, I worry. And that's not the whole picture, either, though I am sure you know by now."

"I think so. You want to tell them, right? About your Crumbleheart?" Elara proposed.

"Yeah, I think that is prudent and for the best. Especially if you are going to be coming and going. I don't want to live a lie, lest I come to believe it myself once more. We know how that worked out for me last time." Ivivin chuckled lightly, tracing his thumb along his chest where Elara had cut him open.

"If it makes you feel any better, I can strike you down again if you need another wake-up call." Elara teased Ivivin, trying to lighten his mood.

Ivivin smiled at Elara.

"I'll hold you to that, then."

380

"Is there anything else?" Elara asked, feeling like, though they had gotten to the heart of the matter, there might be some other organs in need of being wrapped up, perhaps some gizzards.

"Yeah, but it's a little silly." Ivivin admitted.

"If it is bugging you, then it's not silly." Elara insisted.

"Promise not to make fun of me?" Ivivin asked.

"You know good and well I cannot make that promise, you silly boy." Elara answered.

"I suppose I do." Ivivin relented. "Well, I am afraid they won't recognize me. Or, even if they do recognize me, that they won't believe my adventures. I fear they'll think me a liar for spinning such tall tales and a failure for not being coming home a knight."

"It's true, you've changed a lot since even I met you." Elara admitted. "But, I am sure you could convince them even if they didn't believe you. Heck, I couldn't believe half the stuff you said you did at first, but I do now. If nothing else, give it time."

"You're right, Elara. Thanks. Dinner's on me tonight." Ivivin offered.

"Oooh, in that case, I guess I am eating a great big steak tonight. Thanks, Ivivin!" Elara teased as she returned to her own room, satisfied that Ivivin had gotten his worries off his chest.

Ivivin shook his head.

That girl...she's relentless." he thought, petting a tuckered-out Icarus. *"Still, she knows how to make me feel better. I suppose she's earned her steak."*

Ivivin checked his coin-purse nervously.

7

Ivivin and Elara enjoyed a stress-free night. It would be the last they had in this fashion for a while, perhaps forever, so they went ahead and went all out. They enjoyed a dinner together, coupled with overly sweet drinks. Elara cut Ivivin off early, instead taking his drinks as her own. They went for a walk around the streets and even found themselves a nice hill to stargaze from. They sat on the hill, a few yards between them. Still, on this night, at this distance, they felt closer than they ever had before.

Elara and Ivivin took their time getting ready the next day. They had plenty of time to make the trip, after all. When all owls were accounted for and Lili the horse convinced to bear their burdens, Elara and Ivivin left Gemi. However, something was wrong and it took Ivivin a couple minutes into their trip, outside of town, to realize. Elara was wearing her gloves again. He stopped the moment he realized this, surprising Elara at first. One glance at his face, though, was all it took for Elara to realize the jig was up.

"I already know what you're going to ask." Elara preempted.

"Still going to ask it anyways." Ivivin countered.

"I was afraid you'd say that, you nosey arse." Elara responded.

"Why are you wearing the gloves again, Elara?" Ivivin asked predictably.

"Look, just because you and Minerva and Smith can look past the scars doesn't mean everyone can. Even in Gemi yesterday, I noticed people staring." Elara told Ivivin.

"Who cares?" Ivivin tried to convince her.

"I do!" Elara stated, bordering on a shout. "Look, in Smithton, people came to know me first and foremost as Minerva's apprentice. You knew me before the scars. It's easy for you to not see me and think only of my hands. But people I've never met, they see my hands and become fixated on it. I become defined in their heads before they've even met me. Before I ever open my mouth, they've invented a story and speak for me. I do not want your parents to do the same thing...to define me before they've had a chance to know me."

Ivivin hadn't thought of that. It's true. When he thought about it, Elara did tend to attract glances when she walked around without her hands covered. But she had never shown any indication that it bothered her.

"Though..." Ivivin supposed, *"it does seem like the sort of thing that wears at you little by little, rather than all at once."*

"I see...I didn't know it bothered you." Ivivin looked at Elara, seeing the scar he himself had planted on her face. He reached absentmindedly towards it, causing Elara to recoil away from him. Ivivin winced at the result of his own action.

"Sorry, Elara. I just...now that I know it troubles you, I feel even worse about leaving that scar on your face." Ivivin admitted.

Elara was taken aback at the admission, not because she didn't expect such things from Ivivin, but because she had forgotten about the scar. Of course, she could see it when see looked at her reflection in a mirror or in the water, but it never weighed on her mind long and never like her hands. In fact...

"Don't burden yourself with thoughts like that Ivivin. I actually think it's kind of cool" Elara made an admission of her own.

Ivivin laughed heartily. "Of course. How could I be so silly."

Ivivin returned to a serious tone before continuing.

"But why not the hands, then?" Ivivin asked.

"They're different and you know it." Elara said, annoyance clear in her voice.

"I don't think so. If anything, your hands are even cooler." Ivivin posed.

"What do you mean by that? You and I both know they are deformed and ugly." Elara spat.

"I think that, if you do anything worth doing, you risk scaring yourself. Be it scars of the flesh or scars on the heart. To be bold is to put yourself at risk. Scars, then, are just a reminder that you tried doing something important." Ivivin explained.

"The scars on my hand are a reminder of my failure, Ivivin. And of the ills and evils that befell me because of it."

"They don't have to be. They could be badges, emblematic of the fact that you tried to do the right thing, at the right time, the best you could. Failure or not, scars often mean that those who bear them are, if nothing else, interesting." Ivivin asserted.

"I don't think you can understand, Ivivin." Elara deflected.

Ivivin set down his things and removed his shirt, something he was typically against. He was a bit modestly minded, sure, but he also did not want Elara to be reminded of the bulbous scar now adorning his chest.

"You hide that scar, Ivivin. You hide it from me and you hide it from the world. The only difference is that yours is easy to hide—expected, even." Elara stated, her voice becoming wobbly and unsettled, both from the discussion and the sight of what she had done to him.

"I am proud of this scar, even if I gained it as a result of my foolishness, as a result of a mistake. It is a reminder that I fought you and survived. It is a reminder not to lose myself again. It is many things, but it is also a part of me now." Ivivin argued. "And that isn't the only scar I have."

Ivivin approached Elara.

"Look here." Ivivin said, holding out his hands. "They are not so prominent nor from a wound so painful as yours, but my hands, too, are scarred. I got these scars defending Crosstown from the bandit king Xaivier. They were the result of a foolish endeavour and it is nearly entirely luck that I survived. But I am proud of these scars, because they remind me that I can always try to do the right thing, even if it seems impossible."

"That's fin—" Elara started, before Ivivin interrupted her.

Ivivin cut Elara off, pointing to his upper arm which carried a scar, clearly from a burn. "And this one, here? This one I gave myself, after my interference in a squabble led Smith to getting a cut in the same and him having to cauterize it closed. In hindsight, I know that Smith would have been fine and my meddling risked both our lives. But it is also a reminder of the bond I have with Smith and that I should be accountable for the fallout of my actions, even if they were well intentioned."

"Sure, but—" Elara unsuccessfully tried to get a word in.

"And there's this one!" Ivivin said, moving his face unusually close to Elara's. "It is a bit faded because it is the oldest, but on my face, just as yours, I have another scar. This one, from preventing an attempt at the king's life!" Ivivin exclaimed.

Elara expected Ivivin to continue and explain the significance of the scar, like he did the others. But to her astonishment and, eventually, frustration he just sat there with his face too close to hers. She looked closely. The scar was certainly there. Much like her own, she knew it was there but never gave it much thought. She pushed Ivivin's face away.

"And what's so special to you about this one!?" Elara asked sarcastically.

Ivivin smiled.

"Nothing, I just think it looks cool."

It had been a while since Elara had snorted from laughing so hard.

9

Ivivin had checked the fields near his house and saw no one tending the fields.

"Well, it is nearing supper time." Ivivin reasoned.

Ivivin stood in front of his door, Elara behind him. They had let Lili go forage nearby. Icarus was packed firmly in Ivivin's things.

"One surprise at a time. I don't want to give them a heart attack." Ivivin justified.

Ivivin rapped on the door confidently.

"I can't believe you are doing this." Elara sighed, putting her face to her bare palm and shaking it in embarrassment-by-proxy.

"Shh!" Ivivin called to the girl behind him. "We had a deal, didn't we?"

The door opened.

Ivivin's mother stood at the doorway, shocked at what met her there—her son, Ivivin, grown and standing shirtless with the scars on his body highlighted and encircled with mud. Ivivin's own heart missed a beat as he awaited her reaction. She pulled Ivivin in for a tight embrace. Ivivin couldn't help but notice that he was taller than her now.

"Welcome home, my son."

10

After some barebone introductions, Ivivin and Elara sat at Ivivin's family's table as Ivivin's father, tears still sticky on his face, hustled to expand their supper for two into a supper for four. Ivivin and Elara sat awkwardly as Ivivin's mother had gone to clean the tools off for the day, knowing that she would not return to the fields after dinner as she had planned. Ivivin knew not what to say to Elara, nor did he feel comfortable chatting with his frantic father. Still, it felt nice to be home. It was a warmth he had not felt in some time, even if he was unsure how to handle it.

Ivivin's father finished his improvised meal and Ivivin's mother resumed her home.

"Elara, was it?" Ivivin's dad asked.

Elara nodded, obviously a bit nervous. She had never had a father and wasn't quite sure how to deal with one. It was not unlike her inability to handle Abraham comfortably, though perhaps there was a little more to it than that in this case.

He reached out his hand to shake Elara's over the table. "The name's Ivan. I'm Ivivin's father. Though I suppose you already knew that." His hand hovered over the table as Elara hesitated to meet it. She slowly and shakily met Ivan's hand, staring at the table, anxious as to how this man would react upon feeling her hands. When the two collided, Elara felt Ivan shake her hand vigorously up and down before being released.

She slowly raised her head to see that Ivan had either not noticed the irregularity of her hand or, more likely, didn't think it was a big enough deal to react to. She glanced to Ivivin, who met her glance with a smile.

"Nice to meet you, Mr. Ivan." Elara responded with a cautious, but sincere smile.

"Well, go on, eat up you two! We can catch up once our bellies are full! Sorry for the improper meal. I have gotten so used to cooking for two..." Ivan paused and looked to his wife and allowed an uncharacteristically large grin spread on his face.

"Well, two and a half." He added.

Ivivin and Elara both looked to Ivivin's mother. Elara, in particular, looked quite intently at the woman's abdomen. She was not showing as drastically as Able had been, but that same captivating bump was certainly there.

"Oh, dear. You didn't need to bring that up now!" Ivivin's mother scolded Ivan. "I haven't even given our guest my name yet! I know you're excited, but there is a proper order to things."

The woman looked to Elara and likewise reached over the table to shake her hand.

"My name is Vivian. I apologize for my husband, he's a little over-excited. You'd think that we have never had a baby before, the way he acts."

Elara met Vivian's hand with a bit more confidence than she had with Ivan, though she was still anxious that the woman would make a fuss about Elara's hands. Elara was surprised, then, when she herself was the one who thought that the handshake was unnatural. Elara caught a glance at Vivian's hands and noticed that they were very calloused. Elara had noticed Ivan's hands were a bit, too, but this was a whole other level. Naturally, she was a bit embarrassed for having been surprised, but Vivian acted like nothing strange had been encountered by either party.

Elara could relax here.

"Mr. Ivan and Mrs. Vivian, it is a pleasure to meet you both." Elara said, though she had fumbled on the names a bit. It was as if she wanted to say another word but forced herself not to.

"Ivan...Vivian...Ivan...Vivian..." Elara repeated in her head a few times before she realized.

"Ivan...Vivian...Ivivin!" Elara blurted out at the table. Ivivin blushed, embarrassed at the origin of his name, but his parents got a good laugh from the abruptness of her realization.

"See, Ivivin! Someone thought it was clever, didn't you Elara!?" Ivan teased.

Elara saw the childish embarrassment turning Ivivin redder than an apple and couldn't help but laugh along with his parents.

11

After their light-spirited meal, Ivivin's parents inevitably asked him the question that he had been dreading.

"What brings you home, son?"

Ivivin knew he wanted to be honest with his parents and he wanted to do it up front. He looked at Elara, who understood from just the quick glance that Ivivin wanted to be alone with them for this. Neither he nor she were sure of this until this moment, but it seemed Ivivin had decided and Elara would respect this decision.

"If you'll excuse me, I am going to tend to our horse. She is quite the needy little mare. I'll rejoin you in a while. Thank you very much for the meal." Elara recited before leaving the house. She was worried for Ivivin, but had faith he was doing what he thought best.

"I can be there for him afterwards, if he needs me." Elara decided as she brushed Lili.

Meanwhile, Ivivin struggled to get started inside. He looked back and forth to his parents, who were still beaming at the sight of their fully-grown son. Ivivin came up with a plan. We would tell his parents outright, but in a calm and accepting manner, about his illness. If he didn't make a big deal of it, then surely it would be easier on his parents, right?

"Mother, father...I have returned because I am ill. I have contracted a disease called Crumbleheart and there is no cure. I don't know when it will claim my life, but it will. I want to spend time with you before it does." Ivivin said calmly and resolutely, expecting his parents to receive the news in the same manner.

Ivivin looked to his parents and saw horror and pain oozing from every angle. Never had he seen such a look of pain on his parents' faces and never had he seen two people devolve to tears so quickly.

"It seems I have underestimated paternal love." Ivivin thought as he himself was brought to hot and heavy tears not by the truth, but by the pain the truth had caused his parents. They both got up and embraced their boy. For the first time since he had contracted the disease, crying about it truly felt good to Ivivin. And, so, he let himself. Despite how much he had grown, how much he had faced, and how much he had changed, he let himself cry in the arms of his parents, as he had done as a child.

12

By the time Elara rejoined them, Ivivin and his folks had dried their tears and Ivivin had begun telling his tale. When he got to the part when he met Icarus, he remembered that the poor fellow was still trapped in his bag. Ivivin was met with a flurry of frustrated pecks by the now quite peckish, puckish owl.

"Sorry, sorry Icarus. I'll feed you extra today, so just calm down." Ivivin said, attempting to soothe the owl's searing rage. Ivivin handed him some dried fish. Icarus decided that this offering appeased him. The plague of pecking ceased as Icarus tore into the fish.

"These are my parents, Icarus." He said, patting the owls head gently.

Ivivin's parents were not sure what to make of the creature. Ivivin had described Icarus in his story, but that description did not do the feathered fiend justice.

"He's...nice." Vivian lied through her teeth, making a mental note to clean the table extra well the following morning.

Ivivin continued his story and spared no detail until a certain point. And it wasn't the point Ivivin expected to struggle with. He managed to get through his time in Olympia and contracting

Crumbleheart just fine. No, he had a harder time talking about what happened after that, after he returned to Smithton with Smith. In particular, he wanted to tell them all about the times he spent with Elara but found it difficult with her sitting right there. After all, he hadn't told her his feelings for her. Ivivin was sure that he would give himself away if he recounted their times together in front of her. Ivivin's father noticed his son's hesitance and pieced together the truth.

"Go on!" Vivian pestered the paused Ivivin, wanting to hear more about her son's ever impressive story.

"Now dear," Ivan followed up. "they must be exhausted from their journey. They came all the way from Smithton, after all. There will be plenty of time to finish the story later. Besides, you and the baby need rest, since you insist on working the fields still. Here, I will help you to bed. Worry not about the dishes, I will take care of them."

Ivan helped his wife up. She knew that when he brought the baby into it, she would never win and, honestly, found his concern lovely and charming. As Ivivin's dad walked into the next room with Vivian, Ivivin caught a knowing wink from his father.

Ivivin could not believe he was that transparent.

13

Elara had volunteered to help wash the dishes, insisting it was the least she could do for the meal. She had also sensed that Ivivin's father wished to speak to him, though her unfamiliarity with paternal figures meant she was unable to put a finger on what he wanted to talk about. She shrugged it off and focused on the dishes, happy, at least, that Ivivin seemed to be well enough after telling his parents about his illness.

Meanwhile, Ivivin's father drug him outside under the pretense of putting away the tools—a task that had already been completed by his mother. Ivivin knew what was coming, despite never having been in this situation.

"So, who's this Elara girl, Ivivin? She seems nice." Ivan poked at his son.

"Besides the reincarnation of a celestial spirit? She's my apothecary. I didn't get to it tonight, but there is an experimental treatment for Crumbleheart that her master invented. It's supposed to help a little, though not cure it. Elara knows how to make it, is all. She's gonna come by here every so often to make me more medicine and to teach me how to make it myself." Ivivin explained, trying to keep his voice down and his tone level.

"Oh, is that all?" Ivan said, sounding a bit disappointed.

"Well, she's my good friend, too." Ivivin admitted.

"A good friend, huh? I see. That makes sense. You two do seem to get along. You ready to go back inside?" Ivan asked.

Ivivin couldn't believe that his father had dropped the matter so easily, especially after he had called him out here on false pretenses. He almost felt a little guilty, withholding the information. But he just wanted to escape the awkwardness of it all, so he was more than willing to accept that his father would pry no further.

"Sure." Ivivin said, relief clear in his voice.

"Oh, and one more thing." Ivan called to his son, whose hand was already on the door's handle. Ivivin looked at his father, who was sporting a goofy but mischievous grin—one Ivivin had come to know quite well as a child. Ivivin tried to brace himself for what came next, but his father was far too quick to the draw.

"So, are you two sharing a bed tonight or are you going to make your old man get out the extra linens?"

Ivivin slammed the door behind him, leaving the grown man who was far too proud of himself outside to giggle like a child.

14

Ivivin had offered Elara his room, but she denied it vehemently.

"You're going to be here far longer than I am, Ivivin. No need for you to uproot yourself every time I come." Elara declared, instead taking residence in the attic. It was small, but Elara slept there and left her unnecessary belongings in Ivivin's room. And, just like that, Ivivin had made it back home. It was too much for him to process. He wasn't sure how to feel about being home. He had never seen his parents so happy and so sad over the course of a single day. He didn't know how to respond to the prospect of having a younger sibling. He didn't know what to think of having Elara staying in his home. There would be a lot for Ivivin to sort out later. But, for now, he was happy to know that he had made it home. It was what he wanted, after all.

15

Ivivin had anticipated Elara wanting to show him techniques right away but, much to his surprise, she seldom brought it up. Instead, she'd wander the surrounding area with Lili during the day, leaving Ivivin behind. He started helping in the fields again since he had nothing better to do. It was good timing, too, as Ivivin's mother grew closer to bursting with each passing day. Working the fields returned to Ivivin naturally, though he felt like smithing had become even more natural to him. Of course, Ivivin's return to the fields meant a return to his favourite spot—the large tree under which he used to daydream. He laid beneath the tree and allowed himself to dream once more. This time, though, he dreamed not of fantastic knightly adventures, but of half-memories, as Ivivin called them. He thought of things that never happened, but could have and still could. He imagined another tea party with Minerva, Elara, and Smith. He imagined Icarus flying about the farm. He imagined seeing Elara reunite with her sister and the three of them sitting on the roof of their home together once more. He imagined showing Elara the Flor festival, in all its brilliance, and sharing a kis—

Ivivin felt someone kick him in the ribs. He opened his eyes and saw Elara hovering over him, with Lili running about in the nearby fields.

"Hey, been to calling you for a bit now. Shouldn't you be working?" Elara asked Ivivin.

Ivivin sat up.

"Breaks are important. Besides, this is my favourite spot. Here, lay down and you'll see." Ivivin offered. The pair remained stagnant until Ivivin realized what he might have been implying. He sprung to his feet and moved out of the way, gesturing to Elara to take his place. Elara obliged and laid her head on the moss-softened roots.

"You're right, this is nice." Elara said.

"I used to love this place as a kid. I'd lay here after working the fields and dream of being a knight. I'd imagine grand and fantastic adventures, filled with awesome battles and exotic locales. This was even the tree from which I fashioned my gift to the king. I absolutely loved it." Ivivin explained.

Elara contemplated his words a moment before responding.

"And now?" She asked.

Ivivin looked at the tree with new perspective. Ivivin certainly still thought it was large and imposing, but it seemed much smaller than it had in his youth. Ivivin recalled the story of how his ancestors could not rid the land of this tree, but, looking at it, Ivivin felt he could find a way to bring down the tree he once thought invulnerable, if he was so inclined. Ivivin heard the birds singing above, but now he knew which bird was which by their song alone. Ivivin looked at the comforting shade the tree casted onto the ground, but realized it was only able to do so because of the harsh sun above it. Lastly, Ivivin looked at the woman lying in his spot, who finally relaxed enough to allow her eyes to close, despite Ivivin's proximity. But he saw more than just a person resting under a tree. He saw a friend, one he loved dearly, immersed fully in a part of his life he had never shared with any other. Ivivin smiled and answered Elara before resuming the fields.

"I still do."

Idalia

1

Soon after her sister set forth on her journey, Idalia had found herself becoming quite bored. She had done nearly everything with her sister her entire life. In fact, when she got down to thinking about it, her sister was the driving force behind many of their adventures, large and small. With Elara gone, Idalia wasn't sure what to do with herself. Elara and Idalia both were naturally talented people, with many things coming easily to them. Even though Idalia was never quite as outgoing as her sister, they both recognized that, if Elara was talented, then Idalia was a borderline genius. She didn't have the knack for fighting that Elara had, but, in most other matters, Idalia could surpass her sister and most anyone with just a little diligent effort. The issue now clear to Idalia since her sister's departure was that she really didn't enjoy many things, despite having a natural knack for them. Most of the time when she enjoyed doing things, it was because she did so in service of others or with her sister. Her mother pointed this out to her, warning that living for others' sakes and depending on them for your fulfillment was dangerous. She urged her daughter to seek a passion of her own. Idalia respected her mother's wisdom, but found it difficult to pin down a hobby, let alone a vocation. She simply did not find most things satisfying, especially things that came to her too easily. She entertained the idea of martial arts, as she did struggle with it, but violence was something she generally abhorred. So, Idalia found herself trying out more and more varied occupations, crafts, and trades in order to find her calling.

2

Idalia had tried out many of the occupations of the residents of her humble town. It was not a huge settlement by any means, so her options were limited. As a result, she could find nothing that called out to her. Still, passing the time by helping the locals was better than fidgeting around the house. She had tried baking, cobbling, and even smithing. So, she tried to bring new crafts to the town, by means of teaching herself from books. There were things she managed well enough, even if there was no demand for it. She tried becoming a peruker, a thatcher, a lormer, a mason, and even a fletcher. She tried many things, almost as if she were drawing the next occupation from a hat. Still she found nothing to be engaging. The closest she could get was the satisfaction of a hard day's work, which can only get someone so far.

That all changed, though, when she went to the local tavern to learn to become a brewster. She knew much of the drink was imported by merchants, but she also knew that the tavern brewed some of their own. Idalia wasn't much for drinking—not that she had really ever given it a fair shot—but she was interested in learning how the drinks were made, at least. There was not much equipment and the operation was small scale, but it certainly met the town's needs. Idalia gladly learned the trade. She was unsure how she felt about it, to tell the truth, but to make some of the spirits took time and care. That, at least, was incentive enough for Idalia to stick around and give it an honest effort.

And she was glad she did, as the tavern was a lively place. She had spent so much of her life with her sister that she had never really taken the time to get to know the people of her town. Plus, she got to meet with travelers and hear their tales. Idalia hadn't caught wanderlust, but she did find the stories interesting. She found herself at the tavern more and more often, going beyond her duties as a brewster and actually helping to run the establishment. She began keeping track of the income and expenses of the establishment, acting as an amateur accomptant. Her foster mother saw Idalia working hard and enjoying herself. She knew Idalia was capable of much greater things than running a tavern, but, then again, she also knew greater did not always mean happier. Still, she could not help but worry about her daughter. For now, though, she knew she must let her daughter make her own choices.

When Idalia's first batch of aged brew was complete, she decided she would drink from it to celebrate. In fact, the proprietor of the tavern threw a modest celebration for her. She drank with the lively crowd—a mix of regulars and travelers—and found it much easier to connect with them when a little tipsy. Indeed, Idalia was surprised by how much she enjoyed the drink and its effects. She hadn't done half bad for her first attempt. She was proud.

Idalia found herself more and more immersed in the world of brewing. It was fascinating to her, that she could make a drink that could help people become so lively and friendly. She even found herself drinking now and again. She appreciated how it made interacting with others so easy, sure, but it also made uninteresting things interesting. When she had a buzz, she found a renewed interest in things she had previously decided did not entertain here. She made pottery. She wrote stories. She repaired clothing. And so much more. All of these mundane tasks seemed to have hidden value that Idalia could only see with the aid of spirits and she enjoyed enjoying things again.

For a time, Idalia was happy. She began to notice, though, that it took her longer and longer to hit that point. When, before, she needed only one beverage, she now needed four or more to feel the same way. Moreover, she found herself craving a drink all the time. Even when she went to work, she would sneak a bit to tide her over until she finished. At first, Idalia had been setting aside her wages to help her mother, but now it seemed that her money nearly all went back to the tavern. It was like a blur to Idalia. She wasn't sure when she got this way. She even tried to fight it when she began to suspect that she was drinking too much. And it'd work, for a time. Until she relented and allowed herself to have 'just one' for a special occasion. It'd often trigger a binge. Sometimes, she got so drunk she was embarrassed to go home. Idalia knew she shouldn't be drinking so much, but pretended like everything was fine.

"After all, there are plenty of people who are here every day, just as I am." Idalia thought.

And, so, Idalia continued to work at the tavern, spending most of her day and night there. When she wasn't working, she was usually drinking. The tavern's proprietor saw this change in Idalia's behaviour and suggested she spend more time with her mother at home, but Idalia got defensive, thinking that she was no longer wanted around. After that, no one really tried to stop her, even Idalia herself. Even as her work slipped and her mother voiced concerns, Idalia found herself drowning out the sounds with the sharp taste of alcohol.

4

One evening, Idalia was sitting at her frequented spot in the tavern. She had just given up giving up drinking for what seemed like the dozenth time and was in the middle of drinking herself silly. There, she met a man. He was a traveler named Roick, who was only in town for the night. He was headed to Crosstown to live with his uncle and help him as a hunter. However, the journey was long and weighed on Roick, so he, too, decided to let loose this night. The two drank together, telling each other jokes and even dancing that night. They drank and drank and drank.

And the next thing Idalia remembered, it was morning and she lay bare next to this man in the inn near the tavern.

Idalia didn't have to remember what happened the night before to piece it together from the sensations of her own body and the clues around her. She had slept with this man—her first time ever. She gathered her things and rushed from the room, sprinting back home and shutting herself away before her mother had a chance to see her. She cried something fierce. It wasn't that she was against such casual intimacy. It was not even that she felt violated and betrayed by Roick. She found him quite charming, in fact. No, what caused the stone in her stomach and the rivers in her eyes was the fact that it was her first time and she didn't even remember it. That thought and that thought alone made Idalia feel weak-willed and caused her to resent herself. And she had no idea how to change.

5

Idalia struggled in the days following her encounter with Roick. She was so used to things coming easily to her that she was unsure how to approach quitting. It seemed impossible. She worked at the tavern and people depended on her there. Moreover, even though she knew she shouldn't be drinking, she had come to appreciate the atmosphere and people there. When she tried to avoid the tavern, she often found herself becoming lonely. So, she'd often find herself at the tavern anyways. And, when she found herself there, it was likely that she'd find herself drinking there. She was embarrassed and ashamed. She knew she had the potential for so many things, yet she was here drinking her life away. She was even letting the quality of her work there slip.

She looked around the bar and realized for every happy group of people, there was a lone and quiet drunkard—a fact she had willfully ignored when she first came to work here. She saw them and saw herself in them and it distressed her. It distressed her to the point where she no longer had fun at the bar. It was just the only way she didn't feel terrible. Nothing felt interesting anymore, but drinking made the dullness tolerable.

Idalia had her face planted on the bar on yet another night at the tavern. She was feeling ill, having come out for each of the five nights preceding this one. Then, she heard a tune playing from the corner of the room. In the corner was a young man playing a lute. The melody was soft. It reminded her of the song Elara had sung to her when they were young. Strangely relaxed and inspired by the melody and her inhibitions having been numbed by the potency of her beverages, Idalia joined the man in the corner of the room and she sang. She fit the words of Elara's lullaby to the tune and sang. It was the first time Idalia had managed to smile in a while. While she sang, she observed the man skillfully pressing on the strings of the lute and found it enchanting. When the man finished the song, Idalia left the bar. She had momentum and motivation for the first time in a long time and she wasn't about to let it slip through her fingers. She went home and her mother met her with gaunt eyes. She could see Idalia suffering in front of her and she could see a bright future for her daughter, but she knew not what to do for her in the meantime. Idalia had been pushing her away for weeks now and she was at a loss. Luckily, on this night, Idalia had tossed her pride aside and pleaded with her mother for help and apologized for distancing herself until now.

It would be a hard road, but Idalia had taken the first step to recovery.

6

Idalia's mother truly did not know what she could do to help her daughter, but now that she had come forth and asked for help, at the very least, she could hold Idalia accountable without feeling as if she was constraining her. Still, quitting cold turkey was hard on Idalia, even with her mother's help. She was bored, irate, shaky, and feverish. She quit her job because she knew it was enabling her, but it left her without a sense of purpose. Never had Idalia questioned her ability and her worth so much as she did now. She tried to pass the time helping around the house, but there was truly little to be done given the small household of capable women. She attempted some work she could do from home—mending clothes and the like, but they only made her feel more isolated and alone. Idalia missed the human contact she used to get at the tavern. More than that, though, she missed her sister.

Still, Idalia would have to do something. She could feel it. If she kept up on the route she was on now, she would surely lose out to her addiction. Idalia considered leaving, like her sister, but, without a goal, she feared she'd slip back into the habit—this time, without her mother around to help her. She brought up her listlessness and her fragility to her mother.

"Well, if you could do anything right now, regardless of what it is, what would it be? That's where we'll start." Her mother asked.

It was hard for Idalia not to respond: "Go get a drink down at the tavern."

But that itself certainly was a start. Idalia asked herself why she liked to drink and why she liked the tavern so much. The reasoning behind the tavern was simple enough. She felt welcome there and had the opportunity to meet new people and be social in a way she had never been before. She had to ask herself the harder question of what she got from the drink itself. She knew it made things seem more interesting and it made it easier for her to enjoy the company of others. Fundamentally, though, Idalia discovered it was because it allowed a side of her she usually tucked away to be free. It allowed her to express a part of her she found it hard to express. Idalia knew that, if she could manage to find these things in other facets of her life, she could recover. She thought a while to all the things she had encountered in her life, especially recently. She remembered the elation and self-expression involved when she sung with the lute player at the bar. Singing itself was too easy and too simple, but Idalia fell in love with the sensation of singing behind music. After careful consideration, she had an answer for her mother.

"I'd be a musician."

Specifically, Idalia wanted to be able to play the lute or a similar instrument. She wanted to be able to go places like a tavern with a reason other than drinking. She wanted to be able to express herself both through song and through music. She wanted to be able to expose that hidden layer that she had previously used alcohol to channel. Unfortunately, Idalia's hometown did not have any lute players, let alone a luthier who could fashion her an instrument. However, the seer-mother did know of a woman in the village who was a minstrel in her hay day—and for the king no less! However, she did not play the lute. Instead, the woman's partner was a large harp. Idalia decided to pay the woman a visit and, if nothing else, get advice on how to go about learning music.

Idalia was surprised by the size of the woman's house. She had imagined that an old servant of the king would have a sizable estate in their retirement. After all, tales of the king's fairness and generosity were widespread. However, the home seemed small— even smaller than her own mother's modest house. She knocked on the door and waited some time for an answer. She had almost given up and began to walk away when it swung open. A small, frail old woman called softly for Idalia to return. Idalia saw the woman and immediately felt guilty for making her come to the door at all. She was warm and friendly looking, sure, but Idalia felt as if even she could shatter the woman's bones with a well-placed sneeze. Idalia approached the bespectacled woman.

"Hello ma'am. I am so sorry to trouble you, but I heard you were once a great harp player and I was hoping to ask you some questions about music." Idalia asked gently.

"Huh? Pardon me missy, my ears ain't what they once was. Speak up, will ya!" The old woman said.

Idalia was caught off guard by the woman's speech. She seemed so elegant, but she spoke rather inelegantly.

After repeating herself at least a half a dozen times, Idalia was allowed to enter the house. She entered the living area— it served as the bedroom, living room, and kitchen all in one. And it was a calamity. It was not only unorganized, but filthy as well. Idalia could see mold in the corner and old food strewn about.

"Baba is my name, so stop calling me ma'am. What are you here for, again?" Baba called to Idalia as she struggled to make her way to the only seat not sporting a precarious stack on it.

"Please ma'am, allow me to help you." Idalia offered genuinely.

The woman refused Idalia's arm.

"What did I say about calling me ma'am!?"

"Sorry ma'—"

Idalia stopped at Baba's dirty look.

"Sorry, Baba."

"I can get around myself, thank you very little!" Baba barked.

Idalia did not know how to handle this woman and could not think of anything to say.

"So, you came to talk about music, huh missy? You seem a little prudish to be pursuing such an art."

Idalia wasn't sure if she should be insulted or not. Whatever the case, it seemed unlikely that Idalia would get what she was looking for from this woman.

"Sorry to bother you. I must have made a mistake." Idalia told the woman politely

"Oh, now you think you're too good for me, huh, missy? Hiding your condescension behind a cheap veil of politeness. Have you ever even had a friend who you didn't share blood with?"

Idalia recognized that as an insult. For the first time in her life, she was angry at a person. Even the Shaa'Id hadn't made her feel this way.

"I'll be going." Idalia stated headed for the door.

"What, quitting so soon? No wonder you're a drunk. A dainty prodigy indeed, with an ego frailer than my bones. The rare occasion comes where you fail and you can't handle it. A prodigy you may be, but the mantle of virtuoso is so far from the grasp of such a brat." Baba slandered.

"How did—" Idalia started.

"How did I know you were a good-for-nothing drunk? It's in your face, you ignorant little girl."

Idalia's frustration and mild anger swelled to a rage, one that she let loose.

"You homely and bitter old woman, I'll have no more of your disparagement, ma'am."

400

To Idalia's surprise, the woman did not retort. Rather, she laughed weakly but wholeheartedly.

"There we go. Something finally real from this porcelain doll. Still, even your insults are so stiff. Fine, fine. Come with me missy. I'll show you why I was the king's minstrel for so many years."

Never before had Idalia been so confused, but she followed the Baba, bewitched by the sheer absurdity of their encounter.

8

Idalia somehow felt better after having loosed an insult at the old woman. Of course, her patience was tested as she sifted through a mound of junk to follow Baba to the other room in the house. After taking what Idalia swore was nearly a half hour, Baba managed to get her keys out and open the locked door. Idalia expected the inside to be as terrible as the rest of Baba's home, but was surprised at how pristine the room was. Not only was it clean, but it was minimal. There were some drawers, a workbench, and a large, elegant harp in the center of the room. It was truly the most intricate and beautiful instrument Idalia had ever seen, though that wasn't saying much. Still, she recognized it was not an ordinary instrument.

"Did the king procure that for you?" Idalia asked as Baba waddled her way to the instrument.

"Are you daft, missy? Of course that low-life didn't get this for me. I made this myself well before I even met the scumbag." Baba threw words at Idalia as she continued struggling to position herself about the harp.

Idalia, again, found herself at a loss for words. Few people insulted the king, both because it was improper and because few people of this country had qualms with him. Idalia looked at the harp, which stood as tall as, if not a bit taller than, Baba. She was doubtful of the crude old woman's ability to play such a colossal elegance.

Her thoughts were interrupted by Baba screeching at her.

"I bet your pompous arse is doubting my skill. I suppose someone as naive and ignorant as yourself can't help it. Really, missy, you must be a riot at parties." Baba said with a snicker.

Idalia could feel rage building up again in her once more.

"Agitated, are we? Good! Now shut up and listen. Maybe I'll learn you a thing for once in your pitiable excuse for a life." Baba finished, cracking her knuckles before touching the strings.

Idalia was caught halfway between shouting and crying when Baba began to play the harp. It was slow, melodic and, as much as Idalia did not want to admit it, absolutely lovely.

"Of course it is so slow paced, she is an old woman after all." Idalia found herself thinking.

As if reading her mind, Baba winked at Idalia and her hands began to move incredibly fast. Try as she might, Idalia could not keep up with her movements. Baba worked her partner over so masterfully, it sounded as if multiple instruments were playing at once—a vivace fugue played solo. Baba, with her eyes closed, put her whole body into playing. Idalia looked at the woman, who just moments ago she thought spiteful and rotten, and saw grace and allure. Her negative feelings were supplanted by the rich notes coming from every direction. Thoughts left Idalia, her worries and doubt joining them. Baba's playing began to crescendo, hinting again and again at a spectacular climax. Idalia anticipated the release of the tension, but Baba just kept building and building, keeping Idalia on her toes, expectant.

And then, she stopped. Suddenly, the music ceased.

No climax.

No resolution.

Idalia thought she was frustrated at the woman before, but she found a new visceral ire with the woman now.

"Why'd you stop?" Idalia nearly screamed at Baba, who was sweating and breathing a bit heavy, though obviously capable of playing further.

"Oh, sorry, are you frustrated? Not getting the release you wanted? You need a climax?" Baba said, teasing her fingers about the string. "I don't recall being obligated to show you a good time. You should be grateful I helped you feel anything at all, you prig."

Idalia was so worked up, both from the music and from the batty woman in front of her, that she was nearly pulling the hair from her head. Idalia wanted so badly to shout something, but no words she had would adequately express this novel rancor. She clenched her fists, mouth agape, and leered at the woman.

"Get out of my house, you picayune and entitled little brat."

Never had Idalia slammed a door so hard.

9

Idalia spent the rest of the day in a frenzy. She paced around her house, irritated and irrational. It took all her self-control to not lash out at her mother when asked what was wrong for what felt like the thousandth time. Idalia stayed up late into the night fuming. She imagined in her head over and over again all the retorts she should have uttered rather than leaving silently. These imaginings escalated into a full-fledged plan.

"*Yes,*" Idalia thought. "*I'll go give her a piece of my mind tomorrow, the old sour bat.*"

It was only in telling herself this that Idalia calmed enough to finally sleep.

10

Idalia woke early and readied herself in a huff. When it came time to leave the house to go and let Baba have a piece of her mind, Idalia kept finding excuses to put it off. Still carrying her nebulous rage, Idalia tidied up around the house, tended to the garden, and walked about aimlessly. It was only when her mother questioned why she was acting so strangely that Idalia was prompted to actually leave the house and march to Baba's. She stood in front of the old woman's house going over what she was going to say again, when she started feeling guilty.

"*Am I really going to shout at an old woman?*" Idalia asked herself. It took only recalling a bit of the day prior to get Idalia to pound on the door. She had never felt this way before. In a way, it was exhilarating, even if she didn't like the negativity. The suspense tapered off after a minute of waiting for Baba.

"*I forgot she moves slowly*" Idalia thought, kicking at the dirt to pass the time.

The door swung open and Idalia was met face to face with Baba once more. She opened her mouth and pointed her finger at Baba viciously. Unfortunately, Baba was the faster draw in this shoot-out.

"Took you long enough, layabout. I was starting to wonder if you were even coming back, though I guess it wouldn't surprise me."

Idalia stood there blankly, finger still pointing. No words would come to her. Baba started wobbling back inside, leaving the door open.

"Hurry it up missy! Standing there with the door open. Children these days, so rude!" Baba called from the hallway.

Idalia sighed and entered the filthy home anew.

"What have I gotten myself into?"

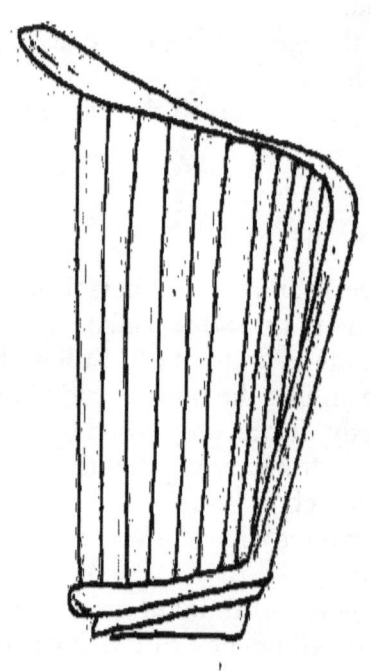

The Performance

1

Idalia deftly dodged a projectile.

"That was close. A little closer and I would have been a goner!" Idalia thought, refocusing on the situation at hand. It was tense. Never before had Idalia been in such a high-stakes situation, including the time facing off with the Shaa'Ra in the cave with Ivivin and her sister.

"One little mistake is all it'll take." Idalia thought nervously.

She knew she shouldn't—that she couldn't afford to divert her attention, but curiosity overwhelmed her as she looked to the object that had nearly made its mark. Before she could process the sight, though, she was alarmed by the sound of shouting. Idalia snapped back to attention, but it was too late. Another, nearly identical weapon had been flung at her and made contact square with her nose, knocking her over.

"Such a worthless girl! Can't play this simple progression. We musta been working on it for days now!" Baba raspily scolded.

As she nursed her nose, Idalia looked at what the old woman had decided to lob at her this time. In front of her sat an old muddy boot. Idalia felt her face and wiped away the lingering mud that had been transferred during impact.

She was seething.

"I'll show you a progression, you homely old hag." Idalia thought as she ferociously plucked away at the harp strings.

2

The harp lessons Idalia had been taking with Baba had been...alright. Baba was talented, but Idalia sometimes questioned her efficacy as a teacher. Still, Idalia could feel herself improving, even if Idalia had to serve as maid and mule to the woman to get lessons at all. Undoubtedly, Idalia found the sound of the harp lovely. She hadn't been able to replicate the mastery, in any sense, that Baba had, but she even found her own music pleasant now, if simple. However, Baba would not tolerate Idalia singing while playing. She insisted that only talentless hacks needed to supplement the delicate strings of the harp with their voice and that she would not teach a talentless hack. Idalia was grateful, if only just, for the lessons. But she wanted to learn the lute or some other, more casual instrument, like that played by tavern-musicians. Sure, it was less elegant, but it seemed so sincere and freeing. She couldn't very well take Baba's harp into a bar—it just wasn't practical.

After some time learning from Baba, Idalia found herself returning to the tavern. This time, though, she outright refused to drink. Each time she went, she was on a mission and having a mission gave her the focus and willpower she needed to resist the call of the brew. Instead, she was there to study and learn. Anytime there was a performer, Idalia would go scope them out and gather what she could from watching them. If they seemed friendly, Idalia would even ask them to show her their instruments or even if she could play with them a bit. She would never sing, though. Idalia had promised herself that the next time she sang, it would be her own sounds supporting her words. Idalia found the lutes and other guitars that passed through to give her the freedom and sincerity she sought.

Two things kept her returning to Baba's for lessons, then. The first was that Idalia didn't own an instrument of her own; harp, lute, or otherwise. The second was enigmatic. Baba had never repeated the caliber of performance she had shown Idalia on her first day. While it was true that Idalia felt the guitar-style instruments allowed her more expression and freedom, what Baba had shown her on the harp surpassed any expression that Idalia had ever encountered in any medium. It was more poignant and emotional than pained tears and it was fiercer than a battle between bitter rivals. Idalia was not sure if she could achieve such things herself, but even just the possibility of hearing Baba play that way again was more than reason enough for Idalia to continue to subject herself to Baba's harsh tutelage.

3

So, Idalia kept up with her lessons. Most days, she was tempted to quit and just go grab a drink, but she kept with it. Days that art and improvement couldn't motivate her, spite for the old woman did. Of course, Baba was quite old and frail, despite her lively mouth. Even so, Idalia was surprised when Baba turned Idalia away from lessons one day as she was feeling poorly. Idalia returned home, listless and unsure what to do with herself. So, she made soup.

And she brought it to Baba. Rather than making the old, sick woman get up, Idalia let herself in. Baba was feverish and pale. Idalia sat by her side and helped feed her soup, all while enduring the usual gauntlet of petty insults and slights.

The next day, Baba felt up to a lesson, though she still seemed sick. Nonetheless, it was silent law that neither of them would talk about the subject. It would become a pattern, as Baba began to get sick more often and stay sick longer. Idalia found herself worried about the old woman, though that worry was forcibly dissipated with each item hurdled at her. Idalia was no fool, despite Baba's insistence that she was. It did not seem like Baba had much time left in the world.

4

One fine afternoon, Idalia was enduring the barrage of criticism that came after each lesson when Baba started a long and brutal coughing fit. Idalia had to throw herself under the woman to keep her from striking the floor. It was only a moment, but Idalia and Baba met eyes and exchanged a knowing. When the fit subsided, Baba wiped moved her hand from her mouth and looked at it.

Blood.

Idalia saw the scarlet stain and rose, presumably to get the physician. Baba grabbed Idalia's sleeve to stop her, though her grip was weaker than ever before.

"Stupid girl, those quacks can't cure ham, let alone the inescapable passage of time. Unless you're as dumb as you look, you know just as well as I do that this is it." Baba insulted Idalia as casually as she always had.

Idalia wasn't sure why she decided now was the time to retort, but it felt right.

"I suppose spite has kept you alive for so long already. Shame it couldn't do anything for your looks, though." Idalia said, covering her mouth after realizing what she had said to the woman.

Baba smiled perhaps the most genuine smile Idalia had ever seen.

"Oh, look, the prude has some fight in her, after all. So strong, reaming an old woman with one foot already in the grave. Your mother must be so proud." Baba retorted.

"Oh, you were a woman? You hide it well. I would have never guessed." Idalia countered.

The two kept at it for quite some time before another coughing fit grounded them both.

"Alright, I suppose I owe you a treat for dying in front of you. Probably not how you wanted to spend your day, after all. Here, help me to the harp." Baba ordered.

Idalia was unsure whether to comply and sat there a moment contemplating whether or not she should actually fetch a physician after all. A wooden spoon to the jaw was enough to get her to help Baba walk over to the harp.

She leaned on it and it supported her, as it always had. The moment that Baba held the instrument, her posture improved and she seemed strong and lively. She sighed in preparation before placing her fingers on the strings. Baba played, each strum producing a rich sound soaked in emotion. She played the same song she played the day Idalia had met her. Idalia fell easily under Baba's spell and marveled at this woman who, just moments ago, was at death's door but was now filling the room with passionate notes. Baba built the song up and up and up, as she had done before and, this time, granted Idalia the climax and resolution. The fierce, upbeat song slowed and the fiery passion cooled into sorrowful and heavy notes. Baba brought the song to its conclusion, playing the notes more and more softly until they became one with silence.

Baba looked onwards, past Idalia, as if to receive the applause of a whole kingdom and smiled, sweaty, before falling to her knees. Idalia rushed over and carried the woman to her instructor's chair.

"That was incredible, Baba." Idalia said, wiping the tears invoked by the music from her eyes. Her effort was fruitless, though, as fresh tears at the feebleness of her instructor spilled from her eyes.

"Of course it was. I composed it myself, after all..." Baba started before seeing the rivers on Idalia's face.

"Oh, dear, look at this sissy here. You act like you've never seen anyone die before. Well, if you insist on disappointing me to the bitter end, then you might as well hop on the harp. Your final lesson, Idalia. Play yourself for me."

408

Idalia was unsure what Baba meant, but approached the harp, trembling. When her hands touched the strings, though, they steadied. She looked at Baba, slumped in her chair.

"Get on with it!" Baba tried to yell.

Idalia made music. She didn't have a plan. She closed her eyes and allowed emotion to guide her fingers. It was clumsy and she made more than a few mistakes, but she played on undeterred. Idalia put her whole body and her whole heart into each note she played. Idalia concluded, exhausted both physically and emotionally. She looked to the chair that held her mentor. Baba was still as stone, but smiling.

Idalia's first song had become an elegy.

5

Baba had no next of kin and she didn't grow up in the area around the village. She was alone, in many ways, but Idalia made sure she would not be alone being put into the ground. She gathered as many that would come, leading to quite a respectable funeral. It was silent, though, with no one speaking on her behalf. Idalia had already said her goodbye in that room with that harp. She felt any words would only taint the experience. Idalia was surprised a few days later by a local official who alerted her that she had been left Baba's estate. Idalia was given a note, written by Baba herself, that explained the decision.

If you are reading this, then congrats! I didn't think you could read. By now I am taking a big ol' dirt nap and you have been alerted that you are now in charge of all my junk. I was going to leave it all to a lame mule, but figured you were worse off. In any case, if I didn't leave it to somebody, it would go to the king and I'll be damned if I let that moron have any of it. I'll never forgive him for forcing me to retire. In any case, all my stuff is your problem now, Idalia, though I have some stipulations. Just two, because I know you can't count any higher than that. Firstly, you can do whatever you want with any of it—pawn it for booze, hit your mother upside the head—I don't care, just as long as the royal family gets none of it. I am bringing this grudge to the grave and beyond. Secondly, before you do anything with the harp, I want you to play it

once more and sing behind it. After that, you can leave it in a ditch
for all I care. I think that is simple enough that even a buffoon could
figure it out. So, if you are struggling, ask your mother—she *might*
be able to help.
  —*Baba*

Idalia was almost infuriated by the note.
"Damn old woman, always has to have the last word."
Idalia went and obliged the woman's last request of her. She
dragged the harp out to the graveyard—a feat that took nearly half
the day itself—and sung to Baba the lullaby that Elara had sung to
her when they were children.
Idalia would have the last word.

6

Going through Baba's belongings was...challenging. Idalia
had been cleaning nearly every time she went to the old woman's
house, but it was still a cluttered disaster. Idalia had asked her
mother what she should do with it all, but her mother refused to
sway her one way or another. The only thing that Idalia knew what
to do with was the harp, which now crowded Idalia's own room.
However, something did catch her attention in the practice room.
The workbench and materials. Idalia yearned to play a lute, but knew
that she would never be able to replicate what she had done the night
Baba passed on such an instrument. The harp was too constraining,
though, and, in truth, she doubted that she could master it as Baba
had. But the workshop, it inspired her. Baba had made that harp
herself. It itself was an expression of self, the sort of thing Idalia
wanted to learn music for. So, Idalia resolved to make her own
instrument.
Idalia did her due diligence in researching the craft. She
knew she would not be able to become a master luthier by books and
tinkering. But she didn't need to or even want to master the craft.
She just wanted to be able to express herself, just this once, in this
way. Many of the materials were already in Baba's workshop and
Idalia used them graciously. But other materials required some
doing. Particularly, making strings was difficult and took a long
time. She used the fibres in animal intestines to prepare catgut
strings, but she had to do it gradually, as animals were not

slaughtered here frequently. She happened upon two carcasses that made her giddy, though. An old bear that ceded its life to age and a young buck that had gotten away from a hunter but later succumbed to its wounds. These, as well as more traditional fibres, served as the strings for her instrument. For things she could not scavenge, Idalia worked for. She resumed her job at the tavern, so focused on her goal that she fought temptation well.

After what seemed like a lifetime of preparation, Idalia had finished her instrument. With all the musicians she watched and in all the books she read, she had never seen an instrument quite like it. It was part-lute and part-harp—a harplute. There was a fretted neck for the lute strings that arched and provided an anchor for the harp strings. Idalia strung her creation, six on the board and six suspended, and plucked at the strings. They were imperfect, as was the construction of the instrument; Idalia didn't need to be an expert to know that.

But, it was hers. She had never been prouder.

7

One of the first things Idalia did after completing her instrument was to play it for Baba. Idalia was sure that the old woman would have torn her instrument to shreds, but imagining how such a scene would play out brought a smile to Idalia's face. But now, it was time for Idalia to test herself. She had arranged to play a show, alone, in the tavern this night. She was nervous and anxious. She had never really performed and being in the tavern made her uneasy. However, she was also more excited than she had been for anything in a long time. She wanted to wrench her emotions out and express herself in a way that she could only with music.

When it was time, Idalia took to the corner of this tiny little bar. She had played a song full of mourning for Baba, when she passed. But she saw this place, cozy and full of friendly faces, and she did not want to sully the mood. Rather, she sought to enhance the positive aspects she found here, despite the negative. So, she played a song that was warm and fond. She thought of her sister and of her mother and the love they shared for one another and used that as a scaffold for her expression. It was a flawed performance—

more than once Idalia struggled to make her instrument bend to her will. But Idalia played passionately and captured the ears of the patrons nonetheless.

When she finished, she was met with applause, which wasn't something Idalia had even considered. She was happy and content with just the feeling of having expressed herself so wholly.

But the applause was nice, too.

8

As days passed, Idalia still knew not what to do with Baba's estate. She had finished her harplute, so she really did not have need of Baba's workshop. But she also had no reason to sell it—her family got by just fine, if frugally. Selling her things just for money they didn't need seemed wrong. Luckily, Idalia would receive a call to action in the form a delivery, brought to her mother by a foreign man bearing a book, a stone, and an assortment of letters. While her mother read her letter, Idalia inspected the stone. It reminded her of a much smaller Tear of Jupiter, which had her quite worried for her sister. When Idalia held the stone in her hand, she felt it become warm, but never hot. It was comforting, frankly. When her mother had finished reading, she handed Idalia a letter addressed to her.

"It's from Ivivin." said the seer-mother.

Idalia read the letter. She was shocked by the contents. Ivivin had apparently found the existence of other tears which, while not inherently dangerous, could be corrupted in the wrong hands. Furthermore, Ivivin had detailed how he had gotten sick from his latest excursion. He said that it was invariably fatal, but that he was still going to pursue his goal nonetheless. Idalia's letter ended with a fond recollection of their time together and kind words about Idalia.

"There's one for Elara, too." Idalia's mother giggled. "Please, Idalia, hand me that stone. According to Ivivin, it is the tear of Ganymede. He sent some research from Olympia and the stone so that I might investigate. I suppose if he went through all the trouble, I should hop to!"

Idalia handed her mother the stone. Her mother's eyes rolled back a bit and she began to tremble slightly. After just a few seconds, she returned to herself, shaking off the fit. "I see..." the seer-woman said.

"Are you alright, mother?" Idalia had seen her mother have premonitions in the past, but this one seemed particularly intense.

"Yes, my darling daughter, I am fine. And I will be fine, too."

"What do you mean?" Idalia asked her mother.

"Well, Idalia, you are to leave this place and meet up with Elara and Ivivin at the castle."

"You saw me on a journey? And I go to the castle?" Idalia questioned excitedly.

"Yes, and so much more too. So, go. It will take you some time to get there, but I know you can do it. Head to the kingdom. It is time for you to start your adventure, too."

"But mother, what about you?" Idalia worried, with fresh memories of Baba's passing populating her mind.

"I said it already, I will be fine, my daughter. Fate calls you. I can sense that you have gotten a taste of something quite unique with your music. There is no better time to grow than the present."

Idalia searched her feelings for a moment. She didn't particularly want to travel or have some grand adventure, but she did want more people to hear her music. She had always considered that she would play at the tavern, sharing her music with those who passed through. But never had she considered being the one to pass through places... No, that was not quite right. She had considered it, but feared losing herself again. She could not deny that she was now infected with an itch to play for many people. She had wanted this from the beginning, but was too scared until now to aim for it.

"Alright then, mother. Can you help me prepare?"

"Of course, but first, take these." Idalia's mother said, handing her the stone, the book, and Elara's letter.

"Why do I need all of this?" Idalia asked, confused.

The old seer woman smiled slyly. "I wouldn't want to spoil the surprise."

1

"*It's strange,*" Ivivin mused "*even though she does nothing but poke fun at me while she's here, I can't help but look forward to her visits.*" Elara had returned to Smithton, having taught Ivivin very little. She came back not terribly long after. As luck would have it, though, Ivivin's mother went into labour just minutes after her arrival. A tired Lili reluctantly aided Elara in fetching a midwife. For the rest of Elara's visit, they did little other than dote on the baby. She only taught Ivivin how to properly grind materials before leaving once more. Luckily, Lili was a strong and swift horse. The other visits had not been more fruitful in teaching Ivivin much of anything either. When Elara would arrive, they'd always get sidetracked in deep conversation, silly escapades, and practice of the swordplay or dance variety. Still, even though Ivivin learned little when she came, he didn't really mind. He figured it just meant she'd have to come again soon. His feelings for Elara were still quite strong and growing stronger still, but he had decided not to tell Elara how he felt. Not out of cowardice or a misguided sense of protection, but because he realized that he just enjoyed spending time with her. He was happy just to spend some time at her side and their relationship was theirs alone—there was no need to put pressure on himself or on her by trying to put labels on it. He was in love with her, sure, but she was also his closest friend.

Ivivin was happy to be able to help his family as his new sister slowly grew. They had named her Ivyiani—another silly name, in Ivivin's opinion. But he had a unique satisfaction and pride in being able to contribute to his family. Between the skills learned as a child on the farm and those he learned with Smith, he was quite the handyman. He would sometimes go into Gemi and do a day's forging there with the local smith, who was more than happy to have Ivivin's skill at his side. And he was paid quite well for his quality work.

Still, as Ivyiani grew and his mother recovered, Ivivin began to find home cramped again. Home was cozy, but home was also constraining. He entertained the idea of leaving home once more, but knew he should discuss it with Elara first; she was his apothecary, after all. So, he did not allow himself to make any firm plans about the future and just carried on, eagerly awaiting Elara's next visit.

2

One evening, Elara arrived at Ivivin's home, tired and worn from the journey. Ivivin was eager to talk about the future with her, but could see the weariness in her face.

"Elara, why don't you take my bed tonight?" Ivivin offered, though he expected her to decline as usual.

"I'll take you up on that, thank you." Elara answered, surprising Ivivin. "I'll be headed there now, if you don't mind."

"Yeah, of course. I'm glad you made it here safe." Ivivin added.

Elara stopped about halfway to Ivivin's room and looked back to him.

"It's good to see you, Ivivin. I was looking forward to coming. G'night."

"Good night, Elara. Rest well." Ivivin responded.

After Elara entered Ivivin's room, he felt a rush of blood to his head, accompanied by a slight giddiness. It was nothing special, but the small, tender words that Elara occasionally let slip made Ivivin illogically happy. He went outside, under the stars, and laid in his special spot with his special bird friend. He had considered proposing the idea of returning to Smithton to Elara. However, Ivivin knew that he had to spend his time wisely. He wanted to think carefully about what he wanted to do next. He thought about the things in his life that he regretted and things he might come to regret. He reflected on his past achievements and wondered if they were enough for the king. They didn't feel like enough to Ivivin, but, as he considered the issue with fresh perspective, guided by the most important things in his life, he decided that, to him, they were enough.

"I will go to Castletown to see the king. And I will ask Elara to come with me." Ivivin decided as the sun broke the horizon.

3

"You want to leave already?" Elara asked incredulously. "It hasn't even been all that long since you returned home."

"Yes, I know, but you know as well as I do that I don't have time to dally. I am happy to have visited home and happier still to have borne witness to the birth of my little sister. It's morbid, but at least I know my folks will have a child, even after I am gone." Ivivin replied.

"Are you going to stop taking your medicine? You are not trained well enough yet and I cannot make that trip to-and-fro as easily as this." Elara retorted.

"About that…" Ivivin looked pleadingly at her.

Elara saw his game.

"You want me to come with you, is that it?" Elara questioned.

"Only if you want to. Even though my fuse is particularly short, we all have limited time. I know you are busy with your apprenticeship, but your company means a great deal to me, so I figured I'd ask. And...if you tag along, I suppose that you might as well make me some medicine." Ivivin stated, only half-joking.

Elara thought long about this proposition. It was not something she had anticipated, after all.

"Can I ask you some things before I decide?" Elara inquired.

"Of course, Elara, you know you can ask me anything."

"How long will you be away?"

"I don't know."

"Will you stay there after?"

"I don't know."

"Will the king even grant you knighthood?"

"I don't know."

Elara was a little frustrated by Ivivin's responses, but did appreciate he was being frank with her. She was afraid he might try and sweet-talk her into joining him. The fact that he didn't made Elara much more willing to consider going.

"What will you do if he doesn't grant you knighthood?"

"I have thought much on what I am to present to the king. I am satisfied...no, I am happy with what I have decided. If the king rejects me, I will ask him why he is displeased. And, if he does not answer me in a way I find fulfilling, then I need not be a knight." Ivivin said resolutely.

Elara was shocked. To become a knight was Ivivin's long-time goal. It was what inspired him to leave home. To hear that he was so willing to give it up so easy alarmed Elara. She could sense there was more to this decision, but couldn't figure out what it was.

"Ivivin, there's no need to give up on your dream if you fail. Even if you don't get it this time, I know you could do it— Crumbleheart be damned." Elara said encouragingly.

Elara's words touched Ivivin, even if they were off the mark. Still, they were potent enough to make him blush.

"It's not about Crumbleheart, Elara. I just know that there are other ways for me to be happy. Places I can see and people I can see them with. It's true that my dream is to become a knight, but there are things I will not give up for that dream. I've come to hold them dearer to me than some title. Still...I know I will regret it forever if I do not at least try." Ivivin opened up.

Elara sighed. Ivivin's words reminded her so much of Elisabeth from Grandia's book. It was almost sweet.

"Fine, I suppose it's settled then. I shall return to Smithton to alert Minerva that I will be gone a while. I will prepare and, on my next venture here, we shall depart, together." Elara planned.

"Why don't I come back to Smithton with you and we can go from there?" Ivivin proposed, not thinking twice about it.

"Silly boy. Stay here with your family a while longer. They've missed you, you know." Elara ordered.

Ivivin knew she was right. He had just gotten so excited to travel with her once more that he got swept up in the moment.

"You're right. Thanks, Elara. You're always keeping me in line. I'll have to repay the favour someday."

Elara thought of how far she had come. She struggled, still, with many things. But each day she grew more comfortable around Ivivin and it translated to being a bit more comfortable and open with everyone. She thought of the satisfaction she got from her work and the kindness she was treated with in his home. She thought of all the nights under the stars, all the fireside dancing (if you could call it that), all the lazy days, and all the conversations. Things weren't perfect, sure, and she was still hurting. Not Ivivin, nor Minerva, nor anyone else could heal her. It was up to her and her alone. Still, it helped to have them around, so confident that she was worth healing.

"You already have."

4

Elara left. She didn't linger or meander about like she usually did, nor did she show Ivivin more techniques. Not that it mattered too much—Elara was not the best instructor to begin with. The pair got distracted easily by more fun things. Even when Elara buckled down to show Ivivin things, he found it hard to focus on the task at hand while she was around. If Ivivin was concerned about learning in a timely matter, he might be better off studying on his own. But, he liked the time they spent together, so he never felt compelled in the slightest to object or complain.

Elara was surprised at herself. She never imagined she would so easily agree to leave Minerva's side—permanent or not. She found herself thinking of the time Ivivin and her had travelled to Gemi together and was struck with bouts of giddiness when she imagined travelling together once more. She also felt strangely guilty, though. It took her nearly the whole trip to realize why. Travelling with Ivivin was fun. And, somewhere in her mind, she still did not believe she deserved to do something simply because it was fun. Elara found it curious, though. The act of realizing why she felt the way she felt itself eased that feeling.

Elara found herself telling Minerva her plans excitedly, rather than guiltily.

5

Although it was an incredibly fast turnaround (much to Lili's displeasure), both Elara and Ivivin felt it took ages for Elara to return. Ivivin had told his parents of his plan to see the king in Castletown. It was not hard for Ivivin to see conflicting nature of feelings. On one hand, they still wanted Ivivin to flourish and seek his goals, just as they did when they first encouraged him to set forth from home. On the other hand, though, the threat to their child's life was no longer vague and nebulous. It had a face and a name and it worried them. It took some convincing and reassurance, but Ivivin managed to help his parents find peace with the ordeal and, in doing so, he had come closer to finding peace with it himself. Talking to his parents so seriously and as equals made Ivivin feel incredibly grown-up. It was an incredibly unique and alien sensation, to know that your relationship with people you had known all your whole life had changed markedly in such a short period of time. Ivivin was happy, though, at his growth. And that growth had not gone unnoticed by his parents, who, though unsure how to fully express it, were incredibly proud of their son. Ivivin and his family spent their days together more relaxed and in more fulfilling manners than ever before. He couldn't help but feel grateful for Elara's insistence that he stay—his departure would have been rushed and he would not have gotten this quality time with these people, his family, who he loved very dearly.

Of course, Elara did return, being the reliable and daring young woman she was. She insisted that she rest a week or so, as the trip had taken a lot out of her. She did so with an ulterior motive, though. A few, actually. She wanted to give Ivivin as much time with them as possible and to make sure he really wanted to leave. More selfishly, though, when she visited Ivivin and his family, she felt like she was home.

Well, not quite.

She felt like this is what home *could have been*. She loved her sister and her mother dearly and with all her heart. But, still, Elara could not remember her birth parents. It was hard to be here and not imagine the way her childhood could have been. She knew she was stronger for the struggle. She trained hard and served as a protector of her little village. She grew fierce and moral and brave. But her fierceness and morality and braveness were the same things that led her into great hardship. If she had grown up in a home like this one, would she be happier? Would she still pain and ache as she did? Such things were not worth considering—Elara knew this, yet she did it anyways. Still, despite less-than-pleasant thoughts it sometimes brought her, Elara felt like the time she spent here, with these people and in this house, was giving her the childhood she never had. She wanted to take in as much of it as she could, even if that made her selfish. She was sure she would tell Ivivin, someday.

There was, of course, one guilty pleasure Elara never wanted Ivivin to find out about. While Ivivin worked the land or helped at the forge in Gemi, Elara would spend time with Ivyiani. Specifically, she would offer to help Vivian put her down for naps. She would lay the baby in the crib and look at her, innocent and untainted by the hardships of the world. And Elara would sing to her. She would sing the same song, a gentle lullaby, that she had sung to Idalia when they were young. Sometimes, she'd even use the music of her stone to support her words. Elara was embarrassed by her own mediocre voice. Her sister was a much better singer than her. But she liked it and liked lulling this child to sleep.

So, she sang. This visit was no different—Elara brought Ivyiani to her crib and tucked her in. She put on the music of the stone and began to sing. This time, though, Ivivin had returned to the house early as he had forgotten something in his pack. As he walked by, he heard singing. It was not the most beautiful or most elegant singing Ivivin had ever heard, but he was drawn to it nonetheless. He stood there, on the other side of the wall, listening to Elara sing her gentle lullaby. It was magic to Ivivin and he tried to figure out why. After a while, it came to him.

"She may not be able to sing, but she sure has soul." Ivivin thought, listening with eyes closed and an earnest smile.

When the music stopped and he could hear Elara shuffling from within, Ivivin spirited himself from the house, counting himself lucky to have heard such a treat. It had been a while since his heart had beat so fast.

6

Inevitably, the time for Ivivin and Elara to depart came. They didn't really have a plan on which day they were going to leave. Rather, one day, over breakfast, they made eye contact and they both knew the other was ready. Of course, they didn't just book it then and there. Ivivin told his parents he would be setting out and they insisted they both wait until the afternoon. Vivian and Ivan both scrambled about trying to prepare. When they finished, Vivian handed her son his favourite dish from home—the same salted fish she had prepared for him when he left home the first time. Likewise, Ivan had made sweetbread for Ivivin and handed him the loaf. The gifts meant just as much this time as they had meant when Ivivin had first left home. Tears came to his eyes.

Elara watched the scene from the sidelines. It was a tender moment, sweet and warm. She was happy for Ivivin and his family and their bittersweet moment. But, at the same time, she was reminded again of the childhood that was taken from her and the thought caused her chest to tighten and ache.

"How childish of me." Elara thought, staving off her own tears. *"I am actually envious."*

Elara almost left the room to compose herself when Vivian walked over and pulled Elara from the sidelines right onto the main stage. There, Ivan handed Elara a bottle full of stew.

"Here, I could see how much you enjoyed this, so I made you some for tonight. It won't keep, sadly, but I figure you wouldn't refuse it for dinner tonight." Ivan said told Elara gently.

Elara was dumbfounded. Ivan was right—the stew that he made was by far Elara's favourite meal she had eaten here, but she had never come out and said it to anyone. He noticed on his own. Elara was even closer to tears than she had been just moments before. Of course, that meant that Vivian turned to Elara and offered her a pouch. Elara opened it slowly and saw it was filled to the brim with blueberries.

"Our son doesn't much care for berries, but I saw you eying them that day we went to Gemi together. We were in a hurry and couldn't stop then, but I took note and promised myself I'd get you some next time I had a chance." Vivian said.

Vivian and Ivan stood side by side, with their arms across each other's back.

"I know it's not much, Elara, sorry. But we wanted to send the both of you off properly." Vivian said.

"You're welcome here anytime, both of you." Ivan added, his face already covered in blubbery tears and his nose oozing.

Elara looked at the pair and at Ivivin. The floodgates gave way and Elara began sobbing, loud and ungracefully.

"Di-did we do something wrong?" Vivian panicked, rushing to Elara's side.

"How long has it been since I cried such happy tears?" Elara thought, letting her emotions surface. She was embarrassed that she was crying like a child, but she was happy to feel just a bit like one, just this once.

And so, Ivivin and Elara set forth on another journey together. This time, though, the journey was a little bit different. On their last trip, they were covering ground that Ivivin was at least somewhat familiar with—they were going to his house, after all. On this trip, however, they were going somewhere completely novel. Neither of them had been to Castletown and neither of them had been further west than they currently were. It was nerve-wracking at first, but as Elara and Ivivin discussed it, nerves turned to excitement as they got to do something entirely new together for the first time. When they looked at the map, they were surprised to find that the distance from Gemi to Smithton was not so different from the distance from Gemi to Castletown. They also came to know Castletown's true name, though no one used it. Jura was, formally, the location they were headed. There was only one small town, Kayon, directly on their route, so that was their first destination.

Ivivin had built this trip up in his head again and again over the course of his long journey. He imagined being confident and resolute, flourishing a full suite of legendary armour while riding an obedient and gallant steed across the country side. He imagined it being an epic and exciting journey, fraught with trouble and obstacles. Instead, he felt very much himself, in armour he made himself. He was having trouble getting 'his' steed to carry any of his things, let alone him. In fact, he was acting as steed to a small, dirty, flightless, and patchy bird.

Their trip to Kayon was normal and unexceptional—there were no grand battles nor majestic sights. Just average days passed with a close friend, a sky-rodent, and a sassy horse. And Ivivin wouldn't have had it any other way.

8

The group arrived in Kayon without incident. Ivivin had become accustomed to beds during his stay at home, so he was yearning to stay at an inn. He and Elara entertained the idea of splitting up for a day, as they had done before. But they decided there was no need—if they wanted alone time, all they needed to do was go indulge in it. They both rented rooms in an inn above the tavern. They usually avoided such inns if they could—the happenings in the tavern often kept them awake later than they wanted to be. However, this time, they both wanted to let loose a little in the tavern. Elara, not wanting to have to carry a useless Ivivin across town after a night of drinking, insisted they stay in these rooms.

"At worst, I'll just have to bring him upstairs." She thought.

They spent the day wandering the town, splitting up and joining together seamlessly and without much concern. When they returned to the tavern to get a meal and start their festivities, Ivivin carried with him flowers—yellow daffodils of sorts. Elara thought for a moment that he might have gotten them for her.

"Did you get those for me?" Elara asked, half-teasingly and half-suspiciously.

"N-no!" Ivivin stammered. "They're for me. A treat of sorts. You know how I love these little yellow flowers."

Elara laughed. Ivivin did like his flowers, sure enough. He always gave them lingering glances in the field and while they travelled.

"Ok, ok. Calm down." Elara said.

"I'm just going to put these upstairs, did you want me to put your things in your room?" Ivivin offered.

Elara nodded and handed Ivivin her key and bag.

"Get us a killer seat, then! After all, we aren't leaving until we are good and drunk!" Ivivin said, headed towards the stairs.

"So, a few minutes for you, then? Might as well just bring one drink up to your room with you—that's all it'll take!" Elara teased as Ivivin shook his head and walked out of sight.

Elara got them a seat and Ivivin joined her not long after, returning her key and joining her at the table. The pair enjoyed their meal (with Ivivin taking a short break to go upstairs and feed Icarus who, for inexplicable and unjustifiable reasons, was not welcome in the tavern proper). And then they got to drinking. Elara helped pace Ivivin and the two enjoyed a wonderful night. Elara talked to strangers jovially—men and women alike. The spirits encouraged her and Ivivin being there made her feel safer, somehow.

Of course, not all the patrons were good-spirited and good-natured. At one point, Elara was tipsily dancing, with a fiddler playing behind her. She lost her balance and knocked into two men carrying their food and brew. Naturally, they dropped their things and were upset. Elara immediately offered to replace the items and even buy their drinks for the remainder of night, but they were not having it. One of the men angrily grabbed Elara's arm. Upon looking the man in the eyes, her chest instantly clenched and breathing became nearly impossible.

"Damn it!" Elara thought, upset that she was succumbing to these feelings once more. *"I know I can take him, no problem, so why am I so scared just because he grabbed me!"*

Before Elara could think further, though, the man grabbing her released his grip and was stumbling backwards.

Ivivin had thrown a sloppy, drunken haymaker at the man.

9

Ivivin was now engaged in his first ever bar fight—his parents would be so proud! Luckily, the two irate men were nearly as drunk as Ivivin was and not nearly half as well-traveled. Elara saw this gap in skill and decided to compose herself, let Ivivin handle it, and go explain to the owner what had happened so that he didn't get kicked out.

Ivivin's punch had bought him time with the first man, but the second one wasted no time in backing up his bar buddy. Ivivin felt as if the portly man was moving in slow motion. As he dodged the man's wild punches, he couldn't help but think of how easy it was to avoid these in comparison to Elara's strikes. He was so amazed by this, in fact, that he carried on with it a bit too long. The other man rejoined the tussle and avoiding blows became much harder for Ivivin. The man he had nailed previously got behind Ivivin and tried to choke him. Ivivin tossed the man over his shoulder and onto the floor, losing balance and hopping on one foot for a moment to recover. He turned to the other, portlier fellow confidently with his hands up, ready to throw a blow.

Just as Ivivin wound his strike, though, he felt a deep and sudden pain in his chest that stunned him. He lowered his guard and clawed at his chest, as if he wanted to tear out his own heart just to ease the suffering. The man still standing took the opportunity to grab the back of Ivivin's head with both hands and slam it into his knee. Blood spurt from Ivivin's nose as he fell to the floor. The pain in his chest had subsided into a dull ache, but he was now dazed from the knee to his face. He tried to regain a defensive position, but the man he had flipped had taken Ivivin's back and prevented him from guarding the other man's punches and kicks. Ivivin could feel his right eye swelling shut and blood trickling down his face.

Just as Ivivin was struggling to decide what to do next, Elara swept in and expertly dispatched the vagabonds. Luckily, the owner had seen what had happened and did not fault Elara or Ivivin for their actions—the men were known to get rowdy from time to time as it was. Elara had noticed, however brief it was, Ivivin gripping his chest. She wanted to ask him about it, but, even with his battered face, he insisted that the continue having a good time.

"I can ask him in the morning." reasoned Elara.

And, so, the pair continued their evening joyfully. Ivivin was gently teased by all the bystanders for Elara having to come save him. He just laughed it off, instead praising Elara's superb combative skills. Elara felt guilty—she knew Ivivin could have taken the pair if not for whatever happened to his chest. She knew she wouldn't be able to stop the teasing—that was just how patrons of this sort of establishment were apt behave. But she did truly feel grateful. If she noticed his chest pain, then Elara was certain that Ivivin only acted because he noticed her having an episode of her own.

"Well, even if I did have to come save your sorry arse," Elara joined in the teasing "at least you did something about it. These scallywags poking fun at you all just stood by and watched!"

The small group that had gravitated around the duo all broke into laughter, playfully teasing each other and timidly offering excuses for their own inaction. In all the guffawing, Elara looked at Ivivin and spoke sincerely.

"Thank you."

10

After Elara finished explaining to a dysfunctional and drunk Ivivin why he could not order drinks after last call, she helped the tipsy fellow to his feet.

"How did I know this night was going to end with me babysitting this lightweight?" Elara thought lightheartedly, still riding her own wondrous buzz.

Elara methodically assisted Ivivin up the stairs and towards his room.

"Where's your key?" Elara asked.

"In muh pockeets." Ivivin slurred.

"Turn them out for me, then!" Elara demanded.

Ivivin obeyed, turning his pockets out clumsily. Change scattered, but no key was in sight. Ivivin looked at the small pile of his pocket's contents intently.

"Huh? Where'd it go?" Ivivin said as if this was the world's most vexing conundrum.

"Come on lightweight, I'm tired. Where'd you really put your key!?" Elara pressed.

"I'm serious, I put it in muh pockeets!" Ivivin insisted. "But..."

"But what?" Elara prodded the drunk Ivivin.

"I don't remember feeling it in my pockets at all after the scuffle with those arseholes." Ivivin confessed.

"Do you think you lost it in the fight?" Elara inquired.

The fumbling Ivivin nodded guiltily.

"Sorrrr."

"It's ok. It's no big deal, you big lug. I'll put you down in my room and then I'll go look for the key downstairs. Worst comes to worst, I ask them to let me into your room for the night and we find the key later." Elara explained.

Ivivin was losing his senses more and more by the minute. A tired grunt was all that Elara got in response.

Elara leaned Ivivin against the wall.

"Stay." She commanded while getting her own key ready. She opened the door and entered to turn on her lantern. She hustled back and found Ivivin had slid to the floor. She sighed and drug the man-child into the room. She hoisted his limp body onto her bed. It reminded her of the time she had to do the same to get him onto Lili's back—just with considerably less blood this time. When Ivivin was finally positioned comfortably, she wiped the sweat from her brow and looked to the nightstand beside him. In a small vase were the flowers that Ivivin had earlier. By them was a hurriedly scratched note.

Sorry. I lied.
—Ivivin

Elara couldn't help but laugh. He really was a terrible liar. She looked to Ivivin. His face was bloodied and swollen, but he was grinning in his sleep.

"So much for a knight! You look just like the troll from Grandia's book!" She told an unconscious Ivivin. She took one of the flowers from the vase and placed it gingerly behind one of Ivivin's ears.

"Thanks, my Oldman. Goodnight."

The Tasks

1

Ivivin woke at the Kayon inn a bit hungover. He inspected his surroundings while coming to his senses and panicked when he couldn't see Icarus or his things. When he saw the flowers in vase beside him, though, everything snapped into place.

This was Elara's room.

"Damn it…" Ivivin thought. *"I was trying to surprise Elara with flowers for when she woke up. How did I get here?"*

Ivivin struggled to recall the end of the previous night, but he was sure Elara had gotten him into bed safely. He touched his face and winced. He had almost forgotten the whooping he had, unfortunately, been on the receiving end of, but the sting and tenderness of his face was a stark reminder. And that reminder led to another—the horrible pain he had felt in his chest. It was brief, lasting only a few seconds, but it was truly painful. The thought worried Ivivin. He really wanted to see Elara to thank her and to talk to her about what happened the night before. He was sure she saw him reeling in pain, after all.

Ivivin poked his head out of Elara's room and looked next door to his own. On the door was a short note.

Gone to tend to Lili. Took Icarus with me. If you need any of your things, I explained the situation to the innkeeper and she'll let you into the room. I expect breakfast to be ordered and ready when I come back.

—Elara

P.S. Don't skimp on the meat, you bum!

Ivivin sighed deeply. This silly note had taken the wind right out of his worry's sail. Even though Ivivin felt a bit grimy and wanted to change clothes, he did not want to inconvenience the innkeeper.

"I can make it until after breakfast." Ivivin told himself as he stumbled down the stairs.

He sat in the tavern and the innkeeper came over. She was a tall and thin woman with a stern face, but kind eyes.

"Woah! You're looking a little worse for wear there, young man. I had forgotten about your skirmish last night." said the innkeeper.

"Is it that bad?" Ivivin asked, delicately touching his face once more.

"Oh, so-so. I wouldn't want to wake up next to you, but I am a little picky." the innkeeper teased.

Ivivin laughed at the joke.

"I must really be a sight to see, then!"

The woman shook her head. "So, are you ordering breakfast then?"

Ivivin nodded.

"Just for you, or will your ladylove be joining?" The innkeeper asked casually.

Ivivin got incredibly flustered. He stood for no reason and knocked about the cutlery and such laid before him.

"I...uh, I mean...she's not..." Ivivin struggled.

"She's not joining you?" The innkeeper tried to finish Ivivin's statement.

"No, I mean, yes! She will be back soon!" Ivivin managed, deciding it was too much effort to correct the woman.

"So, what'll you have, then?"

"Whatever's easiest for you to make." Ivivin responded.

"Oh, how considerate. It'll be right out, then." the innkeeper told Ivivin as she started to walk away.

Suddenly, Ivivin remembered something of dire importance.

"Wait!" Ivivin called.

The innkeeper turned around and faced Ivivin.

"What is it, young man?" she asked.

"Extra meat, please. Just on one." Ivivin added, reaching up and discovering the flower propped between his head and his ear. As he waited for Elara and for his meal, he rolled the flower between his finger and his thumb, smiling.

2

After a satisfying breakfast, Ivivin and Elara decided that they would leave around noon, giving them a short relaxing day of travel where they could sweat out all the poison lingering in their bodies. Over breakfast, it was obvious that both wanted to talk about

Ivivin's fit. But, the fact that they both wanted to talk about it relaxed them and neither of them brought it up until that afternoon while they were walking.

"What happened with those guys, Ivivin? I saw you clench your chest." Elara asked just outside of Kayon.

"I am not sure. It was just a lot of pain in my chest. It left as quickly as it came. I'm sure it has something to do with… you know." Ivivin said.

"Hmm, maybe we should up your dosage, just a little. Minerva warned me that medicine can be a bit fickle. If you get bigger, you'd need more, for instance." Elara proposed.

"You calling me fat?" Ivivin joked.

"Perhaps." Elara retorted. "But, seriously, there are other options too. You're the first person to take this medicine, after all. Minerva suspected that you might start to develop a resistance over time and need more and more. Another possibility is that you had something that messes with the medicine…maybe all the booze?" Elara offered.

"Whatever the case, I'll do whatever you think is best." Ivivin told Elara.

Elara found the response strange. Entrusting her with the decision was akin to trusting her with his life. And Ivivin did so very casually. Elara wasn't sure she deserved such trust, considering she had come close to ending his life before. Still, knowing that he trusted her like she trusted him was reassuring and heartwarming.

"For now, just keep an eye on it. Let me know if it happens again." Elara ordered.

"Yes, doctor." Ivivin said sarcastically. His tone was met with a firm punch to the arm.

3

Elara and Ivivin enjoyed their casual trip to Castletown. There was an incident with some boars that delayed them a smidge and Icarus had a fit of indigestion, but, other than that, they made steady progress. When they finally could see Castletown on the horizon, they both skipped about and celebrated their progress. Even if they had thoroughly enjoyed the trip, it was easy for them to both recognize that their achievement was meritorious. When they arrived in Castletown, though, they quickly realized how strange of a situation they had found themselves in. They were amidst what was arguably the busiest city on the continent, with the nearby Portington port town only adding fuel to the fire. They were in the middle of this grand city with no plan. Ivivin wasn't sure what he had expected, but he had never thought about how he'd go about getting an audience with the king. It wasn't as if he could just walk up to the castle, knock on the door, and ask for an audience. But he wasn't sure what other options he had. He turned to Elara to ask what she thought, but she seemed preoccupied inspecting Lili. In particular, she was looking at Lili's hooves.

"What's wrong?" Ivivin asked.

"Lili is a strong and capable horse, but I fear we've put too much stress on her as of late. Her hooves seem worn." Idalia stated.

"I see. Then let's see if there is a smithy around here. If I can convince them, I'd like to make her some horseshoes." said Ivivin.

"That's a great idea. We still need to figure out how we are going to get you to see the king, after all. This'll give us time to think." Elara remarked.

After a bit of asking around, Ivivin and Elara received instruction on how to get to the closest smithy. They left Lili in the stables and assured her that they would return soon with something to aid her irritated feet.

When Ivivin approached the smithy, he immediately noticed the quality of the armours on display there. In many ways, they resembled Smith's style. Elara wandered about, casually looking at varied contents of the shop that headed the forge proper. But Ivivin was transfixed at the quality of the armour. The sword that Smith made for him was a true piece of art, but any of these armours could be in contention for the title of most well-made piece Ivivin had ever seen. After a few moments, the hammering in the back slowed to a stop and an extremely tall man emerged from the back. He had long hair, tied in the back, and a braided beard. He struck Ivivin as being incredibly serious.

"Be frank with me, young ones, and do not waste my time. Do you intend to purchase anything today or may I go back to work?" the smith said.

"Actually, I was hoping that I might purchase some materials and use a small space in your forge. Our horse is in need of horseshoes and it would be easier for me to do it than for me to get a mold to size her." Ivivin returned the man's directness.

The man huffed. "Fine by me, as long as you don't linger any longer than you need."

Ivivin nodded and followed the man back to the forge. While Ivivin gathered the materials he needed, the owner already resumed his own work. Ivivin was distracted by the man's strokes and techniques. There was something both familiar and foreign about them. It was uncanny and it made it hard for Ivivin to focus on the task at hand. Moreover, it seemed as if the dry fellow sparked to life more and more with each strike of his hammer. Just as Ivivin was about to make his own first strike, it came to him.

"Helmschmied!?" Ivivin asked abruptly.

The smith almost missed his mark, but looked to Ivivin surprised.

"Yes? What is it young man? I'd appreciate it if you didn't interrupt me further. I almost errored because of your outburst."

"Sorry, sorry, just a second..." Ivivin responded, scrambling to pull the chain bearing the ring Smith had given him out from his shirt. He walked over and showed the man the ring.

"Oh? This is truly a surprise. Smith took another apprentice after his son, then?" Helmschmied flatly responded.

"Yes, I just recently completed my own apprenticeship. He had told me about you. The way you smith and the quality of your armour...I figured it had to be you!" Ivivin said, excited to meet this man who knew his mentor.

Helmschmied nodded. "That follows."

Ivivin didn't know what to say next. It was just as Smith had said. Helmschmied was talented, but serious. It was only in his work that his passion manifested.

"May I watch you work a while?" Ivivin blurted.

"Normally, I would refuse. But seeing as how you, too, studied under Smith, I suppose there is no risk in it." Helmschmied agreed.

Ivivin ran back to the front of the store, where Elara was still perusing the wares and explained the situation. Elara nodded and told Ivivin she understood, but did not want to wait about the smithy all day and set off to explore the city on her own, promising to return before sunset.

Excitedly, Ivivin returned to watch Helmschmied shape a beautiful helmet. It was more emotional than Smith's method. If Smith could produce pieces of art, then Helmschmied was able to make an art of smithing. The day flew by as Ivivin observed this master of the craft. It was not until he heard Elara calling from the front that he remembered that he had work to do, too. He hurriedly assembled his materials once more and set to work. To his surprise, Helmschmied stopped what he was doing and watched Ivivin work. While it was bit unnerving to have him there, Ivivin was most comfortable with these sorts of tasks, so he managed to complete it as swiftly and deftly as always.

"Incredible." Helmschmied commented.

"Huh?" Ivivin shook his head in disbelief.

"I have seen many smiths with many talents." Helmschmied explained "There are those who specialize in polearms, in swords, in armour, and much more. But you are the first one I've seen to wield such skill with a simple horseshoe, though I suppose Smith comes close. It exceeds even my own talent."

Ivivin felt himself blush. It didn't feel like anything special, but, then again, while he worked under Smith, he only rarely focused on armour or weapons. Instead, he made tools and other necessities. Now that Ivivin thought on it, Smith had complimented him in much the same way the day he completed his apprenticeship. Ivivin felt a renewed pride in himself.

"Thank you, Helmschmied. It means the world to hear that from you." Ivivin said.

"Thank me not, young man—I only speak the truth. Instead, tell me your name." Helmschmied responded in his typical, serious tone.

"My name is Ivivin."

"And what brings you to Castletown, Ivivin? I need not a partner—I have my hands full with apprentices as it is."

"No, it is nothing like that, Helmschmied. Where are your apprentices? I saw no one else here all day."

"I have two forges, you see. This is my personal forge, but, as I am sure you know, I serve as Smith to the king. I have a forge within the castle's walls. At least once a week, I work here, away from it all. It was a condition of my hire, you see. I can't focus on my art with people constantly asking me questions. My apprentices are not allowed in this forge. It is my haven."

Ivivin nodded.

"You still have not told me what you are doing here in Castletown, Ivivin. It is rare for any to come here without business."

Ivivin was about to thoughtlessly repeat his speel about becoming a knight when he realized that Helmschmied might be able to help him with his issue.

"Helmschmied, I need to speak to the king! He gave me a task long ago and I have completed it. I wish to present him with the fruits, but I honestly have no clue about how to approach him. Can you help me get inside the castle grounds?"

"Yes, but for every task, a price, no? I will help you enter the castle grounds, but, in exchange, you must teach my apprentices for a week. They could use exposure to your style and I could use the break."

"Teach?" Ivivin thought, panicking. *"How am I going to teach them? I feel like I barely know it myself..."* Ivivin recalled that Elara had been teaching him, even though she herself was not a master of her craft. Her courage inspired him to accept, despite his worries.

"It's a deal." Ivivin said, reaching his hand to shake Helmschmied's.

"So it is. Return here at sunrise. I will take you then."

4

Just as Helmschmied had required, Ivivin and Elara returned to the forge the following morning. They walked in silence to the door leading beyond the large wall encapsulating the castle.

"How is he going to get us in?" Ivivin wondered.

Helmschmied knocked on the door, prompting a slit to slide open and revealing the eyes of a guard.

"State your business." the guard recited.

"I am Helmschmied, here to resume my post." Helmschmied responded.

"And them?" the guard followed up.

"This is it..." Ivivin thought anxiously.

"They wish to speak with the king." Helmschmied stated plainly.

"Oh, alrighty then. Come on in." The guard responded, opening the door for the trio.

'That's it?" Ivivin asked Helmschmied as they entered the grounds.

"Indeed. If you wish to see someone, isn't it typical to just knock at their door and see if they're home?" Helmschmied remarked.

5

Once inside the castle grounds, Ivivin was overwhelmed by how large the castle actually was up close. They followed Helmschmied to the forge, but he dismissed them once they arrived.

"I said only that I'd get you into the grounds, the rest is on you." Helmschmied told them.

Frustrated and feeling duped, Ivivin and Elara paced the grounds for a while, with Ivivin sporting a cranky Icarus on his shoulder. They had skipped breakfast to meet Helmschmied so early. However, as they walked around, they came to realize how elaborate and incredible the castle was. There were still many people on the castle grounds, no doubt various attendants of the king doing various tasks. Though Icarus occasionally solicited a second glance, they did not feel out of place. In fact, the walk became pleasant, as the walls were lined with ivy and flowerbeds adorned the grounds. There was a gentle breeze that inspired Icarus to leap from Ivivin's shoulder. He flapped about as hard as he could, but could not prevent himself from tumbling to the ground. It was, however, a little more fruitful than it had been. Ivivin scooped up Icarus from the floor.

"It's ok, buddy. I have an idea you might like. I'll pitch it to you later, ok? For now, let us go and see the king." Ivivin told the frustrated bird.

"That's right, if everything goes well, I will see the king today!"

Ivivin walked up to the front doors of the castle and, taking the lesson he learned from Helmschmied, knocked. A guard opened the door.

"Hello, my name is Ivivin and I am here to see the king." Ivivin announced confidently.

"Are you kidding me? You can't just knock on the door and expect to see the king!" The guard belittled Ivivin, who was now feeling incredibly embarrassed. The guard shut the door in Ivivin's face. Elara wasn't sure whether to laugh at or pity Ivivin. On one hand, it was incredibly funny, but, on the other hand, it was a setback to their purpose here.

She settled on laughing, after all.

She and Ivivin turned to leave the door and regroup when it opened again. A familiar voice called out to Ivivin, though he could not quite place where he had heard it.

"Ivivin, killer of nightmares and savior of Crosstown!" said the voice.

Ivivin turned to give form to the voice. Standing in the doorway was none other than The Free Knight, Miroslav.

6

"Miroslav!" Ivivin said, ecstatic to see that the one-armed knight that he had met more than once on his journey had returned to the castle safely.

"It really is you, young Ivivin! You've grown so much since I last saw you. Please, follow me, you and your guest both. We've been expecting you!" Miroslav exclaimed. The guard who had previously denied their entry was now taking their things for them.

"What do you mean you were expecting us?" Ivivin said as he and Elara followed Miroslav into the castle. Two things immediately caught their attention once in the castle.

Firstly, the entryway was gigantic and absolutely stunning, sporting the same sort of stone Ivivin had encountered in Olympia. And, secondly, in the middle of it all was Idalia, waving at the two of them.

"What the—?" Ivivin started before nearly being run over by Elara, who could not wait to give her sister a hug.

"I can see you are confused, lad." Miroslav consoled Ivivin. "To be frank, I am too. Come, I am sure she will explain everything."

Miroslav and Ivivin met up with the sisters. Idalia began to explain how she came to be in Castletown and in the castle itself, no less. She told them that Ivivin's delivery arrived and caused her and Elara's mother to have a vision. This vision involved Idalia meeting Elara and Ivivin both in the castle. So Idalia set forth, playing music at every town along the way. She didn't mention her struggles leading to it, but she described how she had learned music from Baba, the old minstrel of the king, and figured that the king might like to know of her passing. She approached the castle and entrusted a guard with the note Baba had left for her. The king saw the note and heartily vouched for its authenticity. Much to Idalia's surprise, though, he requested her presence and she obliged. They discussed Baba's death and the king even let Idalia play a song for him. Before she was escorted from the king's presence, she had mentioned how she knew Ivivin and wondered if he had made it to the castle yet. The king, shocked that she knew of Ivivin, allowed her to speak a while more. Idalia assured the king that Ivivin was on his way here and it would not be long before he arrived. The king responded by offering Idalia a place in the castle to rest and assigned Miroslav to accompany her during her stay, in addition to his regular duties.

It was an incredible story that hinged on incredible coincidence, but the three were just happy to see each other. They began casually chatting as if they had known each other all their lives in the middle of the king's castle. It was only when Miroslav cleared his throat that Ivivin and the sisters remembered where they were and the task at hand.

"Come, Ivivin and friends. I will bring you to the king. He is currently watching his children study under my successor—the new royal trainer. He will be happy to speak to you afterwards, I am sure, but let us go to him now."

"That's right...Miroslav lost his arm training the current king in the ways of the sword." Ivivin recounted. *"I wonder what his successor is like?"*

8

Ivivin and Elara followed Miroslav and Idalia down several long and winding passages in the castle. Ivivin occasionally caught sight of art adorning the walls and wanted to take his time admiring the works. Unfortunately, Miroslav would not be hindered from swiftly arriving at his goal and marched on, insisting that the others do their best to keep up. Sour, Ivivin made a note to explore the halls at his earliest leisure.

Miroslav approached a door, behind which the sound of metal striking metal could be heard.

"Alright, young ones. Behind this door is the combative lesson for the king's children. I ask that you all keep your silence until after the lesson concludes so that you do not distract the young masters. We wouldn't want any accidents." Miroslav whispered cheerfully, waggling the small stub that remained of his arm for emphasis. The trio nodded and Miroslav opened the door and led them into the room as quietly as possible. Inside were just four individuals. One was the king, dressed in regal attire with his focus entirely dedicated to observing the bout at hand. Two were children, one boy and one girl. They were, perhaps, twelve or so years old, by Ivivin's estimate. They were both skirmishing with the final figure— a small framed man who expertly deflected the advances of both children while correcting their form on the fly. The king and the children never let their glances stray from the instructor, but the instructor caught Ivivin's eyes for a moment and winked.

"Do I know that man?" Ivivin thought, struggling to recall ever meeting such a person on his travels. Unable to place the man, Ivivin settled for observing—perhaps he could pick up a trick or two as well! However, the longer he observed the man and his movements, the more he was convinced that he had met him somewhere. He just could not for the life of him remember where. When the lesson ended, the two children faced their instructor panting and bowed. While bowing, the children recited in unison:

"Thank you for the lesson, Master Lancelot."

It clicked for Ivivin at that moment. From the wink, to the motion, to the swordsmanship, to the name.

"Could it be...Lance!?" Ivivin considered in disbelief.

The king looked towards Miroslav, the sisters, and Ivivin and waved before escorting his children from the room.

"He'll return after he discusses the lesson with his children. He does this every chance he gets. I'm sure it will be brief, though. They seemed to be doing quite well today!" Miroslav explained. He could not explain, though, why Master Lancelot had started over towards them.

"Miroslav, my predecessor, I hope you are well." Lancelot said approaching the group. "I do hope you intend to introduce me to the two beauties that keep you company this fine afternoon." He looked to Idalia before adding "Especially the lovely lady who I've seen accompanying you the last few days. It is a travesty we haven't become acquainted in that time."

"Lancelot, you scoundrel, introduce yourself! I will have no part in your chauvinistic shenanigans. I suggest you womanize elsewhere—these are friends of Ivivin, the aspiring knight I spoke to you of." Miroslav said, with a hint of shortness in his voice.

"You do me dishonor, Miroslav, suggesting to these fine ladies that I am some lowlife scoundrel. Do you not trust their judgement? If you do, then let them judge me without the lens of your prejudices." Lancelot said slyly before turning to address the two sisters.

"Pardon the rudeness of my senior. He has forgotten what it is like to be young and surrounded by such striking women. My name is Lancelot and I am tasked with training the king's children in the art of swordsmanship. It is, truly, my pleasure." Lancelot said, stretching out his hand for a handshake. Elara did not take the bait, instead opting to kindly wave. Idalia, however, reached out to shake Lancelot's hand. She was surprised, but did not object, when Lancelot bent down and, instead, kissed the back of her hand. He stood back up slowly and locked eyes with Ivivin. They stared at each other intensely for what seemed like an eternity before Lancelot suddenly embraced Ivivin.

"And, how could I forget my good friend Ivivin. I had my doubts when I heard the stories old man Miroslav told me, but it really is you!" Lance jovially proclaimed.

The embrace confirmed it–this man was Lance, the reincarnation of Mars that he met in Olympia. The bracelet could change his appearance, but not his form, after all.

Ivivin smiled, surprising all three onlookers.

"Nice to see you again, Lance. Though I never thought it'd be so soon!" Ivivin responded, glancing quickly back towards Elara, who recognized the name from Ivivin's story.

"Miroslav, my dear mentor. Could you do me the favour of entertaining these lovely women while I catch up with my friend here? A little privacy between men, if you will." Lancelot asked, not waiting for an answer before he whisked Ivivin outside.

Lance led Ivivin away to somewhere private. He looked to-and-fro nervously, confirming they were alone before dispelling the illusion.

"Hello, Ivivin." Lance said in his original form, smiling.

"Lance! This is truly a surprise. I hope you did not drag me out here to end me!" Ivivin responded, only half-joking.

"No, no. I wouldn't want to spoil the gig I have right now."

"How did you come to be here?"

"Oh, you know, wandering the land seeking my fortune…and a chance to do good, just as you asked of me. I am glad to see you are not yet felled to the disease. Has it…progressed much?"

"You needn't concern yourself with my fate as long as you are aiming to do good in this world."

"As a premise of my promise, you are correct. But as someone who considers you friend, you cannot fault my curiosity."

"There is a new medicine that seems to be slowing the progression, but it seems to still be easing forward."

"That is both great and terrible news, Ivivin. I could never apologize enough even if I had a hundred lifetimes."

"Enough of that talk, Lance. Tell me, how have you fared? Has Ojasa's bracelet helped ease the dissonance in you?"

"Yes and no, my friend. I have chosen a form, as you can tell. A little smaller than I would have liked, but necessary to not break the illusion. Though the king already knows of my original form."

"What!? And he granted you the task of training his children despite this?"

"He did. He saw right through my illusion, though I do not know how. He simply remarked that I must have my own reasons for assuming such a form and granted me the position regardless."

"How did you happen upon the job, in any case?"

"I came here, to Castletown, and saw a young homeless child being bullied by some local children. I chased them away and decided to show the child how to defend herself. Soon after, she brought a friend who brought more friends. Before I knew it, I was running a full-blown school! That attracted the attention of Miroslav, who the king had tasked with recruiting a new trainer. And I've been doing both ever since. Twice a week, I travel back into town and give free self-defense lessons to any who come. And, after, I cook for and feed the attendants."

"That is great, Lance. Are you happy, then?"

"Well, the form I have crafted is certainly much better than the one before you. But it's stature ensures that I must rely on my tongue to court. Yes…since that form is immaterial, my tongue is all I can rely on. Good thing I have mastered it, yes?"

"Whatever you say Lance."

"Do not worry, Ivivin. I shan't pursue the clay-haired sister. I can tell you have your eyes on her. But I make no promise about her fair-skinned sister." Lance said, reassuming his illusionary form.

"I do not!" Ivivin instinctively denied.

"Oh? Then you will surely not mind if I win her heart and body, then."

"…"

"Oh! How wonderful that look of jealousy is! Your face betrays your words, Ivivin. Was it not you who told me to be true to myself? Heed your own advice, my friend. It will do you wonders. Now come, I can justify stealing you from Miroslav, but it would be ill-advised of me to keep you from the king."

Ivivin was overwhelmed by the sort of person Lance had become, but was also glad to see how the hate and negativity had been driven from his heart. The pair returned to the training hall just as the king did.

All the people in the training hall converged together in the center. The all began to bow before the king, before he waved the gesture away.

"Ivivin, you certainly have grown since that day in Gemi." Remarked the king.

"You remember me, then, your highness?"

"Of course I do, lad! It's not every day a farm boy saves you from an assassin, is it? I take it you have come here to ask that I make good on my promise to you?"

"Yes, your majesty."

"Very well, then. But before all that, might I show you something?"

"Of course, your highness."

"Splendid! As for the rest of you, please reconvene in the throne room in roughly an hour! We will determine if Ivivin has achieved knighthood at that time."

"An hour!? So soon!" Ivivin thought, becoming nervous. He looked to Elara, who was being ushered away with the others back towards the main entryway. She turned and met his glance just before walking out of sight. She smiled and gave Ivivin a thumbs-up.

"Now then, Ivivin. Please, follow me." The king commanded. Ivivin obeyed and followed the king down new corridors and hallways until they arrived in a room—the bedroom of young children.

"This is where my twins grew spent their youngest days, Ivivin. It was only recently we moved them to separate rooms." The king said nostalgically. "They grow up so quickly…"

Ivivin meekly nodded in agreement.

"In any case, Ivivin, I brought you here to show you this." The king said as he walked over to the mantle. On it were two things—an urn and a necklace of sorts.

Ivivin joined the king and saw the necklace. It took Ivivin longer than he cared to admit, but he came to recognize the necklace as the token he had given the king the day they met. Not only did the king keep it, but he had it on display in his children's' room!

"Yes, Ivivin. It is the trinket you entrusted me with that day in Gemi. And, in the urn, are some of the ashes of the queen—the twins' mother. I kept both these in this room to inspire my children. I wanted to know that, even if their mother wasn't with us any longer, that a piece of her would remain with us forever—I wanted them to know she was watching them from afar." The king recounted, choking up a bit as he talked about his deceased wife. The two stared at the urn a while before the king continued.

"And the necklace you made taught many lessons, too. It taught them to be grateful for the kindness of strangers. It taught them to not judge others by their lineage, but by their character and their actions. It reminded them that, if their mother was watching them from afar, then I was watching them from nearby and that we all needed to watch out for one another. You helped me survive to teach my children and your necklace helped me do so. You have my gratitude, young Ivivin. But, a deal is a deal, no? I will call for a guard to escort you to the room where we have stored your belongings. Are they all with you?"

"Yes, your highness."

"Very good, then. Take your time there to decide what you shall present to me to justify your knighthood. I will see you soon, Ivivin. They will come for you, when it is time."

The king exited the room and were soon replaced by two guards who escorted Ivivin to a small and simple room. Besides Ivivin's things, it held only two things: a bed and a mirror.

11

Ivivin immediately opened his pack freed Icarus. Ivivin had no clue that the guard would take their things at the door, so he didn't have a chance to free Icarus. He fed the little bugger the last of his mother's salted fish as an apology. He carried the owl to the mirror.

"We sure have changed, huh Icarus? For better in some ways and for worse in others." Ivivin said, almost somberly. Icarus attempted to cheer Ivivin up by trying to tear off his ear lobe.

"I had decided on what I was going to present the king before I came." Ivivin said to Icarus. "But now that I am here and he's given me time, should I reconsider?"

Icarus shrugged at Ivivin, but looked at him with great trust in his owly eyes.

"It's just…wouldn't the wise thing be to consider all my options until the very end? Or am I just working myself up for nothing…?"

Ivivin took time once more to reflect on his life. He called his journey from the onset until where he stood at this moment. He recalled his parent's parting words when he first left home and he recalled the king's words to him just minutes ago. He remembered meeting Icarus, Elara, Smith, Idalia, Minerva, and all the others. He remembered spinning tales of Icarus' brave feats and he remembered sharing his pains with Elara. Ivivin did his best to remember every detail, even those that caused him pain and fear. After he had spent a lifetime in his head, he decided that he would stick with his original plan and that he would regret nothing, no matter the outcome.

Just as he made this decision, the guards knocked at the door.

12

In the throne room, Ivivin stood before the king. Elara, Idalia, Miroslav, Lance, and other bystanders were scattered around the sides of the room. Not many subjects knew of the ordeal that was happening on this late-afternoon, but those that did knew how momentous this presentation had the potential to be and ensured their attendance. Not since Miroslav was knighted by the old king had one of common blood become a knight.

"Ivivin. Do you recall the tasks I required of you to become a knight?"

"Yes, your majesty." Ivivin replied.

"Please, announce them to me and to the court."

"First, I was to travel to the eastern edge of the kingdom to the city of Rumi. The citizens there were being plagued by a great and evil creature. I was to fell this being. Secondly, I was to find an esteemed squire to follow me. And lastly, I was tasked with collecting a great and valuable treasure on my travels. Once I accomplished these three tasks, I was to journey to Castletown and present to you the fruits of my travels." Ivivin recited.

"Indeed. That was the agreement we made. So, you shall present the results of your trials and, upon hearing them all, I shall deliberate to determine if you have completed them satisfactorily.

So, then, young adventurer, what proof have you that you felled the beast plaguing Rumi?"

Ivivin had given Ojasa's armlet to Lance and he did not wish to place the burden of proof on Miroslav. Ivivin suspected the king may ask for proof and had a response prepared.

"I have no proof. The only thing I can offer you is my word, your majesty. I am the one who ended Ojasa's reign, even if he were not the grand and fierce monster he appeared to be."

"And this is your final say on the matter?" the king asked.

"It is."

"Very well. Next, present to me a grand treasure of great value you obtained on your journey."

Ivivin had accumulated a number of valuable items on his journey. His shield, given to him by the grateful people of Crosstown and his sword, forged by a master smith were both stellar candidates. Mars' dagger was an option. He also had the tears, which were valuable in their rare magic. Ivivin approached the king with none of these things, however. Instead, he bore his apprentice's ring from Smith, still on a chain, and handed it to the king.

"This appears to be an ordinary ring, Ivivin. What is it truly?"

"It is a symbol of my apprenticeship with Smith, the blacksmith of Smithton. It is a symbol of his trust and allowed me to act in his name." Ivivin recited the response he had prepared.

"You are sure this, of all the treasures you bear, is the one you wish to present to me?"

"It was close, your majesty, between that ring and an old book of constellations. But I am sure of my choice."

"Very well. Only one task remains. Tell me, Ivivin. Which person of esteem have you convinced to be your squire?"

Ivivin reached into his pack once more and approached the king's side once again. Instead of delivering into the king's hand the letter from Arastoo, Ivivin handed the king a disheveled and dusty Icarus.

"Icarus, Imp of the Owls, shall be my squire." Ivivin resolutely stated.

"…you're certain of your choice, Ivivin?"

"Not a doubt in my mind, your majesty."

The king scratched Icarus before returning him to Ivivin. He placed his hand to his chin in an act of deliberation.

"Let me get this straight, young Ivivin. You present to me no evidence other than your own word that you brought down the beast plaguing Rumi, you present to me a simple ring as a great treasure from your journey, and, finally, you present to me a worn-down and dirty bird to be your squire…and you think yourself yet worthy of knighthood?"

"Yes, your majesty. I have tried to live true to my word, so it is as good as any proof I might have otherwise brought you. That ring represents time I spent with a kind man. He taught me his trade and he taught me to read. He did his best to make sure I was prepared for the world and he loved me as he loved his own son. I owe him for so much of the man I am today. And Icarus, the homely and mangy owl you held? He is one of the few creatures, man or otherwise, to have ever knocked me off my feet. He has been with me nearly my whole adventure and he has already saved my life more than once. He is of noble blood and of nobler character. Any other squire would simply pale in comparison." Ivivin said, kneeling before the king.

The court was fell silent and all eyes were on the king. All the onlookers were shocked, save Elara who somehow expected Ivivin to pull something as sappy and silly as this. Still, tension grew thick in the air as Ivivin awaited his judgement.

"Arise, Ivivin." The king commanded.

Ivivin obeyed.

"I can think of no one worthier of this title than you, Ivivin. Be it known to all that, from this day forth, Ivivin is now and forever a true knight of Vasilos."

13

In the moments leading up to Ivivin's arrival in the throne room, the king sat on his throne, adorned in his complete regal assortment, including the ceremonial crowns and scepter. He was not a fan of the bells and whistles, but he knew that it was his duty to his subjects and Ivivin was indeed a subject of his. In truth, the king knew of Ivivin's many accolades. He had sent men to help and investigate many matters, after all. Moreover, Miroslav had borne witness to not one, but two of Ivivin's heroic endeavours. Arastoo, one of the two highest authorities in Olympia, had sent the king a letter personally vouching for Ivivin and verifying that the letter

Ivivin bore promising his son as Ivivin's squire was authentic. In short, the king knew nearly all of Ivivin's story. He knew of his time in Smithton, to fending off the wolves in Wolfelaw, to conquering his fear to face Ojasa, to defeating the bandit-king Xaivier, to sealing away the Shaa'Ra, to solving the Crumbleheart outbreak in Olympia.

There was no doubt in the king's mind that Ivivin's actions merited the title of knight. However, travel and accolades could change the character of man. Entitlement, arrogance, and more could seep into the soul and lead to needless pride and condescension. So, rather than a test of Ivivin's capability, this ceremony would be a test of Ivivin's character. And, as the king admitted to himself, he was genuinely curious about what the boy would present to him. He could not shake the feeling that, at the very least, it would be interesting.

A Wayward Knight

1

It was surreal. Ivivin had accomplished what he had left home for. He was worried, to be honest. The king's short and curt responses had made him almost regret his decisions for a moment. At the very least, Ivivin was not hopeful that the king would accept him as a knight. Now that he was one, he had no idea what he would do. Presently, he was getting ready for what the king described as a 'modest banquet'. Attendants were helping Ivivin into clothes probably worth more than any amount of money he had ever held. He was being bombarded by instructions from all angles, which did not give him much time to sort out his thoughts.

"There will be time later, I suppose." Ivivin thought, resigning to his fate

Ivivin was not the only one being made up for the occasion. Icarus was being washed and groomed. Apparently, the it was tradition that the knight's squire give a speech at the banquet. Ivivin wasn't sure how that was going to play out.

"Tradition sure can be outright foolish, huh?" Ivivin snickered internally as a gentleman scrubbed the owl that, despite his best efforts, never seemed to get any cleaner.

At the same time, Elara and Idalia were also being readied for the occasion. Elara protested the large, poofy dress they tried to stick her in. She insisted on something comfortable and that had pockets—otherwise, she would not go in a dress at all. Idalia, however, allowed the handmaids to go to town, more out of curiosity than anything. It was a very strange experience for both sisters and they silently agreed to never let this happen to them again. But, for tonight and to celebrate the achievement of their friend, they would set aside their reservations.

2

Ivivin was escorted to the banquet hall as soon as he was garbed. Icarus joined him, though he was coated in a thick layer of powder and awfully sore about it. There, Ivivin encountered what appeared to be a handful of nobles waiting in the massive hall. The hall itself was incredible. There were tables littering half of the room, bisected by a monstrous wooden table already bearing some of the night's food. The nobles approached Ivivin, who was still looking around the room in awe.

"You were right, Eugene, he certainly is from the boonies." One man said, obviously not caring that Ivivin was in earshot.

"Oh, hello there. What are your names?" The new knight tried to socialize. One man cringed at Ivivin's words, prompting another to scold him.

"Now Frankfurd, you can't expect him to know proper etiquette. Until today, he was a country bumpkin, after all." The man turned to Ivivin before continuing.

"Please, excuse my associate. In high society, it is considered polite to offer your name first, before asking for the name of others. But you couldn't have known that."

"Ah, my apologies, then. My name is Ivivin. A pleasure to meet you." Ivivin tried, looking to the man who corrected him for affirmation. The man laughed at Ivivin.

"Pardon me, but your ignorance tickles me. You should announce your title when you present yourself, young master."

"My…title?" Ivivin asked.

"You are a knight now, after all. At the very least, you have 'Sir', do you not? And surely the king granted you a title."

Ivivin was starting to feel as if he were playing a game to which he knew not the rules. "Hello, esteemed guests. My name is Sir Ivivin, Knight of Vasilos…?" Ivivin stated, inflecting his voice to make it sound as a question.

"Close, close. You would say 'I am Sir Ivivin' or 'My name is Ivivin, Knight of Vasilos'. You'll get it someday, I'm sure. Just. Keep. Practicing!" The man chuckled jovially at Ivivin's response.

Ivivin was discouraged, but not defeated.

"May I have your name, then, esteemed sir?" Ivivin said, trying to be as proper as possible.

"I am Lord Doosh, Grand Sire of Montenegro, Father of the Wheat, executive patron of the arts and 5th of his name." The man recited proudly.

Ivivin was then introduced to each of the other nobles in turn, their names getting longer and more unwieldy with each iteration. Still, Ivivin was patient and tried his best to remember each one. They spoke to him as if he was a child, but Ivivin tried to ignore it the best he could. They told him that he was to await his introduction from around the corner and then make his way into the hall. They specified that he should wait exactly two minutes for the applause to desist and that he should be waving until such time. Then, he was to face the king and kneel, wait exactly seven seconds before rising and marching confidently to the center of the dancing area. The band would then begin to play a tune. As Ivivin was unwed, he was to dance with each woman for no more than thirty seconds a piece. To do more than that would be considered rude and improper. He would continue dancing until the song stopped, allow his final partner to return to the border of the dance area, bow for precisely five seconds, and join sit at his spot at the knight's table near the king. Ivivin's squire would then speak upon his behalf before the king toasted the banquet.

Ivivin did his darndest to remember all the strangely specific customs of a likely dated ceremony. He worried he would mess up and embarrass himself and somehow get his knighthood revoked. Ivivin nervously assumed his position, out of sight. He heard doors open and the sound of many footsteps filled the hall.

3

Elara and Idalia were approached by the same nobles that had approached Ivivin just moments before. They tried to play the same tricks on Elara and Idalia as they did Ivivin, by seeming offended about their introduction. It took less than a minute for Elara to leave, taking Idalia with her.

"Shove it up your arse." Elara muttered as she walked away.

4

Eventually, the chatter in the banquet area ceased. Ivivin could hear brass horns welcoming in the king. After a few seconds of enduring the cheesy and generic horn, Ivivin heard his name being announced. He hastily turned the corner. With all his nerves, he tripped and fell just moments after stepping into view. He did his best to recover and hurried to stand near the king, remembering almost too late to wave at the attendants. He could see many of onlookers whispering to one another. It made Ivivin even more nervous. Eventually, the applause subsided, but Ivivin continued to wave at the silent masses. He started to walk towards the dance area.

He was about halfway there when he realized that he had forgotten to kneel before the king. Ivivin scurried back and kneeled before the king. Ivivin could feel his face burning. The king met Ivivin's eyes with understanding and compassionate eyes of his own, but also with an air of impatience. Ivivin got the sense that the king did not enjoy this sort of event very much.

Ivivin rose and hurried to the dance floor in less of a confident march and more of an anxious stumble. Ivivin looked around the border of the dancing area. There were at least two dozen women there. Ivivin groaned internally. He was terrible at dancing and, at thirty seconds or so a piece, he would be dancing a while. His outlook brightened, though, when he spotted Elara. She was wearing a dress that was far plainer and far more sensible than any of the other women. In fact, she stood out like a sore thumb amoung the sea of made up women in ludicrous gowns. Ivivin looked about for Idalia and saw her standing alongside the band. She was in full gown, unlike her sister, but looked plenty uncomfortable in it. Still, she gracefully held an instrument Ivivin had never seen before. Ivivin looked back to Elara. She was third in line, if he started in the corner to his right. His first thought was to save her until towards the end, so that he had something to look forward to. However, upon a second inspection, Ivivin saw that Elara was wearing dress gloves and, looking closely, Ivivin felt that she was just as nervous and uncomfortable that he was.

"Perhaps sooner is better, after all." Ivivin thought as the music began to play.

5

Ivivin approached the woman in the rightmost corner and pulled her slightly away from the border. Stiffer than a log, Ivivin tried to dance with the woman, but he must have stepped on her foot a dozen times in the thirty seconds she was his partner. Ivivin could swear he saw her limping back to the border when they had finished. This failure only made Ivivin more nervous. He began to sweat profusely and tensed even more. He reached out to the second woman and tried to lead her from the border, only to have his sweaty hand slip through hers and loose his balance, just narrowly avoiding crashing to the floor. Ivivin danced no more than a bar with her before she led him back to the border, so that she might avoid a broken ankle.

Ivivin looked to his third partner, Elara. He was still tremendously nervous, but it was a type of nervousness to which he had grown accustomed. He took her hand and brought her away from the border a bit. Elara put Ivivin's hands in proper position and began to lead their dance—it was easy for her to tell that Ivivin had lost all his confidence in the last minute. It took Elara about half of their allotted thirty seconds to get Ivivin to relax and loosen up enough to actually call his erratic and uncoordinated movements 'dance'.

But after that? The two started having fun. With what must have been five seconds before their thirty seconds was up, Ivivin whispered to Elara.

"Can I take your gloves off?"

Elara would not meet Ivivin's eyes, but nodded. While they were dancing, Ivivin removed Elara's gloves and tucked them into the waist of his pants. The first thing he noticed was that Elara's hands were coated in a sweat as cold and sticky as his own. Ivivin and Elara both knew that their time was up. Ivivin didn't want to offend anyone and began to dance Elara back towards the border. But his heart was beating so fast and he was having so much fun that he immediately changed directions, lifting Elara just an inch off the ground in the resultant swing. Elara looked at Ivivin confused, but it took only an instant for Elara to realize what Ivivin was thinking. They smiled and danced their way to the center. They danced and danced together, Elara still leading Ivivin. They danced until the song ended. Ivivin bowed to Elara and handed her the gloves, which were promptly shoved into her pockets as she returned to her place on the border.

Elara looked at the other women from whom she had stolen time. The reactions were mixed. Some women seemed relieved not to have danced and others looked entirely indifferent. Still, Elara could not ignore the other malicious glares she felt coming from nearly every direction. She could not ignore them, but decided that she did not care.

Ivivin looked to the nobles who had advised him. Some looked at him with confusion and others with amusement. Still, Ivivin could not ignore the animosity he sensed from some of them at his defiance. He could not ignore it, but he decided that he did not care.

The newly-fledged knight looked towards his king who, for the first time tonight, seemed entertained and in a good mood. Ivivin was right, the king truly did not enjoy trivial ceremonies. Ivivin kneeled before the king and could not help but sass.

"Sorry, my liege. I am but a country bumpkin, after all."

6

After a surprisingly eloquent, coherent, and moving speech delivered by Icarus, the king toasted Ivivin.

"To Sir Ivivin, the newest knight of my realm. Though your blood is not noble, the nobility of your spirit is second to none. May you serve the kingdom well and may it serve you well in turn. Hear, hear!"

"Hear, hear!" erupted the room in near-unison.

"Please, guests, enjoy this celebration in Ivivin's honour. Eat to your heart's content and dance until your legs be weary!"

7

It did not take Ivivin, Elara, and Idalia long to tire of the festivities. Ivivin danced with Idalia once and with Elara once more. He also noticed Lance dancing with Idalia while he introduced Icarus to anyone who would give him the time of day. Still, this whole banquet felt foreign to him and he did not have the sense that he would be missed by any of the castle's inhabitants. Ivivin took Icarus and snuck off to a balcony to properly process having achieved his goal.

"It will be easiest to think under the night sky and in the fresh air." Ivivin justified his escape to himself.

As Ivivin looked up to the stars, reflecting on the day's happenings, he could not help but feel underwhelmed. Not at the banquet or the castle or the king—these things all far exceeded his wildest imaginings. Rather, Ivivin was underwhelmed with how he felt. He was certainly happy and relieved that the king had approved of him. But he didn't feel any different with this new title—this new qualification. He still just felt like Ivivin. Becoming a knight didn't change how he saw himself. It didn't change the fact that he was sick. It didn't change how he felt about Elara. It didn't heal Icarus' feathers. It didn't solve the issue of Jupiter's tear. Really, the only thing that seemed to have change is how some people Ivivin didn't know or particularly care for saw him. And even then, he was sure he was not seen as an equal amoung many of them.

So, yes, Ivivin was a little underwhelmed and it was not exactly a good feeling. Still, looking at the stars with Icarus reminded him of when he first started his journey and all the nights that followed. Not all the nights were good ones. Some were hungry nights. Others pained. Some were fearsome nights. Others lonesome. Still, the thrill of adventure and the possibility of meeting new people in new places excited Ivivin, even today, and far outweighed the negatives. He wanted to meet people and help them and grow even more. That sentiment, too, remained unchanged despite Ivivin's newfound knighthood. And for that, he was glad.

Elara joined Ivivin shortly after he escaped the party.

"Way to go, leaving me alone. Tell me about your escape plan next time!" Elara teased Ivivin as she made her way to his side.

"Sorry, I know you enjoy dancing, so I didn't want to make you feel like you had to join me out here. Besides, I have Icarus out here with me and you know how he hates to share my company with anyone." Ivivin explained, scratching the back of his squire's head.

"I can't believe I have to compete with that powdery mongrel for your attention." Elara joked.

"Well, he *is* your brother." Ivivin retorted.

The pair exchanged banter until Elara became serious.

"Hey, Ivivin. I just wanted you to know that I'm really proud of you. It's a big deal, after all, and you earned it."

Ivivin's heart jumped with excitement. It was rare to see this tender side of Elara. Ivivin found that it never failed to make his heart soar. In this moment, Ivivin felt becoming a knight and all that it required was worth it, just for the feelings brought about by her simple praise. The friends looked at each other and smiled, genuinely happy to be in each other's company. Instinctively, Ivivin leaned in to hug Elara and she seemed to lean in too. However, the moment before they touched, Elara flinched and Ivivin pulled himself away.

"I'm so sorry, Elara!" Ivivin apologized on the spot.

Elara's frustration was apparent.

"It's not your fault Ivivin. I wish to be able to greet you and congratulate you properly. I trust you—I know you mean me no harm, but still…my body will not listen to my reason. It makes no sense, being able to dance with you, but being unable to share a simple hug with you. And I'm so inconsistent! Perhaps yesterday or tomorrow, this same scenario would be fine. It is infuriating and I know it hurts you when I reel away from you as if you were a monster. But I want you to know you're not. You're kind and you're patient. A true friend. I hope that my body comes to know what my mind does, in due time. In the meantime, I am truly sorry, Ivivin." Elara spilled.

"Elara, do not hold these thoughts any longer than you need to. I know that you trust me just as I trust you. We have already shared our scars with one another. Unfortunately for you, my dearest friend, I am in it for the long haul. I look forward to the day where you feel healed, happy, and congruent. Until then, I guess I will have to settle for Icarus. He's the prettier sibling anyways." Ivivin answered, hugging Icarus tightly. His words were met with a roll of the eyes and a familiar punch in the arm.

The two of them stood at the balcony, looking at their stars for a while. It was only when Idalia came and told Ivivin that the king was going to be delivering the closing speech soon that he was prompted to return. Idalia left as soon as she arrived, hoping to find a partner for the final song of the evening.

"Shall we?" Elara asked.

Ivivin looked closely at Elara. She looked very much herself, especially after the time they had spent chatting on the balcony. But Ivivin still thought there was something off about her. It took him a minute, but he realized what it was—her hair. The handmaids must have managed to tame Elara's somewhat unruly hair. Ivivin couldn't help but think it did not suit her as well the way she usually carried it.

"Sure." Ivivin replied.

As the pair walked back into the castle, Ivivin suddenly and vigorously ruffled Elara's hair, returning it to its usual state of moderate messiness.

Ivivin expected a punch, but it never came.

8

The king dismissed the guests of the banquet rather hurriedly. Ivivin could see that the king hadn't the patience for a moment more of these fanciful trivialities. Ivivin and Elara did not get their fill of merriment from the rather stiff banquet. They overheard a gaggle of the rowdier castle workers talking about headed to a nearby bar and decided they wanted to join.

"Idalia, come, we are headed to the tavern to celebrate properly!" Elara prodded her sister.

The blood fell from Idalia's face.

"I am feeling a bit worn, sister. Perhaps just you and Ivivin should go."

"Nonsense!" Elara exclaimed. "I haven't seen you in ages Idalia. I've missed you so! Let's celebrate our reunion as heartily as we celebrate Ivivin's accomplishment!"

Idalia tried to get her sister to understand, without words, but her attempted telepathy failed, falling flat due to Elara's excitement. Idalia composed herself the best she could and smiled for her sister.

"Alright then, Elara. Let's go."

Ivivin, Icarus, Elara, and Idalia all left the castle walls and followed the boisterous castle attendants to a nearby tavern. Once there, the celestial siblings and Ivivin found the locale to be energetic and earnest in ambiance. Elara went to the bar and returned with drinks for all three of them. Idalia held the brew in her hand, resisting it's call. She resented her sister, just a bit, for getting her a drink without asking. She sat there with the duo, just holding the drink and sweated. There was a pressure that surrounded her in this setting and another exuded by her sister to drink. Idalia was terribly embarrassed of her alcohol problem and that embarrassment was only heightened by the fact that Elara did not yet know of it. She knew she wanted to tell Elara someday, but she also did not want her sister to be disappointed in her. She wanted to tell her sister, but she wanted to do so in due time, under her own terms and certainly not under duress.

When Elara went to go dance, Ivivin noticed Idalia had been nursing her drink for quite some time.

"Everything alright, Idalia?" Ivivin asked, concerned. "Do you not like that drink? Would you like me to get you a different one?"

"No, it's not that." Idalia muttered, biting her lip.

"Should I tell him? Maybe he can help me. I can't imagine getting through tonight the way things are going. He'll keep the secret, right? No…I don't want to risk that, but… maybe he'll help me anyways?"

"Is something else the matter, then?" Ivivin questioned.

The sincerity of Ivivin's concern sold Idalia.

"Ivivin, I cannot tell you why now but I musn't drink this night, no matter what. And my sister cannot know that I am not drinking, either. Please, can you help me?" Idalia pleaded speedily.

Ivivin was a bit shocked by the abruptness and seriousness of Idalia's request, but whether nor not to help her was never a question.

"Sure, Idalia. I trust you. What's the plan?" Ivivin queried.

Idalia was relieved. "I'm…not quite sure. I've been too occupied to think of a solution."

"Well, I'll just drink for the two of us tonight! Just leave it to me!" Ivivin said, bursting with an unmerited confidence. Idalia, never having gone drinking with Ivivin, smiled and clapped.

"Are you sure? Thank you so much, Ivivin!"

In less than an hour, Elara and Idalia were carrying Ivivin out of the bar.

9

Never before had Ivivin been so hungover. Ivivin rolled over to keep the sunlight pouring in from the window (in a room whose location he was unsure) from his eyes. Despite the splitting pain in his head and his queasiness, he smiled.

"I kept my promise. Not a drop of alcohol touched Idalia's lips." Ivivin thought proudly, hoping sleep would return and whisk him away from his agony.

Even hungover, it was not long until Ivivin was faced anew with his existential questions. He was now a knight of the king, but he really didn't know what that meant. It was a title, sure, but wasn't it also a job? What would be required of him? He trusted the king, but Ivivin had really no idea what the king expected him to do.

"I really didn't consider what this truly meant, did I?" Ivivin thought, ashamed of his lack of foresight into his own future and decisions. *"Well, no use in thinking myself in circles. I'll just ask the king."*

Just as Ivivin exited the inn to seek an audience with the king, guards approached him on behalf of the king. He was being summoned.

"How convenient." Ivivin thought as he followed the guards to the castle.

Ivivin soon stood before the king, who met the freshly minted knight with a weary smile.

"Greetings, Sir Ivivin."

"Your majesty." Ivivin replied with a small bow.

"I know the ceremony seemed rushed, but, in truth, I did not wish to have the occasion looming over me for days. Better to be quick and minimize the suffering. I can tell we were in agreement by your prolonged absence from the festivities." The king remarked.

"My apologies, your majesty."

"No need for apologies. Save them for when it matters. I called you here not to chastise you, but, rather, to discuss your place in my court from now onward."

"How fortuitous. I was hoping to ask you about the very thing." Ivivin responded, still trying to be as formal as he could muster.

"Well then, no need to beat around the bush. What do you see yourself doing for me?"

Ivivin was taken aback. He was expecting orders and instead received a question.

"I am not quite sure what you mean, my liege."

The king sighed.

"It is just you and I here, now, Ivivin. Please speak plainly and freely. In fact, I command it."

"I thought you'd be telling me what I am supposed to be doing, so why are you asking me what I see myself doing?"

"Ivivin, I know not how to best utilize the talent of all of my knights. Some report to me daily, others monthly. Some stay around these parts and others scour the land. Save your strength of spirit, I know very little about you. So, help me direct you. What do you want to do? If it is within reason and serves the kingdom in at least some small way, I will allow it."

"I...don't know. I hadn't thought about it."

"You have growing up to do, yet, Ivivin. Think on this matter and return to me in three days' time. I expect an answer then."

"I will do my best. And, if I may?"

"Go ahead, Ivivin, but make it quick. I value you but I have much to get done this day."

Ivivin explained the details of the Tear of Jupiter, as well as the existence of other tears and their ability to be corrupted under the right circumstances.

"Hmm, I knew of the existence of tears. They are rare, but far from myth. But I knew not that the tear of Jupiter existed here in these lands nor that it held such power. I will think on this matter and will discuss it further with you when you report to me in three days. Until then, Ivivin, guard the stone and do whatever you need to do to get me my answer. Those are your orders. For now, you are dismissed."

Ivivin bowed slightly and exited the throne room.

11

Idalia and Elara went about town to catch up with one another. Elara did most of the talking. It was easy for her to share her story, pains and all, with Idalia. It was made even easier by the fact that she had already told Minerva and Ivivin, making this her third recital. Idalia did not open up quite so easily. In the plain light of day, with nothing but time, Elara could tell something weighed on Idalia heavily. Eventually, Idalia volunteered the information about her drinking problem and how it affected her. Elara was shocked by the revelation. She had always assumed her sister to be balanced and satisfied, but she, too, held hidden pains. Moreover, this news brought great guilt to Elara about the previous night in the tavern.

"I am so sorry, Idalia. Though I suppose that explains how Ivivin became so worthless so much faster than usual."

Elara paused a second.

"Did you tell him?"

Elara might as well have said: "Did you tell him, *before me*?"

Idalia shook her head.

"No. I asked him for his help and he gave it, despite not knowing why."

Elara smiled.

"Yeah, he is an odd one, isn't he?"

Idalia could sense something new in the way her sister spoke and suspected she knew what it was.

"So, how long have you been together?" Idalia asked casually.

Elara began to drown on dry land.

"What—what do you mean by that?"

"Oh, come now sister! I told you about my recent intimacies, however questionable they all were. The least you can do is return the favour!"

Elara just shook her head furiously.

"You won't tell me? How selfish you are, sister. I thought we shared everything with one another." Idalia pouted.

The guilt trip worked.

"Look, Idalia. I…really like Ivivin. But we are friends and nothing more."

Idalia was shocked to see her sister so timid. The Elara that Idalia had grown up with feared little and was more confident than she likely had any right to be. Idalia was truly happy she saw a side of her sister that she had never seen before.

"Never mind, then, my sister. We can talk about it another time, perhaps. What is your plan from now on, then?"

"That depends on what Ivivin ends up doing. When I went to go shake his lazy arse awake, I learned from the innkeeper that he was summoned to the castle. I imagine that he'll learn his duty there."

"Well, it has been some time since then. Perhaps we should wait for him back at the inn, then?"

"That sounds good, Idalia. I am glad we had this talk."

"Are you? I guess you won't care when I tell Ivivin how much you like him!" Idalia teased.

"Never mind, I regret everything about today my dear sister."

The two continued their banter all the way to the inn, where they met up with Ivivin.

12

"You want to go camping?" Elara asked, incredulously.
Ivivin nodded.

"We just got to town, you do remember that, right mister?"

"Yes, but the king told me to do whatever I thought would help me come to an answer. I don't know if it will help me come to an answer, but I do know I want to spend some time with you both. Who knows what will happen once the king gives me an assignment? I want to make our moments count."

"What do you think, Idalia?" Elara asked

"I have not seen you in such a long time. I will do whatever you do, Elara." Idalia answered.

"Then let's go camping, Ivivin."

Gone Camping

1

Ivivin, Idalia, Icarus, Elara, and Lili all left Castletown and headed west, a bit towards Portington. Elara insisted, as she missed the breeze of the sea. All members of the excursion worried that it would be a bit awkward, but their worries were for naught. The first night that they were out there, they found themselves in the same position as they had been on the roof when first they met. Idalia separated Elara and Ivivin as they lay stargazing by the fire. It was not long before Idalia fell asleep and the remaining conscious pair simply looked to the heavens in silence. When the fire flickered out and died, Elara cuddled up to her sister. Though they were now grown, Elara missed how they used to sleep together. Getting the sense he was intruding, Ivivin moved over to where Lili and Icarus lay. He cuddled up to Lili and fell asleep, content.

A few hours later, Ivivin woke up shivering from the cold of night. Lili had gotten up and moved over to where Elara and Idalia lay. Only a shivering Icarus remained with Ivivin. Ivivin looked at his friend, touched by his loyalty. Just moments later, Icarus got up and booked it over to join the festival of cuddles occurring on the other side of the campsite.

Ivivin sighed as he rekindled the campfire and retrieved his blanket from his belongings. He looked at the sight and felt his heart melt. The scene was adorable. Ivivin wished he had some way to immortalize it. Struck by inspiration, Ivivin retrieved some parchment and some ink from his bag, as well as the luminous tear. Bundled up in his blanket, he let the stone light his lap as he sketched the group. Each of Ivivin's strokes were filled with emotion and captured his exact impression of the scene. He artfully replicated the contours enhanced by the campfire's unique lighting. The parchment was dotted not only with ink from his well, but also from his soul. His passion ensured that his finest creative sensibilities were firmly, but subtly, embedded into his magnum opus. With each finished line, Ivivin grew happier and happier with the product, but his enthusiasm could not fend off sleep forever. Ivivin, with the heavy eyelids that accompany the artist's struggle, lay contentedly in a state of half-sleep, excited to show the others his masterpiece when he woke the next day. The flickering of the fire faded to black.

. . .

Giggling is what woke Ivivin.

Ivivin sat up to see Elara and Idalia covering their mouths, trying to stifle their laughter.

"What's so funny?" Ivivin asked the sisters. Idalia immediately turned away and buried her face in her hands. Ivivin recognized the piece of parchment that Elara had in her hands as the medium that held his pièce de résistance.

"What is this?" Elara countered, showing Ivivin his handiwork.

"I sketched you all as you slept last night. It was a sight so touching I wanted to show you and Idalia. Isn't it good?" Ivivin asked Elara expectantly.

Never had Elara been faced with such a dilemma. She hadn't expected Ivivin to be so proud of his work and she did not wish to hurt his feelings. On the other hand, the sketch was pretty bad and she didn't want to lie to Ivivin. Furthermore, it was tremendously funny, the silliness of it all.

"It looks like a far-sighted child with tremors and a wild imagination drew it." Elara critiqued the work.

Ivivin's heart sank. The words hurt a bit extra coming from Elara, after all. He knew he hadn't talent, but he was so focused and engrossed it his task that he was sure that it would be decent, at least.

"It's cute." Elara said with a gentle smile.

The campers spent the day lazing about. Elara asked Ivivin if she could lend "Elisabeth and the Troll" to Idalia. Ivivin agreed, thinking Idalia might like it. He also wanted to see how the book held up without knowing the backstory of its creation, so he conspired with Elara to make sure Idalia didn't find out until after she finished. Ivivin was interested in the book concerning the tears that he had sent (pointlessly, as Idalia was sure to point out) to the sisters' mother while in Olympia. He propped open the tome and joined Idalia in lazily reading in the grass. Only Elara seemed energetic and restless. She quickly found the campsite and its occupants boring and was spirited away by wilds.

When she returned hours later, as the sun began to fall from its apex, she was dirty and her legs were coated with little scratches. She held a toad out proudly to the other two campers. Idalia found the creature to be ugly and gross. She wanted no part of it, which prompted Elara to chase Idalia around the campsite, trying to force Idalia to kiss it. Ivivin looked at the scene and was charmed. This trip didn't seem to be helping him decide what to tell the king, but it was incredibly fun and wholesome. When Elara finally managed to shove the dizzy toad in Idalia's face, she cheered triumphantly and zipped over to Ivivin to show him her prize.

"Ivivin, look at this fellow! He is a kind of toad I have never seen before! He's in the book Minerva gave me, but there's not much known about this little bugger." Elara excitedly filled Ivivin in.

To Ivivin, the toad looked like all the others, but he saw the way Elara doted on the toad and knew it was something special to her. Her cut and muddied legs meant she likely chased her target through some rough terrain. Ivivin looked at Elara, who was positively beaming and felt his chest burst with warmness.

"It's cute." Ivivin said with a gentle smile.

3

The trio drew sticks to decide who would cook dinner. Idalia lost and had to shoulder the burden alone. Elara was delighted and Ivivin would come to learn why. Elara and Ivivin were both decent at cooking, especially while travelling. But this was camping and they had plenty of supplies, so Idalia could make something quite delectable. Idalia settled on a thick, creamy vegetable chowder since their milk wasn't likely to keep another day. While Idalia cooked, Ivivin and Elara played a game with Icarus, who was still sore that he could not fly. Instead of flying, Ivivin and Elara tossed the owl to one another from all over the campsite. It wasn't the same as flying, but Ivivin could tell Icarus loved it nonetheless.

After dinner, they all sat around the fire. Lili, Icarus, Elara, and Idalia preemptively cuddled up together. Ivivin was envious and felt a bit left out, but he had learned things from his readings that he could share with everyone this day and was eager to, irrespective of his current state of cuddlessness.

"So, I learned a lot about the tears today!" Ivivin said excitedly.

"From the book?" Elara asked.

"Yes, it had information about each of the tears and the lore behind them! It was really interesting."

Idalia almost spoke up. She had read the book during her journey here. She noticed how excited Ivivin was to share and held her tongue. She had nearly forgotten that Ivivin only relatively recently learned how to read. The novelty of novels clearly hadn't yet left him.

"Do tell!" Idalia instead prompted Ivivin.

"We have three of the tears, not including Jupiter's, Idalia. I don't know if you knew that." Ivivin started. Idalia knew of two of them. She knew Ganymede's tear intimately. Ivivin had sent it to her mother and she had travelled here with it, after all. When she felt lonely or, more accurately, when she craved the sensation of warmth and belonging she found with a drink in a crowded tavern, Idalia would sleep with the stone. It would grow warm and the warm was not ordinary. Somehow, it helped Idalia feel wanted and welcome in a world she was unsure of. The other stone she knew of she knew only from Elara's story the other day—the tear that played music. She did not know they possessed a third tear, though.

"I didn't know that, actually. Do you have it? What does it do?" Idalia asked, both out of curtesy and curiosity.

Ivivin donned a scholarly tone before proceeding. "In due time, Idalia, in due time. Let me start with the tear I sent to your mother, the one you brought with you all this way. That tear fell from the eyes of Ganymede, Icarus' past form. Legend has it that

Ganymede grew incredibly close with man during his time away from the heavens. He loved him and he loved spending time with them. They were not perfect nor strong, but neither was he. He came to develop comradery with him far beyond what any other celestial spirit had ever achieved. He gave away his mother's tears to Europa and was slain in the war. As he died, he thought not only of his mother and his sisters, but also of man, who he had come to know so well, and the fire that he lit in his heart. A single tear escaped his eye on his deathbed, the Tear of Ganymede. It is said to contain all the warmth that he felt for man, so that they might truly understand how he cared for them so."

Elara was intrigued by the story, but Idalia was floored by it. She knew about the tear, sure, but having Ivivin summarize it made her realize how much the story resounded in her. She wanted desperately to connect with people and to let her emotion spill forth in a way that people could understand. Before she had much time to dwell on it, though, Ivivin continued.

"Next is the tear that Elara carries. It is the Tear of Callisto, the spirit who Idalia is the reincarnation of. Callisto fought fiercely in the war not for the cause, but because she loathed the idea of misfortune befalling her family. In the day, she would fight beside her siblings the best she could. But her truest talents revealed themselves at night, during the short ceasefires. The horrors of war and the actions that it forced upon them took their toll on Europa and Ganymede. It did not take long before they could not find peace in their peaceful moments. Trauma and regret plagued them constantly. So, Callisto would sing for her siblings. Her symphonic voice calmed their hearts and put them at ease during times they needed it most. Her songs provided the siblings a reprieve from the war and served as a reminder that they were more than just the trauma they carried. Of course, as we know, Callisto eventually gave her share of Jupiter's tears to Europa and she, too, fell during the war. To Callisto, family was the most important thing and what was important to them, was important to her too. So, though she was not as fond of humans as her brother, she shed a tear for them in his honour. In her tear, she wanted to leave her voice. She wanted for those who fought out of necessity and suffered the ills that befell them to that end to find solace in the tear. She knew that man was strong, but even the spirits needed tranquil time to gather their strength and face their evils. She hoped the stone would provide that for man, just as she had done for her siblings."

Idalia found this story interesting, especially considering she had decided to study music and singing prior to learning the story of the tear and independently of her status as Callisto's reincarnation. She was filled with thoughts at how much of life is fated and how much is coincidence. Elara, on the other hand, fixated on the words. The tear had reminded her of Idalia's singing well before she knew of its origin—that was gripping enough alone. However, what really caused Elara to reflect was how much she had used the tear to that end. When she struggled to deal with thoughts of Rumi and the fallout thereof, the stone could provide a reprieve from the nightmares. Its song didn't solve her issues, but allowed her time to adjust and redistribute their weight so that she could carry them more easily and, with any luck, less painfully. She teared up, thinking about the tear.

"And, lastly, is the tear you know not of, Idalia. I came into possession of it by chance not long after I split from you and your sister." Ivivin pulled out the luminous tear and let it glow as brightly as he could.

"This is the tear of Elara...I mean, Europa!" Ivivin stuttered. "Anyway, if you remember the story your mother told us, Europa ended the war by washing it, and herself, away with the tears that came at the news of the death of her siblings. However, the last tear she wept before she herself became a torrential wave was special. It endured afterwards, just as Ganymede's and Callisto's tears did. She mourned the loss of life, both of her siblings, but also of all caught up in the war. Though she had fought as the strongest and most brutal of the siblings, she had come to know the pain of causing harm to others. In her final moments, she wondered if ignorance was not the cause of all this suffering. If all beings could come to understand one another and to learn from their surroundings, perhaps the fear that led to conflict could itself be exterminated. So, Europa's final tear before ending the conflict carried in it her hopes that such conflict could be prevented from happening again. She gave to man a light to help illuminate the unknown. She knew that knowledge was only part of the battle, that those seeking knowledge must be able to acknowledge their ignorance with humility if they wanted to derive the wisdom and wit to prevent calamity. But her light could, perhaps, help them recognize their fear and deal with it, not as an enemy to be vanquished, but as a puzzle to be solved." Ivivin finished.

Idalia and Elara looked to the sky to internalize the stories. They were fantastic and it reminded them of the stories they would spin with each other about the stars in the skies. Ivivin, on the other hand, only realized how much that the story and the tear related to him. It had given Icarus the means to face the fear of death and save Ivivin from the snowstorm. It had allowed Ivivin to educate himself by its light. It had helped Ivivin face his fears, even if he didn't always win, as was the case when he passed through the grand forest en route to Olympia. It had illuminated Ivivin's world literally more times than he could count, but it had also illuminated his world figuratively, too.

Ivivin joined his eyes to the skies with Idalia and Elara, each of them grateful for the gifts left by those before them.

4

Ivivin felt himself getting drowsy and the chatter of the sisters had long subsisted. He looked to them and saw them sleeping once more, cuddled together with Icarus and Lili.

"This is my chance!" Ivivin thought. *"I will try sketching them again. I know I can do better!"*

And so, Ivivin attempted to capture the sight with ink and paper once more. He was more deliberate in his approach and tried to recreate the scene perfectly as he saw it. When he finished, he looked at his work. He looked at it as objectively as he could. It was, in earnest, a bit better than his first one. But he felt nothing when he looked at it. He looked back to the one he had done the night before and remembered the passion he had when creating it. He smiled and threw this night's work into the gentle embers of the dying fire.

5

Ivivin and the others woke late. Early on, they enjoyed a day of merriment, but the knowledge that, first thing in the morning, they would return to Castletown set in. Idalia had wanted to explain herself to Ivivin properly, feeling that he deserved to know why she refused to drink. But it was a difficult conversation to have, even with the inspirational stories of the tears fresh in her mind. She hadn't even properly thanked him yet!

Elara worried too. She was doing better in a lot of ways, but she felt that her progress might be stalling. Moreover, she was unsure of how she would react to the various scenarios Ivivin might encounter tomorrow. She had feelings for him—she could admit that to herself now that Idalia wrenched it out of her. But what place she wanted those feelings to occupy in her life and whether she wanted them to guide any of her decisions was another matter entirely.

And, of course, there was Ivivin. He was faced with not having any clue as what to say to the king tomorrow. He had not an answer for him. Moreover, Ivivin's illness cast a shadow on any discussion of the future. He hadn't told the king and wasn't sure that he should. All that he knew was that, if the king assigned him a task that he loathed, he would be wasting much of the likely little time he had left in this world. This knowledge just pressured him further to search for an answer for the king, but the pressure pushed him further away from any such answer.

Though they enjoyed each other's company and their interactions buried their worries, when night inevitably came and they settled down to sleep, the isolation of their own minds quickly unearthed these worries.

Idalia was the first. She, Elara, the owl, and the horse were all huddled together, as they had been in the previous nights. However, despite the radiant warmth of the three creatures around her, she shivered. She was frustrated that she hadn't managed to approach Ivivin at all this day and missed her chance to open up to him. She could communicate through music, sure, but there are situations where only words would suffice and she had failed to even try and use them. Despite being next to her sister and despite Ivivin being a stone's throw away, she felt incredibly isolated. She held Ganymede's tear and let it warm her shivering body for a while. She took a deep breath and resolved that she would talk to Ivivin on the walk back to Castletown, no matter what. Sleep evaded her now not because of her frustration, but because she was planning on what she would tell him when the sun eventually did rise.

Elara was the second. Allowing her feelings for Ivivin to dictate her actions, even a little, made Elara feel like she was not in control. Even though she knew and trusted Ivivin, a fear crept up in her that, if she yielded anything to him, that Ivivin would become like Ajaxx. He would take advantage of her and the position she allowed him to have. She worried Ivivin, just like Ajaxx and others she had encountered, simply wore a mask of civility and she was just too daft to see it. It was illogical and Elara hated herself for feeling it. After all, when it was untainted by these negative sentiments, she very much enjoyed the way she felt about and thought of Ivivin. His friendship was unique and indispensable to her. She worried that if she could not force herself to heal, she would inevitably drive him out of her life. She held Castillo's tear to her ear and let it play its gentle music. After the melody had repeated itself a few times, Elara managed to stave off her fear for the night. She realized that, if she was this worried about tomorrow, Ivivin must be struggling something fierce. She resolved to offer her ear and her advice to her friend tomorrow. She resolved to try to continue healing at her own pace while believing in her friends. Anticipation of the day to come, rather than fear of it, kept Elara up.

And Ivivin was the last. When he could not sleep due to his worries, he sat up and looked at the pile of warmth on the other side of the campsite. The sisters were as still as stone, though Ivivin could hear Castillo's tear playing music. He suspected that Elara was having a tough time sleeping. He swore at himself for not being able to solve that problem, either. After all, if he couldn't even solve his own problems, how was he going to help his friends with theirs? He wanted so badly to help Elara, but could think of no way to do it. Likewise, he tried to search himself for an answer to the king but the uncertainty about his own future prevented him from finding it. Ivivin could not sleep and he could not solve his problem, so he decided to distract himself. He would try to sketch the group one last time to immortalize the scene. He could make out their figures by the fireside, but would need light to see his drawing, just as he did each night before. Ivivin pulled out his supplies but, just before he made Europa's tear illuminate, he looked again to the sisters, Icarus, and Lili. His life was short and his time was limited. But so was everyone's. It would be neglectful and foolish of Ivivin to ignore his disease—that much was true. But if he allowed it to cast a shadow over all his actions and decisions, then not even Europa's tear could light the way for him. Rather than fear uncertainty and impermanence, Ivivin resolved to try and revel in it. He knew not what he would tell the king tomorrow, but he would answer the king the best he could with who he was tomorrow. That's all he could do.

That's all that anyone could do. In an attempt to accept the fleeting nature of life, Ivivin put away his paper and ink. He looked at the heap of creatures and smiled. He pulled out the Europa's tear once more. This time, rather than wanting to use the stone to preserve the moment forever, he aimed to use it to simply see them better to more fully enjoy the moment. Ivivin let the stone shine. At that moment, the Tear of Jupiter, still affixed to Ivivin's bag, began to glow and shake loudly, prompting all the campers to spring to life and look its way.

6

All but Elara were immobilized by shock. Elara, though, charged the stone, hoping to pacify the strange phenomenon. The stone broke free of Ivivin's bag and levitated just a meter or so out of her reach. Soon after, the three tears of Jupiter's children joined the Tear of Jupiter in the air and began to revolve around the stone. Ganymede's tear grew hotter and hotter, such that the three adventurers on the ground below could still feel it's comforting warmth. Callisto's tear began to play a melody far more intricate and layered than Elara had ever heard it play and at a volume that rivaled the king's band. Europa's tear shone brighter than it had ever before, illuminating the area as bright as if it were day, but with a far gentler hue.

The moon tears revolved faster and faster around Jupiter's tear, their effects becoming more and more pronounced and exaggerated until, suddenly, the campers were exposed to a wholly new and unexpected sensation. In their mind's eye, they saw without seeing. Their horizon expanded from their field of view to one nearly fully spherical as ribbons made of colours unknowable to man interwove and danced with phantasmagorical wisps all around them. Every infinitesimally small point on their body was filled with a different sensation, some familiar and some indescribably foreign. A hypnotizing melody sounded not in their ears, but in their hearts. The beat sent tremors through their whole being as the masterful musician plucked on the strings of raw emotion. Each moment brought a carefully selected sentiment that, when arranged together, told nearly every story, from the most tragic life to the most passionate of loves.

In a singular instant, Ivivin experienced what seemed to be an eon. Interspersed between the ethereal and ineffable sensations, he had flashes of lives unknown to him. He was a young girl, clinging to another and crying amoung the still burning remains of a village. He was a free-spirited and hooved beast, wind blowing through his mane as he roamed the fields near Smithton. He was a searing pain and the scent of burning flesh in a time of desperation. He was a wing from which feathers were haphazardly ripped by kin. He was a musician, singing from the bottom of her heart in a gentle, high-pitched voice and he was the sound of children giggling. He was a deity, crying over death and he was those that had died. He was so many things, so quickly. Some things, he understood. Others were a fleeting experience, unable to be captured beyond the instant he underwent them.

The nonpareil marvel reached a crescendo before fading. Ivivin and the others began to regain senses typical of man. Disoriented and with their senses saturated, their gazes remained affixed to the revolving tears hovering in front of them. The tear of Jupiter began to flash, slowly at first, but more and more rapidly until it shone blindingly. With a nearly deafening boom and an incredible force that knocked to the ground all in attendance, the Tear of Jupiter shot to the heavens above. Its return sent ripples through the night sky itself. Stars split and merged and scattered about the sky unpredictably.

The three tears of the celestial siblings tumbled to the earth in an oddly mundane and ordinary fashion.

No one moved after being knocked down. Ivivin was struggling to remember how to be himself—how to move and who he was. Like a toddler, he wobbled to his feet. Every second that passed, he felt more and more himself and could recount less and less the specifics of the wonder that had befallen them. He knew, for instance, that he had seen through the eyes and felt through the skin of beings not human, but could not replicate the sensation in his memory. He knew he had relived moments of a life not his own and he knew that he had truly lived them in their entirety—with every sense and sensation, but he could only recall them as blurs and vague emotion.

Slowly, the others, too, returned to this plane of existence. Upon discussion of the experience with one another, none could properly find the words to describe what they had been through.

They suspected that they had lived parts of each other's past, but also those of Lili and Icarus and even the celestial siblings themselves. Each of them was floored by the experience, but also frustrated in a way. Ivivin knew for a fact that, for the briefest of moments, he understood Elara's trauma as if it were his own—it was his own! But that understanding was gone, leaving behind only the knowledge that it was once there. It taunted him, like a childhood memory that may or may not have been imagined. Still, for him and for the others, it was nothing short of a miraculous experience. Moreover, Ivivin thought it curious. In having both left and returned to himself, he had a rare clarity. His feelings were now unclouded and sharp.

Unable to sleep after such incredible stimulus, they looked again to the stars to pass the time. The arrangement of the stars was different than it was before. The campers had been part of an event that had literally shaken the heavens. Elara took out her charting materials and began to document this new night sky as Idalia and Ivivin both watched. Idalia found the courage to tell Ivivin about her drinking problem and Ivivin found the compassion to comfort her.

The moment the sun began to light the land, even before it broke the horizon, they packed their things to return to Castletown. They each held one of the tears. Out of curiosity, Ivivin tried to light Europa's tear once more. It was faint—fainter than it had ever been, but the same comforting light trickled from it. With much to report and an unforgettable experience between them, they set forth to Castletown.

Closing the Distance

1

As the trio walked, Elara asked Ivivin what he planned to tell the king, both about the tear and about his plan. Ivivin didn't really know and let Elara know that much, but he seemed much more at peace with the idea than before. Elara paused after hearing Ivivin's response and thought back to new arrangement of the stars in the sky. Elara felt the gravity of the situation in full. The stars were no longer a guide that could be relied upon for navigation. They would need to be re-charted and their movements throughout the year re-described if they were to ever be useful to man again. The sun and the moon seemed unchanged, so rudimentary navigation with those bodies would still be possible, but it would not be precise. In particular, nautical voyages would likely be risky. When Elara thought about what she wanted to do, irrespective of Ivivin, she knew that she wanted to travel the lands, documenting and studying wildlife in the days and charting the stars in the night. So, she let Ivivin know as much. He had chased his dream and inspired her to do the same. Ivivin responded encouragingly to Elara's dreams, though neither wished to discuss the ramifications thereof. There would be time for that later.

2

Ivivin stood before the king, just as he was commanded. The king looked tired and flustered. Ivivin spoke plainly, just as he was commanded.

"You seem tired." Ivivin opened their conversation.

"Yes. I had a rare night where I slept rather soundly, only to wake to a crowd of people concerned that the stars themselves had been rearranged. If it had only been one or two people, I would have dismissed them as drunkards or pranksters. But there must be merit to their claims and I have spent much of the day resenting that I was not awake to look for myself."

"About that…" Ivivin said, almost shamefully.

The king's face morphed into one of grave realization and again into one of weary amusement.

"You had your hand in this matter, too, Ivivin? Leave it to our newest knight to vacation and return having reshaped the sky itself! Speak. Tell me what happened! And where is the Tear of Jupiter?"

Ivivin did the best he could to recount the events of the previous night. Words failed him, at times, but the king seemed to get the practical gist.

"So, the Tear of Jupiter returned to the sky with such force that even the spheres above were shaken and strewn, that is why the night's sky is changed?" The king asked in confirmation.

Ivivin nodded.

"On the bright side, at least we don't have to worry about the Tear of Jupiter falling into the wrong hands. I don't think anyone could reach it if they tried!" Ivivin tried to joke.

The king smiled.

"Solved one problem but created a whole new set. I cannot fault you, my knight. No one could have imagined such an event to occur. It will be difficult to recover, but man is resilient and we shall manage. So then, we have but one other matter to discuss today. What to do with you?"

"I know what I would like to do, if you'll hear my suggestion." Ivivin stated with a confidence he lacked less than a day ago.

The kind nodded for Ivivin to continue.

"I want to travel. I want to see this land and others and all of their people. I want to help those I can, when I can."

The king sighed.

"It that all?"

Ivivin nodded.

"Approved. Ivivin, wander these lands and others beyond. Help our people and others still. I ask only that you identify yourself as a knight under my command as you travel. Represent me and yourself well. Use your title in a way befitting your position and remember that you are welcome here."

Ivivin was shocked at the ease by which the king approved of the solution to the problem he struggled with for so long.

"Where do you plan to go first, my knight?" The king added.

Ivivin knew right away where he wanted to go. "My companions, the two sisters, are going to set forth on a journey to re-chart the stars. I will go where they go, if they'll have me."

"Oh? New charts of the sky will assuredly be needed. Navigation will be difficult and dangerous, for a time. That is a more productive task than the one I had imagined you'd undertake. You have my blessing. Tell your compatriot that the kingdom of Vasilos will pay her well for copies of those charts. Good-bye, Sir Ivivin."

"Thank you, my liege." Ivivin said, bowing and headed for the exit. The king called to Ivivin at the door, prompting him to turn and face the king once more.

"Be safe! That's an order!" The king commanded.

"As you wish." Ivivin responded with a smile.

3

Ivivin returned to the sisters, who were waiting for him in the nearby inn.

"How did it go, Ivivin?" Idalia asked

"It went well, surprisingly." Ivivin responded, still stunned by the encounter.

"Well, what did you say? What are you to do?" Elara asked cautiously, unsure if she was ready for the answer.

"I…Elara, would you have me along with you on your journey? You have supported me and my goal for so long. It is one of my deepest wishes to return the favour."

Elara certainly wasn't expecting that.

"What do you mean, what about the king's task?" Elara managed, flustered as she was.

"I asked the king if I could travel the land and help whoever I happened upon. You are the first one I want to help." Ivivin responded.

Elara's heart was pounding. Though she had told Ivivin what she wanted to do, she hadn't yet grasped it as a reality she was to pursue. But, with him asking this, it became much more real. Elara was more nervous than she had been in a while, but also more excited, too. She hadn't realistically considered the possibility of travelling with Ivivin, but here the chance was, right in front of her.

"I don't know if it's for the best, Ivivin, but I'd be happy if you came along." Elara responded unusually meekly. She turned to Idalia and quickly added. "What about you, Idalia? What do you want to do? What is your dream?"

"I really do not know. I need time, I think, before I settle upon such matters. I just know I want to return to our mother's side." Idalia said.

"Then home is our first destination. Objections, Ivivin?"

Ivivin smiled and shook his head.

4

Ivivin had to make good on his promise to Helmschmied before they left. They had considered splitting up, with Idalia and Elara getting a head start to Smithton to inform Minerva that Elara would not be completing her apprenticeship. But with the new arrangement of the stars, they knew it would be safer to travel together. So, while Ivivin worked in the forge doing his best to instruct Helmschmied's apprentices, Elara and Idalia prepared for the voyage. While sorting through their things, Idalia pulled a crumpled letter, still sealed, from her bag. When she realized what it was, she went pale a moment and turned to her sister.

"I forgot…" Idalia told her sister.

"What's that?" Elara asked.

"It's the letter that Ivivin sent you while in Olympia. In all the excitement and hullabaloo, I forgot I had it." Idalia said, handing it to her sister.

Elara flattened the letter out the best she could and broke the seal. Reading it invoked a whirlwind of different emotions, not least of all was happiness.

Dear Elara,

I hope this letter finds you well. I am writing from Olympia, the country to the south. I think you would like it here—it is very different from your home, though! I know we haven't known each other long, but I consider the short amount of time we did spend together a blessing. I hope it doesn't sound strange, but I think of you often. I have read the book you gave me many times over. Somehow, I feel closer to you when I am beneath the stars, like we are watching them together. I don't know if I will ever see you again and that is a tremendously saddening thought, but a lot has happened since we parted ways. I just wanted to let you know that you have inspired me. The strength you showed in the cave of the

Shaa'illi and the tenderness you showed for your sister both emboldened me. You, knowingly or not, helped me find strength and comfort in times I needed it most and, as a result, I've had an amazing adventure. I hope that you get to have one, too, and that it is exciting and fulfilling in every way you can imagine. If you do, I hope that I, too, can inspire you, even just a little (though I don't think you'll need it). You are strong and you are kind and I hope you realize how incredible you really are. I don't really know how to end this note, so I suppose I will leave off with this—No matter where my story goes and how it ends, I am so very happy I had the honour to share a page with you.

Your friend,
Ivivin
P.S. I hope I am not being too presumptuous in calling us friends.
P.P.S. Icarus says hello!

5

On the night before they were to depart on their new adventure, Idalia had managed to secure a gig at a local tavern at the very edge of Castletown. Ivivin was weary from the intensive instruction, but he and Elara both wanted to support Idalia. They went to the tavern, together, and listened while enjoying a single drink each—they had learned their lesson about excess before days of travel. Idalia had a beautiful voice and her song was full of soul. At the end of her set, Idalia came over to the pair to thank them for coming to support her. But that was not her only purpose. She told Ivivin and Elara that she really wanted to stargaze with them tonight, maybe even play a new song for all of them to share. Elara and Ivivin agreed excitedly. Idalia insisted that they go get a small fire set up at the top of the nearby hill and that she would be there after she played a short encore and cleaned up. She also wanted them to leave Icarus behind so that she didn't have to scale the hill alone. Elara and Ivivin obliged Idalia's requests, taking their leave and leaving the owl.

Shortly after they left, Idalia packed away her instrument and returned to the inn with Icarus for the night.

6

Elara and Ivivin sat on the hill on opposite sides of the fire, waiting for Idalia to join them. They chatted and joked about all manner of things. After a while, Elara realized her sister's ploy, though Ivivin did not.

"Man, I wonder what is taking Idalia so long?" Ivivin remarked.

"I don't think she's coming." Elara informed the dense child.

"What do you mean she's not..." Ivivin figured it out just short of finishing his question.

"Oh..."

"Yep." Elara quipped.

"Just us then, huh?" Ivivin found himself getting nervous.

"It seems that way." Elara also found herself getting nervous.

"Let's not let it ruin a perfectly good night of stargazing!" Ivivin insisted, laying down and looking to the stars. He heard the shuffling of grass and footsteps. In an attempt to ignore the slight awkwardness of the situation and to try and stay calm, Ivivin did not break his eyes away from the sky.

Suddenly, he heard Elara plop down right beside him, just inches away. She, too, laid down to look up at the stars. Moving at the rate of about an inch per hour, the two shuffled a bit closer to one another. Elara placed her hand in Ivivin's and he squeezed it gently. He had felt her hand before. It was rough, callous, and scarred. But, more than that, her hand was warm. His senses began to overload. He wondered if the tears were not up to their mischief once more. He shimmied his leg over just a hair, so that they now touched at the knee as well.

The couple laid there, hand in hand and knee-to-knee, happy, in their own way, eagerly anticipating the dawn of a new day and the beginning of a brand-new journey.

Epilogue

Ivivin sighed as he looked in the mirror and found yet another grey hair on his head. He walked to a desk sporting a lit candle, ink, and a bound, but empty, book. He reflected on the life he had lived so far. So many incredible people and so many incredible places! He had lived a life far richer than he could have ever wished for and it was not over yet! Icarus flew in through the window and landed on his shoulder. Ivivin scritched his friend's chin before putting his pen to the book's first page.

Icarus sighed as he wiped his brow and looked longingly to his favourite spot on the farm—an elder Oak tree nearly as tall as a barn. It served as a sort of reminder of his ancestors. His great grandparents had settled this land, clearing it of trees to be tilled and used for crop. They had succeeded in clearing all the trees in what is now their family fields. All but one, that is. Still standing was this behemoth of a tree. There were axe marks lining the westward facing end of the tree—a memento preserved from Icarus' ancestors' attempts to bring the beast down. In the end, they failed to conquer the giant and left it be, as did his grandparents and even his own parents. While Icarus found this familial tale amusing and would oft think of it fondly, the victor from that ancient scuffle had another purpose that Icarus found much more appealing. It was a perfect place to lay under for a nice rest. Birds of all varieties came and went, their songs bringing life and peace to an otherwise mundane landscape. The roots of the tree were mossy and unexpectedly soft, making them a perfect place to lay one's head. Naturally, such a large arboreal wonder would not be complete without a thick canopy of leaves providing respite from the scorching sun of summer.

• • •

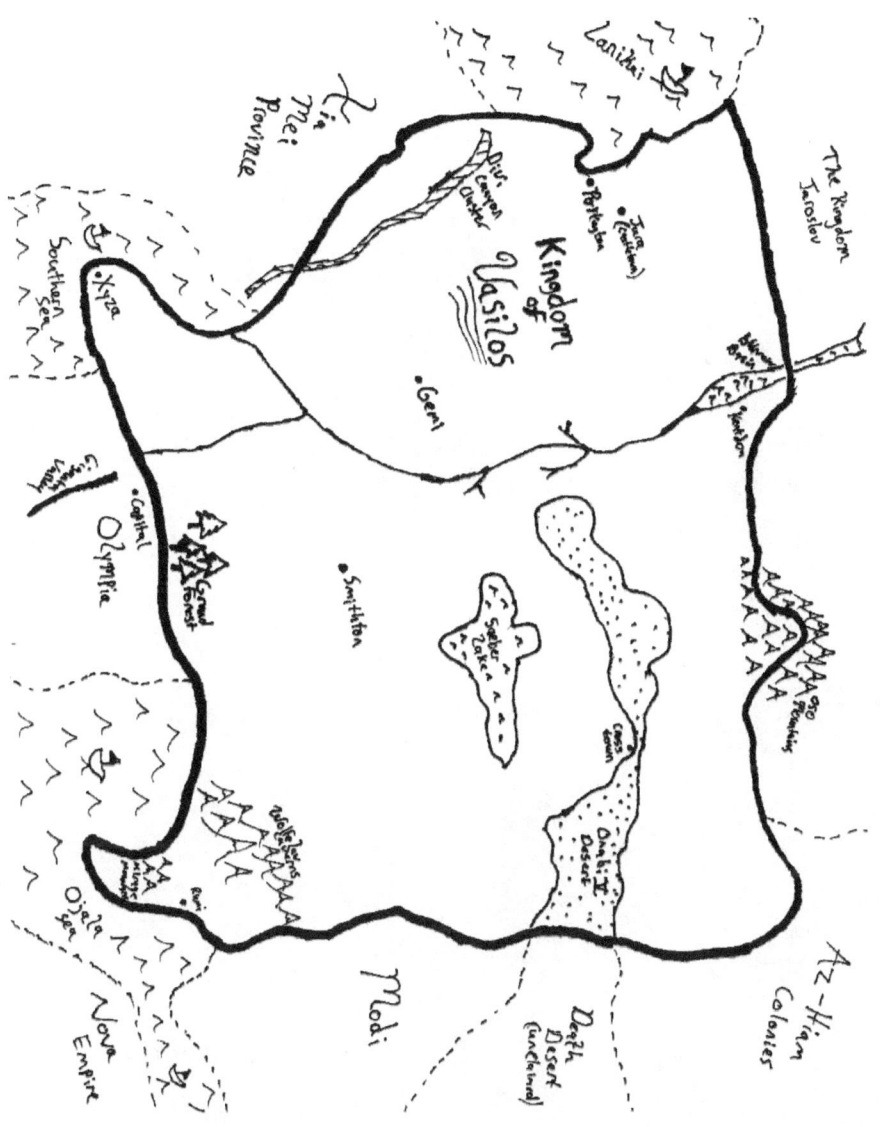

About the Author

J. Nick Fisk is a resident dweeb, scientist, poet, bird fanboy, and all around dorky fellow. While *Ivivin* is his debut piece in fiction, Fisk has published scientific works in journals such as *CBE-Life Sciences Education* and *BMC Evolutionary Biology.* He anticipates publishing a collection of poetry within the galactic year.

Fisk graduated from the Rochester Institute of Technology in 2016, from where, as legend has it, he holds a Master's degree in Bioinformatics and a dual Bachelor's degree in Biotechnology/Molecular Bioscience and Bioinformatics. Here, Fisk also *arguably* enjoyed an *arguably* successful four-year stint as a NCAA wrestler. He is presently pursuing both a Ph.D. and a sense of humour at Yale University.

Fisk is best known for his groan-inducing puns and his inhuman coffee consumption. Visit him at *jnickfisk.com*

About the Illustrator

◆

Orlando Guerra is a native of Las Cruces, NM. He attended and enjoyed an athletic career as a NCAA-DII wrestler at New Mexico Highlands University. In addition to his studies relating to fitness, nutrition, coaching, and leadership, Orlando is a talented visual artist. He currently operates under Space Case Press. His artistic capabilities and sensibilities range from traditional illustrative art, as seen here, to truly psychedelic. Guerra welcomes inquiries about freelance projects and artistic endeavours.

Follow the Space Case Instagram:

https://www.instagram.com/space_case_press/